IRRESISTIBLE YOU

She guided his hand to her waist. Instinctively, he pulled down the right side of her thong, then repeated the action on the other side. Satisfied that the stockings, garter and strappy sandals would stay on, she slowly unwound the tie from her hand, then released it from his wrist, freeing him to explore at will. And explore he did.

He sat up. With ease, he adjusted her body on his lap. Then, eye to eye, she sat, still straddled across his body. With ardent dedication and masterful skill he touched, teased, and tantalized her until she called his name in rasping pleas of pleasure. Knowing her body as well as he did, he stroked every softness, sending moans of rapturous desire tingling over her skin.

"Now," she whispered. Then shifting her weigh, she reached for him . . .

Irresistible You

Celeste O. Norfleet

BET Publications, LLC
http://www.bet.com
http://www.arabesquebooks.com

ARABESQUE BOOKS are published by

BET Publications, LLC
c/o BET BOOKS
One BET Plaza
1900 W Place NE
Washington, DC 20018-1211

All Kensington Titles, Imprints, and Distributed Lines are
available at special quantity discounts for bulk purchases for
sales promotions, premiums, fund-raising, and educational
or institutional use. Special book excerpts or customized
printings can also be created to fit specific needs. For details,
write or phone the office of the Kensington special sales
manager: Kensington Publishing Corp., 850 Third Avenue,
New York, NY 10022, attn: Special Sales Department,
Phone: 1-800-221-2647.

First Printing: August 2004
10 9 8 7 6 5 4 3 2 1

Printed in the United States of America

Fate & Fortune

ACKNOWLEDGMENTS

To my mother, Mable Johnson, and in memory of my father, Otis Johnson, thank you for everything. Your love and guidance encouraged me all of my life. My dream was to make you proud.

To my readers, thank you for your encouragement and support. You are truly the best.

Prologue

Juliet waited in line for nearly half an hour. There were dozens of people behind her, all frustrated, all annoyed, and all stranded. She looked up at the mountainous man in front of her. Tall and wide, he talked loudly and nonstop on his cell phone, as did the man behind her, albeit a bit quieter. It was just her luck to be stuck between the only two people in the city with uninterrupted cellular service.

Inching forward as she heaved her huge travel bag higher up on her shoulder, she finally saw the gleam of the front marble counter. She was almost there. She was tired and her feet hurt. She'd been walking for forty minutes and had gotten less than thirty blocks. That's when she had decided to duck into the nearest hotel instead of walking another thirty blocks to her stepmother's apartment.

She eagerly looked toward the front desk again. The man stationed there was irritable and short tempered, but who wouldn't be? This was New York City, the biggest and brightest city in the country. And unfortunately in a few hours, for the first time in decades it would also be the darkest.

Juliet looked around impatiently, then peered out through the shaded glass windows in front of the building. It was still light outside, but it wouldn't be for long. The sidewalks were packed as the mass of humanity ambled by, all forced out onto the streets at one time, creating mass confusion.

New York City at rush hour was madness enough; New York City in the midst of a blackout was insanity. Angry pedestrians, irate motorists, and those looking to take advantage of the situation were things Juliet had no intention of witnessing.

She turned just as the huge man took his key and walked away. Thank God she was next.

"Can I help you?" the desk clerk asked dryly, already knowing the answer.

"Yes, I'd like a room, please," she said, although the word *duh* would have been a more appropriate answer.

"We have one room left, fifteenth floor." He slapped a key on the counter. "That'll be two hundred twenty-five dollars, up front." Juliet pulled out her wallet and handed him a credit card. "Sorry, cash only. In case you hadn't noticed there's a blackout; that means *nada* electricity."

She looked at him sternly. "Yeah, duh, I noticed. This place doesn't have backup generators?"

"Only for emergency use—stairways, hallways, like that. Cash only for the rooms."

She slammed her large bag on the counter and began digging into her wallet and purse, all the while praying that she had enough to cover the room. Two minutes later she was still digging through her things.

"Look miss, do you want the room or not?" The front desk clerk said as he looked at Juliet with annoyance along with the rest of the line behind her. "I can't hold it for you forever."

Juliet continued to dig in the bottom of her bag. So far she had found sixty-three dollars and some change. "Hold on, I'm still checking."

The clerk turned away from her and asked to help the next person in line.

The man with the cell phone attached to his ear disconnected, closed the phone, and stepped forward. "I'd like a room, one night, king-size bed, top floor, no smoking."

The clerk looked at Juliet as she glared up at him. "Sorry, lady, I told you that I only had one room left. First come, first served." He looked back to the man. "That'll be two hundred and twenty-five dollars." J.T. dug out his wallet. "Cash up front," the clerk emphasized as he looked over to Juliet.

"No credit cards?" he asked.

"Look around. No electricity, no credit cards."

"Fine," he said as he began pulling bills from his money clip. He quickly peeled off seven twenty-dollar bills, then looked at the rest of the cash in his hand. He counted a ten-dollar bill, a five and five ones. He reached into his pants pocket but came up empty. He proceeded to check his suit jacket, then his briefcase.

"Here, I found another five, that's sixty-eight," Juliet said as she placed the cash on the counter.

"Good for you," the clerk said sarcastically.

"I'll take anything you have: single, double, presidential, honeymoon suite, anything."

"Sorry, like I said, I only have one room left, and this gentleman just asked for it." He turned back to the man. "That's two-twenty-five."

"I was here first. I have the cash, just not all of it."

"Sorry, lady." He focused his attention back to the man. "So do you want the room or not?"

"Yes, I have one hundred and sixty dollars cash. I can get you the rest plus a nice tip when the banks open tomorrow."

"Sorry, next." The clerk looked to the next person in line.

"Wait," Juliet said to the clerk, "just give me a second." She leaned over to speak with the man now standing at the counter beside her. "Look, there's only one room left. I don't have enough for the full room rate and apparently neither do you. Why don't we make a deal?"

"What do you suggest?"

"Simple, we pool our cash and get the room together before someone else gets it. We can work out the details later. I don't know about you, but I don't want to spend the rest of the night walking the streets trying to find another hotel room, or fighting some vagrant for a park bench, do you?"

It took less than a second for J.T. to decide. He slid his cash across the counter. "We'll take the room."

The clerk immediately placed a no vacancy sign on the counter and handed him the key. He took it, turned it over in his hand, and smiled. With the advent of computer automation and keycards, he hadn't actually seen a hotel room key in years.

"Sorry folks, no more rooms available. You can sleep in one of the lobby chairs for twenty dollars each. Next."

Juliet shook her head at the clerk's audacity then smoothly took the key from her new roommate's hand. She read the room number, then walked off down the hall heading toward the elevators. "I hope you're not some crazed lunatic with delusions of being on the front page of the *Enquirer*, the *Globe* or the *New York Times*," she threw over her shoulder as she pushed the elevator button several times.

"Hardly," he said calmly as he stopped at the first door and pushed it open. "This way," he said holding the door to the stairway open while waiting for her to realize that the elevators wouldn't work in the blackout".

Juliet turned to him, then back to the elevator. She shook her head, then walked to the staircase. She looked him up and down as she approached the doorway, making a quick assessment of his character.

He was a professional, no doubt, tall, dark, and handsome. He reeked of money. He wore an expensive tailored business suit and carried a pricey leather briefcase. She paused a moment to see his eyes. Brown, framed with long, black lashes.

"I'm about to share a hotel room with a strange woman, whose name I don't even know while in the middle of a New York City blackout."

She walked up the stairs then stopped on the first landing and turned to him. "Juliet." She held out her hand to shake. "Let's leave out the last names for the time being, okay?"

"Fine with me. We can just play it by ear. J.T.," he responded grabbing her hand evenly. They each nodded in agreement that they'd make the best of an unusual situation.

"Shall we?" Juliet prompted.

"After you," J.T. said as he allowed her to lead the way, leaving him free to continue making his own assessment as she walked up the stairs.

She moved confidently, carrying a large leather bag over one shoulder, and although she wore a nicely fitted business suit with high heels, she didn't look like she belonged in an office. She seemed to have way too much bravado for that.

J.T. smiled and nodded. This was definitely going to be a night to remember.

Chapter 1

The new CEO of Evans Corporation, known as E-Corp., J.T. Evans was a certifiable workaholic when it came to business and a rogue when it came to love. From coast to coast, he'd left a trail of broken hearts like the exhaust fumes of his latest sports car. Known as a corporate player, he had enough charm and charisma to seduce the wings off an angel while processing computer algorithms.

Taylor Evans was worried, and knowing her son's faults didn't make it any easier. Seeing him continuously splashed across the society pages with a different woman made her realize she had to do something. A part of her knew that it was the right thing, but still there was another part that just wasn't sure. J.T. was adamant about bachelorhood. Even though she and her husband, Jace, had a loving marriage, J.T. always equated love with being tied down.

The thought of what she was planning made her brow furrow. She looked around pensively. The stillness of the moment did little to ease her worries. She had waited long enough for her son to make a move, but he was always too busy. So now, it was up to her to make the first move. In less then twelve hours, she would have done just that.

Taylor closed her leather binder and placed it on the desk in front of her. J.T. had taken her to lunch, and they had spent the last twenty minutes coordinating their schedules and deciding which corporate events required his attention and attendance. Looking down, J.T. continued to make notations in his calendar.

Deciding that this was the perfect opportunity, she forged ahead. "I stopped by Crescent Island a few weeks ago and spent a lovely afternoon with Louise while your father and Colonel Wheeler planned their fishing trip," Taylor began.

J.T. stopped what he was doing and looked up. "No."

"No what?"

"Just that, no," J.T. said emphatically. "I'm not participating in one of Louise's latest get-married schemes. She can go find Kennedy. She's in Africa somewhere hiding out."

"What are you talking about, what get-married scheme?"

"You know exactly what I'm talking about. Now that I'm here in the area, I knew that it was only a matter of time before this came up."

"Don't be ridiculous. Believe me, Louise isn't after you to get married."

"I'm not so sure about that. I can name several people who said the same thing, and look what happened to them. Tony and Madison, Raymond and Hope, and now Dennis and Faith. The answer is no."

"J.T., you're beginning to sound paranoid. Louise and I went shopping, checked out some local museums, and saw a few tourist attractions on the island. We talked and laughed and had a great time. I'm sure she has absolutely no intention of pairing you up with anyone. Tony and Raymond are her grandsons. Of course she wanted to see them married and happy. And Dennis, well he was just a nice surprise for all of us."

"As I said, I'm not so sure about that. But just in case, please tell her thank you but no thank you."

"You can tell her yourself," Taylor said. "She's coming for an extended visit when Colonel Wheeler and your dad go fishing all next week. She's staying at the house so that we can keep each other company."

J.T. opened his mouth to object, but before he could say

anything his phone rang. "This isn't over," he said firmly. "I have no intention of following in Dennis's footsteps." He looked at the caller ID. "I've been expecting this call, but it won't take long." He excused himself and picked up the receiver.

Taylor noticed the grimace on her son's face as he spoke on the phone. He was obviously unsettled by her week-long houseguest, just as Louise said he would be. She smiled triumphantly. The seed of suspicion had been successfully planted. She picked up several computer magazines from his pile of mail and flipped through the pages. Advertisements, product articles, and industry news breezed by. Then, on page seven of *Computer Tech* magazine, her son's handsome face smiled back at her.

Boyishly charming, just like his father, he had classic features, a strong angled chin and a determined jawline with soft brown eyes and smooth rich cinnamon-toasted skin. He had a mischievous glint in his eye that came from his father, and a stubborn streak that he had most certainly gotten from her.

She shook her head, knowing the effect J.T. had on the opposite sex. She had observed several female employees who had gone out of their way to get her son's attention as they walked in from lunch. It was as if a company-wide e-mail had been sent announcing that J.T. was back in the building.

It had been the same earlier at lunch, when two drinks and several business cards had arrived at their table. One woman had even gone so far as to offer to pay for their meal in exchange for his phone number. From the hostess to the waitress to the other patrons in the restaurant, they all clearly let their interest be known. Her son was apparently now on the Washington, D.C.'s, *new bachelor in town* menu.

After all, this was D.C., the nation's capital where women outnumber men seven-to-one. This was also Chocolate City, where the ratio was almost eleven-to-one in favor of African-American men.

So when an eligible bachelor arrived in the city, women

knew about it. But when J.T. Evans, the newly named CEO of Evans Corporation, arrived, it made the front page of the *Washington Post* business section and, as usual, the society pages.

Tall, dark, and handsome, J.T. was every woman's dream and his mother's unending concern. Add to that, he was comfortably wealthy, with an impressive list of credentials and a bright future in a family-owned computer software company that bested most of Silicon Valley. He had a way with woman that left them panting and weak in the knees while making her, his mother, a nervous wreck.

Featured in virtually every society page in nearly every major newspaper, he was the bachelor-businessman most likely to leave a broken heart. Like clockwork, every three months there'd be a different woman on his arm, the relationship ending just before things turned serious or tedium set in. Then he'd move on to someone new. Taylor loved her son but she knew that he could be as detached and unfeeling as the computer systems he designed.

J.T. always made it clear from the beginning of each relationship that he was never getting emotionally involved and that it was nothing more then a distraction for him. His attention was solely on business. The hopeful ones, intent on changing his mind, accepted his conditions without reservation, but were sadly disappointed when the truth became reality and he moved on, as he always did.

Taylor had comforted many young women who had lost their hearts as they faded from J.T.'s radar. They cried on her shoulder for days, and sometimes weeks, all in hopes that she could persuade her son to return to them. Of course, it was always futile. The only consolation was that they knew what they were getting into. Still, the pain was real.

To his credit, J.T. was always honest and up front about his intentions. Business always came first. Ambitious to the point of obsessiveness, for the past ten years J.T. had focused all his attention on a single, solitary goal, the growth, expansion, and advancement of Evans Corporation. Much to Taylor's chagrin, her son's single-mindedness left little room for a serious and lasting personal relationship.

Oh, he had what he referred to as relationships, but in reality they were little more than momentary attractions, flings, or dalliances in the dating pool. At nearly thirty-three, he was no closer to settling down than he had been when he was in his early twenties.

Taylor waited patiently as J.T. continued his phone conversation while she continued to flip through the computer magazine. She prided herself on being patient, or as patient as any mother could be under these circumstances. But enough was enough.

Seated in front of his desk, she frowned as she looked around the office. Lifeless and sterile, it was a depressing space. It looked more like an empty computer wasteland than a Fortune 500 executive's office. She shook her head, still unable to get used to the redecorated disaster.

Standing, she moved to the large single window across the room. She pulled the cord, opening the dark-hued vertical blinds that covered the windows, and let the late afternoon sunlight stream in.

Spring settled peacefully against the backdrop of the Evans Corporation complex. She smiled as she stood at J.T.'s office window and looked down at the surroundings. She was greeted with a magnificent view. Two interconnected office buildings and two warehouses were spread out over thirty-five acres around her. She watched as a large truck drove through the front gate and wound its way toward the warehouse entrance.

After years of planning and two years in the making, the complex was finally complete. Evans Corporation was finally under one roof, with just a few satellite offices scattered around the country. Now it was time to turn her attention to something else, namely her son and a little plan she and a friend had hatched a few weeks ago.

From the beginning, Taylor knew that she needed help, and who better to lend expertise in the art of matchmaking then the expert herself? Louise Gates. Smiling confidently, Taylor remembered the exact moment she'd decided on the undertaking.

Three weeks ago, she'd been visiting Crescent Island, sitting out on the dock with Louise and discussing her concerns about J.T.'s new position as CEO.

"He has used his hectic work schedule as an excuse for not finding that special someone for years. I'm afraid that now that he's CEO, he'll never find happiness."

"I'm sure he'll be just fine," Louise said, assuring her.

"Tell me, Louise, exactly how long have you been matchmaking?"

Louise smiled proudly. "I've been doing this for over fifty years, sixty if you include me and my Jonathan." Louise smiled as she usually did at the thought of her late husband.

"And it always works?"

"More or less," Louise said after a sip from her glass.

"What do you mean, more or less?" Taylor asked as she sipped her iced tea and turned to face her.

Louise watched as several colorful, fluttering butterflies danced over the surface of the Chesapeake Bay. "I mean that love is as unpredictable as it is precious. The treasure of the heart is often steeled and protected by pain or fear."

Taylor thought about Louise's words as she watched the butterflies dance until they disappeared into the reeds by the water's edge. "J.T. doesn't exactly fit into the broken-hearted rebound or the commitment-phobic categories. Neither is he openly adamant against love; he has just detached himself from the idea of love. He seems to think that his busy schedule and lack of time thwarts the development of a meaningful relationship. In his words, 'I'm too busy with business affairs to have one of my own.'"

"Sounds like you have matchmaking on your mind."

"I most certainly do," Taylor smiled and nodded. "His brain has overruled his heart all his adult life, and it's about time I do something about it. I helped him crawl. I helped him walk. Now I think it's time I help him find that special someone to love."

"Well, to start with, J.T. is going to need a remarkable woman to break through that ironclad excuse of his."

Taylor smiled warmly. "I agree, and Juliet Bridges is a remarkable woman."

"Juliet Bridges from the Capitol Ballet Company?"

"Yes."

Louise smiled, "She just might be perfect for him." Louise nodded in agreement. "But remember, the elements of matchmaking aren't an exact science. Our job, your job, is to encourage the attraction that's already there. Ultimately, a spark is essential. If the participants don't feel that spark of possibility, then there's nothing anyone can do. But," Louise smiled knowingly, "if by chance the spark of possibility occurs, then love will surely follow."

"A spark of possibility," Taylor repeated.

Louise nodded. "That's all it takes."

"How do I encourage sparks?"

"You don't. That part is all up to them."

"How do you know if the spark of possibility occurs?"

"That's easy. We'll see it in their eyes."

"Louise, J.T. is analytical, single-minded, and methodically driven. He's not easily fooled. And after Tony, Raymond, and now Dennis, he's going to be anticipating this. More likely than not he'll see right through it."

"Of course he will, they all think they do. That's why a distraction is imperative. He needs something else to focus on. As with Tony, he was distracted by suspicion, and Raymond was distracted by his concern for my health. Everything you've told me shows that he's the perfect Lancelot type, the hero looking for a damsel to rescue. You'll need to supply him with a damsel."

"That would be Juliet, right?"

"No, that would be you."

"Me?" Taylor asked completely confused.

"Well, actually it will be both of us, at least for the moment."

"But he'll be skeptical as soon as he sees you."

"Yes, he'd surely suspect me of matchmaking, but not you. Matchmaking is like magic. It's all smoke and mirrors. Misdirection is the key." Louise arched her eyebrow.

Taylor smiled and nodded with understanding. "Misdirection, of course. He'd never suspect me."

"Precisely."

"Still, the only problem I foresee is J.T.'s complete lack of interest in anything pertaining to the arts. His idea of a perfect evening is reconfiguring a computer."

"Things change," Louise said, "you'd be surprised."

Taylor shook her head. "The closest J.T.'s ever come to the ballet is signing a check for the corporation's charity sponsorship. I'm not so sure we're not setting ourselves up for failure by choosing Juliet," Taylor said.

"Juliet is perfect for him. You chose well."

"They're complete opposites."

"It's not just an old wives' tale that opposites attract. There's a lot of truth in that old adage. Trust me, they have a lot more in common than you think. It's been my experience that the sparks shine brighter with opposite personalities."

Taylor nodded her head absently. "Sparks," she said aloud. Encouraged by the memory, she watched as the truck backed up and maneuvered its way into the warehouse bay. Even though it was late spring and a crisp snap was in the air, it was a glorious afternoon and the perfect day to start a new venture. Everything was in place. It was now or never.

"Did you say something?" J.T. asked her, interrupting her thoughts.

"No," Taylor said innocently.

"Sorry about that," J.T. said, standing at the window beside her. He glanced out briefly, unaware of the perfect brilliance of the day. "That was the West Coast office regarding a company we're interested in."

"Are we selling or acquiring?" She asked.

"Acquiring," he said, looking down at the expansive complex.

Taylor looked over to J.T. and smiled brightly. "It's wonderful to finally have you back home."

J.T. turned and looked at his mother oddly. "I'm here all the time," he said, then returned to his chair behind the large mahogany desk. He reached over and pressed several buttons on the keyboard, then entered a code bringing his four desktop monitors to life.

"A few days here or there, and a week or two now and then isn't exactly being here all the time," Taylor said. J.T. nodded absently, then turned to open a file in his computer. "Having you here permanently and your father semiretired frees me up to implement other options I've been planning for several years," she said as she casually turned and followed him back to his desk.

It's now or never, she reminded herself as she artfully changed the subject. "Did I mention that I've decided to invest in some property?"

She stopped in front of his desk and stuck her finger into the soil of an orchid she'd placed there a week ago in hopes of bringing a little life to the bleak surroundings. The abundant, perfectly formed flowers were still in bloom, but the moss-covered soil was as dry as the Sahara.

"No," he answered simply and began scanning his computer screen.

She went into the office's private bathroom and filled a glass with water. When she returned to the office, she found her son at his desk and completely engrossed in work. "It's a wonderful opportunity that just came up for sale a few months ago. The location is perfect. It's just across the street from the art gallery. It's an old, vacant community center."

"Sounds great," J.T. said as he continued to surf through several screens of e-mail messages and meeting notes, his eyes never leaving the monitor.

"Oh, it is. I already have some wonderful ideas planned for the center. As a matter of fact, since I always wanted to open a neighborhood art and dance facility and sponsor major recitals and exhibits, this is the perfect vehicle."

"Really," he grunted.

"Oh, yes, I'm hoping that the entire center will be completely self-sufficient. Sets, costumes, printing, dance instruction—everything could be handled in-house."

"Good," he said, nodding absently.

Taylor knew he wasn't paying any attention, but she continued talking as she poured half the water onto the moss, then waited as the dried moss and soil soaked in the water. "We're planning to open it in about twelve months or so. We already have a very impressive list of prospective students." She rearranged the glass marbles and river stones, then added the rest of the water.

"Uh-huh."

"It's a lot of work, but ultimately it's going to be a labor of love, a wonderful opportunity, and a tremendous investment." She glanced at her son, waiting for a response.

"Aha," he muttered as his fingers began clicking the keys in front of him. She went back into the bathroom to return the glass.

"The basic premise will be to offer an after-school and weekend dance-and-arts program to help promote the arts in the community," she said as she returned to the desk.

"Really."

"But as with most programs, it will be expensive. The cost of sets, costumes, and instructions can add up. The average

ballet can cost anywhere from twenty-five thousands dollars
to several hundred thousand dollars. Of course we intend to
raise scholarship money with patrons, sponsoring fashion
shows, auctions, and other events including an annual Fairy
Tale Ball.

Taylor fingered the orchid gently, turning the ceramic dish
for the best effect. "To begin with, we'll offer a fine-arts and
graphic-arts program, sculpture, painting, and drawing. And
for dance, we'll offer ballet, modern, jazz, and of course, to
get the kids interested, hip-hop classes. Then, in the following years, we're going to develop a music and drama
program," she added, knowing that she didn't have his complete attention.

"Sounds nice," he said, still concentrating on the computer
monitor.

"Of course I'll head the arts program," Taylor continued as
she dusted a speck of nothing from her lapel and sat down,
"And I have a wonderful partner who was a dance professional. She's a choreographer now and she has an amazing
classical and traditional dance program already in place."

"Aha," he said as he typed in new information.

"She's the perfect partner. Her name is Lena Palmer. She
was a prima ballerina for the Alvin Ailey American Dance
Theater, the American Ballet Theatre, and the Capitol Ballet
Company. She's absolutely brilliant. She already has a dance
studio in New York."

"That sounds great," he mumbled. The constant clicking
picked up speed, sounding more like machine-gun fire than
computer code.

"I've already put in an offer on the property." Taylor
watched as J.T.'s eyes were transfixed on the monitor.

"Un-huh." The keyboard clicking grew louder and faster.

She smiled. "I got it for the amazingly low cost of a million dollars." Her smile broadened as she finally got a
reaction from J.T.

He froze. The air stilled around him as the silence became

deafening. He stopped typing, with his hands unmoving and poised in midair just inches from the keyboard. His body was motionless. His eyes were lowered and focused, as if still concentrating on the screen. "Say that again?" he asked, now fully focused on his mother's voice for the first time since she had unexpectedly shown up to his office and insisted he take her to lunch.

At last, now she had his undivided attention. Taylor smiled slyly and brushed at that same speck of nothing on her suit lapel. "Which part, dear?"

"The part about the million dollars; never mind, just tell me you're joking," J.T. said, still staring at the screen.

"You know that I never joke about the being a patron of the arts."

J.T. raised his head slowly and, for the first time, looked into his mother's soft brown eyes. He knew instantly that she was completely serious. "You put in an offer of a million dollars for a dilapidated community center to open a dance studio?"

"Oh for goodness' sake J.T.," Taylor said, brushing off his reaction nonchalantly, "It's no big deal. It's only money, and heaven knows we have plenty of it. A small philanthropic endeavor would be good for us."

"Mom, thanks to you, E-Corp has a very prestigious list of charitable organizations to which we regularly, and I might add, very liberally, contribute. If you'd like to add a particular organization to the list, please feel free. As you are well aware, we review the list regularly. We have always handled our responsibility as a community leader with great generosity and pride."

"J.T. please," she chuckled, "You sound like a bad corporate commercial or some hyped-up press release."

"What about the art gallery?"

"It's doing wonderfully."

"And your painting?"

"I still paint from time to time, when inspired."

"But what about—"

"Sitting on committees and making recommendations was fine, but now it's time for me to get involved."

"Have you discussed this with Dad?" he said, changing his tactics.

"Your father has nothing to do with this."

"Of course he does, he's the chairman of the board. Any substantial disbursement or expenditure must be cleared by the board of directors."

"This is a personal investment. It's for me, not the company. Evans Corporation has nothing to do with this."

"Personal?"

"Yes, personal."

"Mom, personal or not, a million dollars is out of the question."

"Of course it's not. It's an investment for the future."

"That's not the point."

"It is as far as I'm concerned."

"Okay, what about this business you want to get into. You don't know anything about managing this type of business, or for that matter, dance."

"I don't have to know anything about dance. I have a partner for that. We've already asked Lena to look over the proposal. She's as excited as we are."

"You need more to start a business than a proposal and an ex-dancer."

"Lena wasn't just a dancer, she was a prima ballerina, there's a difference."

"Okay," he yielded to semantics, "a retired ballerina, whatever. What could she possibly know about an undertaking this size?" he added sarcastically.

"That's where you come in."

"I don't have time to baby-sit a ballerina."

"Sure you do."

Frustrated, J.T. buried his face in the palms of his hands. He took a few moments to calm down, then continued more patiently. "Mom, how can you just write a check for that amount of money without consulting me first?"

Taylor smiled, then looked at her son sternly. "You weren't here, and since when do I need anyone's permission to spend money?"

"But a million dollars isn't just petty cash," he said exasperatedly. "To open an art and dance studio?"

"We know exactly what we're doing. We've researched and developed several feasibility plans."

"We? Do you have more than one partner?" J.T. asked.

"Yes."

"Who else is involved?" he asked.

"Does it matter?"

"Yes," he said firmly.

"Louise Gates is going in with me."

"Mamma Lou?"

"Yes."

J.T. opened his mouth, then closed it instantly. Now it was beginning to make sense. If Louise Gates was involved in this, then it had to mean that there was a matchmaking scheme going on somewhere. A knowing smiled eased across J.T.'s lips.

Taylor scowled at her son. She recognized the smug expression on his face. He had rightly assumed that Louise was matchmaking. So far he had done exactly as Louise had anticipated. He was about to come to their rescue.

His smiled broadened. "Can I presume that this whole thing is another one of her matchmaking schemes?"

"Not this again. Matchmaking for whom? Her grandsons are both married."

"If I'd venture a guess I'd say she was trying to play matchmaker for me."

"Why would she want to match you up with someone?"

"Because that's what she does. Her fixation has now become her obsession in life."

"Don't be ridiculous, J.T. With her grandsons already happily married and your sister expecting, Louise doesn't have time to play matchmaker for you or anyone else. She and I are both on the Arts Council and we both love art and dance. It's as simple as that. I assure you Louise is not matching you up, this is strictly business."

"We'll see." The skepticism on his face was obvious.

"Louise, Lena, and I are serious about this."

"That's another thing. How do you know you can trust this ballerina person? There are scam artists everywhere, in every line of business. Huge companies fall prey to them every day. All they need is an opportunity and a willing subject."

"Okay, J.T., you made your point. I'll tell you what. I'll make you a deal."

"What kind of deal?"

"I'd like you to be personally involved with this. I only made a small down payment on the property and we're in the very beginning stages of financing, so I'd like you to meet Lena for yourself. She's a delightful woman, and I truly treasure her as a friend. Also I'd like you to attend a dance performance and get a feel for the business. Then, if after a period of time you still feel that it wouldn't be prudent for us to invest, I won't."

J.T. considered the proposal for a moment, then agreed. "Deal, but first I'd like more information on your ballerina friend. I'll send her name to Trey and have him look into it first thing in the morning. A thorough investigation shouldn't take more than a few days. He can forward you the report." J.T. reached across his desk and began making a notation in his calendar.

"No," Taylor responded, "the deal is for you to handle this personally. Your cousin can handle the final paperwork."

"Mom, Trey's company is far more experienced and capable in investigating acquisitions than E-Corp. We just don't have the time or the expertise."

"Find the time, and I'll trust your expertise."

"Okay, I'll put someone from legal and auditing on it first thing."

"I said personally, J.T. That means you."

"That's impossible, Mom. I told you before that I don't have time to baby-sit an ex-ballerina." J.T. shook his head adamantly. "It's literally my first few weeks in the office on a permanent basis. We're right in the middle of a product launch, we're developing new encryption software for a voice-recognition prototype, and we're in talks to acquire another company's satellite lease. I need to stay on top of everything."

He paused and waited for her to show signs of relenting. She didn't. The expression on her face was unmistakable. She wasn't going to budge on this point. "I'll have the company's best . . ." he began, then stopped short seeing Taylor's brow arch as she steeled her gaze. "Okay, fine," he said, throwing his hands in the air to surrender, "I'll handle it, personally."

"Good." Taylor smiled brightly as she stood. She reached into her purse and pulled out a ticket, a playbill, and an invitation. "You can begin this evening, there's a charity ball and private fundraiser. Juliet Bridges will be performing as Carmen, that alone is worth your time this evening. Afterward, there'll be a fundraiser in the main hall of the arts center. Lena will more than likely be attending the performance and event." Taylor came around from behind his desk and placed the ticket, invitation, and performance playbill in front of him. "Lena Palmer. You can meet her at the fundraiser."

He stood. "What if I already have plans for this evening?"

Taylor turned, smiled, and winked. "You'll work it out."

"Do I really have to be there?"

"Yes, E-Corp is sponsoring tonight's performance and fundraiser. A representative from the company must attend, and as newly named CEO, that means you."

"But," he began as she raised her brow and continued.

". . . It's in your job description; read the fine print. It's right under the six-figure salary, company car, stock options, and use of the corporate jet."

J.T. laughed. "I must have missed that list of perks. I'm sure I would have remembered the jet."

"I'll speak to you this evening."

"By the way, I don't have a job description."

"You do now." She waved as she exited. "Don't be late."

J.T. slowly sat back down, shaking his head. He looked at the computer screen, and for the first time saw nothing he cared to see, as the computer's binary code language of zeros and ones blurred into a mass of confusion. He automatically saved and exited the screen. Shaking his head, he stood and went into the bathroom. He turned on the faucet and let cool water run. He grabbed a towel and dampened his face. As he looked up he caught a glimpse of his reflection in the mirror.

He squinted his eyes and leveled his chin from side to side, then stroked his clean-shaven jaw. A shadowed rim drifted just below his eyes. He looked tired. He'd been working too hard again. Apparently, twenty-hour workdays had begun to wear on him. But his fortitude had always driven him to the edge and given him ample rewards.

This time his focus had been on new software with an interior and exterior perimeter-protected security system. And in another two years he intended to have it on the market under the Evans Corporation brand.

He tossed the damp towel on the sink and walked out. As he stood at his desk, he looked down and picked up the ticket his mother had left. "A million dollars," he said aloud and shook his head slowly. Something definitely didn't feel right about his mother's sudden interest in real-estate investing. J.T. had always relied heavily on his gut instinct, and it told him now that there was something else going on.

His mother had always had a passionate interest and had been an ardent supporter of the arts, and for her sake he had relented and had given generously. But enough was enough.

As a professional artist and painter, she had exhibited her

work in the finest galleries across the country and overseas. Her oil paintings were still extremely popular. They sold at auction houses and galleries for generous sums. Although she seldom painted now, she was still very much involved in the visual and performance arts. But this sudden decision was uncharacteristic of her. She'd never been interested in investments before. So why now?

As the cultural liaison and representative for Evans Corporation, she was a member of several boards. She had continually represented the company in its community involvement and generosity, and E-Corp had earned major recognition through her efforts. Without even trying, Taylor was, by far, the company's biggest public relations asset.

Mamma Lou, as his mother's partner in the new venture, still gave J.T. pause. If she was involved, he had a gut feeling that matchmaking was the primary focus, but to whom? And exactly who was his mother's other partner, Lena Palmer? Maybe she was the one Mamma Lou wanted to match him up with. "Of course," he smiled, delighted that he'd figured her plan out so quickly. *Gotcha!*

He looked down at the ticket and playbill. A stylized graphic of a sexy woman seductively posed instantly got his attention. There was something familiar about the woman's figure.

The cover read, *Peter Flemings presents Juliet Bridges as Carmen.* Juliet Bridges—he'd remembered that his mother had mentioned the name earlier.

He picked up the playbill and flipped through the pages. Biographies and photographs whizzed by as he fanned the pages to the end. Then he stopped. His heart jumped as he leafed through the pages of the booklet again, a little more slowly this time. *It can't be.*

He slowly turned the pages until a picture of the star performer's smiling face appeared. His heart pounded again. Beneath the photo he read, *Juliet Bridges, prima ballerina.* He couldn't believe his eyes. He read the notation again, than quickly read the short biography, only half believing what he'd just read. How was this possible? After all this time, she was right here all along.

Her biography was impressive and read like a who's who celebrity profile, even to his limited knowledge of the dance world. She'd danced with Alvin Ailey, Dance Theatre of Harlem, the American Ballet Theatre, in Russia, Japan, London, Australia, all over Europe, Asia, and in nearly every city in the U.S. She'd danced before kings and queens, dignitaries, diplomats, and presidents.

The last notation in her biography announced Juliet's official retirement at the end of the current season and her final stage performance, which had been sold out since the announcement.

J.T. noted the dates listed in the brochure. Ten months ago, when they'd met in New York, she was just returning from a six-month tour in London, France, and Italy. Apparently she was on her way to D.C. when the blackout occurred.

J.T. shook his head in disbelief. Dozens of trips to New York, seeing dozens of Broadway and off-Broadway performances, constantly searching for the one woman who had captured his heart, and here she was, right here in his own backyard.

He sat down slowly, still not believing his eyes. He reread the biography twice more. The photo was slightly grainy, but he was sure that it was the same Juliet. Never giving up his quest, he had searched for her for months. He knew that she was out there, that she'd said she was a dancer, but she'd never mentioned ballet and he'd never guessed.

But he should have seen it: her perfectly refined posture, her elegant poise, and her graceful movements. It was all there, and he'd missed it. He smiled and nodded as he reached over and pushed the intercom button on his desk. His secretary answered immediately. "Clear my schedule for the rest of the afternoon and evening. I'll be out of the office until tomorrow." He waited for her acknowledgment, then placed his briefcase on his desk. He paused, then pressed the intercom again: "One more thing, get my cousin Trey on the phone for me."

Chapter 2

"Send him in," Trey said as he stood and walked over to the door. He'd cleared his last few appointments when his cousin J.T. asked to see him as soon as possible.

It had been at least seven months since Trey had seen J.T. The perpetual traveler, had been on the road for E-Corp for nearly six years straight.

In that time, he had generated a sizable reputation as a force to be reckoned with and a master at negotiations. Never living in one place for long, he had called New York City his home up until a month ago, when Jace had officially announced his semi-retirement and persuaded him to return to the D.C. area permanently.

J.T. had decided that it was time to come off the road and settle into the new corporate offices in northern Virginia. And three weeks ago, he did just that. He leased his apartment in Manhattan and temporarily moved into the Ritz-Carlton Hotel.

"Come on in, have a seat," Trey said after he greeted his older cousin, then ushered him into his office. Since the two were as close as brothers, Trey was delighted to hear that J.T. was returning to the area. Everything Trey had learned to make his business a success, he had learned from his cousin. And everything he had learned about women, he'd also learned from his cousin.

"Welcome back home, finally. It's been what, like six years since you've settled down in one place for more than a few months. That's a long time to be on the road." He began handing J.T. his usual drink—coffee, black.

"Thanks, it's good to be back, but I'm sure I'm gonna miss being out there on the road." He absently picked up the latest edition of *Barron's* sitting on Trey's desk and flipped through the pages.

"I hear you're staying at the Ritz."

J.T. nodded. "For the time being, until I find a place," he continued. "Tony offered his place in Alexandria, now that he's living in Philadelphia. But hotels have always seemed more like home to me."

"Are you settled in yet?"

"Pretty much."

"How's Madison and the baby?" asked Trey.

"I haven't seen her in awhile, not since Raymond and Hope's wedding reception. But I hear she's getting big and that she and Tony are still acting like newlyweds." He tossed the magazine down and sipped from his cup.

Trey shook his head. "Raymond got married. I still can't believe it."

"Tell me about it. Marriage and settling down is the last thing on my mind at this point in my life," said J.T. "I agree with Keni, I need my freedom."

Trey nodded. "And how is Kennedy these days?"

"Still hiding out in Africa, I spoke with her the other day. She said that she intends to be there indefinitely, or at least until Mamma Lou finds a new target."

"It's a good thing Mamma Lou isn't our grandmother. We'd be in serious trouble."

A moment lapsed as both men silently reassured themselves that they were happy as bachelors for life. "Dennis's engagement blew me away," Trey finally added. "How did that happen? I thought Mamma Lou was just concentrating on Raymond?"

"No one saw it coming, least of all Dennis."

"Sounds like Mamma Lou is really good," Trey said. "I

gotta give her props. She's made excellent matches so far," Trey confessed.

J.T. arched his brow. "Are you planning on being next?"

"Me, no way, man! I'm way too young for that. I've got my whole life ahead of me, and I intend to keep it that way. I have no intention of being shackled down 'til I'm eighty or ninety years old." Trey said decisively. "You, on the other hand . . ." he chuckled, leaving the statement open.

". . . Have no intention of finding myself walking down the aisle anytime soon. I just don't have time for a wife and family yet," J.T. said.

Trey continued to chuckle. "Famous last words. I believe Dennis said the same thing. Now look at him. He's meeting with wedding planners, picking out china patterns, and choosing lace doily invitations." Trey shook his head sympathetically at his friend. "I tell you, man, this is totally unacceptable."

J.T. smiled. "That's right. you two used to run the clubs together. Now you're on your own."

Trey shrugged, "No biggie. Just means that there are more lovely women out there for me."

"Until Mamma Lou turns her attention in *your* direction," J.T. said pointing across the desk to Trey.

"It'll never happen. I'm way too smooth for that. You forget who you're talkin' to. I am the man when it comes to sidesteppin' that commitment thing. My record is clear, never even been challenged," Trey said, boastfully.

"I suppose that's due to another one of your infamous theories, no doubt."

"No doubt." Trey stood and cleared his throat. "You see, you gotta know how to move on before the commitment thing even becomes an issue. Therefore, your opponent loses the element of surprise. That's what gets you caught. The, *oops I slipped and fell in love* surprise thing. Once the surprise thing happens, you're lost."

J.T. gave his cousin a *you are out of you mind* look. And the look said it all. Both men laughed with the not-so-sure knowledge that Mamma Lou would not be interfering in their lives.

"So, what's on your mind?" Trey said as he sat back down behind his desk.

"Actually, believe it or not, it's Mamma Lou. I'm not so sure she's not up to something. She's coming to visit this weekend, then staying the week with Mom while Dad and Colonel Wheeler go fishing, and that can only mean one thing."

Trey looked at him sympathetically and nodded. "Match-making," they replied in unison.

"Exactly, I think she's using Mom's love of the arts and dance to throw me off guard."

"So you *are* next," Trey said bursting into laughter as he hit a few keys on the keyboard, bringing up a betting grid. "I need to check the stats to see who had you within six months' time."

"Not so fast. I'm not down that aisle just yet."

"So, what do you intend to do?" Trey found it difficult to wipe the grin from his face.

"Beat her to the punch. I think Mamma Lou might attempt to set me up with a woman named Lena."

"And you want me to run interference while you slip out of town?"

"Good plan, but not viable. I have too many things on my plate right now to leave town. Plus I need to get her off my back once and for all."

"How?"

"I don't know yet. It's a shame I can't make a preemptive strike, like in Sun Tzu's *The Art of War*."

"Now you're talking," Trey agreed, "*The Art of War* should be considered the primer for all commitment-avoidance relationships. It's a war out there, man, and our side's losing."

"Not another theory," J.T. said as he shook his head.

"I'll tell you about that one later," Trey promised. "What do you mean, preemptive strike?"

"I mean, go on the defense before she makes her first move."

"Why don't you?" Trey said.

J.T. smiled broadly and nodded with interest. The idea had merit. The tactic would put her totally off guard and just might put her off matchmaking for good, or at least for the time being. "It can't be that difficult," Trey paused. "Do unto others—" Trey added.

"Before they do unto you," J.T. said nodding his head as an idea began to form. His mind whirled with possibilities. Then, one idea stood out. It was absolutely perfect. All he needed to do was throw her off guard by producing a woman who was already in his life.

"A good sting ought to do it. But just long enough to throw her off guard. A few days should work. Surely Mamma Lou wouldn't interfere with true love already in bloom. She's too much of a romantic at heart to do that."

"A sting?" Trey asked.

"A rope-a-dope," J.T. replied.

"You intend to do a Muhammad Ali and punch her out?"

J.T. looked at Trey, who was grinning like a Cheshire cat. "Of course not, the rope-a-dope was fooling the opponent into thinking that they had the upper hand. Then, when your opponent is worn out, you turn the whole thing around so that you're showing one hand while the other hand basically does all the work."

"You've completely lost me," Trey said as he leaned on his desk further.

"What you see isn't always what you get."

"Alright," Trey threw his hands up. "Enough of the cryptic strategies. What do you have in mind?"

"Advertisers and magicians do it all the time. Think of this as the old bait-and-switch. All I'll need is a pitchman to help set it up, and a pawn to play the part of someone willing to be in love with me for a few days."

"That's perfect. I can do the pitchman, no problem, but who you gonna get for the pawn?"

"Good question."

"It has to be a pretty convincing act. Everything is going to have to hinge on the perfect person playing the role."

"Exactly. I'd need someone already in town to make it look more convincing. She doesn't necessarily have to be my type, but nothing too drastic, or it'll raise suspicions. She needs to be beautiful, independent, sophisticated, intelligent, and sexy."

"Yes," Trey agreed readily. "She has to also be an excellent actress able to pull this off."

"Agreed, but not a working actress, and certainly not someone I've already dated. The last thing I need with this is more complications."

"True," Trey agreed.

J.T. pondered a few moments, then smiled and chuckled. "I'll have to give this some more thought. The right person is crucial if this is gonna work."

The room went silent for a moment as J.T. considered his pawn. He reviewed all the women he knew, but eventually dismissed all of them. Trey mentioned a few women he knew that might fit the bill. But they finally decided that they needed someone new, someone without previous ties to either of them.

"If this is going work," Trey warned, "you're going to have to put some time into this charade. You can't just set it up and move on to business as usual."

"You're right, I have to make this look good or Mamma Lou will see right through it, and she'll have me be back on the trail to wedded bliss in no time."

"What's the first step?"

"In any good plan, the first step is simple, know the enemy. I need some information on someone."

"On who?"

"Lena Palmer."

"Lena Palmer," Trey muttered, recalling the name.

"She's a dancer."

"No, actually I believe that she's a choreographer now."

"Whatever," J.T. tossed out nonchalantly. "Do you know her?"

"Yes, indirectly, I know of her. She and Aunt Taylor are on the Arts Council together, and they're interested in purchasing a property here in town."

"Yeah, I just heard. That's what got me curious in the first place. Mamma Lou is the third partner, and when she's involved with anything, matchmaking can't be far away."

"Wait, you think Lena Palmer is the lucky lady she's going to try to match you up with?" J.T. nodded. "No way, I don't think so."

"Why not?"

Trey grinned. "Well, first of all, I think Lena Palmer lives in New York City; then there's the fact that you have nothing in common with her; and, of course, there's the obvious, she's about fifty or sixty years old." The chuckles instantly erupted. "You're starting to get a little paranoid, man," he said as the laugher continued.

"So this thing Mom's doing is real. She's serious about the property and the money?"

"She's serious," Trey confirmed.

J.T. shook his head. His gut feeling still told him that there was more to his mother's sudden interest in investing in real estate than met the eye. His thoughts raced to the one intersecting point of all three women, ballet.

"Tell me about this property."

Trey reached over to his computer and brought up the details—architectural floor plans, construction records, and schematics. He listed the area's pros and cons, including the fact that the area was just beginning to experience a new wave of interest. To be fair, he also outlined the problems. "I can e-mail you a copy of all this, but the project has been in the works for months."

J.T. nodded in appreciation. "Tell me about the Art Council."

Trey shook his head. "You *have* been out of touch a while. About two-and-a-half years ago, Aunt Taylor and several artist friends of hers in different fields developed the Arts Council as a way to generate more interest in the D.C.-area arts community. They also endow scholarships and sponsor cultural events and institutions."

J.T. asked several questions about the Arts Council, Lena Palmer, and the planned community center art-and-dance studio. He shook his head each time Trey responded.

"Where was I when all this was happening?"

"New York, London, Hong Kong, Los Angeles, Chicago, Seattle, San Francisco, shall I continue?"

"No, I get the point. So basically, Mom got bored with painting and decided to create something a bit more substantial."

"No. I don't think so. Aunt Taylor is a brilliant artist and an extremely astute businesswoman. You're not giving her enough credit. Don't underestimate her. For example, the Arts Foundation she founded a few years ago is an extremely valuable asset. If it were traded on the exchange, it would be worth an immense amount. As a tax deduction alone, it's invaluable, and the council has raised an enormous amount each year for the arts."

"She's giving Lena Palmer a million dollars to open a dance studio."

Trey's interest piqued, "She's purchasing property, there's a difference."

"I don't care what it is. I will not stand by and have my Mom taken advantage of."

"I don't think Aunt Taylor is being taken advantage of. This is her heart. She loves art. She loves ballet. It's a natural for her."

"That's exactly what I'm afraid of. She loves the arts so much that taking advantage of her would be easy."

"There's nothing you can do."

"Yes there is."

"What?"

"Stop it before it goes any further."

"That might not be the best idea. Aunt Taylor really wants this."

He ignored Trey completely. "One more thing, Juliet Bridges, have you ever heard of her?"

"Sure. What about her?"

"You know her?"

"Yes, I know her. An acquaintance introduced us a while back." Trey smiled openly at the memory. J.T., noting his expression, frowned but was curious. "By that smile I assume you know Ms. Bridges well."

"Well enough."

"Are you two together?"

"No."

"Have you dated her?"

"No."

"Tell me about her."

"What do you want to know?"

"Everything you know."

Trey flexed his fingers, propping his chin in his hands as he smiled. "Juliet Bridges is a principal dancer with the Capitol Ballet Company. She's danced most of her life, and won many awards for her performances. She's ambitious, determined, driven, shrewd, smart, and extremely good at what she does. She's beautiful and has a wry sense of humor. And she can be extremely dangerous with her tongue."

"What does that mean?" J.T. asked.

"Rumor has it that she's broken more than a few hearts and crushed a hell of a lot more," Trey said, noting J.T.'s consuming interest. "One would have to be beyond exceptional to get and keep her attention."

"Sounds like you're listing for a dating service."

"You tell me, am I?" Trey asked.

J.T. mulled over the question but decided to let the answer rest for the moment. He still wasn't convinced of Mamma Lou's motives when it came to his marital status. And any woman associated with Mamma Lou could be a possible target for matchmaking.

If it wasn't Lena, then maybe it was someone else, maybe even Juliet. Juliet—the idea had merit, but suddenly he wasn't exactly sure if he was annoyed or pleased at the prospect of the target being Juliet. "Does Juliet have a connection with my Mamma Lou or my mom?"

"I doubt there's a personal connection. I'm sure they know of each other. Obviously, Juliet is the CBC principal dancer. Both Mamma Lou and Aunt Taylor are on the board, but that's it. Other than ballet, I can't see them traveling in the same circles. Besides, Juliet has a small circle of close friends. She pretty much keeps to herself aside from the dance world."

"Any outside interests?" J.T. continued.

"Oh, she does have a small children's dance center in D.C. I heard that's like her second home when she's not performing."

"Where is it?"

"In D.C. someplace," Trey said.

J.T. nodded. "What about her personal life?"

"She drinks coffee twenty-four hours a day, seven days a week."

J.T. looked at Trey's smarmy expression. He knew exactly what type of information J.T. wanted to know.

"More personal than that," J.T. pressed.

Trey smiled. "The past few months, she's supposedly been connected with Senator Randolph Kingsley."

"Supposedly?"

"I can't see the connection."

"Who is he?"

"I know him, he's a good guy. We often travel in the same circles. A newly elected senator from California, apparently he and Juliet are both originally from the San Francisco area, but they didn't connect again until he moved to D.C. a few months ago when his term started."

"What's his angle?"

"He's ambitious, with a squeaky-clean reputation."

"What about his connection to Juliet?"

"They're seen out a lot together, and she attends some of his major functions. If you ask me, they seem more platonically associated than anything else." Trey shrugged, reiterating the obvious. "But then again, he's a red-blooded male. She's gorgeous. You make the call."

"What about you?"

Trey smiled. "With Juliet?" J.T. nodded. "As I said earlier, one would have to be beyond exceptional to get and keep Juliet's attention. I didn't even get up to bat. She is very selective. Not just anyone walks into her life and stays for a while." Trey watched closely, seeing J.T. process the information. He knew his cousin well. This was more than the usual show-and-tell session that they'd done from time to time. For one thing, this wasn't business; it was most definitely personal. "Your turn to show and tell."

J.T. stood and walked over to the window. He looked out at the traffic traveling down Pennsylvania Avenue. The rush of the financial district was constant. Surrounded by the most powerful financial institutions in the world, K Street was the power center of the District, and Trey's office was right in the center of it all.

Noticeably tucked between The World Bank and the International Monetary Fund headquarters, Evans International Finance, Trey's brokerage firm, was right in the middle of the action. J.T. looked up at the Department of the Treasury building across the street. Imposing in its power and prestige, the view from the window was ideal.

As a financier and investor, Trey Evans was brilliant in his investments and lived well from his financial savvy. He had learned young that money, power, and Washington, D.C. were an ideal link. So, as a teen, he began his love affair with the stock market, and found that he was more than just lucky after making a quarter of a million dollars in ten months.

Quietly reserved, Trey sat in silence at his desk and waited attentively for J.T. to speak.

"A while ago, last summer, I gave a speech at a conference. It was only supposed to be one night."

"But something happened, I'm presuming," Trey added.

"Yeah, there was a blackout."

"New York, end of August, right?" Trey asked. J.T. nodded. Trey smiled. "Let me guess. In a city of millions, you and a yet-unnamed lucky lady connected."

J.T. nodded again. "Traffic was crazy. I couldn't get back uptown to the appointment, so I left the car in the street and stopped at a nearby hotel. She was in line in front of me. The hotel was cash only, and neither one of us had that much, so we made a deal and pooled our funds and got the last room."

"You shared a room together?"

"Yeah, we did."

"Okay," he smiled, impressed. "I get the picture. Cut to the next morning. Which one of you left first, you or her?"

"I had to go move the car and take care of a few things. I needed to know if the blackout affected E-Corp. When I came back to the room, she was gone." J.T. paused.

"So, what happened then?" Trey asked, watching J.T. closely.

"I looked for her when I returned to the hotel. She'd already left the room." J.T. cleared his throat, then hesitated. "I wanted to make sure that she would be okay."

"Of course," Trey said, not at all fooled.

"She'd said that she was a dancer, so I went to a few Broadway and off-Broadway productions."

"You," Trey asked, astonished by J.T.'s remark, "on Broadway?"

"Yes, me, on Broadway," J.T. said, slightly annoyed.

"Wait a minute, is that the *occurrence* you mentioned?"

"What occurrence?"

"That's what you called it. Apparently something happened in New York a few months back, and you asked me to refer you to a local investigator."

J.T. instantly remembered the situation and his overly vague request. "Yeah, that's right, she was the occurrence."

"Did you ever find her or see her again?" Trey asked.

"Yeah, earlier today, right here in D.C., I found out that she's dancing with the Capitol Ballet Company in a production of *Carmen*." He tossed the playbill onto Trey's desk.

Trey picked it up read the cover, then laughed out loud at the irony. "You and Juliet Bridges shared a hotel room in the New York City blackout. That must have been an interesting *occurrence*."

J.T. sat down and sipped his coffee while eyeing his cousin sternly, but the laughter continued. "Okay, you found Juliet, now what?" Trey asked when he finally settled down.

"That's a good question." J.T. paused for a moment as a thought dawned on him. "She'd be perfect."

"What do you mean?"

"I could use this."

"Use what?"

"Bear with me," J.T. paused, stood, turned laughed then turned back to Trey. "What if Juliet and I pooled our resources again? What if I offered her money in exchange for services rendered?"

"Last I heard that kind of thing was illegal, even inside the Beltway."

"It says in there that she's retiring from the stage soon. Ballet dancers can't make much; surely she could use a part-time job."

"You're talking about Juliet as the pawn, aren't you?"

J.T. nodded. "Exactly, but what would her incentive be?"

"She could use a backer," Trey offered.

"A backer?"

"Yeah," Trey said, "Its well known that Juliet is interested in opening a new dance company when she retires at the end of the season."

"That's right. So if Mom can help finance a community center, surely I can do the same for Juliet's dance company, right?"

"So Juliet's the pawn. She gets a small endowment to help sponsor her dance company. How perfect is that? You already have a working relationship with her, so to speak. You've joined forces before for the greater good, no emotional ties, no romantic baggage."

J.T. frowned and searched for a flaw in the plan. He sat down and looked across the desk to his cousin. "It's too easy, too obvious."

"Not necessarily, sometimes simple is best."

"How long are we supposed to have been involved?"

"Not long enough to be serious, but not too short to make it sound frivolous."

J.T. smiled, then chuckled. "Ten months, perfect." Trey joined in, and they both nodded in agreement. It was perfect, simple, and direct, and was guaranteed to get Mamma Lou off his back before she even got started.

"Okay, I'll do it, I'm supposed to go to the ballet tonight to meet Mom and Lena Palmer, and I'll also talk to Juliet while I'm there. Hopefully I can settle everything tonight."

J.T. stood to leave as Trey opened his top drawer and pulled a small round packet from the desk. "Hey," he called, getting J.T.'s attention. J.T. turned just as Trey tossed the packet to him. He caught it easily, then turned it in his hand to read the contents.

"Thanks, it just might come in handy."

"In that case," Trey reached into the drawer and tossed him two more, "enjoy."

Chapter 3

Thunderous applause silenced all doubts about Juliet Bridges' performance. Tonight age was apparently just a number because she was sheer perfection. Juliet held the smug smile as she arched her back straighter and pointed her toe. She stood in fourth position, her right foot slightly in front of her left, toes pointed in opposite directions, back straight, and neck and head held high and confident. She knew without a doubt that she had danced brilliantly.

The heavy curtain rose slowly, and two perfectly paired figures modestly skipped from center to front stage at the centerline as the remaining corps de ballet took a modest step forward and nodded appreciatively. The audience leaped to their feet having thoroughly enjoyed the dance vignettes narrated by the company's artistic director, Peter Flemings.

Taken from several classical and modern ballets, the company presented shortened dances from several well-known ballets. Juliet performed the dual roles of Odette and Odile in *Swan Lake*, Terpsichore, a muse, in *Apollo* and Kitri in *Don Quixote*, then as a soloist in *Stars and Stripes*. But it was her signature role of Carmen that ended the program, and she was brilliant. Not since Dorothy Dandridge had a role been so perfectly performed. The brash, brazen harlot she played seemed to come alive with Juliet's spirit. She smiled brightly and curtsied low, gracefully extending her arm, bending it for effect.

A plump, round child hurried on stage from the left wing,

carrying two dozen roses in her chubby little hands. With golden Shirley Temple ringlets, wearing a dress a size too small, and carelessly clicking her patent leather heels, she glanced at the audience, then froze midway. Her rose-colored cheeks brightened and reddened to full bloom. Her perfectly paired lips formed a deliberate *O* as her baby-blue eyes filled and were about to burst. Then she caught sight of her grandmother waving to her from the wings, prompting her to continue to the pair waiting at center stage.

She hurried to Juliet and clumsily handed her the bouquets, then backed away slowly. She turned, smiled at the horde of smiling faces in the audience, then ran offstage into her grandmother's open arms. Everyone laughed at the cherub.

"Where do they get these kids?" Richard Griffin asked, breathing hard, his British accent more pronounced than usual. He tilted his head slightly and bowed thankfully to the audience as his expression froze in a perpetual stage smile.

"Be nice," Juliet said, still smiling graciously to the audience. Still poised in fourth position, with an aura of accomplishment surrounding her, she curtsied gracefully.

"Yes, yes, I know," Richard said, holding her hand firmly, then letting go to allow Juliet to take two steps forward and bow solo. "Her grandmother is one of our largest patrons. She's got about fifty million dollars and loves the ballet."

"Exactly," she confirmed.

Richard, the other half of the *pas de deux* and Juliet's friend, was from the British Ballet Company in London. Born to British and Caribbean parents, he was an enigma in the dance community. He was a straight man who took full advantage of his auspicious position. Like a child in a candy store, he had spread his favors and granted private audiences with most of the women in the cast and on the patron's list, and in a great number of dance companies around the world.

His shameless reputation preceded him. And when Juliet took the summer to guest dance in London, he was the perfect tour guide and gentleman. When the Capitol Ballet

Company made a special request for him to perform in Washington for the season, he jumped at the opportunity, and Juliet reciprocated his kindness on this side of the Atlantic Ocean.

Although he and Juliet had been friends since they met in London, she never fell for his particular charms. Hence, after months of attempts to seduce her, he finally gave up and instead became her friend.

"But do I care?" he continued.

"You'd better," Juliet said as she returned to his side. "The company needs the cash."

"Don't they always?" he said, with a similar smile plastered across his face. The pair took one last bow as the curtain came down. They hurried offstage and were replaced by the company's solo dancers, Vanya Kastavah and her partner, Damon Hall.

Juliet and Richard stood in the wings, gently dabbing the moisture and perspiration from their brows and necks, careful not to disturb their delicate stage makeup. They watched as Vanya and Damon bowed to generous applause.

Richard peered over Juliet's head and looked into the prime orchestra center house seats and the center parterre box seats. "Is your illustrious congressman here yet?"

"You know perfectly well that he's a senator," she corrected dryly. "And I have no idea. He said he might show up tonight if he could get away."

"I don't see him."

She peeked around the heavy curtain, then squinted out at the applauding crowd. The house lights were still turned down so only those sitting in the very front rows were visible. "They all look like a bunch of screaming faceless lunatics from here."

"Now, now, go on there, that's not the right sort. Where's your gratitude? This is your public, they adore you. Just look at their faces."

"You look at them, I'm exhausted. All I can think about right now is my pillow and about fifteen hours of sleep."

"I know you're not missing the fundraiser tonight."

"What's one more fundraiser? Let them use Vanya. I'm sure she'll be delighted to play diva for the evening."

"Our black Russian princess would absolutely love that. She can't wait to fill your tutu and become company principal."

"She needs a hell of a lot more than what she has to fill this tutu and be a sole principal. Her feet are questionable and her technique could use some serious detail work. Not to mention she's got a major anorexic thing going on."

"Hold on, now, do I sense a catfight coming on?"

"Hardly. Vanya is the least of my worries. She's so far out of my league, she needs the psychic hotline and a bloodhound to find half the techniques I've already forgotten."

"You two are too much alike to be such mortal enemies," Richard observed.

Juliet smirked and shook her head, then turned to him. "Mortal enemies. Mortal enemies. Where do you get these corny lines from?"

"Sorry, love, I was watching the BBC again."

"You're mental."

"Of course I am. And you adore me for it."

Juliet chuckled and shook her head. She focused her attention back on stage as she watched Vanya go through her usual postperformance ritual. "Vanya does remind me of myself at that age—so hungry for the spotlight yet still needing to grow up emotionally."

"You need to mentor her."

Juliet's sudden burst of unexpected laughter caught even her by surprise. She quickly controlled herself and continued to wipe the perspiration away.

The curtain fell again, cuing Vanya and Damon to leave as the chorus hurried onto the stage. The curtain rose, the chorus members took their bows, stepped forward, and bowed again just as the curtain lowered a third time.

The crowd continued to roar, raising its collective voice.

Juliet took Richard's hand as Roger Payne, the stage manager, beckoned wildly for them to return to their position at center stage. As the red velvet curtain rose again, they skipped downstage, then to each side, giving the entire audience full view for one last curtain call.

Juliet stepped forward and bowed gracefully. As she returned to Richard's side, the pair took several steps forward, separated, then opened their arms and saluted the conductor, the orchestra, and the assembled dancers behind them. When they came together again, the conversation continued. Together, they took two steps forward. He took her hand again and they both bowed.

"Still, she's breathing down your neck, love. She attended every gala and fundraiser this season and is seriously sucking up to Phillip Waverly."

Juliet pulled a single rose from her bouquet and handed it to Richard. He took it and gracefully bowed to her. "So let her. I'm tired of being trounced around like a show pony just to please a bunch of moneybags."

"Hey, don't bite the hand that feeds us. Besides, some of those moneybags aren't half bad."

"You didn't?" Juliet said just before they parted and stepped aside. Vanya and Damon returned to the stage and the chorus hurried off.

Each performer took a solitary bow. Then Damon took Juliet's hand as Richard took Vanya's hand. Each man bowed to his dancer, then they returned to their respective partners.

"Beg your pardon?" Richard said as soon as he and Juliet were reunited.

"Don't play innocent with me. You know the rules. Never, never touch the purse strings. Just make sure that the powers that be don't find out." She chided him, then instantly begged curiously, "Which one?"

"A gentleman never kisses and tells."

"Since when are you a gentleman?" Now alone on stage,

they prepared for the final bow, sending the roaring audience into hysterical applause.

"You are in a seriously nasty mood. PMS?"

"Shut up."

"Ooh, you are cheeky tonight," he shivered jokingly. "Sounds like you've still got some Carmen left in you."

"Carmen ain't got nothing on me."

"Apparently not."

She circled around him, going farther downstage. After a deep bow and curtsy, they stepped back and waited until the final curtain fell.

As soon as the edge of the curtain hit the floor, Richard leaned over and kissed her forehead. "I will still see you at the fundraiser this evening?" he asked, emphasizing each word, making his meaning clear, knowing her tendency to change her mind when it came to pubic appearances.

"I promised Patricia that we'd go tonight," Juliet said as she began moving her mouth animatedly to relax the strained muscles from her fixed smile and perfectly poised expression.

"Good, I'll see you later then," Richard said. Juliet nodded.

As soon as Richard walked off, the lead wardrobe mistress, Nadine Palmer, hurried on stage to meet her. "You were wonderful, Juliet."

"Of course I was," Juliet said confidently.

Nadine shook her head, not at all surprised by the flippant remark. "Your friend Patricia Franklin called twice, and Senator Kingsley regrets that he is unable meet you this evening," Nadine said as she took the two bouquets and handed them to her assistant. She wrapped a thick terry cloth robe around Juliet's shoulders and handed her a soft white towel.

"Thanks," Juliet smiled tightly, then responded automatically while waiting for the inevitable. It came as expected.

"Oh, before I forget to mention it, that last *pirouette* at the end of act two, scene one should have been a full rotation longer. It should have been two triples, not a triple and a double." She turned to walk away, then paused and returned. "Oh, one last thing, your final *fouettés* were noticeably weak. You were clearly winded. You need to focus on that in the future."

Juliet continued to pat her face with the towel. "I'll make sure to work on that," she sneered sarcastically.

"Just a thought," Nadine said nonchalantly.

"You might want to keep your thoughts to yourself next time."

"I wouldn't count on it. We've known each other too long for that, haven't we?" Nadine said as she smiled smartly, then turned to walk away, heading in Vanya's direction.

Juliet arched her eyebrow and smirked, pulling her lips tightly to one side, a look that usually caused even grown men to steer clear. Few people had nerve enough to criticize her performance, let alone comment on a particular missed routine. Nadine was the exception.

Nadine was fifteen years her senior. They had known each other since Juliet first began with the company. Nadine, a former chorus dancer with lead potential, had taken the position as wardrobe mistress when an injury had ended her promising career on stage. Unlike most, she had remained in the company and had forged an unusual bond of friendship with Juliet.

Both had a biting wit and a determination and respect for excellence, yet it was Juliet who had gained the reputation as an arrogant, temperamental, difficult, and even volatile prima donna. The title came solely because of her desire for perfection. She expected the best of herself and of others around her. Only when time was being wasted and the level of excellence was seriously being compromised did she become aggravated.

But never did she show her annoyance without good reason. No matter what others said about her, she knew her craft. She had the talent, ability, and skill that made and kept her a star performer and a prima ballerina on stage and off.

At five-foot-seven she was of average height, with an accelerated metabolism that, no matter how much she loved to eat, always kept her around her target weight of one hundred and fifteen pounds, the perfect weight to perform the arduous lifts without straining or breaking her dance partner's back.

By the time Juliet had dabbed the moisture from her face, Nadine and her assistant had scurried off in another direction, leaving her alone at center stage.

As if in slow motion, Juliet looked around her. A sense of loss gripped her. Nadine was right, the routine had required a longer pirouette but she was just too exhausted. Another turn and she would have fallen on her behind. She looked up at the rafters, then to each stage wing. How was she going to survive the rest of her life without this world? This was all she knew, and all she ever wanted. She looked down at her trim, neat body. It had betrayed her. At the age of thirty-two, her stage life was over.

Suddenly the stage around her was a bustling hive of activity. Grips and backstage hands quickly removed the scenery as the stage crew and attendants secured the lights and prepared for the next performance the following night.

Juliet walked through the backstage throng, greeting and being greeted by her ensemble, dancers and visitors. They all congratulated her on another brilliant performance. The frozen smile returned on cue as she accepted the accolades while moving closer and closer to the solitude of her dressing room.

Juliet noticed her young rival, the Russian-born principal-troupe apprentice named Vanya Kastavah, standing to the side, stretching out her long, thin legs. At only five-foot-three she was all legs, willow thin, and chalk white from her heavily applied makeup. Always sullen and brooding, she insisted on perfecting the role of tortured rising star being held down by the world. One would hardly guess that her mother was a plump African-American woman with the fun-loving, gregarious personality of a cheerleader.

Juliet smiled as she witnessed Vanya's glare and the childish roll of her eyes as she refocused on her raised leg. Vanya grabbed her towel and stomped off. Juliet nearly burst into laughter again at the juvenile display.

She shook her head in pity. Apparently Vanya had a lot to learn about this business, about life, and about her. The recent antics she performed in order to bring attention to herself were truly pathetic. She was a child in a woman's body who used it to her advantage, driven toward a single goal, to dance center stage as the Capitol Ballet Company's prima ballerina. Juliet shook her head with sincere sympathy. Youth was truly wasted on the young.

As Juliet continued walking to her dressing room, the backstage manager, Roger Payne—appropriately named— appeared at her side carrying his usual clipboard and pen. With mousy blond hair that was too long and always needed to be trimmed, and wire framed glasses falling from his nose, he had a heart of gold, but his last name would indicate otherwise. At twenty-five, this was his first real job out of college. He had fish pale, belly white skin that freckled like polka-dot wallpaper every summer and an impossibly wide-eyed, rose-colored vision of the theatrical world that was idealistically naïve. But he gave credence to a dream she once coveted before the reality of stage life came along.

"Juliet," he quickened his step to keep pace with her long stride. "Your friend Patricia called, said she'd call again later. Also Senator Kingsley called. He sends his regrets. He won't be available this evening. He's unavoidably detained on Capitol Hill."

"Yes, thank you, I heard," she said as she brushed him aside and continued walking.

"One more thing, Chester's looking for you.

"What else is new?"

"There's someone he wants you to meet."

"I bet," she smirked without breaking stride.

"He said that this was important."

"It always is," she muttered. Chester Banks, the company

publicist, had been after her since the day he'd been hired. It seemed his sole purpose in life was to drive her crazy and get her to participate in as many of his promotions and publicity events as humanly possible.

"They're on the way to your dressing room." Roger stopped. Juliet stopped. He knew that would get her attention.

She turned to him. "Who's on their way to my dressing room?"

"Chester and his guest, tonight's performance sponsor."

"He's taking someone to my dressing room?" Juliet said slowly, enunciating each syllable. The look in her eye was unmistakably fierce.

Roger shifted the clipboard awkwardly. He recognized the look instantly. He had just lit her fuse, and an explosion was imminent. He just hoped that he wasn't anywhere near when she blew.

Juliet had a reputation for being temperamental on her good days, but after a performance, she could be absolutely impossible. And now Chester had crossed the line by invading her personal space. Roger took a step back. "Hey, don't shoot the messenger. I'm only giving you a heads-up."

She glared at him a moment longer, then continued her quick pace. "Thanks, messenger," she said sarcastically and walked away.

Knowing how Juliet hated being paraded around like a show pony, he didn't take offense. "One more thing. I need to know what time to expect you this evening. Phillip has several major patrons that have already requested to meet you tonight. Chester says that it's extremely important that you be there this evening. What time?"

"How about quarter past never?" she said as she was engulfed by other dancers hurrying down the hall to the cast dressing rooms. "But I might be late."

Juliet smiled to herself. This was one of the few fundraisers that she actually intended to attend. Her friend Patricia was dying to get out of the house, and this was the perfect opportunity, so she readily agreed to go with Juliet. But she refused to let Roger or anyone else know, just in case she changed her mind.

"You have to be there tonight. It's important," she heard him call out after her. "You know as soon I tell him you're not going, he's gonna have a fit, don't you?"

She waved her hand, ignoring Roger's usual paranoid rant and turned down the labyrinth hall into the belly of the theater. The last corner brought her to the dressing room door with the painted star. She smiled at the familiar sign of respect. Her name was proudly painted just above the golden star, *Juliet Bridges, principal dancer*. Using the soft white towel, she wiped the perspiration from her top lip, then patted at her chest and hung the towel around her neck as she entered. She gasped.

Chapter 4

He stood there with the most perfectly smug smile she'd ever seen. Her mouth still open, she stepped inside her dressing room and held the door open behind her. She tilted her head as she sized up the man standing there. He hadn't changed a bit. He was still as tempting as sin and just as gorgeous.

Standing there like he owned the world, she couldn't help but remember their first meeting. It was in New York City nearly ten months ago, and without a doubt the most memorable night of her life. But questions remained. How did he find her? What was he doing here? And what did he want?

She never expected to see him again. But she was wrong. She had seen him many times since then, in her dreams and her fantasies. He haunted and enticed her, but she refused to give in. It was a one-night stand, nothing more, nothing less. They'd agreed to give only first names and occupations that night. She told him that she was a dancer, but she never specified. She knew that since they'd met in New York, he'd naturally assume she was on Broadway in the theater.

One night was all they promised each other. But she knew before the words left her mouth that there was something special about that night. The night the lights went out and they spent the evening together in a hotel room. They'd touched each other somehow. In that short span of time, there was something that had drawn them together.

She could see when she looked into his eyes that the possibility of more than a simple attraction was there. Maybe it was a peculiar bonding that happened in the crisis. Whatever it was, it was strong and would only get stronger over time. That's why she had to leave when she did. She felt it, and she knew he did, too.

But one night was all she could give him. The circumstances presented themselves and they had spent a glorious night in each other's arms. When the lights came back on she had left, never looking back, never stopping to reconsider, but always wondering what might have been.

She watched as he stood motionlessly, across the room staring quietly. He hadn't been holding flowers; that was different. They all brought her flowers; why, she had no idea, but they did. The dressing room already looked and smelled like a mortuary. Randolph was the worst. He'd sent her enough bouquets in the past two months to fill a dozen flower shops ten times over.

Tall, dark, and gorgeous was an understatement. At six-feet-two, he was regal. He was stylishly dressed in a tailored dark blue suit with a matching shirt and tie and studded cufflinks. She liked that. He looked dangerous, which was arousing.

She watched as he leisurely and seductively raked his dark brown eyes over her face and down her body. Few men had the audacity to openly ogle her body. She, as any good performer, opened her robe to give him a better view. He accepted the invitation willingly.

Still dressed as her character, Carmen, she had a fringed shawl wrapped around her hips and a colorful bright red midriff peasant top provocatively slung off her shoulders. A red silk rose was entwined in her hair, which was characteristically left pulled back into a classic ballerina twist and bun.

His boldness sent a spark through what had long been a

cold façade around her heart. This was very different and very familiar. But why him, and why now?

She paused. Upon further scrutiny, she smelled the delicately subtle scent of wealth, sophistication, and self-absorbed arrogance, all of which she had long ago learned to avoid.

J.T. shook his head. With a stilted smile in, the only word he could think to describe this woman was, *irresistible*. Heart-stoppingly, knee weakeningly, breathtakingly irresistible. She stood before him as a vision from his dreams and fantasies.

He remembered her well, too well. Every inch of her body had been *seared* into his memory in just one night together. She had a candid street-smart persona wrapped in a slick, cultured package. As a ballerina she was poised and dignified, but he could still see the fire spark and burn in her eyes. It was the same fire he saw ten months ago. A fire from a night that he remembered all too well and had never been able to duplicate no matter how hard he'd tried.

The instant she stepped out on stage she had captivated the audience. Juliet Bridges had a presence beyond anything he had ever seen. Enthralled by her beauty and mesmerized by her body, she danced like liquid silk. Gliding gracefully across the stage all eyes were on her as she held the audience in the palm of her hand.

Despite her polished performance he saw something different. He saw trouble, and that excited him. Something about her sparked a primal need inside of him. This was the woman who had stolen something from him that night. Without even knowing it, she'd taken his heart with her when she walked away.

"I believe one of us took a wrong turn," Juliet said as she sashayed into the dressing room, moving closer to those gorgeous eyes. She stared at him as she closed in on her target. A crooked smile appeared on her lips. This was going to be easy, she thought. Seductively, she licked her lips, purposely allowing her tongue to linger longer than necessary. She moved to just inches from his body. They usually backed up by this time. But he didn't. She smiled. She always enjoyed a challenge.

"I once heard that if you wait long enough, everything comes back." Juliet openly looked him up and down. He hadn't changed a bit. "I guess it's true."

J.T. smirked and chuckled at her obvious insinuation. "I came back for you, but you were gone. So technically, you left me."

She nodded absently and reached up and ran her finger along her lips, then traced his lips and smiled, expecting a reaction. It didn't come. A glint sparked in her eyes. On impulse, she reached up and kissed him, hard and long. It was sexy and sweet and just as she remembered.

After the kiss, she leaned back to observe the shock. There was none. She shrugged. "Curious, I just wanted a taste to remember." She turned to walk away but felt her arm caught in a viselike grip.

J.T. pulled her back hard against his chest. Holding her waist firmly, he boldly looked into her eyes. He smiled for the first time since he had entered her dressing room. He leaned in to kiss her again. She leaned back; then for reasons she couldn't fathom, she threw her arms around his neck and kissed him with all the passion she felt inside. Just as full as the first, this kiss left nothing to the imagination.

When the kiss ended, she stepped back and walked toward the open door. She stood with her hand on the inner doorknob, waiting for him to leave. "Goodbye."

But before J.T. could speak, Chester Banks suddenly appeared at the open doorway. "Juliet, darling, there you are." Breathless and anxious, he hurried to her side, expecting her usual fury at finding a stranger in her dressing room. But, to his amazement, the room was calm.

"You were absolutely brilliant this evening," Chester began cautiously. "Truly the best I've ever seen you perform," he gushed awkwardly. In his typical drooling, one-man-fan-club, publicist persona, he air-kissed her three inches away from each cheek, then bear-hugged her with the strength of a sleeping two-year-old toddler.

"Yes, I know," she said dryly. She grinned sweetly as she met J.T.'s smile head on.

Chester stepped further into the room and closed the door behind him. He watched the two as their eyes remained connected. A chill shot through him as he felt as if he'd just interrupted something major.

"Chester, how nice of you to join us," Juliet said, still staring at her guest. "J.T.," she smiled smugly.

"Juliet," he responded with a curt nod.

Chester looked between the two again, pointing to each in turn. "Do you two already know each other?"

The obvious question drew an answer from both of them. "No," they responded in unison.

Chester's mouth opened, then clamped shut. Speechless and confused, he suspiciously looked from J.T. to Juliet, then back again. There was definitely something going on. "Okay," he said, prompted when a moment of silence followed. "Then where are my manners," he began, anxiously now hurrying to J.T.'s side. "J.T., this is the Capitol Ballet Company's principal ballerina, Juliet Bridges. Juliet, this is my guest, J.T. Evans, and tonight's special fundraiser performance sponsor."

Juliet nodded tightly, her eyes piercing.

J.T. nodded in return, fixing his gaze on her.

"Hoo-kay," Chester said with reserved glee, still totally confused, yet completely elated that Juliet hadn't done the usual and insulted his guest. Granted, he had no idea what was going on, but that wasn't anything new for him when it came to Juliet and her artistic mood swings.

Hastening to fill the void, Chester began a long monologue detailing the merits of the Capitol Ballet Company, then recalling his PR spiel point-by-point. Without warning, Juliet opened her robe and unsnapped the satiny shawl from her slim waist. J.T. watched as she let the shawl drop to the floor and stepped away. Now in just her top, tights, and pointe shoes, she moved to sit down at her dressing table.

She looked up to see J.T.'s eyes watching her intensely. Juliet nodded at her own reflection in the mirror. J.T. returned the gesture. An understanding had been reached.

She smiled coyly at the acknowledgment, then looked back as the bright naked bulbs glared back at her perfect reflection. Barely listening to Chester as he continued to rattle on, she removed the paste jewelry, the large red flower bobby pinned in her hair, then shrugged the robe onto the back of the chair. J.T. smiled in appreciation, as she knew he would.

She picked up a large white jar from the table and twisted the lid off. She dug her fingers into the creamy white goop just as a knock broke the staring competition between the two. "Come," she called out.

Roger stuck his head inside. "Juliet, have you seen, oh, there you are, Chester." He stepped inside with his usual clipboard attached. "Peter needs to speak with you as soon as possible. I think that it has something to do with Vanya's auction basket." He turned to leave, then changed his mind, directing his attention to Juliet, seated at the dressing table. "Oh, and Juliet," Roger's voice rose with added inflection, "Peter needs to talk to you before the party this evening."

"Why can't they get anything right? Don't move, I'll be right back," Chester mumbled before disappearing through the door, dutifully followed by Roger.

Juliet proceeded to remove the thick pancake makeup from her face as J.T. stood staring. With her face now covered in white cold cream, she looked up to him. "If I ignore you, will you go away?" He smiled and shook his head but didn't answer. "So, Mr. Evans, do you talk or would you like to just keep standing there staring at me while I remove my makeup?"

"Chester was right. You were pretty good out there tonight."

"On the contrary, I was phenomenal, but I wasn't fishing for a compliment," she said, now with a handful of tissues wiping the cream from her face.

"It was a statement of fact," he said plainly.

She looked directly at him in the mirror's reflection. "Let's cut to the chase, shall we? We know each other well enough not to beat around the bush. What do you want?"

"Excuse me?"

"Get to the point. What do you want: an autograph, a signed photo, another quick lay with a prima ballerina, what?"

His brow rose with interest. "Are you always this direct?"

"You should know."

"You're right, I guess I should."

Their eyes met in the mirror again. He smiled, remembering just how direct she could be. "It saves time in the long run." With her face now perfectly clean, she spun the chair around to face him. "Well, what's it gonna be, Mr. Evans?"

His smile turned to a knowing chuckle. "It's J.T. As you said, we know each other well enough."

"Okay J.T., what's it gonna be?"

"Why don't we play it by ear for the time being?"

Juliet stood to face him, remembering that those were the exact words he had used ten months ago when they shared a hotel room. "That was a long time ago."

J.T. walked to the door. He grabbed the knob. "Ten months isn't that long ago, Juliet." He turned the knob and opened the door.

"It was one night," she said as he stepped into the hallway.

"Some say that one night can be a lifetime. We'll talk later," he answered as the door closed behind him.

"Bet on it," she said to the empty room as the idea of attending the fundraiser began to appeal to her. She owed J.T. Evans. No man had ever walked away from her like he did.

She grabbed her robe from the back of the chair and a fresh towel from the cabinet in the small bathroom. She reached into the shower stall and turned on the cool, refreshing water. She removed her clothes and stepped inside, letting the water wash away her stress. Tonight promised to be an interesting evening.

Chapter 5

J.T. walked around the huge open space, officially named the Washington Cultural Center, in amazement. Although he'd been here just two years earlier to celebrate a product launch, he barely had time to appreciate it then. The open, airy space with huge plate-glass windows afforded an excellent view of the gardens and promenade outside, while keeping the attendees cool and refreshed inside.

Built in the mid-sixties, and typical of that era, the main promenade and lobby had a vaulted ceiling at least two stories high, with live ornamental trees and Italian marble flooring polished to a reflective sheen. Monochromatic in its stark minimalism, it was traditional and classical, and ironically the perfect complement to the evening's elaborate performance.

J.T. stood by one of the long cloth-covered tables topped with cascading floral arrangements and a variety of appetizers, hors d'oeuvres, and aperitifs. Talking with several businessmen and women, he watched as, one by one, cast members entered and joined the gathering. To his disappointment, Juliet had yet to arrive.

Beset by several members of his mother's professional arts organization who had instantly recognized him, J.T. attempted to be as attentive as possible.

They asked about Taylor's whereabouts. J.T. offered her regrets and apologized for her uncharacteristic absence. She'd called him at the last minute to say that, due to unforeseen circumstances, she was unable to attend, but for him to go ahead without her.

They expressed their concern, then began talking endlessly about the Art Council's projects, their high regard for his parents, and, as he expected, about the merits of his becoming a more active member of the organization.

J.T. quickly and expertly sidestepped all of their attempts to pin him down about attending the next meeting, citing his heavy work and travel schedules and his mother's arduous dedication to the organization. He nodded attentively, while continuing to focus his attention on the still-arriving guests.

Afterward, he excused himself and walked over to the bar. Standing there gave him an unobstructed view of the entrance. As each dancer arrived, a wave of excitement rippled through the crowd. The most intense was when the second leads, Vanya Kastavah and Damon Hall, arrived.

Smiling brightly, Vanya looked around the room in earnest. Juliet was noticeably absent, as usual. A self-satisfied feeling swelled inside of Vanya. She had delayed her arrival as long as she dared. Making a grand entrance took ingenuity and timing, both of which she was blessed with. Having guessed that Juliet would pass on the gala by showing her usual contempt for the company's patrons, Vanya was pleased that it left her solely in command of the center stage.

She was born for this, her mother always told her. Her mother, an African-American diplomat's assistant who'd married a Russian dancer, knew as soon as she sent her daughter to her first ballet class that she would be a prima ballerina. Holding her head high, Vanya looked around. Remembering her mother's words well, she took her place at center stage.

She worked the room like the true professional she was. She had learned from the best. Madame Jacqueline was an exceptional instructor with an eye for talent. She was the founder, artistic director, and choreographer of the Cheva Ballet Group, a small, poorly maintained studio in the southwestern part of Russia. The moment Madame Jacqueline laid eyes on Vanya, she was spellbound. Vanya had been her pupil for the next six years, and in that time she had learned a lot about dance and about life.

At the tender age of thirteen, she had left her father's homeland and come to America to dance with a world-famous company. But now, at the age of eighteen, instead of fulfilling her mother's prophecy, she had been relegated to the second position and soloist because Juliet Bridges was jealous of her talent and her youth.

Everyone knew that Juliet was well past her prime and that her overrated talent was waning, along with her youth. But no one had the courage to stand up to her. It was time for new blood at center stage, and the new blood was her.

Vanya greeted her fans with all the poise and grace of a queen ascending her throne. She smiled and laughed while strategically planning her next move. She held her hand out to be kissed as soon as she walked up to her fans. They loved it, they loved her.

The women, thrilled at meeting her, marveled at her petiteness and her small, waiflike frame. The men were attracted by her body and sexuality, and were excited by the possibilities. She knew the game, and played it to perfection. Every new face in the crowd noticed her; she made sure of that. As Madame Jacqueline always said, the more the patrons loved you, the further your star will rise and the brighter it will shine. She learned early that, as in most industries, money moved the ballet world, not talent.

Vanya swayed her narrow hips across the room and stood by Chester. She raised up on tiptoe to whisper in his ear: "Who is that man? I've seen him before."

Chester leaned down and inched closer to Vanya. The nearness of her tiny body sent a lustful shiver down his spine. He couldn't wait to get out of there and take Vanya to his bed. As a dancer she was limber, as a woman she was seductive, and as a Russian she was her father's child.

"What man?" Chester asked.

"Him, over there in the blue, talking with Peter and Richard," Vanya pointed out.

Chester looked across the room and found J.T. in her line of vision. "You probably do recognize him. That's J.T. Evans from E-Corp."

"What's E-Corp?"

"It's a major player in the computer software industry. J.T.'s in the business section of newspapers or magazines a least once a month. His family is one of the wealthiest African-American families in the States."

An interested smiled tipped her full lips upwards. The moment he mentioned wealth her interest level was piqued. He was just what she was looking for; all she needed was a wealthy personal benefactor, and Juliet would be out of her way. J.T. Evans was perfect. All she had to do was pay him a little attention and she'd have everything she ever wanted. She smiled sweetly as Chester continued. "He came to meet Juliet."

"What?" Her sweet, innocent expression instantly faded.

"Juliet, he came specifically to meet her."

"Why her, why Juliet?" she demanded.

Chester shrugged. "I don't know. I got a call from his office requesting that I set up a meeting tonight."

"But Juliet's not here, so he hasn't met her yet."

"No, they met earlier in her dressing room. I introduced them right after her performance. I wonder where she is?" Chester began looking around through the crowded room.

Vanya rolled her eyes. Again Juliet was the topic of conversation. "I want to meet him, introduce me," she insisted.

"Okay," Chester agreed reluctantly. The two made their way across the room just as Richard was pulled away. "J.T.," Chester began, "I'd like to introduce you to the company's next great star, Vanya Kastavah. Vanya, this is J.T. Evans of E-Corp."

Vanya stepped closer and raised her hand for J.T. to kiss. He took her hand, lowered it, and shook it. Her disappoint-

ment was obvious. "How do you do, Monsieur Evans?" she
added with a pert nod and fluttering lashes.

"Nice to meet you, Vanya," J.T. said looking down on what
seemed to be a child pretending to be an adult. He arched
his brow knowingly. He'd certainly noticed Vanya earlier. She
entered the room like a star. He noticed how she connected
with every businessman in the room, and now, apparently, it
was his turn. This was a woman on a mission. She was definitely after something. He knew her type instantly. Young,
hungry, for more, and eager to get it any way she could.

But J.T. was definitely not interested. She was far too
young, too bold, and too hungry for his taste. Besides he had
recently acquired a taste for a certain prima ballerina, Juliet
Bridges to be exact. Her boldness excited him and her brazen
bravado enticed him. She said exactly what was on her mind,
and each time he looked forward to hearing more.

"If you'll excuse me," J.T. said, then turned and walked toward the doorway.

Vanya huffed indignantly as she watched J.T. walk away.
She was so tired of Juliet getting everything. But not this
time; this time she was going to have everything she wanted
and deserved. She turned away as Peter and Chester began
talking. It was time to get to work, seeing that the perfect person had just walked in.

"Phillip's here," Peter said as soon as Vanya left.

Chester looked around the immediate area. He spotted
Phillip smiling and greeting patrons as they passed by. Vanya,
ever savvy, had attached herself to him like a Siamese twin.

"I know I saw him earlier, he's already asked for Juliet."

"I know, he asked me too."

"She is coming tonight?" Peter asked.

"I told her how important tonight was," Chester insisted.

"So, where is she?" Peter hissed gritting through clenched
teeth.

Chester shook his head and shrugged. "I have no idea. I
sent Roger to look for her."

Peter nodded and scanned the immediate area for Juliet. As he turned behind him, Phillip appeared and stepped into his line of vision.

Phillip Waverly, the Washington Cultural Center's president, approached, slightly startling the two men. Carrying a glass of champagne but never drinking a drop, he smiled his customary Cheshire cat grim. "Gentlemen," he announced with his usual grandness, "this is truly a great event. *Carmen* was an excellent choice to perform for the show's finale this evening. What a profound experience, truly inspiring. I am truly pleased, as were the patrons that accompanied me. We were all truly touched and truly blessed."

Then, as usual, he recounted every scene and act of the performance, giving a full rendition of the various interpretations and putting the ballet in context for each. He went on to critique the costumes, lighting, and scenery, including a general critique of the dancers. He ended by giving his full analysis of possible alterations, noting his years on stage and in the business.

Smiling and thanking Phillip for his astute knowledge and excellent taste, Chester and Peter hesitantly waited for the appropriate moment of reflection, knowing Phillip's next remark.

"Speaking of which, where is our lovely leading lady?" Phillip asked finally.

"She'll be here momentarily," Peter assured Phillip.

"She's probably still getting changed. You know how long it takes for Juliet to get down here sometimes. She's usually the last one to leave and the first one here in the morning," Chester added.

"I hope so," Phillip warned. "I have several patrons looking forward to meeting her this evening. I'd hate for them to be disappointed."

The veiled threat was understood as Peter and Chester looked at each other, then once around the room quickly, then finally back to Phillip.

"I'm sure she's just a few minutes away. She knows how

important tonight is," Chester said, hoping he didn't sound as desperate as he was.

"See that she does, I'd like to keep this money in the room." Phillip turned on a dime and welcomed a passing patron with an exaggerated greeting. He instantly threw his arm around him, grabbed a waiter with a tray of champagne, and placed a glass into the man's hand.

Chester and Peter looked at each again. A shadow of concern covered their faces. They were pretty much at the whim of Juliet's mood, and attending after-performance events wasn't exactly high on her priority list. Tonight didn't seem to be any different.

"She's not in the main lobby," Roger said as he hurried to Chester's side.

"This is ridiculous. The rest of the cast has been here for the last twenty minutes." Chester looked around, scanning the room for Juliet. "Can't you do something about this?" he said, looking to Peter.

"What do you suggest? Strap her down and drag her here? Juliet is a grown woman. If she chooses not to attend, so be it."

"Look, I know she's your lead dancer, but there are times that the company needs her for publicity reasons, and this is one of those times. She goes to those rundown inner-city studios more than she attends these patron functions."

"She enjoys teaching the young dancers."

"That's fine, just as long as she's here when we need her. We pay her to be here."

"Why don't you tell her that? I'm sure she'll be interested in your opinions of how she spends her free time away from the company."

Chester ignored Peter's suggestion. The last thing he was going to do was confront Juliet about how she spent her time. The last time he suggested she be more accessible at his publicity events, she nearly took his head off. "The guests are getting anxious. Did you impress upon her the importance of her presence this evening?"

"Yes," Roger said, nervously looking from Chester to Peter.

"Then where is she?" Chester anxiously asked again.

"Maybe she's in one of the back studios," Peter offered to Roger.

"I already checked there."

"Go see if you can find her again," Chester insisted.

"I'll head back to her dressing room, then make a sweep around the back stage exit, then head back to the—"

"Whatever, just hurry up and find her," Chester said, cutting Roger off and drawing the attention of those standing close to him. He smiled, greeting them, then introducing himself as he watched Roger disappear through the doors leading to the rehearsal studios and office areas.

Juliet sat in her dressing room staring in the mirror at the place J.T. stood earlier. Her heart still pounded from seeing him again. She took a deep breath and let out a ragged sigh. No man had ever made her feel so nervous and panicky inside. She knew the feeling, she remembered it well.

Seeing him standing there in her dressing room brought a flood of memories back. When she awoke the morning after the blackout to find him gone, she was insulted and ran. And now here he was again, but unlike before, there was no place to run. She needed to face her attraction to him once and for all.

A muffled phone began ringing, taking her attention away from her troubling thoughts. She grabbed her dance bag and began digging through the cluttered piles as the phone continued to ring. When she finally found it, she flipped it open and answered. "Hello?"

"Hey, girl," her best friend, Patricia Franklin, said in her usual cheerfully manner.

"Hey, yourself, I got your message and you're late. You

were supposed to be here half an hour ago. And don't tell me that you can't go."

"I can't go."

"You talked me into going to this fundraiser tonight, so if I have to deal with this, I'm not doing it alone. Get your butt here now."

"That's what I called to talk to you about. Kimberly isn't feeling well. I'm gonna have to pass tonight."

"What wrong with her?"

"She and Jasmine went shopping at the mall. They couldn't find anything to buy, so they ate dinner at the candy store."

"Sounds delightful," Juliet said. "Is she going to be okay?"

"Yeah, it's just a stomachache. I just don't want to leave her here alone tonight."

"Of course, I understand. Thanks to Phillip and Chester, there'll always be another fundraiser."

Patricia chuckled, knowing Juliet's aversion to Chester's one-on-one performances for the public. "How was the performance tonight?"

"Great."

"Great, as in Nadine said it was great, or great, as in you got major ovations."

"Both, although according to Nadine I'm slowing down."

"According to Nadine everyone's slowing down."

"Tell me about it." Juliet smiled, knowing that Patricia knew all about Nadine's idiosyncrasies.

"Are we still on for dinner this week?" Patricia asked.

"Sure, I'm looking forward to it." Juliet's voice seemed distant and distracted, Patricia noticed.

"You sound stressed; are you okay?"

Juliet took a deep breath, then exhaled slowly. "Patricia, tell me something, years ago, with Pierce, did you know he was the one for you from the very beginning?"

"I wasn't quite thirteen years old when I met Pierce, you know that."

"Yes, but did you know that he was the one?"

"No, of course I didn't know. I was a kid. I only hoped and dreamed it, just like any other young girl with a crush on the most popular boy in middle school."

"It was more than a schoolgirl crush?"

"Are you asking if I believe in love at first sight?"

"Yes, do you?"

Patricia smiled, remembering the first time she'd seen her husband sitting in math class in the eighth grade. The moment she saw him, she was smitten. Although it took nearly twenty years for them to find each other again, it was well worth it. "Yeah, I guess I do." She paused again, then continued. "Are you asking for a particular reason?"

"Mom always said that she fell in love with Wyatt the first time she saw him."

"That's so romantic."

"He'd just gotten a divorce after being married sixteen months. Then he and Mom dated and were married within four months, and then they divorced just a few years after that."

"Okay, maybe not quite so romantic. So, what's with all the love-at-first-sight questions? Have you?"

"Have I what?"

"Fallen in love at first sight?"

"No, me, never," she stammered out too quickly to be believed. "Just curious, that's all. I never really believed in the whole eyes-meet-across-the-room, instant love thing."

"I know better than that, Juliet. You're the perfect romantic. Your entire life revolves around the theme of romance: *Giselle, La Sylphide, Swan Lake, Sleeping Beauty,* and *Beauty and the Beast.* You specialize in classic love for a living. How can you not believe?"

"Easy, you forgot the tragedy part. You can't have love without a tragedy. Every one of those love stories is full of pain and suffering. Which I'd say typifies the whole idea of love and romance in a nutshell. See, you can't have one without the other."

"Ah, yes, but each is also a classic morality tale. Need I even mention that your name comes from the ultimate classic romantic tragedy, *Romeo and Juliet?*"

"Yeah, I know all that. She dies, he dies, she dies again, pure tragedy. I rest my case. I'm the personification of Freud's id theory. I live in the world of ballet, filled with dreams and fantasy, where happily-ever-after doesn't really exist, and on some level I crave detachment from the real world."

"Hardly. Psychoanalysis is my domain, not yours. If you ask my professional opinion, I'd say the childhood fairy tales you dance to remind you that there is love and romance out there to be found. Thus, ballet is the hope of finding love and happiness in world filled with drama."

"My mom believed in love at first sight when she married Wyatt. Then three years later, he divorced her because he felt trapped. So if all that's true, where was their happiness?"

"I don't know. Only they can answer that question. As for you, you may not have met him yet, or you might have already met him and by chance your paths will need to cross again."

Juliet was immediately reminded of J.T. and the feeling in her stomach the instant she saw him this evening. She knew that there was a strong attraction to him, she just wasn't sure what to do about it.

"I think I'm gonna pass on the fundraiser tonight. There's someone that will be there that I'm not quite ready to see yet."

"Crossed paths before?"

"You could say that."

"Since when are you a coward?" Patricia asked.

Juliet looked at her watch. The gala was just getting started. "Since about ten minutes ago."

"Can you do that, just decide not to go?"

"Of course I can, I'm Juliet Bridges, I can do anything. I'll talk to you later. Give Kimberly my love."

Juliet hung up and turned on the music, slow and sultry. It

was filled with emotion. The blues stirred her soul as she walked around the room, tense and anxious. She thought about what she and Patricia talked about earlier. The feeling of being trapped drove her from the dressing room. She didn't want to go to an empty house, so she chose the only place in the world were she could be in complete control.

She needed to dance, and going to the small, dark practice studio afforded her the perfect opportunity. It was the therapy she needed to recover her lost composure. Flustered since she walked into her dressing room, she needed to regain control. The sight of J.T. again after so many months was too unsettling. Dressed in her comfortable practice clothes, she wrapped her dance shoes around her lower leg and stood in the silence of the darkened room.

She breathed deeply, gently took the barre with her left hand, and in one graceful action, leaned in, going all the way down to the floor. She rose up, exhaling slowly, then she raised her arm past her ear and leaned back as far as her body would allow. She closed her eyes and willed herself to concentrate as her thoughts trailed back to New York City.

At the time, ten months ago, it seemed only right for the entire East Coast to suffer her dark mood. So, as far as she was concerned, the blackout couldn't have come at a more perfect time.

Dance had always been her therapy. So when Lena asked her to dance in a special performance of *Carmen*, she willingly agreed.

She'd just finished her final matinee performance when, in the dressing room, the lights dimmed, then fluttered, then went out completely. After the initial shock, she found herself walking and wandering the streets along with millions of New Yorkers.

She had done something stupid and pretended to be someone she wasn't. The possibility of a one-night stand with a stranger had always tantalized her imagination. It was the night and the lights. In darkness she could do anything, be anyone. She got caught up in the fantasy. One thing led to another and an adventure was born.

That night their escapade was sealed by their anonymity. No last names, no personal information. It was perfect until the impersonal became personal and the attraction became real.

Lost in the music, Juliet turned and repeated the action with her right hand on the barre. Her focus wavered again. The pull of those New York memories was just too strong. She stopped, walked to the corner, and changed the music. She dropped a CD into the player and waited. The slow, sexy sounds of a tenor saxophone rippled through the dimmed room. Perfect. She let the music move her body, taking over her mind and her soul. Dancing would always be her release, so she did just that—she danced.

Chapter 6

J.T. had been wondering around the dimmed corridors of the Cultural Center for the last ten minutes. The lobby where the main reception was taking place, was crowded, and he needed to get some air. He walked up the stairs to the balcony that surrounded the open hall and looked down on the festivities.

Seeing the crowd of dressed-to-perfection patrons left him just as distracted. He felt prompted to explore further. He circled the balcony and found the elevators. Going to the first floor, he knew, he'd find the main offices, so he decided to start his solo tour on the top floor.

Large, empty studios filled both sides of the enormous wing. This wasn't what he had in mind as an evening's entertainment, but anything was better than being in the main lobby. He found a stairwell and went down a level to the smaller, apparently private studios.

He wasn't sure what he was looking for; he was just looking around. Although he did know *who* he was looking for, he was looking for Juliet. Apparently, Ms. Bridges wasn't the partying kind of girl, at least not tonight. While at the fundraiser, he'd heard conversations about her constant absences from these affairs. At the last one she had attended, she'd announced her pending retirement.

He turned down a darkened hall, drawn by the low, sexy sound of a saxophone. Pulled along as if in a hypnotic trance, he stopped to gain his bearings and listen for the music again.

It stopped as he came to a room at the end of the hall. As he passed the small rehearsal room he heard a brushing sound, and stepped back to investigate.

He walked to the open doorway, paused, and looked around. The room was empty. He turned to walk away, then stopped again. At the last second, out of the corner of his eye, he saw Juliet. She was standing alone in the far corner toward the back of the room. The room was dimly lit with only gentle beams of moonlight coming through the chiffon-covered windows. She stood in silence, with her head bowed low. Her slim body cast a dramatic shadow across the wooden floor. Quietly J.T. moved further into the room, staying to the deep shadows against the wall.

Gone was the audacious Carmen costume from her evening performance. Dressed simply, she'd changed into a light-colored leotard and tights with a scant chiffon-like material over her slim hips. She wore ballet shoes tied with ribbon around her lower leg. Her hair was pulled up into a tight bun at the base of her neck. She looked like the ballet dancer he had expected to see earlier. Mesmerized by the new woman, he watched as she slowly began to move.

She looked up at her shadowed reflection in the wall's row of mirrors. She placed her hand on the barre, then pointed her toe and lifted her leg slowly.

In ordered form she began her ritual, turnout, into position one, two, three, four then five, then *demi-plie*, *grand plie* with *port de bras*, and finally, *releve*, in first position. She turned and repeated the short exercise, then began a new series: *chasse tendu*, *efface*, *arabesque*, and *ecarte*, followed by *chasse releve*.

Elevating her movement she performed a *sous-sus*, *tendu a la quatrieme devant*, a *developpe a la quatrieme devant*, then rose up *en pointe*.

The slow refined motions made it seem like her body had been pulled through the air with a marionette's wire. Her leg reached waist level. She paused, then spun around suddenly and released her hand from the barre. In an *arabesque,* she balanced herself, then began a series of incredible movements.

To J.T.'s amazement, he found himself mesmerized by her fluid movements across the floor. The music stopped and she slowly walked to the center of the room and struck a dramatic pose. He waited silently as the soft jazz music began again.

She moved, slowly at first, then her pace quickened as the music's sizzling tempo increased. With more and more determined steps, she danced, then slowed and rose up onto her toes and stood there, statuesque and majestic, arms braced apart at shoulder length, her head bowed low and tilted to the side. The music changed again. She turned suddenly, skipped forward, then began spinning around and around, first up on her toes then back down, then up on toes again. She stopped, then ran toward the far corner of the room. She turned ran and leapt into the air.

It wasn't any type of ballet he'd ever seen. The dance was more like a mix of Latin salsa, modern jazz, ballet, and hip-hop. She twirled around several times, then stopped, ended with her body doing a grinding motion, then fell to her knees and eased to the floor. She lay down a second, then pulled up, arching her back first, then kicked one leg up and instantly sprang to her feet.

As the tempo increased, so did her movements. She raised up on her toes and performed a type of ballet step; then she spun around and ended by leaping into the air.

Leap after leap, jump after jump, she flew around the room with the grace and natural agility of a gazelle. Higher and higher she flew as the music's crescendo enveloped the room. She danced and he watched. Every move she made sent his heart thundering in his chest. He'd never seen anything like it before. She was more than a dancer, she was an artist. Her body painted a picture of beauty, grace, and elegance that easily vied with her amazing feats of athleticism.

She danced a private dance. But he was there and he

watched, enjoying what he saw. She was erotica personified as her body swayed and gyrated to the sweet, sexy rhythms. The music climaxed and she threw her body against the barred mirror. He stepped forward. She turned awkwardly, detecting the reflection of an intruder for the first time. As the music continued, she stared and then squinted across the room. Their eyes connected. She knew who it was even before he spoke. There, standing in the shadows, she recognized him instantly.

His private dance was over.

Juliet walked over and turned off the music, then grabbed her towel and slung it around her neck. She looked up at the shadows dancing across the far wall and sighed heavily, catching her breath. "This room is off limits," she said into the darkness, knowing that he was still standing in the room. With her back to him she began gathering her things into her bag.

He ignored her comment. "That was beautiful."

She dotted her face and neck with the towel, turned, then walked toward him as he stood at the open door. She paused briefly and looked up at him. "I know."

J.T. chuckled, "Your confidence is limitless."

"I know that, too." She brushed past him and headed down the hall. He followed.

"We need to talk."

She sighed loud and long, seemingly from boredom. "Look, rich men are a dime a dozen," she threw out over her shoulder. "I'm not interested." She continued to walk.

"Of course you are." He continued to follow.

She stopped and turned. "Enough. You're obviously a man who gets exactly what he wants. You want something from me or you wouldn't be here. What is it?"

He nodded. She was just as he remembered. Smart, quick, and determined. "You're right, I do want something."

"What do you want?"

"Your time," he said.

"My time is valuable."

"You'll be adequately compensated, I assure you."

"I think this conversation just slipped into either an indecent proposal or vice-squad entrapment. What is it that you want?"

"The question Ms. Bridges, is what do *you* want?"

Her expression didn't change. She turned and continued walking. After several turns, they were back at her dressing room door. She opened the door and turned to him. "I don't need or want anything from you. Goodnight, Mr. Evans."

J.T. nodded and stepped back as the door closed in his face. He smiled as he walked down the hall. Just as he turned the corner, he walked into Roger.

"There you are," Roger said rushing breathlessly. "We were afraid that you'd already gone. We're just about to close the auction."

"Auction?"

"Yes, a silent auction. We hold several throughout the season each year. It's a way to generate continued interest and raise additional funds for the scholarship program."

J.T. was only half paying attention. His thoughts were still on the private dance. "Sounds like a worthy cause."

"Oh, it is, it is. Everyone participates. Basically, the company auctions-off a dancer's basket, which usually contains an autographed photo, playbill, ballet slippers, and in some cases, as with our principal dancers, a personal studio visit or tour of the company, invitations to exclusive dancer and executive social events, principal's dinner, and exclusive dress rehearsals. The total highest bidder of the night receives dinner with the dancer of choice and admittance to our special platinum partners programs."

"Does Juliet Bridges participate in the fundraisers?"

"Not lately. But if I'm not mistaken, she does have a basket this evening. Oddly enough, she used to participate all the time. Believe it or not, the whole silent auction thing was her idea a few years ago. Of course, now it's grown to include a wide range of fundraiser perks, including personal tours from dancers and even the shadow dancer program."

"Shadow dancer program?"

"Yes, very popular, but very expensive, if, of course, you're lucky enough to be the evening's grand winner." Roger went on to elaborate about the activities available for the evening's entertainment.

"What's usually the top bid?"

"That depends. It could be anywhere from five hundred to eight hundred dollars. When Juliet is auctioning, the bids go as high as two and three thousand."

J.T. nodded. As they approached the open reception area again, J.T. noticed that a table had been set up on the side of the room covered with several baskets of ballet slippers. Beneath the baskets was a clear glass bowl filled with small folded pieces of paper.

Roger grabbed a blank paper and pen, then handed them to J.T. "Interested?"

J.T. took the pen and paper, wrote a bid then walked down past the table of slippers. He stopped at Juliet's basket. It was already filled to capacity. He smiled knowingly and dropped his paper into the overflowing glass bowl.

"I hope you have a bid for me as well," Vanya said as she eased in front of him, drawing his attention. "I assure you I am very accomplished. I will certainly be worth your while."

J.T. looked at her, understanding her meaning perfectly. Her green eyes and slightly bronzed skin glistened with a shimmer that covered the rest of her overly made-up face. Small in stature, she seemed more like a child begging for table scraps than a professional dancer. "Maybe next time," he said, suppressing the urge to pat her on the head and send her on her way.

"It is a shame to grow so old," she said as she glanced down at Juliet's overflowing basket. "People tend to pity you."

J.T. followed her line of vision to the basket. "Juliet is certainly not old."

"Yes, I'm afraid she is. This business is for the young, and age is very important. Juliet Bridges is very old. In dancer's terms, she is well past her prime."

"I find that very hard to believe."

"It is true. A professional dancer can dance for ten years, more if she is very careful and avoids injuries. Juliet has been dancing ever since I was a child of two, nearly sixteen years now."

"But her performance tonight was very good."

"Carmen is an excellent piece, and it is very forgiving to those who do not see and understand its subtle eccentricities."

"I see."

"Her body can not continue to take the rigorous punishment of the dance. Practices and rehearsals alone can be brutal. A masterpiece like *Carmen* is physically and emotionally draining. Juliet is probably resting now from the grueling performance this evening. I doubt she will last until the end of the season. She will certainly have to retire soon."

"Leaving you center stage, of course."

"Of course, I am the soloist. I am the obvious choice."

"So what happens to Juliet then?"

"I understand she has already found a benefactor who will take care of her needs. A senator, I believe. This is good." A muscle in J.T.'s jaw twitched and tightened. "I wish her luck." Vanya added smugly, then turned and walked away. She paused and turned. "But for now, if you are waiting for her to join us, I am afraid that you will be disappointed. She hardly ever attends these fundraisers. I doubt she'll attend tonight."

Instant applause rang out, drawing everyone's attention across the room. With the mass of heads turning, J.T. had no idea what was happening. Excited whispers and chatter traveled through the crowd like wildfire.

Roger walked back over to where J.T. stood. "That can only mean one thing," he said breathing a sigh of relief. "Juliet has arrived."

Smiling like a perfect angel, Juliet entered the room to a

whirlwind of praise. Dressed in show-stopping red, she was instantly surrounded by a crowd as she commanded attention as soon as she walked in. Smiling, laughing, and greeting her admirers, she was the perfect celebrity, and it seemed that everyone adored her except for one. J.T. watched as Vanya glared angrily, turned, and stalked away.

J.T. looked after her curiously. Her age belied her true nature. She might be young, but she had the killer instinct of a seasoned professional. His concern shifted to Juliet. He wondered if she knew what her understudy was up to.

As if magically transformed into a joyous celebration, the once somber room was lively and crackled with energy. All because the vivacious Ms. Bridges had arrived. Like to a queen bee they swarmed to her: her fans, her admirers all begging for a glance or a touch from the supremely divine Ms. Juliet Bridges.

She was an expert on stage and in every setting. Every smile became brighter, every laugh merrier as her eyes twinkled with joy. She was unattainable yet approachable. Those who met her for the first time instantly fell in love; those who knew her, reaffirmed their adoration.

J.T. watched from across the room as conversations continued all around him. He was again amazed by her ability to charm. Bubbly, bright, and intoxicating, she entranced everyone in the room.

As the cocktail chatter circled around him, J.T. half listened and participated as he continued to watch Juliet work the room. To his relief, the conversation was interrupted by the company's publicist, Chester Banks, congratulating him on not only winning Juliet's basket, but also on having the highest bid of the evening. Soon after, Peter Flemings and Phillip Waverly approached, adding their congratulations as well and extending an open invitation to visit the company rehearsals at any time.

Never yielding an opportunity, Phillip immediately went to work citing the merits of becoming a platinum patron for the

Cultural Center. As J.T. endured a session of long-winded fundraising chatter, he watched Juliet across the room. J.T. promised to mention his financial interests to his company's community relations and development division.

Phillip turned to see what or who had drawn J.T.'s attention as he continued. A dedicated professional, Phillip was tenacious. Seeing that his fundraiser attempts were fading, Phillip grabbed the passing Juliet in a last-ditch effort to garner additional donations from J.T.

"Have you met our Juliet Bridges yet?" he said to J.T. as he nearly lassoed Juliet's arm and pulled her to him.

Juliet's mind raced. *I am not a coward. I can do this.*

J.T. turned. "Yes, we met earlier."

Juliet smiled innocently and nodded graciously to him, then smiled at Phillip. "If you'll excuse me, I need to speak with someone across the room." She stepped back in an attempt to leave.

"Nonsense," Phillip insisted as he guided Juliet to stand beside J.T. again.

"This is a perfect opportunity for you two to talk. Juliet, J.T. not only won your basket but he was also the evening's top bidder, winning the shadow dancer prize program. You two will be spending a great deal of time together in the coming days."

Juliet looked at the smiling J.T., "Congratulations." Her smile and salutation were anything but genuine.

"And he's chosen you as his dance sponsor," Phillip added.

"Is that right, oh goody for me," she added, as the decidedly acid tone in her voice drew a chuckle from J.T.

"I'll leave you two to get better acquainted." He gently guided Juliet closer to J.T.'s side. "Juliet, why don't you tell J.T. here how important it is to demonstrate leadership in the community and be a true catalyst for cultural growth in the nation's capital."

He turned to leave, then instantly turned back, "And that each tax-deductible philanthropic donation goes to a very worthy scholarship applicant that will enable that student to further their career in the performance arts."

Juliet looked at Phillip's very serious expression then turned to J.T. "What he just said," she said, nodding her head in Phillip's direction, and smiling innocently.

Phillip's mouth dropped open. He reached over and took J.T.'s hand. "J.T., it was a pleasure meeting you. Congratulations again, our scholarship program can always use an added boost. I look forward to seeing soon. Juliet . . ." he prompted, his bushy brows wiggling like two caterpillars stuck on a fishing rod.

J.T. nodded, humored by Juliet's latest performance. "My pleasure, Phillip, and thanks for the invitation. I just might take you up on that offer," he added.

"Any time, any time, just give my office a call," Phillip continued as he handed J.T. a business card, then walked away in search of more donations.

Juliet looked at the card in J.T.'s hand guardedly. "What invitation?" she said as she smiled, responding to and greeting a passing supporter.

"I've been invited to attend a rehearsal."

She smiled brightly as several patrons walked by and congratulated her on a brilliant performance. "You realize, of course, that this is a private party."

"Yes I know, I was invited," he said.

"By whom?"

"A friend."

She looked around the immediate area for any women who might appear to be waiting for him. Although several eyed him admiringly, none appeared to be with him at the moment.

She turned to him prepared to respond but found her breath caught in her throat. She looked away quickly. A wave of heat rushed through her. "What are you still doing here?" she whispered breathlessly, still refusing to look at him.

J.T. leaned down to catch her eye. He smiled when, annoyed, she turned away further. "You look sensational this evening," he said, admiring her simple thin-strapped fire-engine red slip dress with a colorful fringed chiffon scarf draped over her almost-bare shoulders.

"We need to talk," he said.

"My sentiments exactly," she said as he began looking around the room. "Meet me in Phillip's office in ten minutes. It's through the main doors down the hall on the left."

"It's a date. By the way, which one of these ladies is Lena Palmer?"

Juliet turned to him instantly. "Why, what do you want with Lena?"

"It's business."

"What kind of business?"

Before he could answer, J.T.'s name was announced and applause erupted around them. Phillip beckoned for J.T. and Juliet to come to the center of the room so that she could personally present her basket to him. J.T. placed his hand on the small of her back and guided her toward Phillip.

Juliet took the basket from Roger, smiled graciously, then handed it over to J.T. He took it then grabbed her hand and kissed her adoringly. She curtsied. Applause increased as the pair in the center performed admirably. As they each walked off in different directions, the attention was now on the next basket to be awarded.

Ten minutes later, J.T. followed Juliet, as she knew he would.

"Okay," she got right to the point. "I brightened up your miserable little life a while back, move on. Right now, you can't be here," she said as soon as they entered Phillip's private office. J.T. closed the door as she walked across the room and stood at the desk. She kept her back to him and lowered her head. "You have to go, now."

"Why?" he asked simply.

J.T. looked around at the small, quaint office surrounded by poster-sized playbills of dancers in motion. He stepped up closer to a now-familiar figure of a woman in a white tutu, white leotard, ballet shoes, and a feathered tiara-crowned cap. Her expression was somber and majestic. She was suspended in midair, and her arm was gracefully extended out from her body at midshoulder while the other was arched up and above her head. She faced forward, looking directly at the camera.

J.T. leaned closer to get a better look at the poster. Juliet was sheer perfection. The grace and elegance of her body sent a thrilling spark of excitement through him.

"Go back to New York, there's nothing for you here."

"You asked me what I wanted earlier. I need a favor from you," he said automatically.

"A favor. You've got to be kidding."

"Actually, I'm not."

"Short of telling you where to find the closest bridge and detailing exactly how you should jump, I'd say that you were out of luck."

J.T. chuckled and shook his head. She was exactly the same. "Be that as it may," he decided to forge ahead and ask anyway, "I need favor, I need you to—"

She spun around quickly. "Look, do you think I'm kidding here? I don't have time for this, for you. Whatever delusions brought you here, forget it. Just leave, that's what you're good at."

"Yes, Juliet, ten months ago I left you in a hotel room, I admit it. I had to leave. I needed to take care of some business, but when I came back you were already gone."

"How convenient, this time I'll give you the opportunity of watching me leave. Good-bye, J.T." She brushed past him, preparing to leave, but he grabbed her arm as she passed. He handed her a business card. "In case you change your mind, day or night."

"Don't hold your breath," she warned before opening the door and slamming it behind her.

J.T. smiled, realizing that he was enjoying this little distraction. The challenge of the chase had long since subsided over the years. He wasn't used to being the pursuer. Things always came easy for him, maybe too easy. Women threw themselves at him on a daily basis, and the boredom of it had long since grown tedious. This curious turn of events had stimulated a long-dormant fantasy of his as the challenge of pursuit had begun.

Chapter 7

J.T. looked over at the sofa where he had tossed his suit jacket over two hours earlier. It was still laying there exactly where he'd dropped it. Frustrated, he loosened his tie and rubbed his hands over his face, then looked at the clock. It was after one o'clock in the morning, much later than he thought. The time had slipped by quickly, and he was exactly where he was hours earlier. He'd been working on a program for two hours and hadn't gotten any closer to a resolution.

Computer software programming had always been his escape. He could lose himself in a binary code and not look up until the program was totally configured. But for the last few hours he'd been going around in circles, typing, deleting, modifying, and retyping, only to delete every meaningless line.

The distraction of seeing Juliet again had affected him more than he realized. As soon as he got to the hotel he knew that there was no way he'd be able to sleep, so he decided to stay up and get some work done. Unfortunately, he'd just wasted two hours writing meaningless data, going around in circles, arriving at the same pointless conclusion.

He looked at the clock again, then looked at the laptop screen and shook his head miserably. then his finger hovered over the delete key for the sixth time that evening. With less consideration then it took to write the data he pressed the button and sent the data into the recycling realm.

J.T. stood up, walked over to the window, and looked out

across the city. It was the same view he'd seen for the last seven years. He'd been on the road too long, but that was where he had always chosen to be. Although both his mother and father insisted that he reduce his traveling time, he refused, explaining that the only way to stay on top in the computer business was to be in the center of the action.

It wasn't until recently that being on the road began to pale and stability beckoned. He knew exactly when the feeling hit him: ten months ago when he began searching for Juliet. J.T. rested his palms on the windowsill and leaned down. A familiar, melancholy feeling washed over him as he looked fifteen stories down into the night. Cars lined the streets and traffic thickened to an endless line of red and white lights along the side streets. It was two o'clock in the morning and the city was just as busy as it was at noon.

He turned and looked around. The hotel room, considered the best in luxury, was adorned with every modern amenity and convenience imaginable, but still it seemed empty. The glamorously styled living room, dining area, sitting room, and bedroom all replicated the comforts of home. He walked back to the desk, which was prominently positioned in the corner of the living room and sat down heavily.

He sighed in frustration as he punched a few keys, connecting with his office computer. Ordered and perfectly detailed as always, every minute of every day was planned to achieve optimal efficiency. He scanned through his schedules. He had several meetings planned in the morning, including a marketing meeting with his father. He made several additional notations for the meeting, then closed the laptop for the night.

He reached up and turned off the desk lamp, grabbed his jacket, and walked into the bedroom. The dimly lit lamp on the bedside table was on, but the room was still deep in shadows. Going straight to the closet, he hung the jacket up, then pulled the tie from around his neck. As he began unbuttoning his shirt, he stopped midway.

Going back into the living room, he turned on the desk lamp and opened his laptop. The computer instantly blinked to life. He entered a few codes, then waited. He hadn't used this program for years, not since he realized exactly what it could do. When the screen changed he entered another series of codes and waited. He smiled, amazed that he even remembered the sequences.

By the time he'd completed the computer dance, the screen listed in perfectly concise order every known detail of Juliet Bridges's life including salary, taxes paid and, medical and bank records. Nodding at his success, he connected to the laptop's phone system while scanning down the six-page report, searching for the one piece of information he needed. Finally finding it, he highlighted the numbers and pushed a button on the keyboard. The system automatically dialed Juliet's unlisted home phone number.

A chill went through him when, after the fourth ring, the answering machine clicked on. He decided not to leave a message, then disconnected remembering the last words they spoke as he gave her his business card with his Ritz-Carlton room and phone numbers.

A part of him expected her to contact him, hoped she'd contact him. But she didn't. He turned off the desk lamp and walked over to the window again. He stood there and just stared out into the night. The same night that had brought them together.

The lights of Washington, D.C., reflected in his eyes. But in reality, it looked like any other city as far as he was concerned. The only difference was that somewhere out there Juliet was sleeping peacefully.

Juliet entered the Ritz-Carlton Hotel and went directly to the bank of elevators. She had no idea what she was doing there. After the fundraiser she drove home, parked, and walked, her standard routine. After a performance she usually walked to relax her muscles and release pent-up energy. But tonight, not even her walk helped. The elevator arrived. She stepped on and pushed the button for the fifteenth floor. J.T. Evans was still on her mind. All she kept thinking about was their night in New York. The night they spent together on the fifteenth floor.

She looked at the business card in her hand and turned it over several times as she impatiently waited for the elevator to stop on the fifteenth floor. She looked up and watched the numbers as they slowly ascended: seven . . . eight . . . nine. Then, at the tenth floor, she panicked. What was she doing? She pushed the lobby button, but the elevator continued to go up. When it reached the fifteenth floor and the doors slid open, she just stood there, her heart pounding in her chest.

Just as the elevator doors began to close, she hurried and passed through. More adrenaline pumped through her at that moment than when she stepped out on stage as a solo principal for the first time. There, standing in the hallway, she stood until she made up her mind. Taking a deep breath, she looked at the card again, took note of room 1514, then looked at the wall listing the room numbers and directions. She turned the corner and walked straight down an empty corridor, then turned again. Three doors down, she came to her destination.

Juliet stepped up to the double doors, raised her hand to knock, then hesitated again. She looked at her watch. It was late but she knew he'd be up. After all, he was expecting her. Then without a second thought, she knocked and waited.

Juliet's heart pounded. What was she doing? What if he was asleep? What if he had company? What if—

She heard the lock withdraw.

J.T. answered the door seconds later. When it opened, she didn't speak. She just brushed past him and walked right in. He smiled. He loved this woman's audacity.

The room was still dark, with the only light coming from the bedroom's side table lamp, the full moon outside, and the city lights through the window. He watched as she stood a second to gather her bearings then move to the open drapes.

"I know it's late, but . . ." she began.

"I'm glad you came," he said as he watched the slow, easy sway of her hips that instantly brought images of their New York night to mind. Her sexy hourglass figure sent a shiver of desire raging through him.

He smiled, delighted that she hadn't changed clothing. He wanted the pleasure of peeling the red dress from her body all evening. Snug on her hips, the dress danced on her thighs, dusting her bare legs with gentle wisps of fabric with each step she took. She wore high heels that matched the fire-engine red of the dress. And the shawl, which had been casually tossed over one shoulder all evening, was now wrapped securely over her chest, around her neck, then over her shoulder.

He followed her to the large living room window and stood behind her, smiling in delight with the dress. "Can I offer you something?" he asked, too dazed to specify.

"No thank you," she said as they stood in silence, watching the night sky sparkle with twinkling diamond-studded stars.

He nodded. "You look beautiful, as usual." He moved closer, speaking to her reflection in the clear glass.

"We can skip the polite small talk, don't you think?" She altered her focus, answering his reflection. Their eyes connected and held as they did earlier in her dressing-room mirror.

"Whatever you say," he readily agreed.

She turned to him and looked into his eyes. The memory of New York caused her stomach to stir. Nervously, she bit her lower lip and walked away from him. She circled the living room, then stopped in front of the bedroom doorway. "You said that a friend invited you tonight."

"Yes, I did."

"Is she here?" Juliet asked, noticing the dimmed bedroom lamp and the bed turned down.

"No, she's at home."

Juliet nodded slowly. "Sorry I didn't have the opportunity to meet her earlier."

"You will in time, if you haven't already." He smiled knowingly.

She nodded again, slightly puzzled by his admission. But he had confirmed what she had suspected. It was a woman who had invited him to the ballet this evening, and that was all she needed to know. "Are you going back to New York?"

"No."

She took a deep breath and continued to hold her ground. "Why not?"

"Because I've decided that Washington suits me better."

"I thought you lived in New York."

"I did, among other places—Paris, Los Angeles, Hong Kong."

"What about New York?"

"It's still there."

Juliet turned away. This wasn't going as she expected. "Yes, I suppose it is." Her voice softened. "Why did you come here?"

"Work."

"Ah, yes, computers, I remember. You program computers, right?"

"Something like that."

"So your company transferred you here to D.C."

"You could say that."

She nodded and continued to walk around. "Is that the only reason why you're here?"

He moved, positioning himself in her path. "If you're asking if I knew that you lived here, I didn't." She nodded. "If you're asking if I knew you'd be dancing tonight, I did. I wanted to see you again."

"Why?" she asked. J.T. smiled, tilting a single corner of his mouth upward as his brow arched. The provocative expression had answered her question. "We need to talk," she said.

He reached out and pulled her into his arms. "We will," he assured her. Then before she could say another word, he gripped the back of her head and leaned down to kiss her, but she turned at the last second.

"Are you trying to seduce me?"

"Definitely."

"Just so you know, I don't usually go to men's hotel rooms in the middle of the night."

He nibbled her earlobe and snuggled into her neck.

She continued, "Indiscretions make us who we are."

"Not me. You don't seem like a woman who lacks inhibitions."

"You'd be surprised. But then again, you don't know me very well."

He stopped kissing her and looked into her eyes. The stilled seriousness of the moment gripped him with the truth. "I'd like to."

"Spoken like a true bachelor."

"I get the feeling that you don't you trust me."

"Should I?"

"Of course not."

Juliet smiled and laughed, taken off guard by his honest remark.

"Are you going to tell me what you want?"

He dipped his head to her cheek and inhaled deeply. The exotic scent filled his senses. He remembered her perfume well. It was an exotic mix, one he had never smelled since. "You."

Juliet's heart began pounding wildly. This was definitely not going as she'd planned. The whole idea was to walk in here and demand that he leave and go back to New York. But her hands didn't care as they reached up to him of their own volition. She wrapped her arms around his neck and drew him to her, quickly dissipating the space between their bodies.

They kissed. Juliet's body quivered with anticipation as she felt his hands encircle her body, drawing her even closer. The kiss peaked in intensity as desire surged and passion overwhelmed them. A tangle of hands and arms touched and teased, leaving little question as to where the moment would lead as her shawl fell to the floor.

Intoxicated by the taste of him, Juliet moaned as his mouth sank into the curve of her neck. He nibbled, licked, and kissed a path down and across her shoulder. Then suddenly, he pulled back and stroked the side of her face. "Stay with me tonight," he said.

Juliet smiled coyly. "We'll see." She reached up, spreading her fingers wide across his half-unbuttoned shirt. "You don't need this, do you?" She began unbuttoning the rest of his shirt. When she finished, the shirt hung open, exposing the satiny feel of his cinnamon-toast chest.

She ran her hands up his well-defined chest and over his broad shoulders, releasing the shirt to freely fall to the carpet, joining her shawl. The solidness of his body felt like pure heaven. Juliet smiled in private delight; she'd forgotten just how good this felt, the intoxicating power of passion. It had been too long for her. But now he was here, and he wasn't a dream. This was real, and she intended to take her fill of his body.

Her hands drifted to the band of his pants. She slowly pulled at the clasp, then unzipped the front. J.T. reached down and stilled her hands. Then, in one easy swoop, he captured her in his arms and carried her to the bedroom. She tucked her body and melted against his, feeling the pounding of their hearts beating as one and the excitement of the moment intensify.

Wrapped in each others' arms they kissed, heaven beckoned, and they felt passion swell inside of them as the power of the emotions they felt was revealed. Desire pulled them and they went willingly. The passion of their kisses increased beyond expectation as every tense muscle in his hard body secured her tighter.

When the kiss finally ended, he savored her neck and shoulders sending sparks of pleasure through her body in lightning-fast impulses. Juliet closed her eyes and sighed as the torturous pleasure she felt filled her heart, and her body soared, spinning into a falling dizziness of desire.

J.T.'s overwhelming compulsion for her grew beyond anything he'd ever expected. For the first time in months he had the woman of his fantasies in his arms, and he intended to take full advantage of this moment. The onslaught and ravishing of her body drove him beyond reason. His single, solitary thought was to fill her body and bring her to the same earth-shattering climax he knew would surely come for him.

As he approached the bed and relaxed his hold, he sent her slowly drifting down his body to the side of the bed. She felt the hardness of his need through the thin layer of her dress. An excited thrill surged through her, knowing the power she possessed.

She sat, he stood, and then he lowered himself before her, kneeling at her altar as a knight kneels before his queen. She reached out to him, touching the smooth muscles of his chest and feeling the solid firmness of his body. The feel of her hands roaming over his body excited her. Like a child in a candy store, she wanted more.

His mouth sought and found her lips as his body eased forward and parted her legs. His tongue, firm and rigid, entered her mouth and danced in delight at their union. Tasting the pure nectar of her mouth pulled low, even groans from his throat. Swimming in ecstasy, he closed his eyes and drifted on the sweet sensation of their desire.

As the intensity of the kiss deepened, Juliet wrapped her arms around him, raking her nails in passionate patterns across his back while sinking deeper and deeper into the throes of passion. She held on to him with all her might. The dizzying feel of falling gripped her again. Her heart burst with emotion just as it had before. The same feelings had returned with the intensity of a sledgehammer. Off balance, she was falling again.

The light of reason dawned, as if a penlight turned on in the shadows of desire. "What am I doing here?" she mumbled, weakly dazed by his kisses on her body.

"I think you know," he muttered, nuzzling his face against her neck and down between her breasts as his hands held and stroked her thighs beneath the red dress.

"I came to talk to you," she said, unwillingly arching her back, giving him free access to his destination.

"Um-hum," he moaned against her neck, and he pulled the thin spaghetti straps from her shoulders. He reached around and pulled the zipper of her dress downward, freeing her breasts and sending a burn of eagerness through him. A sound of pleasure mixed with the ache of wanton desire echoed around them as a stilled moment of shared destiny enveloped them. Then, in fierce anticipation, they tore at each other's clothing, removing the last barriers to their attraction.

Juliet lay back on the bed, and J.T. sat on the side. He opened the top drawer of the nightstand and pulled out one of the packets that Trey had tossed to him earlier. He smiled thankfully. He opened the packet and protected them. When he turned to her, the sweet passion in her eyes burned with desire.

In a moment of patient clarity he relaxed his pace and slowed the rhythm. He needed to savor this moment and make it last. He leaned in to her. The velvety kiss was slow, sweet and sexy, stimulating the need to chill the fury of their hastened passion.

He kissed her lips, then purposely traveled downward, laying a trail of passion across her shoulders to her chest. He took her into his mouth and savored her sweet taste. Small and delicate, just the right amount, her breasts centered his passion as his hands roamed her body.

Juliet closed her eyes, willing his hands as they scorched her body. His mouth lowered to her tight abdomen. He tenderly nibbled and licked firm muscles as he gradually moved closer. Juliet gasped and moaned, feeling his hands drift closer and closer to the core of her pleasure. She pulled away, grabbing his tortuous hand and holding it, but his relentless focus found his treasure again. His fingers stoked her inner thigh, then upwards, drawing a quick gasp. He tantalized the tiny hair covering.

"J.T.," Juliet moaned, and she rubbed his neck and arm.

"Umm," he groaned inaudibly, too intent on pleasing her to answer.

"J.T.," she gasped as his fingers found her tender treasure and began stroking her gently. She reached for his hand again, but he captured her and intertwined his finger with hers.

"Shhh," he muttered, "let me love you." He heard the sizzle of her quick breath and felt the moisture of her readiness.

She opened her eyes and found him staring at her, just inches away. He hovered over her, preparing to enter. She reached down and found his hardness. Gripping solidly, she guided him to the entrance of her treasure. He lowered his body, easing himself into her, drawing from her a gasp of exquisite pleasure.

Juliet's body shuddered and arched upwards, taking him in fully as she instantly felt the full force of his passion. Tight and taut, her body accepted him. Her nails bit into his shoulder and her thighs wrapped around his waist.

His lips fastened to hers as his body pulled back, then thrust again. He sank deep into her as the next thrust joined them again. Juliet bit at her lower lip and J.T. took and held her hands on either side of her shoulders and suckled, sending her over the edge of elation.

He rocked his hips to her rhythm as the ancient dance continued. The swelling of rapture filled them as their bodies moved as one, joined in a single goal in furious abandon. The frantic pace cadenced and continued until the ultimate crescendo took them, like a tsunami, over the edge of the world in a climatic explosion.

Their bodies tensed, then released, as the last remnants of passion drained from his body. He gathered her into his arms and tucked her to his side as he rolled from her body, pulling her with him.

Later, after her breathing returned and her heart stopped pounding, she opened her eyes. She assumed that she had fallen asleep because the room had changed. She was under the covers and J.T.'s arm was protectively over her waist.

With gentle ease, she removed his arm and sat up. It was time to leave. She found her clothing draped neatly on the back of a chair and assumed that J.T. had placed it there. Dressing quickly, she slipped into her shoes, grabbed her shawl and purse, and silently closed the door behind her.

An hour later, she lay in her own bed with the images of that night indelibly printed on her memory.

A satisfied sigh curled through Juliet as she smiled, remembering their first night. Never had a man made her feel the way he had. She smiled silently, then snuggled deeper between the sheets, cocooned and bathed in the warmth of her thoughts. As thousands suffered through the blackout, she had been blissfully content in the arms of J.T. Evans.

That was until morning came and she rolled over leisurely to the coolness of an empty bed. With her eyes still closed, she'd reached out to feel if he was still there. He wasn't. She sat up suddenly and looked around. The desk lamp and the lamp in the corner were on, along with the air conditioner, but the room was very certainly empty.

"J.T.," she had called out, then waited for a response. The silence told her that she was definitely alone. She gathered the sheet around her bare body and stood. Walking to the bathroom, she glanced in. Shiny black marble and polished chrome sparkled. She went back into the bedroom and checked out a half hour later.

It was as if fate had placed them together, sending them to the hotel at exactly the same time. It was fate that led them to each other's arms, and it was fate that let her wake up alone.

Everything added up to one big coincidence after another—the blackout, the hotel room, and now, finally, the biggest coincidence of them all. J.T. had come back into her life.

Chapter 8

J.T. glanced at his watch as he sat in the meeting for over an hour, listening to the best and brightest minds in the company planning strategy for their latest software release. Months had gone into the software's conception, production, and implementation. This was the exciting part, the marketing of a new product. Unfortunately, J.T. didn't have the slightest clue what was going on at the moment. For the first time in months, his thoughts were miles away.

Like in so many of his dreams and fantasies, Juliet had come to him and they had made love. The memory of the red dress in his hand brought a knowing smile to his face. When he picked it up off the floor he brought it to his face and inhaled the sweet perfume of her body. She was sweet and sexy, and his body yearned for her again. But he had decided to wait and let her rest. The morning would be soon enough.

Then he would take her into his shower and they would make love again. Afterward he'd dry her body with his hands, lay her back down on the bed, and make love again, the perfect start to his day. But it didn't happen that way. Instead, he woke up alone to an empty bed. The fantasy of making love again to Juliet had vanished like a thief in the night.

J.T. picked up a paper in front of him and refocused his attention back on the men and woman surrounding him at the conference table. They were all capable and proficient, yet no matter how hard he tried, he couldn't grasp the simplest software concept they presented. *This is ridiculous*, he thought to himself as he picked up and shuffled the papers again.

He had never been so distracted by anything or anyone in his life. Except, he thought knowingly, months ago when he'd actually gone as far as to hire a private investigator to find his elusive New York dancer. Thinking that it was business, Trey had suggested it after realizing the change in him. At that time he had been totally preoccupied with a single thought, finding Juliet.

Now, here he was again, with Juliet on his mind. But this time he knew exactly where to find her. The question was, what was he going to do about it? He mulled over the question in his mind as he impatiently tapped his pen on the table, drawing several eyes in his direction. There was only one way to find out the answers to his question. That was to go directly to the source, Juliet Bridges.

He looked at his watch again, impatient for time to move. But it only served to frustrate him further. "Why don't we take a break and pick this up again tomorrow, same time?" he suggested, instantly ending the meeting and dismissing everyone. Amid nods, closing folders, and glances of concern, the marketing and sales teams began leaving the conference room.

He stayed seated as the others gathered their folders and returned to their respective offices. Within minutes, the conference room was empty except for J.T. and his father seated on opposite ends of the long mahogany conference table.

J.T. dared to look up into the gripping eyes that mirrored his own. Although years apart, the family resemblance was obvious. After all, he was his father's son. Unfortunately, the last thing he needed to see right now was his conscience reflected back at him through his father's eyes.

Jace gathered the presentations into a folder. "You want to tell me what that was all about?" he asked as the door closed behind the last person to leave.

J.T. didn't bother to look away. "Nothing." He looked at his watch for effect. "I have another appointment across town and I just wanted more time to consider our options."

Jace looked at his son skeptically. He'd noticed all morning that J.T. was behaving oddly. He wasn't his usual calculating and single-mindedly business-absorbed self. This, the end product, the final stage, was always his favorite part. He usually had dozens of brilliant ideas for promotions and marketing concepts. Yet this morning he barely opened his mouth. And the statement *considering his options* was completely out of character.

Now, like his wife, Taylor, Jace seldom concerned himself with the day-to-day operation of Evans Corporation, having recently appointed J.T. as CEO. He was now free to leave the bulk of the daily concerns of the business to his son. The business, E-Corp, was a multibillion-dollar conglomerate that had successfully converted a multitude of research-and-development ideas into viable products, and hence, a Fortune 500 software company that influenced nearly every aspect of the computer industry.

J.T. was a maven when it came to computers. Analytical and disciplined, he was a prodigy at the age of twelve. He won the *Computer Times* Whiz Kid of the Year award four years in row with his innovative software concepts. Now, adept at every aspect, he was considered among only a few true computer geniuses.

So, to see him totally distracted during the launch of a new product that he himself had designed and developed, and to watch him lose focus in the middle of an important meeting was more than a little troubling.

Jace stood and walked over to J.T. "Now, you want to tell me what's really going on?" He laid his folder down on the table and took a seat at his son's side.

J.T. shrugged easily as he entered a few keystrokes and waited a few seconds for an image to appear. He spun the laptop computer in his father's direction. "The product is perfect." He smiled as he glanced at the computer simulation, proud of his latest achievement. "We're going to revolution-ize the industry with this one. We just need to develop the perfect launch. After that, it will practically sell itself."

"That's not what I'm talking about," Jace said, then pressed a key sending the image back into the abyss of computer-generated encryption.

J.T. looked at his father, completely taken aback by his con-cern. "What do you mean?" Insulted by the obvious delaying tactic, Jace arched his brow, remaining silent yet determined. J.T. looked at his father's unyielding expression. There was no getting around it. When it came to willful and stubborn, Jace Evans was the master.

"I had lunch with Mom yesterday. She told me about her latest venture."

"And?" Jace prompted.

"And? Dad, aren't you the least bit concerned that she's being taken advantage of with this community center arts thing?"

Jace smiled and shook his head, remembering the feeling all too well. He had felt the same way many years ago when it came to Taylor's love of the arts. As far as he was concerned, it was a waste of time and energy and lacked the thrill and ex-citement of analytical software programming and data sequencing. But that was a long time ago, before Taylor had opened his eyes to a new world through her art. "Community center thing?" he questioned sternly, making his point clear.

"You know what I mean."

"Don't underestimate your mother. I learned a long time ago not to make that mistake." He shook his head and chuck-led at a distant memory. "I suggest you not do the same." Jace stood and gathered the folders in front of him.

"A million dollars?" J.T. followed his father's lead. He gathered the folders and laptop in front of him, then stood and walked to the conference room door.

Jace turned to his son. "Is it the money that concerns you?"

"No, of course not."

Jace continued to the door, smiling, knowingly. "You never did develop a passion for the arts, did you?"

"You need to talk to her about this."

"And what exactly do you want me to say?" he asked with a smile.

"Anything, tell her how short-sighted a venture like this can be."

Jace smiled and chuckled, humored by his son's remark. He shook his head in reply. "You've obviously been on the road too long."

"There's no way she's prepared to undertake something like this. With something this big, every bogus and phoney company on the East Coast will be coming out of the woodwork in hopes of getting her to invest. She's making a mistake by being so trusting."

"Believe me," Jace opened the door, "your mother seldom makes mistakes. As a matter of fact," he thought for a moment with a broad smile on his face, "I have yet to see or hear of one." The two men walked down the hall of the executive wing side by side. "And as for trust," Jace continued, "Fort Knox has a better chance of opening its doors for a going-out-of-business sale." Both men chuckled. "I'm sure Taylor knows exactly what she's doing."

They rounded the corner, nearing J.T.'s office. "That's precisely what concerns me. Exactly why is she doing this?"

"Believe me, your mother knows what she's doing. The property she's interested in is listing for $1.4 million. She's getting it for a bargain at one million even, an excellent price considering the neighborhood's promising future."

"What promising future? She told me herself that it's an old condemned community center."

"Diamond in the rough," Jace reminded him. "It's not the building per se, it's the land. The entire area is primed for an artistic renaissance, and your mother is the visionary leader who can make that happen. Since her art gallery opened, there have been a number of promising companies attracted to the quaint waterfront location. The tourists love the historic quality and genuine family, neighborhood feel. It's a goldmine.

"Mark my words, in ten years that area will be the next Georgetown. So, in other words, your mother's million-dollar investment today will quadruple in less than five years without her even touching a single brick."

J.T. was impressed; he had no idea that his mother's instincts were so good.

"You need to have a bit more faith, son. Open your eyes, there's a lot more to life then computer code. I learned that the hard way." Jace looked at his son's still-troubled brow. "You're still not convinced?"

"My gut tells me that something's not right."

"You think there's more to this?"

"I'd bet that million dollars on it."

Jace knew that look well. When Taylor painted, her eyes would sparkle as the creative process developed. J.T. was just like Taylor in that respect. Whenever he felt that he was on to something, he'd get that same spark in his eyes. In business he was notorious when it came to developing new and innovative software concepts, and each time his instinct led the way.

"Like what?" Jace asked.

"I don't know yet."

"You must have some idea. What are your thoughts?"

"Nothing substantial yet, I just have some curious concerns at the moment, one being Mamma Lou." he said.

"Louise Gates? She'll be visiting for a few days to keep your mother company while Otis and I go on that fishing trip."

"I know, and that's what concerns me."

Jace chuckled. "That's it, isn't it? It's not Taylor you're trying to save, it's yourself, from a nice old lady." He shook his head, still chuckling. "You think Louise is trying to match you up with someone, don't you?"

"The thought had crossed my mind."

"So, not only will Taylor, Louise, and Lena be altering the landscape of D.C.'s cultural scene, but Louise is using Taylor and their new investment as a way of getting you down the aisle?"

It sounded ridiculous, silly and paranoid. Even J.T. had to admit to that. "As I said before, I don't have anything substantial, yet."

Jace nodded, still chuckling. "You'll let me know when you do," he offered.

"Mom invited me to the ballet last night," J.T. said as they approached his outer office.

"Yes, she told me. I couldn't make it, and your sisters are both away, so the responsibility as CEO now falls to you." Knowing that J.T. considered the arts as a waste of time, Jace was surprised that he even agreed to accompany Taylor in his absence. "What did you think of it?" Jace asked as J.T.'s secretary handed him his messages.

J.T. nodded absently. "Interesting," he smiled slyly, remembering the private dance in the dark studio and the passionate kiss he and Juliet shared in her dressing room.

"That's an odd way to describe the evening, particularly *Carmen*. I've heard the performance is extremely moving. And the lead dancer, what was her name?" he pondered thoughtfully.

"Juliet, Juliet Bridges," J.T. responded.

"Yes, that's it, Juliet Bridges, she's supposed to be breathtaking."

"She is that," J.T. muttered just loud enough for his father to hear. His smile broadened. Juliet Bridges had certainly taken his breath away on more than one occasion.

J.T. opened the door of his office, allowing his father to enter first. Jace stepped inside and looked around at the newly redecorated office. He frowned, disappointed and stunned by the lack of warmth and personality around him. The office was open and airy, decorated with sparse, ultra-slick, modern furniture. Several computer monitors lining the desk. It was, given J.T.'s personality, functional and sterile and exactly what he'd expected to see.

J.T. walked over and stood behind his desk. He punched in a few keys accessing the multiscreened computer system. In unison, each monitor blinked to attention. A final access code was keyed in with an encryption cipher, giving the system life.

J.T. shuffled through the messages his secretary gave him, putting them in order of importance. He read through the notes, focusing on two in particular. One was from Trey, and the other was a request to join Phillip Waverly at the theatre later that afternoon. "Tell me about the Arts Council?"

"It's your mother's pet project. She and a few friends conceived, developed, and organized the commission as a way to generate interest in the arts."

"Have you met Phillip Waverly?"

"Yes, he's the president of the Washington Cultural Center."

"What exactly does he do?"

"Money," Jace stated plainly. "His main objective is always to raise as much money as possible, as often as possible and as quickly as possible. He has an uncanny knack for attracting funds from wealthy patrons while forging lucrative alliances. He's also a very talented man when it comes to producing the arts programs in the center, but his primary objective is money."

"This is D.C. Money is everybody's primary focus."

"True, but Phillip is an enigma of sorts. Unlike a great number of lobbyists in this area, personal gain has never seemed to be his forte. He is, in my opinion, an unequivocally dedicated lover of the ballet, the opera, and the symphony, and has always put their respective funding above everything else." J.T. nodded, understanding the connection, as Jace continued.

"On occasion, Trey does a thorough investigation of the organization for your mother, just to make sure everything is still copacetic."

"What's his relationship with Mom and her new venture? Wouldn't that be considered a conflict of interest by taking money from his programs since she obviously won't be as active with the cultural center?"

"Not at all. As a matter of fact, Phillip was delighted when Taylor told him about the idea." J.T. looked at him oddly. "Remember, Phillip is foremost a lover of the arts. Another program to advance the arts in the community only adds to his delight. His only endeavor, and seemingly main mission in life, is to bring the arts to the world any way he can," Jace said, noticing the orchid on the desk for the first time.

Like an oasis in the middle of the desert, it was delicate and alive and as far from J.T.'s business style as it could be. In a room filled with solid teak wood floors, cold brushed chrome, smoked glass, and charcoal leather, it was completely out of place.

It was also obvious that it had been placed there by his wife. Jace smiled, knowing her taste well and assured that the look of the office would change in the coming weeks. Then, after a few months and without J.T.'s awareness, Taylor would have completely redone the room, bringing a touch of life and vivacity into J.T.'s structured, ordered world. Jace reached out, gently touched the white blooms, and shook his head knowingly; Taylor had done the exact same thing to his office, and he couldn't be happier.

J.T. sat down at his desk. He watched his father's animated face and frowned at the orchid, wondering why he hadn't discarded it. Jace pointed to the plant. "It was a gift," J.T. said.

"From your mother, I presume?"

J.T. nodded and shrugged. "It's different."

"Very, get used to it." Jace looked at his watch, then stood. "I need to get to another appointment. I'll see you tomorrow evening."

"Tomorrow evening?"

"Yes, Louise and Otis are coming to visit for a few days before we go fishing. You're mother is having a small dinner for them. She's invited family and a few friends to join us."

"Friends," he asked quizzically with a hint of paranoia, "as in matchmaking?"

Jace smiled and chuckled, knowing exactly what J.T. had in mind. "Friends, as in people we know. Other than that, I have no idea. I'm only extending the invitation."

"I think I'll consider bringing a guest, just to be on the safe side." J.T. stood and came around to the front of the desk to walk his father to the door.

"Someone you met recently?" Jace asked, continuing to the door.

"Yes and no, a friend from New York."

Jace nodded, "I'm sure there'll be no problem to add one more setting to the table. I'll let your mother know. In the meantime, think about those proposals. Some of them sounded promising, after a few minor changes, of course." As J.T. opened and held the door for his father, Jace turned to him. "J.T., if this venture of your mother's is really concerning you, check with Trey. He's been on top of this from the beginning." J.T. nodded as he walked Jace through the reception area.

"Dad," J.T. began, then paused a few seconds. "Have you ever met Juliet Bridges?"

"Yes, in passing, a couple of times." The two began walking toward the elevators. "Although I didn't know that you knew her."

"What makes you think that I know her?"

Jace, not answering, gave J.T. a knowing look.

"I mentioned her name and it was written all over your face." He nodded his approval at his son's apparent new choice in women.

"What was your impression of her?" J.T. asked.

"Son, I believe the question is, what's yours?" Jace smiled

at J.T.'s expression. He reached out and hugged his son, then nodded with pride. "It's good to have you back home."

"It's good to be back."

J.T. watched as his father stepped into the elevator and the doors closed. He turned. Mamma Lou visiting, a million-dollar investment, and a ballet dancer to die for. How did his life get so totally out of control in just twenty-four hours? But one thing he knew for sure, there was definitely something going on, and it looked like whatever it was, he was right in the middle of it.

J.T. walked over to his secretary's desk. She looked up from the computer monitor. He said, "I'll be out of the office the rest of the day." She nodded wordlessly and went right back to her computer.

Chapter 9

The night had been long and endless as Juliet's thoughts centered on seeing J.T. again after so long. Dawn had come and gone and sleep had eluded her since she'd gotten home as one question played over and over again in her mind. Why, after all these months, had he suddenly shown up? Now, when her life was spiraling out of control, the center of the fantasy she'd always held on to, J.T., had appeared out of nowhere.

A slow, silent tear fell down her face and onto the pillow-case. He had come back into her life at a point when everything was falling apart. When the biological clock that had seemed so far away for so long was now betraying her by quickly bringing to an end the only thing she had been good at. Everything was changing. Everything was gone. She had lain in her bed, wide awake, staring into the darkness, the same darkness that had brought them together.

She closed her eyes, hoping to erase the image of their bodies locked together in passion, but the memory was too vivid. She sat up in bed, then stood and walked to the window. The early morning was still as she looked down onto the dark, empty street. She asked the question again. Why had J.T. returned to her life? She looked at the clock. Six in the morning; it was going to be a long day.

Two and a half hours later, she was paying for her sleepless night, and all the coffee in the world didn't help. With bags under her eyes as heavy as steamer trunks, she walked down the bright hallway. Between sips of hot, black coffee she glanced up at the portraits of herself and others lining the hall like a monument for the dance company.

As she reached the end of the hall, she came to the poster of her friend and mentor, Lena Palmer, who was by far the most talented dancer in a generation. She'd danced in classics like *Giselle, Romeo and Juliet, Carmen* and *Swan Lake,* to name a few. Each performance was sheer perfection. This particular poster was of Lena in the role of the flirtatious and enticing Kitri from *Don Quixote*.

Charming and alluring, she had danced with perfect technique and masterful styling. The critics raved that she, with her dazzling, playful portrayal and whimsical interpretation, had forever claimed the role as her own.

Juliet stood in front of the poster and smiled. As a young dancer, Lena was the best. She had danced with Nureyev and Mikhail and had traveled the world, displaying her unique talent. Then the day came, as it always did, when she retired, never to perform on stage as a principal dancer again.

Juliet turned away slowly. The solemn thought that she would one day soon be relegated to the end of the hall had quickened her pace.

She dressed and entered the practice studio quicker than usual. Sipping her large coffee, she looked around. The room was empty. She was the first one to arrive, as was customary. She walked across the wooden floors and dropped her towel and bag along the back wall, then sat down on the floor. Stretching and pulling, she prepared for her strenuous daily workout.

The elasticity of her body conformed to the punishing positions. She extended and folded her body, straining muscles to their limit as, slowly, other dancers began to join her. Twenty minutes later, Juliet sat against the mirrored wall, her knees to her chest, as Richard came in and sat down by her side. She pulled out her pointe shoes, scissors, needle, and thread, and began her usual ritual. She cut the shoe's ribbons, elastic, and shank, and then began sewing the ribbons on in a more comfortable position.

"Good Lord, love, you look like week-old fish and chips," he teased with way too much honesty.

"Aren't you sweet?" she said facetiously. "I thought you decided to change your usual pick-up line?" She yawned her reply as she leaned over, pulling her hamstring tight, then releasing it slowly. The exquisite pain of the movement prompted her to repeat the action until the pain subsided.

"Seriously, love, I wouldn't tell you if it weren't true. When's the last time you actually slept? Obviously, it wasn't last night. You look a fright."

"Harsh, very harsh," she said.

"But accurate."

Juliet frowned, adjusted the kerchief, and tucked the stray hairs behind her ears. "Is it that obvious?" She asked. Richard gave her an *are you joking* look, then chuckled inwardly, shook his head, and looked away. She sucked her teeth, pulled the pink and white kerchief from her head, tossed it on top of her bag, and smoothed her hair back, securing her bun. "Better?" she asked hopefully.

"Not by much," he confirmed, then laughed. Juliet lay her face on her pulled-up knees. "Right, now all you have to do is get rid of those humongous potato sacks beneath your eyes, pull your knickers up, get your face out of your hands, stop yawning and . . ." Like a jack-in-the-box, Juliet's head instantly popped up. She smiled, miserable, and bit her lip. ". . . and stop gnawing at your lower lip."

"Alright, alright, I get the picture, enough already."

"Not quite. The good news, love, is that there's possibly someone in Tibet who hasn't yet noticed your frightful appearance. I do hope he was worth it. We have a long day ahead."

"He who?" she questioned innocently.

"J.T. Evans."

"I have no idea what you're talking about," she lied as she

pulled her scissors out again and began cutting the satin tips of the shoes, then roughing them with sandpaper for better traction.

Richard laughed, drawing a few eyes in their direction. "You realize, of course that half the company saw how the two of you looked at each other last night. Then, of course, there was the oh-so-obvious slipping out together."

Juliet buried her face in her hands again. "We did not slip out together, and it's not what you're thinking."

"How do you know what I'm thinking?"

She looked up at him. "Are you kidding? You're about as transparent as plastic wrap." He chuckled. "I just didn't get much sleep last night." She began banging her shoes to soften and loosen them for wear.

"A slight side effect, but well worth it." He smiled.

"Would you please get your mind out of the gutter for five minutes. I couldn't sleep, really couldn't sleep, as in being awake all night."

Richard reached out and drew Juliet into his arms. "I'm sorry, love, that was terribly cruel of me. Where are my manners? So tell me, wazzup, my Nubian sistah?" he questioned seriously.

Richard's slang took her off guard. "You have got to be kidding me," she said, looking at him as if he'd lost his mind.

"What?" he asked innocently. "This is me being a concerned friend."

"No, this is you watching those old seventies reruns again." She shook her head sadly. "You've seriously been in the States too long. You're starting to talk like a *Cooley High* reject."

"A what?" he asked.

"*Cooley High*, it's an old movie from the seventies, great soundtrack, lousy film, tear-jerker with Freddie "Boom-Boom" Washington from the Sweathogs." She paused, awaiting his response. It never came. "Oh never mind. The point is you need to either chill out on the *Soul Train* reruns or trash your television," Juliet said, knowing Richard's fondness for sitting in front of the television the moment he had free time and soaking in anything and everything about American pop culture. "That idiot box is beginning to penetrate that corny stuff into your brain."

"No one touches the telly, lassie. The lovely ladies adore my sexy British slang at the corner pub. I'm phat, livin' large, and dope, so don't be trippin' and dissing me."

Juliet laughed until tears moistened her cheeks. When she regained control, she looked at him and began laughing again. "Okay, first of all, I don't trip, I'm way too old to diss, and the lovely ladies you spoke of only want to get into your pants, Mr. Phat-living-large dope," she teased, emphasizing the last word for effect.

"You say that like it's a bad thing," he said jokingly.

Richard laughed again as Juliet tried to keep a straight face. It was a Herculean feat at best, and the more serious she appeared, the more humor he found in the situation. Finally she gave in. They laughed and talked easily as they continued to stretch and prepare for the morning's rehearsal. Fifteen minutes later, they relaxed and cooled down.

"Have you decided what happens next?"

She looked at him, questioning, then understood, "No, not yet."

"Is that what kept you up all night?"

"Yeah, some. That and other things."

"Look, love, I've got a sweet little nest egg saved in a lovely little bank in Switzerland." He leaned over and whispered closer to her ear: "And a very large nest egg in the Caymans." She looked at him confused. "If you need a little cash, I have some saved, roughly about five million pounds, give or take a few shillings."

"So what's that in real people's money, a dollar and ninety-five cents?"

"Ouch, apparently lack of sleep has made you positively

vicious. And here I thought you adored me," he said, pretending to be offended.

"What gave you that idea?" Smiling, she playfully leaned over and bumped her body into his, then turned to him before he finished. "Richard, thank you, but I'll be fine, really. Maybe I will or maybe I won't open my own dance company. There are plenty of other things to do. I could teach class or even be a choreographer. Lena has been after me to join her in New York or even here in her latest venture. So don't worry, I'll be fine."

"I'm really going to miss you, love."

"I know."

He turned to his reflection in the mirror behind her. "It took me almost three months to train you to my style and raise you to my level."

"I beg your pardon?" she asked indignantly.

"Now I have to start all over again." He looked away, distressed by the possibility. "Hopefully I won't be stuck with some no-talent hack that will make me look bad."

"You don't need a no-talent hack to make you look bad," she teased. "You do that all by yourself," Juliet joked with a chuckle as she wrapped her toes and feet with tape, then secured cotton to the balls of her feet with tape. She slipped on her ballet shoes and tied and secured the ribbon around her lower leg.

"You know I make you look good, even on my bad days."

"That's true." She paused to bend her toes and test the flexibility of her taped foot. "If you're lucky, you'll get Vanya."

"Vanya, *pas de duex* with me? Hardly, many have tried, few have succeeded."

"But you and she—"

"Yes, yes we had a moment. But as a dancer, she's no where near my talent."

With all of Richard's outlandish boasting and conceit, he was absolutely correct. He was by far the best dancer in the company. Having trained and studied at Mikhail Baryshnikov's School of Classical Ballet, he was a master of the art. He did much more than lifting and steadying his partner, which was usually the job of male dancers. He was a bravura dancer, the best of the best.

"Stranger things have happened," Juliet warned, knowing Vanya's determined ambition. "She wants lead principal so badly she can taste it, and to *pas de duex* with you would be icing on the sugar-coated cake."

Richard looked up and across the room. "Here comes our fearless leader with his latest patron troupe du jour," Richard said as Phillip walked in followed by several very excited patrons. He nodded and waved as the dancers, including Juliet and Richard, acknowledged his presence.

With a five-thousand-dollar suit and a cheap toupee, he saluted the dancers like a conquering hero returning from battle.

As the president of the Washington Cultural Center, Phillip was responsible for attracting arts patrons while securing funding for the ballet company, the opera company, and the symphony.

The company's rehearsals were usually closed to anyone not associated with the company. Of course that didn't pertain to Phillip and his latest crop of prospective patrons. He used every trick in the book, and then some, to get additional funding.

"Greetings, all," Phillip began his usual speech of the day with his arms opened wide, seemingly embracing the entire room. For him, every entrance was another opportunity to make a speech, give a testimonial, and name drop at least three semi-pseudo-famous people all at once.

His speech, one they'd all heard before, lasted upwards of five minutes with the usual truly pleased, truly touched, and truly blessed finale.

"Five, four, three . . ." Richard began.

"Stop it," Juliet whispered as she watched.

"Two . . ." Richard continued, slowing his countdown.

Vanya, who'd been stretching across the room, instantly jumped to her feet and hurried over to Phillip. She kissed each cheek, then waited anxiously to be introduced.

"One. I'm impressed, she beat her own brownnose record."

"Stop it." Juliet warned again, trying hard not to laugh and encourage his behavior.

Several well-dressed men and woman circled the room, then took seats along the back wall. They smiled gleefully, recognizing many of their favorite dancers. Among them was the esteemed Senator Randolph Kingsley.

Randolph was a newly elected and extremely well-recognized senator who had a serious political future ahead of him. At present, he was the toast of Washington, D.C. Everyone who was anyone wanted to be with or near him. A bachelor with visions of the White House, he was a magnet for power and women, and enjoyed every bit of it.

Having known Randolph all her life, Juliet knew first-hand his obsessive drive for success. It was the same drive she'd witnessed in her own father as she grew up.

"Then right straight to Randolph Kingsley, what a surprise," Richard added sarcastically, drawing Juliet's attention again.

"Jealous?"

"Please. Don't believe everything you hear. Vanya and I were over long before he or anyone else stepped into the picture."

"Randolph's a nice guy. He and Vanya will probably be perfect, together," she said.

At that moment, Randolph looked across the room and spotted Juliet standing next to Richard. He smiled and nodded his head. She returned the greeting.

"But it's a lost cause," Richard began as he watched the subtle interaction between Juliet and Randolph. "What is it between you two?"

"Believe it or not, he's my big brother."

"No really, you two have this strange on-again, off-again relationship. You take convenience dating to a whole new level."

"Believe me, Randolph is in love with Randolph and the idea of furthering his career. I'm the token every man needs to avoid serious commitment. I'm a politically correct, perfectly polite, prim and proper politician's arm candy. When he needs an ornament I'm there, and vice versa. It's the perfect friendship."

Vanya stepped into Randolph's line of vision and stuck a practiced pose. Her *pas de deux* partner instantly hurried to her side, and together they gained everyone's full attention, dancing in the guise of an impromptu practice.

"That is so sad," Richard said as he watched the couple in the center of the room.

"Be nice and smile," Juliet said as she stood up and made a circular motion with her ankle, bending her foot in either direction and feeling the secured tightness of the ribbon around her leg. She flexed and bent her foot, then eased up onto her toes and leaned over, repeating the action.

Richard stood by her side, took her waist, and spun her until she stopped, extended her leg, and bowed low with him still supporting her hand and waist. "I always feel like we're on display to the highest bidder," she complained.

"We are," Richard said.

"I really hate this part."

"Don't we all," he said as he spun her around again, then stopped face to face.

"Don't even try it. You love this, don't you. Twenty people drooling over you as you dance, who are you trying to fool?"

"Can I help it if these people have exceptional taste?"

"You are so full of yourself," Juliet chuckled.

"Jealously is such an ugly trait."

"Me? Jealous of you? Oh please. I have more talent in my fingernail than you have in your whole conceited body."

"Prove it."

Peter Flemings entered, clapped his hands, several times, and nodded to the pianist sitting in the corner. Morning rehearsal began.

Chapter 10

Phillip excused himself to take a phone call, leaving J.T. sitting alone in the almost-empty theatre watching as the muted stage slowly came to life before him. The dimmed lights and shadowy mood gradually lifted when, as if on cue, a flurry of activity began.

Above him the electricians and lighting crew adjusted the spotlight intensity and modified the colored lighting films that subdued the atmosphere on stage. Now a serene blue with gentle beams of purple and red, the stage was set with a familiar scene from the performance he'd seen the night before.

It was from the first act of the performance. Set outdoors in a makeshift plaza surrounded by trees and storefronts, the props and scenery told the story of a gathering in the busy marketplace. When the character Carmen had arrived the swirl of activity stopped, and Juliet's solo dance began. Dramatic in its intensity, the lighting softened and diminished, giving the stage an almost surreal, dreamlike quality.

J.T. smiled as he imagined Juliet dancing across the stage in her seductive Carmen costume. He could almost see her spins and turns as she moved to the music. His smile broadened. She was good, very good. And the beauty of her body added to the perfection of her movement. Slim and svelte, but not thin, toned but not overly muscular, shapely and curvy with the right amount of feminine accents that had kept him dreaming of her for the past ten months and rattled as soon as he realized she left his side in the middle of the night.

Suddenly his smile faded as he remembered what Trey had alluded to earlier. Maybe he was right, the fact that he had even bothered to search for Juliet the nights following the blackout attested to the fact that there was something more than just a passing physical attraction.

If that night had been as meaningless as he'd tried to convince himself, and merely one night of passion as they had originally agreed, then he should have easily just walked away. But he didn't, he couldn't. There was more. Even now, ten months later, no woman had even come close to making him feel that way, not that he had even given another woman an opportunity.

Suddenly the stage brightened, with white lights getting his attention as the crew of workers now standing on the stage focused on the props and scenery. Three carpenters carried in a painted prop of a large fountain and positioned it center stage. They stood back, looked, then shifted it to the side, looked again and shifted it back to center stage, then called to someone in the wings.

Roger, the stage manager, hurried across the empty stage carrying a clipboard with an earpiece in his ear and a wire connected to his belt loop. He approached the assembled men. They spoke for a few minutes. Then Roger pointed to the lights above the stage and turned his attention to the men adjusting the scenery. He nodded, spoke into his earpiece, then hurried off the stage as quickly as he had arrived.

Phillip returned and immediately began his usual name dropping, having just spoken with the mayor's office. He went on to elaborate the city council's interest in the ballet company giving a special performance for some dignitaries who were coming to the city soon. To change the subject, J.T. asked him to explain what the crew was doing with the new sets. He did, in great detail.

Moments later, several dancers walked out to center stage.

Laughing and talking, some sat down while others stood and listened to Peter as he and his assistant detailed movements. He drew broad strokes with his arm motions, giving the dancers an idea of what he had in mind. Afterwards he clapped his hands, and all of the dancers stood in preparation. In position, they began rehearsing the first act. The rehearsal was filled with laughter and play, with brief interruptions. It continued for the next thirty-five minutes.

Phillip returned just to leave moments later, much to J.T.'s delight.

As the dancers began clearing the stage, J.T. watched as Juliet and her dance partner walked onto the stage. They stopped and spoke to a few of the departing dancers, then with Peter's assistant for a few minutes. Then they walked off stage to stand in the wings. J.T. watched intently as Juliet looked around, nodding her head several times, then pointing across the stage as she and her partner seemed to map out a performance and block out their steps.

The echo of his thoughts faded as his eyes centered only on Juliet. Dressed in black tights, a thin-strapped midriff tank top, a flimsy short shirt, and ribbon ballet shoes, she stopped his breath.

She stood focused, completely oblivious to his or anyone else's presence, just as she had been the night she danced alone. She was beautiful beyond words, graceful beyond reason, and sexy beyond imagination. He felt the familiar quiver dance through him as his thoughts raced and he remembered the feel of her body beneath his just hours earlier.

Juliet stepped onto the stage as the piano began to play. It was a different dance and a different performance. Graceful and serene, with timid steps, she gently glided across the floorboards on her toes. She was a new character but still the essence of loveliness. She was shy and coy, timidly playing the character in a childlike manner.

J.T. followed her every movement, his eyes cemented as the exquisiteness of the dance intensified. Never blinking, never diverting, ceaseless and constant, he stared in an almost trancelike state. She was perfect. He smiled, realizing that his appreciation of ballet had been turned completely around. He could literally watch Juliet dance forever.

"Beautiful, isn't she?"

Startled by the unexpected intrusion, J.T. turned to see, for the first time, a lovely older woman sitting in the seat next to him. He was so enamored with Juliet that he didn't even notice when she came in and sat beside him.

"Yes, she is," he answered.

The woman smiled and tilted her head admiringly but kept her eyes trained on the stage performance. "Are you familiar with ballet?"

"No."

"A novice, how splendid. I shall let you in on a little secret." She lowered her voice and leaned in closer. J.T. looked at her with curious interest. "Ballet is like a beautiful woman. And like any woman, she can give both pleasure and pain, ecstasy and anguish."

J.T. smirked and turned back to the performance. So much for his newfound respect and appreciation of ballet. "That's an interesting analogy," he added skeptically.

"Confident, seductive, the intensity and passion of her movements has been known to bring men to their knees."

"Is that right?" he added, mildly amused by her remark.

"Yes. She can awaken the coldest heart and soften the hardest soul and then free the spirit trapped beneath." She paused as Juliet's tempo picked up and she twirled across the stage. "I have known men who were intensely obstinate turn to ardent lovers as soon as that curtain rose. But she is a jealous and demanding lover who does not tolerate unfaithfulness. Once she is in your blood, you are forever hers."

A curious shudder gripped him. Suddenly the conversation hazed. Were they still discussing ballet, or was the woman referring to his relationship with Juliet? There was no way she could know anything about them because technically, there wasn't anything to know, yet. J.T. finally decided that he was just letting his imagination get the best of him. The woman was obviously still referring to dance.

They sat in silence, watching Juliet as she pirouetted across the stage, then twirled gracefully, then leapt into Richard's arms. He lifted her up into the air above his head with one arm, turned gradually, and then slowly lowered her down against his body. A sudden rush of jealously spiked through J.T. as Juliet glided to the floor.

"You obviously know her very well," he said tightly.

The woman smiled and chuckled gently. "I do, she is an undaunted spirit that will forever be my heart. I'm sure you will agree as soon as you experience your first performance."

"I have. I saw *Carmen* last night."

"Ah, yes, Carmen, the gypsy seductress full of life and adventure who meets a fatal end because of love. It is a magnificent ballet, and Juliet is exquisite. It's her signature role, and she is undoubtedly the finest Carmen in a decade. The role has made her both allegro and adagio."

"Meaning?"

Lena smiled, "Meaning that Juliet has the ability to excel in roles that require both precise and quick movement such as Kitri in *Don Quixote* as well as graceful and classical roles such as Odette and Odile in *Swan Lake*. *Carmen* is somewhere in the middle. But to truly experience *Carmen*, you must see the actress and character as one. Did you enjoy it?"

"Yes," he said, impressed by her knowledge and expertise.

She nodded. "Bold and beautiful, both a seductive temptress and an impossible mistress, *Carmen*, like its characters, is addictive. The ballet, like Juliet, is the heart and soul of this company. Unfortunately, most men confuse the two and instantly fall in love with both the character and the woman." She leaned back then glanced at J.T.'s stoic profile. "Tell me, which one has captured your heart?"

The question, meant rhetorically, reverberated in J.T.'s mind. Had Juliet Bridges captured his heart? No, he assured himself. He was intrigued, yes, enticed, yes, most definitely attracted to her, but there was no way that a dancer could capture his heart.

They slipped into silence as they watched Juliet and Richard dance. Slow and methodical, they moved across the stage in measured steps, capturing the somber, solemn feel of emotion. "I don't remember this scene in *Carmen*. The set is the same one from last night, but this dance looks different. It looks . . . somehow . . . sad."

"Very good, that's very observant. You see, you're learning quickly. You are correct. The company is still presenting *Carmen* for matinees and evening performances, so the set must remain intact. This evening Juliet and Richard are blocking out the choreography for something else, something very special." A gentle smile stole across her face as if her thoughts momentarily moved to the stage.

Following her eyes, J.T. looked back toward the stage. "So it is a different dance."

Lena nodded and smiled again. "Yes it is. It's from a ballet called *Swan Lake*, and it's by far the most beautifully choreographed and performed dance in all of ballet. Executed properly, it can tear your heart from your chest. Tender, heart-wrenching and tragic, it's a love story beyond all others." She paused, nodded, and smiled knowingly. She watched the dancers closely, then turned her attention to Juliet as she stood in the wings preparing for her reentrance. "Juliet is phenomenal in this ballet." She nodded her head, seeming to agree with her own assessment of Juliet's talent while remembering her own glorious career.

J.T. leaned forward in his seat and watched Juliet as she returned to center stage. The music softened. On the point of her toes she seemingly floated across the stage, her arms gracefully reaching out to her partner. J.T.'s heart softened as he watched the perfect scene. She was truly beautiful.

Each step she took was precise in its flawless execution. Disciplined and structured to perfection, she was sharp and exact in her movements. The technique was mastered through years, he assumed, in study, practice, and performance.

"You're not a dance student, that much is obvious. You're not press; I can smell a critic a mile away. A patron, perhaps." She smiled and winked. "But I thought I knew all the attractive male patrons from Phillip's list." She nodded and arched her brow. "Apparently not."

J.T. smiled to himself. If nothing else, she was a charmer.

She watched J.T.'s reaction with interest. "Do you work here at the CBC?"

"No, I'm in the computer industry," J.T. said, using the patented elusive answer he'd come up with years ago in order to avoid more questions. He'd learned long ago that the average person seldom delved deeper, fearing that more questions might mean serious contemplation on their part.

"Software, hardware, peripherals?" Lena asked, curiously ending his assumption.

J.T. smiled. Apparently she wasn't the average person. "A little of each, but I primarily create software dynamics."

"So tell me, why does a computer specialist come to a CBC dance rehearsal in the late afternoon when he should be busily preparing the next generation of computer software? Are you a friend of Juliet's, perhaps?"

"We've met."

"Is that right?" She said looking at him slyly, pleased with her new knowledge. Her brow rose with interest. "In San Francisco?"

"No, we met in Manhattan."

"Really, I wasn't aware that Juliet had been in New York recently. I guess she and I need to have a nice little talk to catch up."

When J.T. didn't respond, the woman smiled and nodded again. There was definitely more to this story than he intended to admit. She made a mental note to have a nice long talk with Juliet as soon as possible. She leaned forward and glanced at J.T.'s profile. He seemed to be entranced by Juliet's stage dance.

Lena nodded, realizing that she wasn't going to get any more information about their curious relationship from him. "I'm a New Yorker myself. Do you still live in Manhattan or in one of the outer boroughs?"

"I did live in Manhattan, Upper West Side. I just recently moved."

"Nice neighborhood. I presume by your move that you now reside in the immediate area."

"Yes." He said beginning to wonder about the apparent third degree.

Juliet twirled, than ran across the stage and jumped into the air as Richard followed. Lena smiled proudly. "Bravo, my dears, bravo, excellent," she said in an almost whisper. Then, to him she added, "That particular jump was called a *full grand jete*. And Richard has just performed a *grand allegro*. They are extremely difficult jumps that must be timed and executed perfectly."

"Do all the jumps have names?"

"Yes most do."

"Here, see, she enters again," Lena said, pointing to Juliet as she began dancing across the stage. "An *arabesque*, triple *pirouettes* into a *brise*, then finally a series of *fouettes*."

J.T. nodded, impressed with the dance and translations.

Lena chuckled, "The French have such wonderful words to describe such simple acts. In essence, Juliet walked onto the stage, spun around three times, ending in a final, slower spin, then rose on her toes and fluttered across the stage a bit, then ended with a long series of spinning turns."

J.T. chuckled along with Lena,. "You're right, the French terminology does make it sound a bit more impressive."

"Indeed," she answered, then changed the subject entirely. "You wouldn't happen to be associated with Evans Corporation, would you?"

He turned to her completely. "Yes, as a matter of fact, I am. Why do you ask?"

Lena tilted her head and chuckled. "Interesting," she simply stated. "Where are my manners, my name is Lena Palmer. And I believe you are . . ." the woman said as she held out her hand to shake.

J.T. turned and took her hand and gently shook it, "J.T. Evans, nice to finally meet you, Ms. Palmer."

"Yes, of course, I suspected as much. Taylor's son. She mentioned that you were now in the Virginia office after traveling extensively for years. Taylor is a brilliant talent and a wonderful person. I have several of her pieces hanging in my New York home."

"I'm glad we're finally meeting, Ms. Palmer. I'd like to talk with you about this community center and dance studio you're opening with my mother."

"Of course you would, but please, call me Lena," she said as she waved her hand for him to sit back and relax. "I reserve Ms. Palmer for my students and the press."

"As I was saying, I'd like to talk with you about my mother's investment."

"Yes, the community center, we're very excited." Suddenly the music stopped abruptly, turning both their heads back to the stage.

"Madame Lena Palmer," Roger announced, then began applauding exuberantly.

Lena stood and waved as the cast joined in applauding joyfully. "Time to go to work." She grabbed her purse and shawl, then looked back at J.T. before leaving. "It was good meeting you, J.T. We'll talk again soon."

He stood politely. "You too, Madame Lena. I'll look forward to our next conversation and my next lesson."

"As will I."

As soon as Lena went on stage, Phillip came and sat down in the seat beside J.T. "Sorry about that. I needed to take that call. I've been trying to get together with Senator Randolph

Kinsley for some time. He wants to sponsor a small gathering on the Hill to raise funds for the upcoming season."

J.T. smirked at Phillip's obvious fondness for name dropping. Before he'd left to take the call in the front office, he had mentioned at least three senators, four congressmen, and a Supreme Court justice.

"As I was saying to the mayor just last night at dinner," Phillip continued, "we truly need the funds. If you want this city to compare to the rich cultural institutions in cities around the world, then you're going to have to come up with the funds needed to truly support it."

J.T. nodded absently, keeping his eyes on Juliet as she talked with Richard, Lena, and a few other members of the company. Eventually the stage cleared and Phillip suggested that he and J.T. continue their discussion in his office.

"Taylor and Jace have truly been our greatest and most faithful supporters," Phillip said as he and J.T. walked down the corridor to his office. Their generous foundation grants and personal gifts have truly been phenomenal. We, the arts, are truly appreciative of their donations."

"I'm sure my parents will continue to support your programs."

"Marvelous. Truly marvelous, although I must say, J.T., I was delighted when you took me up on my offer so quickly," Phillip said as he held the office door for J.T. to enter. "We're truly delighted to introduce you to the world of ballet." Phillip rounded his desk and offering J.T. the seat across from him. "I've already been approached by Vanya. She is anxious to personally show you our world."

"Actually, Phillip," J.T. said, "I understood that I would be shadowing Juliet Bridges."

"True, true, but if you're truly anxious and ready to get started, then Vanya is available now. Vanya is a rising star here at the company. I'm sure she'll be very instructive. Juliet is working on a very important program for the season's finale. She'll be extremely busy over the next few weeks. I've already made arrangements for Vanya to show you around. As I said, she is truly a star in the making."

J.T. smiled tightly. "That is unfortunate." The firmness in his tone left little to be misinterpreted. "Thank you, but no thank you. It was good meeting you. I'll give your best to my parents," he said as he stood to leave.

Phillip instantly panicked, seeing hundreds of thousands of dollars in donations walk out of the door. He stood and hurried to J.T.'s side. "Let me see what I can do. I'm sure I can impress upon Juliet the importance of your interest. I assure you, she'll be more than happy to comply."

J.T. smiled knowingly. With money came power, and with power, almost anything was possible, including buying and selling favors. Unfortunately, wielding power without abusing it was often the challenge for most. He used his only as a last resort. J.T. paused, turned to Phillip, and smiled. "That would be acceptable."

"Granted, she may not have as much time with you this evening, but if she's still in the building I'll have her come and discuss more conducive arrangements satisfactory to both of you."

They shook hands as Phillip left to find Juliet.

After the door closed, J.T. turned back to the empty room. It was the same office that Juliet had led him to the night before. He walked over and looked up at the poster of her again. Serene and still, it was almost luminous. His thoughts instantly went to Juliet's solo dance in the dark shadows of the studio. The sadness of her mood struck him again. There was definitely more to her than the smart-talking woman she allowed the public to see.

Chapter 11

Lena perched on the dressing table, crossed her long legs, and smiled as she admired her taut, even skin in the mirror. Soft and supple, she leaned in, moving her face from the left and right, then rolled her chin upwards, pulling her neck tightly. She smiled knowingly and patted the underside of her chin several times. Her reflection was perfect.

At near sixty, she was still as attractive and vibrant as ever. Styled and mannered, she was a character right out of a Tennessee Williams' novel. A cross between Maggie and Blanche Dubois, she was all southern charm, but with the bite and attitude of Maggie the cat, she wasn't one to be easily fooled.

She surveyed Juliet's dressing table. A bevy of cosmetic supplies littered the counter. She gathered the powder brushes and colored pencils and placed them back into the glass holders. Then she picked up and closed the various colored eye shadows, face powders, and lipstick casings. Lastly she gathered combs, decorative silken flowers, and tiaras and placed them in the small velvet-lined case next to the large CD player. Satisfied that she had successfully cleaned the mess on the table, she grabbed a couple of tissues, removed her red lipstick and replaced it with one from the table. Smoked raspberry. The new lipstick color gave her face an added sparkle. She puckered and eyed her full mouth, nodding her approval as she decided that the color was perfect with her chic outfit.

She leaned back and sat up straight, holding her stomach tight and pushing her slight chest out. Thin but firm, her body reflected of her many years as a dancer and now a ballet choreographer.

She reached up and stroked the thin, laced veil of gray that accented the front of her hair. Usually pulled back tight into a bun, today she had it loose, gently brushing her shoulders. "Do you what to tell me what that was all about?" she called loudly to Juliet, still dressing in the next room.

Juliet paused a moment to think, then continued dressing. "What what was all about?" she asked innocently, knowing exactly what Lena was implying. But denial was always her first choice when it came to answering Lena's question regarding her dance performance.

The morning's rehearsal was horrendous. Lack of sleep and exhaustion were only part of her troubles. Having always been a quick study, she suddenly found that the detailed nuances of *Swan Lake* were a struggle to grasp. Missteps, misdirection, and bad timing had led Richard to suggest that they go down to the stage for the afternoon rehearsal. When the session was over she had hurriedly retreated to her dressing room.

For the first time in her life, she was actually delighted when rehearsals were over. Dancing with pain had never been a problem, difficult rehearsals and performances were merely challenges, and exhaustion seemed to give her more energy. But it seemed that being with J.T. again last night had proved to be more of a problem than she had anticipated.

Apparently getting him out of her system with one last night wasn't such a great idea. Her dancing and concentration lacked focus. It was obvious to her as well as others. The simplest routine had challenged her, leaving her frustrated.

All she kept thinking about was the night before with J.T. A frown crossed her brow. She needed to do something about him quickly, or her retirement would be a lot sooner than she planned.

Lena turned to the open doorway. Her pale gray eyes sparkled radiantly as she anticipated Juliet's usual evasive answers. "The distraction, of course. You had absolutely no focus today. I've never seen you so completely diverted."

Juliet came to the door of the dressing room. "I'm just tired, that's all. I've been overdoing it lately." She sighed loudly to give added emphasis, then returned to dressing.

"Are you sure?"

"Of course," she said. "I have a lot of things on my mind. I'll be fine. A good night's sleep and I'll be as good as new."

Lena nodded, not completely assured by Juliet's excuse.

Juliet changed the subject immediately. The last thing she needed was Lena asking more questions. "How's the community center coming along?"

"It's going to be wonderful. Louise and Taylor are incredible, and we have so many great ideas."

"Sounds like the three of you really complement each other."

"We do, I couldn't have asked to work with two nicer women. I'm really excited to get this off the ground. It'll be nice to settle down in one place for a while."

"You'll miss the road."

"I don't think so. Ballet was wonderful in its time. Choreography was just as satisfying. Now it's time to do something different, to give back. I really wish you'd reconsider and join us. You'd be marvelous teaching the children."

"I do teach children at the workshop, that's enough."

"Juliet, you're wonderful with children. Seeing you at the children's workshop and at my studio in New York is truly a joy. You delight in molding those sweet young minds and feet into the next generation of dancers. The little ones adore you, and the older ones want to be you. You were born to teach. Think about it, join us."

"We'll see."

"Seriously, think about it. We've already discussed having several young children's dance classes at the center. You'll be perfect to head the youth program. We could do wonderful things together."

Juliet didn't respond. Thinking about her future was all she'd been doing for months. At the moment, her options were limitless—teach, choreograph, travel, do guest performances, or even start her own dance company.

Juliet looked up and stared at the poster of herself hanging on the wall. In it she was five and just starting in dance. Even then her petite body showed the promise of a career in ballet. She smiled at her wide-eyed wonder at it all. At that age, she thought that dance was the most wonderfully exciting thing in the world. She still thought so. Maybe passing that feeling on to the next generation was for her after all.

"I heard an interesting rumor a few weeks ago," Lena called out again as she sat down at the dressing table, picked up a large makeup brush, and fanned its bristles with her long fingernail. "Apparently your father's getting married again. I seem to have lost count, is this wife number six or number seven?"

Juliet stopped dressing, sat down on the stool, and took a deep breath, then let it out slowly. She waited, trying not to let her annoyance get the better of her. She loved and adored Lena and would forever be grateful to her for introducing her to the wondrous world of dance, but lately her constant insinuations and innuendos where her father was concerned had gotten out of hand.

Wyatt Bridges, Juliet's father, was the perpetual rolling stone. Handsome to the point of mesmerizing, he had women falling in love with him constantly. Even at sixty he was still considered handsome. He was charming and debonair and unfortunately loved the idea of divorce just as much as he loved the idea of marrying. Juliet's mother was wife number two, and Juliet was his only daughter.

As a father he was doting, loving, and kind, and treated her like a princess, giving her everything she ever wanted except his time. Then as a teen growing up, she spoke to him rarely and saw him even less. As an adult she barely spoke or saw him unless, of course, it was by wedding invitation like the one she received a few weeks ago.

Born to affluence with a platinum spoon in his mouth because of his grandfather's keen eye for investments, Wyatt was fourth-generation old money, which had given him a unique perspective on life and love. Spoiled and selfish, with no sign of actually growing up and taking responsibility for his actions, he enjoyed a life of privilege, free of monetary concerns, and devoted his time to the important task of finding happiness. As far as she knew he was still searching.

Lydia Cane-Bridges, her mother, was born to a middle-class family and worked for Wyatt's father. She always said that with Wyatt it was love at first sight. As soon as she saw him, she knew that they'd be together. Unfortunately, love at first sight didn't last.

Ultimately Lydia had lost her heart and herself in Wyatt's shadow. After the divorce and a less-than-generous settlement, Lydia went back to work, and Juliet rarely saw her father, who was always off romancing his next bride-to-be.

Two years later, after a whirl-wind romance, Lena became wife number three and Juliet's ballet mentor. A year after that they divorced, and he was on to his next romance. Just like Lydia, Lena had always seemed to regret the divorce more than the marriage.

"You know perfectly well that it's wife number eight," Juliet finally called out, knowing exactly where the conversation was going.

Lena smiled and shook her head ruefully. She absently fingered the fresh flower arrangement beautifully displayed on the counter. "When will my dear ex-husband ever grow up?"

"I doubt he ever will," Juliet said as she continued dressing.

"True, true, he does still have those pesky commitment issues."

"Boredom, attention deficit, or maybe he just lacks focus.

Either way, making a commitment has never been an issue for Wyatt; on the other hand, keeping a commitment has."

Lena laughed, agreeing wholeheartedly with Juliet's assessment of her ex-husband. "Will you be attending this wedding?" she asked, anxious for firsthand gossip.

"I haven't decided yet."

"You haven't missed one yet."

"True." Juliet had attended every one of her father's wedding since his marriage to Lena when she was five.

"You'd better decide soon, I hear the wedding is coming up."

"Why don't you go in my stead? I'm sure that would liven up the wedding reception. Ex-wife number three meets new wife number eight. Better yet, why don't you arrange for one through seven to attend, that would really show solidarity."

Lena smirked at Juliet's dry humor. "I'm sure it would." She chuckled at the image of her ex-husband's face at seeing her at his wedding reception.

"If nothing else, you'd all get a spot on Jerry Springer's show."

Lena laughed joyfully. "I might just do that. But I'm not sure I could gather the rest of the Bridges wives." She laughed again. "We do, indeed, have a remarkable family tree." She paused for a response from Juliet, but received none. "Speaking of men, I met a very attractive friend of yours earlier today."

Finally dressed, Juliet came back into the room, walked over to the dressing table, and dropped her bag on the chair across from Lena. "Who was speaking of men?"

Lena ignored her remark and continued to smile happily. "A very handsome friend," she taunted knowingly.

Trying not to look interested, Juliet busily transferred a few items from her rehearsal bag to her oversize purse. "Really?"

"Aren't you curious as to who I met?"

"Not really."

Lena smiled and spun the chair to face Juliet. "He said that you two were old friends." Not getting the curious reaction she expected, she continued. "From Manhattan."

Juliet froze as her heart thumped against her chest. *It couldn't be.* She remained silent and continued stuffing her purse. *He wouldn't dare.* When she finished she pulled out a lipstick tube, leaned closer to the mirror, and ran color along her bottom lip, then puckered. Seeming uninterested, she glanced over at an anticipating Lena through the mirror's reflection. "Okay, I give up, who did you meet today?" she asked, already knowing the answer.

"J.T. Evans." Lena watched as Juliet paused for an instant, then went back to puckering her lips in the mirror. "Care to elaborate?"

"There's nothing to say. We met one evening about ten months ago in New York. I hadn't seen him since then." She dropped the tube of lipstick into her purse and gathered her jacket.

"Interesting coincidence," Lena said as she stood, and gathered her purse, and casually tossed her shawl over one shoulder. She turned to catch a glimpse of herself in the mirror.

"What's an interesting coincidence?" Juliet asked as she picked up her bag.

Lena smiled, adjusting the shawl. "That's exactly what he said."

Juliet looked at her and smiled. "Exactly."

"I know you, Juliet. There's more to this than a simple coincidence. I can see it in your eyes, and Lord knows, I saw it in your dancing. Be careful, dear. Remember, patrons are off limits."

"Are you finished?" she asked.

"For the moment."

"I thought you mentioned that you had dinner plans with Phillip this evening?"

Lena shook her head, noting the abrupt change of subject. "I do." She glanced at her watch automatically.

"Well, shouldn't you be leaving about now?"

"I get the feeling that you're trying to get rid of me."

"Of course not," Juliet said nicely.

Lena looked at her and smiled as she walked over to the door. "Don't forget we have dinner plans tomorrow evening. I understand that there's someone very anxious to meet you."

"Who?"

She shrugged. "I don't know. We'll find out tomorrow night."

"I hope this isn't another one of your attempts at setting me up. I'm still reeling from meeting the last man you introduced me to."

"I won't have to keep introducing you if you'd just go out on a date once in a while. When's the last time you went out?"

"It hasn't been that long."

"It's been nearly a year."

"Are you keeping track?"

"Somebody has to."

"Well for your information, I'm going out to dinner tonight."

"Hanging out with Patricia isn't what I had in mind."

"No, what you have in mind is another blind date."

Lena smiled innocently. "As I said, we'll find out tomorrow."

Before Juliet could respond, a quick knock on the dressing room door got her attention. "Juliet," Phillip called out as he knocked again.

"Come in," Juliet said, relieved at the interruption.

Phillip opened the door and peeked in. "Lena, I thought I'd find you here." He greeted Juliet, then kissed Lena on both cheeks. "Are you ready to go? Our reservations aren't for another hour, but I thought you might enjoy meeting a truly huge fan of yours."

"Sounds divine," Lena said smiling brightly, always willing to meet a fan. She took Phillip's extended arm as he led her to the door. She stopped in front of Juliet, and they kissed warmly. "Good night, dear. Enjoy your evening."

"Good night."

As Phillip followed, he stopped a moment. "Juliet," he began as Lena kept going, offering to meet him in the lobby, "you have a guest."

"Oh?"

"Yes, J.T. Evans is in my office to see you." Juliet's heart began pounding as her stomach lurched. "He's the gentleman who won your basket at the fundraiser last evening. His family is also a major patron."

Juliet nodded. "I know who he is. What does he want?"

"You agreed to donate a basket to the fundraiser. J.T. is here to discuss arrangements."

"Is this really necessary?" she asked.

"Completely, he wants to learn about the world of ballet. You're the perfect instructor."

"But I'm sure Vanya would be delighted to take my place."

"He asked for you personally. I'd take that as an honor."

"I have plans this evening—"

"That you'll simply delay."

"But." She tried to quickly come up with another excuse, but failed miserably.

"Thank you," Phillip said as he turned to leave. "He's waiting for you in my office."

Ten minutes later Juliet walked into Phillip's office. "You're like a bad penny," she said as she entered the office and closed the door behind her. "You just keep turning up."

"It's my charm," J.T. said as he stood and turned to face her. He smiled as soon as he saw her. Just like the woman he'd met in New York, she was magnificent. Dressed in fitted denim jeans and a sleeveless knit shirt and sandals, she was straight off the cover of a magazine and right into his fantasies. This was definitely the woman who had crept into his dreams, thoughts, and fantasies for the last ten months.

"Yeah, must be." She moved around to the front of the

desk. "Phillip mentioned that you're interested in learning ballet."

"Learning *about* ballet," J.T. corrected. "There's a difference."

"What do you want to know?"

"When are the performances?"

"The average series of repertoire performances for most ballet companies consists of four or five per season, October through May. There are additional performances such as preview performances, auditions, and special seasonal performances like the *Nutcracker* and *Spring Flings* and, of course, special charity balls and fundraisers."

"What are the specific days?"

She looked at him sternly. "Performances are usually Friday, Saturday, and Sunday evenings, with Saturday and sometimes Sunday matinees, unless, of course, the company is between performances, as we are now. Then there are rehearsals in preparation for the next series of performances."

"That would make you free for dinner tonight?"

She frowned, refusing to admit to herself that he looked even better than he did last night, if that was possible. She placed her fists on her hips and walked past him. "No." She sat back, leaning against Phillip's desk, then crossed her arms over her chest defiantly.

Juliet refused to turn away from his intense stare. The desire in his eyes seemed to penetrate right through her. "It was just supposed to be just one night, remember. That's all we promised each other. We shared a hotel room."

J.T. approached, standing right in front of her, his eyes centered on her face. "Funny, I remembered we shared more than that. Didn't we, Juliet?" J.T. asked.

"One hotel room, one night," she reiterated.

"I beg to differ, two hotel rooms, two nights. And each time we made love." His voice softened to a whisper as his body trapped her against the desk. "You remember last night, Juliet, don't you?"

She looked away. "Last night was a long time ago."

"You remember the feel of our bodies sealed together." She looked away, finally unable to continue seeing the desire in his eyes. "Do you remember?"

"Yes, I remember," she ventured.

"We made love all night long," he added.

She looked back at him eye to eye. "Things have changed."

"My mouth on yours," he continued with the memory. The attraction was still there, he was sure of it.

Juliet shuddered inwardly. The memory of last night was still too vivid for her. "Last night was physical, not personal," she said.

"Your mouth on mine," he added, just inches away from her lips, "touching, feeling, tasting, wanting." He licked her lips, coaxing her to respond to him. "All night long."

"It was just one night," she said as she looked away from him.

"What happened between us was more than just one night. I felt it, you felt it," he admitted.

A quiver of want went straight through her as her stomach fluttered and her pulse quickened. Yes, she remembered. Every touch, every feel, every night since that first night she had lain in bed with the memory of being wrapped in J.T.'s arms and caressed by his touch. "I have a date, I have to go."

A tense muscle twitched in J.T.'s jaw. He didn't like hearing that she had someone else in her life. It didn't sit well with his plan. "Juliet," J.T. prompted as he reached out and stroked her face.

She leaned into his touch then, suddenly straightened up and backed away. She pushed past him and moved to the door. "What do you really want, J.T.?" She hesitated, then turned to meet his eyes. "And I know it's not the history of modern ballet."

"I have a proposition for you."

Her interest was slightly piqued. "Do you?"

"Yes."

She smiled. "Well, as I said, I have a previous engagement."

"This won't take long."

She looked down at her watch. "Talk fast."

"All right," he agreed. "I'd like to employ you."

"Are stock options and health benefits included?" she joked.

"No, but I'm sure we can come to some accord on the personal perks."

Juliet went silent for an instant. Of all the things he could have said, this was the last thing she expected to hear. "Maybe you didn't notice, I already have a job."

"It's part-time. It won't interfere with your career."

"I'm not an escort service."

"I can make it worth your while."

A cockeyed smile tugged at her lips. This was too intriguing to just walk away, she had to know more. Curiosity got the better of her. "Doing what exactly, being a dance teacher for the computer savvy?"

"Not exactly. I need a woman."

She purposefully looked him up and down and smiled, nodding approvingly. Dressed in a dark charcoal pinstriped suit with a pristine white shirt and gray tie, he was as immaculate as ever. "You're definitely not the kind of man who would have a problem getting a woman."

He smiled. "I don't want just any woman, I want you. I'll be more specific, I need you."

"To do what?"

"I need a decoy."

"What kind of decoy?"

"I need to get a matchmaking grandmother off my back. If she sees that I already have a woman in my life, she'll leave me alone and happily go back to her little island with the knowledge that all is well with the world."

"And that involves me how?"

"It's a simple distraction maneuver. You, the decoy, pretend to be my current love interest, and the matchmaker leaves me alone. There are other elements, obviously, but we can discuss those later."

"I see, okay." She seemed to mull over. "I understand how this little scheme of yours benefits you: You get to walk away trouble-free. The question is, how would it benefit me?"

"We once pooled our resources to benefit both of us. I'm suggesting we do it again."

"Go on," she said, intrigued by the conversation.

"I understand that you want to open a dance company in a few months. I can see to it that you're financially able," he said before revealing more of the plan.

"Tell me something. You're apparently well off financially, you're attractive, and you don't exactly appear to be a former resident of a dog pound. Why not just get an old girlfriend to play the part of your lover?"

"She'd see through it. She and my mother talk. She knows the type of woman I typically date. I need someone that's totally the opposite of my usual taste. I need to get her attention and hold it. Only a new and different face will do. I think you'll be prefect."

"I'm flattered," she said sarcastically.

"I didn't mean it the way it sounded. What I meant was—"

"I know what you meant, keep talking."

"Dance can be very expensive—thousands of dollars for pointe shoes, sets, costumes, lighting, and teachers. I can help with that. Interested?"

"Let me get this straight. You want me to pretend to be your lover, and in exchange you'll help finance my dance company?"

"Exactly."

She looked into his soft brown eyes. His sincerity was not exactly overflowing. The feeling that he was up to something had most definitely crossed her mind. Yet the whole idea intrigued her. No one would go to all this trouble just to get rid of a matchmaker. There was definitely something else going on. This so-called simple plan of his was a lot more than what it seemed on the surface. "What else is involved?" A hint of mischief sparked. It made her smile.

"Dinner, dancing, a few parties, nothing overly difficult," he assured her. "Just think of it as a romantic adventure."

She paused a moment, then turned away from him. The idea of pretending to have feelings for J.T. would be more than dangerous. The question was, could she handle it? The answer came instantly. She turned back to him. "Sounds too complicated."

"On the contrary, it couldn't be easier. All you have to do is sit back and enjoy." He reached out and took her hand, stroking her fingers with his thumb. It was a familiar act. He'd done it before as they walked the dark streets of New York City, and he knew that it made her feel safe and protected.

"Be more specific, what exactly would I have to do?"

He smiled. *It worked.* "First, I have a dinner invitation tomorrow night and another obligation the night after. Several more will follow. I pick you up, we go together as a couple," he said.

"And do whatever couples in love do, I suppose?" she finished his thought.

"Exactly."

"And after that?"

"Dinners, family functions, whatever it takes to get the job done. Mamma Lou will be here for about a week. It's shouldn't take much longer than that. Still interested?"

"Maybe, keep talking."

"There's one more thing."

"There usually is," she said dryly, anticipating the other shoe preparing to drop.

"Once it's over, it's over, no strings, no attachments, no expectations, and no exceptions. My work is my sole commitment. I'm not looking for a relationship, alright?"

"I'll have to think about it. Call me later." She reached across Phillip's desk and grabbed a piece of stationery. She scribbled her phone number on the paper, then handed it to him. "I'll let you know." She brushed by him.

"Juliet," he whispered.

She turned to him. "I need to be fair to you, J.T., I don't do the happily-ever-after love thing."

He smiled and half snorted. "Perfect, neither do I. Love isn't part of the deal."

She nodded, turned to walk away, then stopped and spoke without turning back. "Call me later."

Chapter 12

The rush of cool air conditioning quickened her step as Juliet walked into the restaurant and looked around. She spotted her friend instantly. Patricia sat in a booth at the far end of the restaurant. She waved as soon as she looked up and saw Juliet enter.

Dressed in a tailored business suit, her signature single strand of pearls and a wedding band with a doorknob diamond on her finger that could easily have paid the restaurants' rent for the next three months, Patricia was the newly married bride of Pierce Franklin.

"You're late," Patricia said as she lowered the menu and glanced up at her friend as she quickly sat down.

"I know, sorry," Juliet said as she took the menu from the waiter and placed a drink order, "I was unavoidably detained." A sly smile eased across her face. Patricia watched it spread wider and shook her head knowingly.

She and Juliet had known each other and been best friends since Ida B. Wells Academy. They had seen good times and bad times and had always been there for each other through thick and thin. So when Juliet arrived late, which she never did, and she smiled that particular smile, which she seldom did, it could only mean one thing: she was up to something.

The waiter returned, sat a glass of lemon-flavored club soda in front of Juliet, and refilled Patricia's iced tea. He patiently waited, took their meal orders, then hurried away.

Patricia observed her friend for a few minutes. A very familiar sparkle shone across her face. Patricia continued to shake her head slowly. "Oh-oh."

Juliet looked across the table, then around the dining area. "What oh-oh?" she asked.

"Whatever it is, I don't think I want to know about it," Patricia warned.

"I have no idea what you're talking about," Juliet said innocently.

"Do you think I don't recognize that mischievous glint in your eye? You're up to something, or you're about to be. Either way I know something's going on, and whatever it is, I don't what to know."

"Of course you want to know," Juliet said decidedly. She smiled and waited the few seconds it would take before Patricia surrendered to her curiosity. Seconds later she began laughing, and Juliet immediately joined in.

"Okay, alright, I give up, what is it? What happened?"

"Do you remember about ten months ago, when I was in New York?"

"You mean the blackout?"

"Yes, I told you about the man I shared the hotel room with."

"Yeah, I remember. Of course I remember. That had to be by far the dumbest and most senseless thing you've ever done. I still can't believe you did it, blackout or not. He could have been a nutcase or a crazed lunatic."

"He wasn't a nutcase or a crazed lunatic."

"You know what I mean," Patricia said firmly.

"Yes, but the point is—"

"The point is," Patricia stopped to breathe and relax, "don't ever do that again. You nearly gave me a heart attack when you told me afterwards."

Juliet shook her head sadly and rolled her eyes to the ceiling. "You have seriously turned into such a parent. you must drive poor Kimberly crazy with your constant nagging."

"I do not nag," Patricia stated firmly. "And Kimberly is

doing just fine, thank you very much. She, unlike some people, has better sense than to share a hotel room with a strange man."

"Getting back to the story," Juliet said, quickly diverting her friend from another five-minute lecture, "Yes, I know it was stupid and dangerous, I admit it. I've learned my lesson, and I'll never do it again."

"You could have gotten yourself killed or worse."

"What's worse than getting myself killed?"

"I'm serious, Juliet, you hear about stuff like that on the news all the time."

"I know, I know. Would you let me get back to the story please?" Patricia nodded and was quiet. "Okay, it seems that the guy I shared the room with showed up and wants me to do him a small favor."

"Oh God," Patricia fretted. "What's he want, money?"

"Actually just the opposite, he wants to pay me to pretend to be his love interest so that he can get his matchmaking grandmother off his back."

The waiter appeared with their meal and placed it in front of them. He refilled their glasses, then asked if there was anything else they needed. Both Juliet and Patricia said no, so he nodded, smiled, and moved on.

"And you believed him?" Patricia said, continuing the conversation as if they had not been interrupted.

"Yes, of course I believed him. Look, this guy, J.T., is actually some big shot in the computer business. Pierce probably even knows him. He works for E-Corp," she said, remembering his business card logo.

"Evans Corporation?"

"That's right."

"Over a million men in New York City, and you meet up with J.T. Evans?"

"You know him, too?"

"Yes, and you're right, J.T. is huge in the industry. Pierce and I went to the opening of the E-Corp complex a few years ago. I met him there, and you're right, he's definitely something else. He was there with some tall, thin model type and even then, he had women falling all over him. I don't get it, why you, why now?"

"Thanks for the vote of confidence."

"You know what I mean."

"So," Juliet leaned over closer to Patricia. "What's his story?"

"What's his story? Are you kidding? You don't know?"

Juliet shook her head and shrugged. "I know he's handsome and sexy as hell. Sometimes I think that he's wound a bit too tight and obviously emotionally closed, but other than that, not much."

"You assume all men are emotionally closed."

"And I'm usually right."

"How can you spend the entire night and half the day with a man and not know a thing about him?"

"Those were the rules we went by, no last names and no major details about family and occupations. All I know is he has two sisters, one married and one not."

"So what exactly did you two talk about all night?"

"Everything else: politics, television, sports, movies, travel, music." Juliet smiled, remembering the conversations they'd had while sitting at the hotel room window, fifteen stories up, looking out on a blacked-out city. "We even talked about having children, and what our children would possibly look like."

"Let me get this straight, you two talked about having children, together?"

"Yeah," Juliet smiled brightly and said the word matter-of-factly as she nudged a green pepper to the side of her plate.

"And," she prompted. Juliet fell uncharacteristically silent. "What else did you do? "

"We went back outside into the streets."

"Wait a minute, after all that, you went back out into the dark streets?"

"Yeah, and surprisingly the people were pretty cool. I mean, I didn't see any looting or crime unless, of course, you want to count that front desk clerk, who was charging people twenty dollars to sleep in the wingback chairs in the lobby."

"So, you and J.T. just walked the streets?"

"Actually, we went in search of food. Neither one of us had eaten all day. We stopped by a restaurant that was having a clearing-out-the-kitchen sale. We sat out on the curb and ate, then took dessert back to the room."

"Juliet," she paused a second to sip her tea. "Did you two…?" Patricia asked, not fully finishing the details of her question but letting her inquisitive expression suggest the rest.

Juliet blushed, smiled, then nodded slowly, "Repeatedly." Patricia's mouth dropped wide open in surprise as Juliet continued. "It's a good thing we found condoms when we went out for food."

"You didn't tell me that before." Juliet shrugged innocently. "I can't believe it. You never told me any of this before."

"Since I'm confessing my slight indiscretions, I might as well tell you the rest. I accidentally went over to the Ritz-Carlton last night."

"To do what?" Patricia asked innocently. Juliet answered with a wink and knowing smile, leading Patricia's imagination to fast-forward to the obvious. She opened her mouth and gasped. "No, you didn't . . . you didn't . . . you did!" Patricia squealed loud enough for the diners seated at the two nearest tables next to them to turn and look in their direction. She and Juliet burst into laughter reminiscent of their teenage days. "You didn't," Patricia ended with a whisper.

Juliet nodded slowly each time.

"I can't believe that you didn't tell me this before."

"Well, it isn't exactly a conversation starter. Besides, the first time you were going too ballistic over the whole share-a-hotel-room thing. How could I tell you the rest?"

"Okay, okay, wait a minute. If you didn't give last names, how did he find you here in D.C. all the way from New York?"

"I don't know. It was probably a coincidence. He was at the *Carmen* fundraiser last night."

"So, okay, now J.T. shows up again. What now?"

"That's the interesting part. He wants a favor."

"That's right, the grandmother thing."

"Yep, he wants to hire me."

"Are you serious?"

"Yes," she nodded, "and apparently so is he. The point is, J.T. thinks I need the cash."

"You told him that you don't, didn't you?"

"Not exactly. He wants me to play the part, so I'll play the part."

"Are you actually considering doing this?"

"I told him I'd think about it."

"But you're gonna do it, aren't you?

She shrugged, "I don't know yet, maybe."

"It doesn't take a psychic. I can see it in your face. Why even consider it?"

"Why not? Look, I'm over thirty, my career is over. I realize that. I need something, anything, a distraction to keep my mind off the inevitable. In a few weeks everything I've ever loved will be gone."

"You can still dance. You can have the dance company you always dreamed about. You talked about opening a dance studio since we were kids. Do it, you're great with kids."

Juliet chuckled. "Temperamental, critical, and outspoken aren't exactly the best qualifications for a children's dance teacher."

"True, you're all those things, plus caring, determined, patient, and loving. So stop the pity party, get off your rump, and do it. But first, getting back to the subject at hand, lying to J.T. isn't the best idea."

"I'm not lying, exactly. He assumed that since I was a

dancer I didn't have a lot of money. It's not my fault that he assumed wrong. Besides, how's he going to figure out that I'm a trust-fund baby? It's not exactly common knowledge that my father's grandfather had better sense than my father does."

Patricia shook her head regretfully. "So what exactly are you supposed to be doing?"

"He wants me to have dinner with him tomorrow night. That's where he wants me to pretend that we're together."

"And after that, what's next?"

"What do you mean?"

"I mean, what happens after that? Do you continue with the charade or what?"

"Yes, for about a week, or until the matchmaker leaves." The mischievous glint sparkled again.

"I know that face," Patricia pointed and wiggled her finger across the table. "What exactly are you up to?" she asked.

Before she could answer Juliet's cell phone rang. She opened her purse, pulled it out, and said hello. She smiled easily. "Yes," she said before closing the phone and putting it back in her purse.

Patricia watched, witnessing the instant glow on her friend's face as soon as she recognized the caller. It was evident to her the J.T. was on the line. She nodded knowingly. There was definitely more going on with this than just a simple distraction.

"That was him, wasn't it?" Juliet nodded. "And you're going to do it, pretend to be his love interest?" She nodded again. "Just for the record, I'll hold off on saying 'I told you so' when this doesn't exactly turn out like you expect it to."

"What could possibly go wrong? It's a couple of dinners and maybe have a few laughs. No one gets hurt."

"Famous last words. What happens if emotions get involved?"

"Over dinner, somehow I doubt that. Unless, of course, it's on the menu," she joked.

"Juliet, just be careful. Emotions have a way of popping up when you least expect them." Patricia stopped and opened her mouth. "Unless, of course, they already have." Juliet looked across the room, suddenly fascinated by a busboy clearing a table.

Silence hung over the table for the first time since Juliet sat down. Patricia was getting too close to guessing the truth of her actions. Juliet finally turned back to her friend. "Don't say it. I know what I'm doing."

"Do you? You know in all the years that you and I have been friends, and there are many, you've seen me through drama after drama with men, both professionally and personally. Even from the very beginning, until just recently when Pierce and I got back together, you've been there for me and my relationship trials. But you've never had a serious relationship. Oh, you've had relationships enough with some really great guys, but they never lasted. You never let them."

"So I'm reserved. I keep to myself."

"You're not reserved. You refuse to even open up to the possibility of a relationship."

"Psychoanalysis again?"

"I don't have to. I'm your best friend. I know you better than anyone, sometimes even you."

"Meaning?"

"Meaning, Juliet, that your heart's been in a deep freeze for about thirty years, ever since the divorce. It broke your mother's heart and froze yours. You cover it up with sarcasm and humor, but it's still there, frozen solid. No man has ever gotten in until maybe now."

Juliet looked away as her eyes threatened to well with tears. Patricia took her hand. "Dance was your outlet, your escape. It ruled your life for as long as I can remember. The audience, the applause, and the adoration were a quick fix. Now that your stage career will be ending soon, you're lost."

"You're right, I am lost. My dancing is important to me.

Yes, I've had to make sacrifices along the way. But in the end, my career on stage always came first."

"So what happens when you're no longer on stage and don't have an excuse?"

"I can handle it."

"Juliet, sometimes you're your own worst enemy. Your independence and don't-give-a-damn, I-can-do-it-all-alone attitude aren't always the best. One of these days, love is gonna sweep you off your feet and you're gonna have no choice but to just let go. Maybe ballet has done you a disservice in making you too independent and strong-willed.

"You've been pushing those who love you away all your life. You keep everyone at arm's length. Every romantic relationship ends when the man gets too close to your heart, sound familiar?" Patricia wanted to say more, but she stopped abruptly, knowing that it all stemmed from Juliet's relationship with her father. His distance in loving her and her mother's fierce independence was the catalyst for a lot of her problems.

"By all means, Patricia, tell me what you really think and feel," Juliet smiled and joked the truth away as usual.

"I didn't mean to get so serious, but you're my best friend and I want you to be happy."

"I am happy," she lied to herself as she always did.

"You're obviously already attracted to him, or you wouldn't even consider such an outrageous offer if you weren't. All I'm saying is, just be careful." Patricia reached over and grasped Juliet's hand. "You're my girl. I don't want you getting hurt."

"I know, and I won't. It's a simple favor, no strings attached."

"I hope so."

Juliet looked away as Patricia spoke to the waiter about the dessert tray's offering. A frown creased her brow. *It was only a couple of dinners. It's not like I've fallen in love in a single night.* She didn't believe in love at first sight.

Later that evening, Juliet's thoughts rested heavily on Patricia's words. The anxiety she'd always felt at others getting too close had always been her shield. Like her father, she felt relationships were best when dispensed of quickly. When things got too complicated with love, and love was always complicated, she walked away.

Chapter 13

Taylor hung up the phone and walked back to the kitchen table. She sat down heavily. "That was Lena. She just got a call from Juliet, and unfortunately Juliet has another engagement this evening and won't be able to attend."

"That's unfortunate," Louise said.

"It gets even better than that. Jace told me earlier that J.T. has decided to bring a guest this evening." She sighed heavily as she picked up her tea and sipped.

"Did Jace say who his guest was?"

"No, only that he'd be bringing a friend from New York." Taylor frowned. "So much for my brilliant plan."

Louise reached across the table and patted Taylor's hand lovingly. "I'm of the opinion that all things happen in their own time. J.T.s'. meeting Juliet wasn't a given. If they were destined to meet, believe me, nothing would have gotten in the way."

"Except maybe his friend from New York," Taylor injected dryly. "How could I have so completely missed the fact that he was already involved with someone? I never even asked, I just assumed."

"He's been away for some time, Taylor. There's no way you could have guessed that he was already involved with someone. Is it serious?" Louise asked.

"Jace didn't say, he only said that J.T. would be bringing a guest this evening."

"Well, as long as he's happy."

"Exactly, ultimately that's all you wanted in the first place."

Both ladies paused a moment to reflect on the new development. "Maybe it's for the best," Louise said. "These things happen for a reason. Whatever's meant to be will be." Taylor nodded her agreement. "Do you know if J.T. even met Juliet last night at the fundraiser?" Louise asked.

"I don't know, and Jace didn't say. I haven't spoken to J.T. since I had to cancel after giving him the ticket and invitation." She paused. "I wonder who she is," Taylor mused aloud.

"Well, we'll know soon enough."

Louise turned and looked out of the kitchen window just as two catering vans drove up and parked at the back door. Four women got out of the van and went around to the back and opened the van doors. Two other women looked up at the house and began climbing the back stairs to the kitchen door. "The caterers are here," Louise announced. Taylor turned and followed her gaze.

Taylor stood and opened the kitchen door. She greeted the caterers and explained her last-minute-changes to the two women. The supervising cook and lead chef, dressed in bright white T-shirts with the company logo imprinted on the chest, aprons, and baseball caps, stood listening. The other women from the van, the waitstaff, dressed in all black, continued unloading and bringing in supplies.

Taylor asked a few questions as the workers finished emptying the van of supplies. A group of plastic-covered trays, large industrial pots, and bouquets of flowers lined the kitchen counter and table as setup quickly began. The once still and quiet kitchen came to life in a blast of energy.

Taylor picked up the empty tea cups and placed them in the dishwasher. She walked back to the table, watching as the preparations for the evening continued. "I think everything's pretty much set here. Are you up to do some last-minute shopping? I have a list that could choke an elephant."

Louise chuckled. "I thought you'd never ask." She got up and followed Taylor out of the kitchen.

Taylor paused and looked around the large, formal dining room. Stately and majestic, it was the centerpiece of the Evans home. Usually filled with joyous laughter from many cocktail parties, celebrations, and family gatherings, it had lately been silenced by long work hours and busy, conflicting schedules.

The long brushed mahogany dining table usually sat ten, but for the evening it would sit fourteen. Taylor gripped the smooth velvet chairs and leaned over to adjust the three floral centerpieces. Of white and sky blue fresh roses and a sprinkle of baby's breath, simple and elegant, they were perfect, just low enough for comfortable conversation and just high enough not to crowd the low-hanging crystal teardrop chandelier.

Taylor circled the table once, checking each place seating. The china, silverware, and settings were all properly in place. Nodding, she looked up in the wall mirror that reflected Louise's smile as she stood behind her.

"Everything looks beautiful," Louise assured her.

"It's been so long since Jace and I have had the time to entertain. With his busy schedule, it's just impossible to invite friends over even for a simple meal, let alone a dinner party."

"Now all that will change since J.T. is CEO."

"Yes, thankfully," Taylor said smiling. "Jace has worked so hard all his life. I think it's about time he began taking some time to enjoy the fruits of his labor. And he's been really looking forward to the fishing trip with Colonel Wheeler."

Louise smiled. "Otis goes at least twice a year. He and his Marine buddies have an absolute blast telling tall fishing tales and old war stories."

"Sounds perfect, I'm so happy Colonel Wheeler invited Jace to go along. He loves fishing but just never takes the time to go."

"It'll give Jace, Matthew, and Ray a chance to hear what

I've been going through all these years." Louise laughed. "Oh, the stories they tell," she lamented woefully. "Sharks, pirates, and heaven knows what else."

The two women laughed again as Taylor looked over the table one last time. "I didn't realize how excited I was until now." She picked up Juliet's place card setting and put it in the buffet drawer along with the extra candle sticks and napkins. "Well," she sighed heavily, "so much for my choice, as long as he's happy."

"I'm sure whoever she is, she's just as lovely a young lady as Juliet."

Chapter 14

Old Town Alexandria was exactly that, old. Reminiscent of a bygone era, it still honed and clung to the antique qualities of historical traditions while mingling the relaxed charm of the modern age. Historically sound and steeped in heritage and history, the area was now a thriving contemporary community of affluent colonial and Georgian homes.

J.T. drove around the block several times before he found an available parking space. The quiet residential street was a far cry from the hub of activity he had grown used to over the years. Traveling constantly and calling hotel suites home, he'd forgetting the quaint charm of simple middle-class suburban living.

Suddenly the idea of living at the Ritz-Carlton Hotel wasn't as appealing as it once was. The cold, standard cookie-cutter rooms in hotels had always given him a transient feeling that he had somehow incorporated into his own life and relationships. Always knowing that at any given time he could pick up and leave gave him an artificial sense of power. But recently, the feeling had begun to subside and left him empty and unfulfilled. The idea of permanence was becoming more appealing.

To that end, he decided to give serious consideration to his brother-in-law's offer to move into his house on the waterfront, where peace and the slow pace of permanency beckoned.

Admiral's Way was an address of style and class. The luxury home anchored a row of stately town houses with river-front views. Having played poker there twice a year, J.T. felt the idea of moving in began to take hold. He made a mental note to talk to Tony about his generous offer.

With a flick of his wrist, he silenced the engine but eased back into the leather seat and listened to the sounds of smooth jazz being played on the CD. The sultry saxophone filled the car while the memory of Juliet's dance filled his thoughts.

What was he doing? He questioned himself again as he had a hundred times in the past two days. Finding Juliet was dangerous enough, asking her to pretend to be his lover was outright insanity. The feelings she aroused in him were too real.

The truth was he wasn't sure if he could pull off the charade. One dark night with her had already led to months of sleepless nights. And now, after last night, he was back to the old feeling of needing to see her as often as physically possible. Could he really afford to have her this close without summoning the same feelings he'd yielded to ten months ago? The panic of not seeing Juliet again chilled his heart. He decided to deal with that later. For now he had Juliet, at least for a while.

But this was business. And the focus was a simple deterrent. Mamma Lou's incessant matchmaking needed to be stopped, and this was a way to do it. He looked over to the gift he'd bought. It was unorthodox and would make an interesting impression. Determined to see this through, he picked up the wrapped package, got out of the car, and began walking.

Surrounded by historical homes, churches, and businesses, J.T. saw the charming street was quaint and picturesque. Gray slate sidewalks and pristine marble steps welcomed residents and tourists through the narrow streets. Lined with three-story red brick brownstones, slate and brick sidewalks, and cobblestone paths, the streets were heavily shaded with century-old oak and maple trees. Bordered on both sides with the latest model cars, he half expected to see a horse and buggy turn the street corner.

Arriving early, he leisurely strolled toward his destination. He glanced up at street numbers, counting down to Juliet's. He turned into her small front courtyard, and looked upward. Elegant, he expected nothing less. He walked up the stone path, rang the doorbell, then knocked on the front door and waited patiently for an answer.

Like a kid on his first date, he was uncomfortable and nervous. He anxiously peeked through the beveled glass doors, then turned and looked around, noticing the neatly kept garden of colorful flowers as the sweet smell of spring blooms scented the air. He heard the lock click. Then he turned, seeing Juliet open the inner door. She smiled pleasantly and crossed the narrow vestibule to open the front door. She was breathtaking.

"J.T."

"Juliet."

She looked at her watch. "You're early."

He looked at his watch. "You're right."

"Come in," she instructed and backed up, allowing him to step inside the marble tiled foyer. He entered.

The sound of his shoes on wooden floors echoed through the empty house as he moved through to the living room. He smiled and chuckled as he glanced around the empty space. He was surrounded by mirrors on three sides.

An ornate cornice surrounded the parlor and capped a beautifully gilded antique chandelier that hung from the ceiling. Only crown molding completed the interior adornments. "I have a friend who apparently used your same decorator." His deep voice echoed laughter in the emptiness.

Juliet smiled as she stood and watched him looking around at her in-home ballet studio. "You'd be surprised how much I save in furniture polish and cleaning supplies."

J.T. turned to her. They each smiled, amused by her remark.

Then their eyes met and held for a second until she cleared her suddenly dry throat.

"Is that for me?" she asked, pointing to the wrapped package in his hands, "or do you always walk around holding on to small gift-wrapped boxes?"

"It's for you," he said and handed it to her.

"How thoughtful," she took it excitedly and pulled the ribbon off. She ripped open the tissue and laughed aloud. "It's perfect, how did you know?"

"A friend told me that you liked only the best." She immediately opened the package and dipped her nose into the bag. The rich aroma was uniquely flavorful and filled her nostrils. "It's the best I could find, it's called 'Wallenford Estate Jamaica Blue Mountain.'"

"Umm, delicious, it's perfect. I can't wait to try it. Thank you, this was very sweet of you." They stood in silence for a few seconds. "Can I get you a glass of red wine, or would you prefer coffee?" She held up her gift of coffee beans.

"Sure," he paused briefly to watch her glide across the floor to the kitchen, "red wine would be fine."

After a second or two, he finally tore his eyes from her as she disappeared through swinging doors into the kitchen. He smiled or rather, leered, then shook his head of his wolfish thoughts. He noticed she was dressed in an elegant charcoal-gray low-cut fitted dress showing her perfectly shaped legs. He corrected his first mental impression instantly. She was more then simply breathtaking. She was stunning.

Her hair was gathered up in a twist as usual, with tiny white pearls scattered about her hair and loose tendril locks flowing to her shoulders. She wore simple jewelry at her throat and long, thin dangles on her earlobes. Strapped high-heeled sandals were clasped around her lower legs.

J.T. walked over to the fireplace mantle and looked up at his reflection in the beveled mirror. What was he doing, he questioned himself yet again. In a lot of ways Juliet was a lot more then Mamma Lou's matchmaking. He was certain that his plan would work. But he needed to remain focused on the end result. When this was over, Juliet, like all the others, would be a distant memory because work would always come first.

Juliet returned to his side before he even noticed. She smiled up at him through the mirror's reflection. "I'd say a penny for your thoughts, but that would be just too easy." She offered him the glass of red wine.

He took it and sipped the bitter and full-bodied richness, hoping for a distraction. "I was just thinking about this evening, our arrangement, our business arrangement," he clarified further.

"And," she coaxed as she placed her drink on the mantle. He followed her lead, placing his drink beside hers.

"And to make this look real, we need to be more comfortable with each other." She nodded in agreement.

She turned away and smiled slyly. "I'd say that was pretty much a moot point after New York and the other night."

Just as she said the last word, J.T. grasped her upper arm and swung her around to face him. He pulled her firm against his body. He knew that she felt his very obvious excitement. "We're gonna be late," he said.

His lips touched hers with easy awareness. Soft and firm, he pressed himself to her mouth, imploring entry. She opened to him, surrendering to her desire. She wrapped her arms around his neck, pulling him closer, pressing, pulling, and molding their bodies firmly as one.

Weak and breathless, she rolled her neck back, giving him full access. Long, gentle nibbles inched down her neck, burning right through her skin. Seductively slow, he teased her body as she leaned his back against the mantle, trapping him with her body. She felt his hands as they caressed her fully. When he spread his hands open feeling the round firmness of her bottom, pressing his hardness against her stomach, she gasped. Her body burned with want. A moan of unsatisfied desire escaped as her heart pumped wildly.

"Yes, we're gonna be *very* late," she said as he gathered her up in his arms and walked toward the stairs.

He walked up the stairs slowly while planting passionate kisses on her neck and shoulder. She snuggled closer, feeling the strength of his arms around her. She was safe and secure in the only arms she ever wanted to be in.

When J.T. got to the top of the stairs he stopped. "There," she muttered and pointed aimlessly toward her bedroom. He followed her direction, walking down the dimly lit hallway. He bumped the door open with his shoulder, letting their kiss drift off slowly. Subdued lighting surrounded them in a warm glow of soothing calm.

They both took a deep breath as he slid her body down his. They looked into each others eye's. This was the point where minds changed and clearer heads prevailed. But not tonight, not this time. Juliet reached up and gently stroked his smooth cheek. Firm yet soft, she continued down his neck to the silk tie expertly tied there. She slowly pulled at the knotted noose and freed one end, then pulled the material from his shirt. She draped the tie around her neck, then began unbuttoning the top button of his shirt. She looked up to gauge his expression. He looked back at her, his eyes smiling with encouragement.

Satisfied that she had gotten and would keep his attention, she continued. At the last button she pulled the shirt from his pants, then off his shoulders, letting it drop easily to the floor. Then she loosened his belt and pants clasp. The hardness she felt against her hands was boldly evident. He wanted her. Biting at her lower lip, she smiled, anticipating the pleasure his body would bring.

J.T. placed his hand on her shoulders and attempted to lower her dress's thin straps. She backed away, leaving his hands to drop to his side. She pulled the tie from her neck and slowly wrapped it around his wrist. She tied a gentle knot, then wrapped the remaining fabric around her hand, securing and joining them together. Now in firm control, she walked him to her bed.

Turning him around, she placed the flat of her palm on his bare chest and backed him up until he collapsed heavily onto the bed. He smiled his curiousness as to what she intended to do next. She stood over him and slowly pulled on the tie, bringing his hand to her mouth. She kissed his hand. Then guiding him, she caressed his hand against her body, slowly allowing him to feel the satiny smoothness of her shoulders, waist, arms, and legs.

She loosened the tie from her hand, then turned around, giving him her back. Tossing the tie over her shoulder, she felt his tied hand pull down the dress zipper. As it lowered, she unwrapped more and more of the tie from her hand. Using that same joined hand he removed the shoulder straps and guided the dress down her body.

Sheer stockings, a lace garter and a satin thong welcomed him. She was more than breathtaking or stunning. She was mesmerizing. She peeked over her shoulder, smiling a wily grin. "So tell me, what does J.T. stand for?"

He blinked, taken off guard by her out-of-the-blue question. This was pure Juliet. In the midst of the most arousing seduction in his life, she asked him about his full name.

"Later." He spun her around to face him, fitting her body between his legs as he remained seated on the side of the bed. Their bodies were now against each other, bare chest to bare chest. He reached up to her breast with his untied hand. She leaned back, smiled, and shook her head no, silently mouthing the word. He reached up with his tied hand. She leaned back in. She nodded her approval.

So this is how it works, he mused, smiling, enjoying the new adventure of her dominatrix role. He stroked his tied hand against the swell of her breasts. She gasped her delight. He fingered the tie, pulling it and wrapping it around his palm. When their hands were almost touching, he reached behind her, taking her hand with his.

He carefully pulled her body toward his. When she was near enough, he captured her into his mouth, suckling the brown sweetness of her scented skin. Like a starving man, he gluttoned himself on her perfection. She arched back, giving him full access to his pleasure.

Relaxing the tie's hold he leaned back on a ninety-degree angle. The strength of his muscled arm bore the brunt of her body lying against his. Then with his free hand, secured on the bed behind him, he allowed gravity to hold her body firmly against his mouth.

Unbound rapture spurred their desire as she savored the delight of his body and she relished the feel of his mouth on hers. He slowly relaxed completely back, bringing her flat against his chest. He prided himself on his ingenuity and being a fast learner.

Slightly dazed by the experience, she crawled up onto her bed, and he followed. Kneeling, she began wrapping the tie around her hand again, until he, comfortable, lay down beside her.

Then, with the innocence of an angel and the wicked smirk of sin, she inched up and straddled him, perching atop his firmly muscled abdomen. He reached for her with his hand, and she allowed it. A slow, measured groan rumbled in his throat. She leaned over, winding the tie around her hand until their hands clasped together as one.

Gradually, tenderly, purposefully, she licked his parted lips, then nibbled the underside of his chin, drawing the groan that rumbled in his chest. When she leaned up again, she noted the tense pull of his jaw. She decided that she was going to be either the pleasure of him or the death of him.

Together they pulled his pants and briefs free, then she reached their hands over to the nightstand and pulled a small packet free from the drawer. Together, despite the awkward difficulty, they covered him and protected themselves. Having succeeded, she took his tied hand to her mouth and kissed it affectionately.

She guided his hand to her waist. Instinctively he pulled down the side of her thong, then repeated the action on the other side. Satisfied that the stockings, garter, and strappy sandals would stay on, she slowly unwound the tie from her hand, then released it from his wrist, freeing him to explore at will. And explore he did.

He sat up. With ease, he adjusted her body on his lap. Then, eye to eye, she sat, still straddled across his body. With ardent dedication and masterful skill he touched, teased, and tantalized her until she called his name in rasping pleas of pleasure. Knowing her body as well as he did, he stroked every softness, sending moans of rapturous desire tingling over her skin.

"Now," she whispered. Then shifting her weight, she reached for him. Feeling him hard and throbbing, she guided him to lie back down on the bed. Then she inched higher, then lower, and placed her moist readiness above the pinnacle of his manhood and the obelisk of her pleasure. She grasped him firmly and sheathed herself, feeling her body fill completely. She held her breath in a gasp of pure pleasure, hearing his sigh of satisfaction and anticipation.

She leaned down over him. His lips fastened onto hers as a blinding toe-curling kiss stoked the already burning fire inside of her. She arched her body, sending a tremor of delight through them. Then she rocked her hips, slowly at first, then picking up to the rhythm of his movements. He held her waist firmly as she pumped the life force of desire from his body.

He took her breast into his mouth as she leaned over. Playfully he cupped her, kissing both, then sucking each one separately. The feeling, a blinding panic, seeped through her, building a flaming rocket of explosive pleasure. She rocked harder as her nails bit into his shoulders. Then in wild, passionate abandonment, their love cadence quickened to a tense, frantic pace.

The wave of ecstasy erupted and a blur of brilliant white lights washed over them as their bodies twisted, tensed, twitched, then shuddered, surrendering to the inevitable. Ecstasy washed over them.

Breathless, she collapsed onto him. Moisture glistened their bodies as wicked, knowing smiles dragged lazily across their faces. "So, what did you say J.T. stood for?" she barely rasped out.

J.T. laughed heartily, causing her body to bubble and bounce along with his. He pulled her down to his side and gathered her close in a fierce embrace. He kissed her forehead and gently stroked the loosed ringlets of tousled hair from her face. "Later," he promised.

Chapter 15

Juliet looked out the window into the darkness. "Where exactly are we?"

"McLean, Virginia."

"What's in McLean?"

"Your first performance."

She nodded. "So tell me now, what are the initials J.T. short for?" He didn't answer. "Is it really that bad?" He remained silent and just smiled in the darkness. "Okay, you've forced me to guess," she thought a moment, smiled and began, "Jethro Thurston Evans, Jonah Thaddeus Evans, or maybe, Jeremiah Truman Evans?"

She caught him off guard. He laughed, then chuckled, shaking his head while remembering her last few attempts to gain that information. Making love with Juliet was like heaven on earth. She was playful and audacious with a sexy streak of adventure. They didn't sleep afterwards, but they did lay in each other's arms talking until moments turned into hours. "Few people know that dangerous secret," he warned.

"Ah, but I'm not just any people, I'm the woman who captured your heart, the love of your life."

J.T.'s heart pounded as he grasped the steering wheel tighter. The truth of her words took him by surprise. It may have been just a casual remark to her, but for him it continued a chain reaction that had been slowly building for ten months.

She was more truthful than she knew. Lying on her bed

with her wrapped in his arms was a fantasy he would play over and over again in his mind. A simple twist of his silk tie had captured his heart.

"Question," she began interrupting his thoughts, "who else knows about our production?"

"My cousin Trey."

"Trey Evans?"

He nodded and turned to her, gauging her reaction. She had none. "I understand you know him."

"Yes, a mutual friend introduced us a while back."

"A male friend?"

She looked over at him and smiled wide. She inched over and placed her hand on his thigh. "Don't tell me you're jealous already, sweetheart." Her voice softened to the barest whisper.

He turned to her again. "Of course I'm jealous."

"Well, no need to be. Senator Kingsley introduced us."

"Oh, a U.S. senator, is he my competition?"

"There is no competition," she stated honestly.

"That's good to hear."

"Will Trey be here tonight?"

"I don't know. I'm not sure who's on the guest list."

"Is that it?" she asked as he drove through a large iron gateway. Several parked cars lined the long, narrow road. He steered steadily as a van quickly zipped past them, headed back to the main road. Juliet watched the van and read the wording on the side. "Oops," she giggled. "I believe that was the catering truck from dinner."

"Oops," he repeated.

"So, what excuse shall we use, the car broke down, traffic on 95 was unbearable, we got lost, or the every-popular we were driving by a burning pet store and stopped to save the puppies."

"How about we made love, then lay in each other's arms, unable and unwilling to move."

Juliet blushed in the darkened car as a quiver of flutters

went through her stomach. She quickly looked out the side window into the darkness. Truth was sometimes painful, particularly when it came too close to the heart. Her father was an expert at steeling his heart from others; surely she must have some of her father's qualities. If ever she needed to distance herself it was now. "You choose."

J.T. looked to her and grimaced. "What, no smart, sassy reply, no sarcasm?"

"No, not this time."

The car pulled up in front of the Evans home. Juliet was relieved to end the conversation before it began. But she needed to gather her acting ability and stage persona for the next few minutes. The first act was about to begin.

J.T. came around to her side door. He opened it and extended his hand. She grasped it firmly and he pulled her into his arms, taking her breath away, again. He gathered her into his arms, leaned in, and kissed her, caressing her back lovingly.

When their lips parted, Juliet glanced over his shoulder and saw the curtain in the front window drop. "Perfect timing. I believe we just got our first review, although I couldn't tell who just saw us."

J.T. looked away. The thought of pretending was the furthest thing from his mind. He kissed her because he wanted to, needed to, had to, not because it was expected as a performance. He stood holding her in his arms.

Juliet looked to the house again. "We'd better go in."

He nodded wordlessly, took her hand, and guided her down the illuminated brick path, up the steps, and to the front door. Juliet looked up at the three-story edifice. "This is beautiful," she said as he grasped the brass handle and held the door open for her to enter.

The foyer was brightly lit. J.T. took Juliet's wrap and laid it across the hall chair. He reached over and took her hand and paused a second. "Are you ready for this?"

"I'm always ready," her eyes sparkled with added meaning.

"I'll have to remember that." He brought her hand up and kissed it. "Here we go."

Taylor's brow furrowed with added concern as she closed the kitchen door. Dinner had been over for nearly two hours. Dessert and coffee had been served, and most of the invited guests had already left. The catered help had cleaned the kitchen to its usual spotless, pristine glow, loaded their truck, and had pulled around the circular drive that surrounded the house.

Louise, Colonel Otis Wheeler, and Jace sat in the living room talking as Taylor returned after seeing the caterers out. She sat down and looked at her watch as she had done all evening. "I can't imagine what happened to J.T. and his guest." Taylor said.

Trey smiled knowingly as he came back into the room. "I'm sure he's just unavoidably detained."

The slight smile on his face gave Taylor pause. She turned to Trey as he sat down beside her. "You know something, don't you?"

Trey shook his head and rolled his shoulder, shrugging innocently. "All I know is that he is late."

"He's more than late, I'd say," Jace added.

"Who's this guest he's bringing this evening?" Taylor asked Trey.

"A friend."

"What kind of friend?" she continued the interrogation. "A good friend. Whom he's known long?"

"Long enough."

"Where did they meet?"

"New York, I believe."

"Have you met her?" Taylor asked.

"Maybe."

"Maybe? What does that mean, what kind of answer is that?"

"It means maybe," Trey said.

"Taylor, Trey," Jace interrupted their cop-and-bandit routine. "Are you two going to do this point-counter point, interrogation, comic, evasive maneuver the rest of the evening?" Jace asked.

Louise smiled and chuckled, and Colonel Wheeler was full-out laughing.

"As I was saying," Trey continued, "maybe you should ask him yourself. His car just pulled up outside."

"Good evening all, sorry we're late," J.T. offered as he and Juliet entered. All eyes turned to the doorway. Taylor's mouth dropped. Louise's mouth dropped. Trey chuckled openly as Colonel Wheeler and Jace stood to greet the newly arrived couple.

"Well, hello," Jace said as he approached, "Come on in, welcome."

"Dad, this is Juliet Bridges. Juliet, my father, Jace Evans." Juliet smiled brightly as they shook hands.

"Yes, we've met, nice to see you again, Mr. Evans."

"And this is Otis Wheeler, a friend of the family."

"Call me Colonel Wheeler, everyone else does. It's a real treat to meet you. I've seen you dance. Marvelous, just marvelous."

"Thank Colonel Wheeler. It's good to meet you, too."

"And you know Trey Evan's, my cousin."

"Of course, nice to see you again, Trey."

"The pleasure is mine, I assure you." He took her hand, bowed, and kissed it.

"Always the charmer," Juliet said, smiling at his exaggerated manners.

J.T. looked at his mother and Louise. Their mouths were open in shock and they were still sitting on the sofa and staring at them. "Mom, Mamma Lou, this is . . ."

Louise recovered first, she smiled broadly. "Juliet, hello dear."

"Mrs. Gates," Juliet said, recognizing Louise. She had no

idea that the Mamma Lou J.T. spoke about was the company's president emeritus, Louise Gates. "Good evening, how are you?" She walked over and hugged her warmly.

"Just fine, thank you, dear. I had no idea that you'd be here this evening."

"Me either, when J.T. invited me this evening he didn't tell me where we were going. It's good to see you again."

"Taylor," Jace said as he turned to see his wife still completely stunned by J.T.'s guest. "Taylor?"

"Juliet Bridges," she began with a broad unending smile, then stood and walked over to greet them. "Welcome to our home." Taylor opened her arms wide, hugging Juliet warmly.

"Thank you, it's good to see you again, Mrs. Evans. Thank you for inviting me this evening. Your home is absolutely lovely. I had no idea I'd be with such illustrious company this evening. Apparently J.T. forgot to mention to me that you were related." She looked at J.T. sternly. In all of their conversations, he'd never mentioned that his family actually owned E-Corp, only that he worked there.

"You two must be ravenous. Why don't I heat you up something to eat? The caterer left plenty of leftovers." She stood. "Louise, would you like to give me a hand?" Louise nodded mutely and followed Taylor.

As soon as the two women entered the kitchen, Taylor went to the refrigerator and Louise sat down on a stool at the counter. Taylor gathered some containers in her arms and came back to the counter. Seconds went by before either one of them spoke. Then, as soon as Taylor looked to Louise, they both burst with giddy laughter.

"I can't believe this, how did this happen?" Taylor asked rhetorically. "I can't stop laughing," she said as a sudden giggle bubbled up. "Can you believe the coincidence of something like this happening?"

"I've never witnessed anything like this before," Louise admitted. "But it can only mean one thing, J.T. and Juliet must certainly have been meant to be." Taylor nodded her total agreement as the two broke into laughter again.

Juliet smiled and listened attentively as the men talked about weather, sports, traffic, the stock market, the theatre, and Virginia politics. She laughed, nodded, and smiled. J.T. stood by her side the entire time. When the conversation steered toward computers, investments, E-Corp, and an upcoming fishing trip, Juliet began looking around the large room.

She moved to the far wall, spotting a large, elaborately adorned birdcage in the corner. She inched closer, seeing a large blue and gold bird sitting on the top wooden post. "Hello Gorgeous, miss me?" it said. Juliet smiled, leaning in even closer to the bird as it flew to the nearest perch. It side-stepped closer to her and scratched its beak with its feet. She chuckled as it repeated its greeting several more times. "Hello, Gorgeous, miss me?"

"Juliet, meet Gorgeous," J.T. said as he came up behind her, placed his hands on her shoulders, and massaged her gently.

"Hello Gorgeous," she replied eyeing the bird's iridescent feathers carefully. "He's so beautiful. What is he? She?"

"He's a South American macaw, and the family pet who loves to flirt with beautiful women." J.T. stuck his finger through the bars and stroked the bird's chest feathers.

"Really?" she turned to him.

"Um-hum," he hummed while tilting her chin upwards.

"You think I'm beautiful."

"I think you're irresistible."

"I see Gorgeous isn't the only flirt in the Evans family."

"What can I say? Beautiful women are a delight, but you, Juliet, are my weakness." He leaned down as he tipped her chin up to meet him. The kiss was tender and loving.

"Hey, you two, enough of that, get a room," Trey said as he approached the kissing couple. "Some of us didn't bring a date."

Juliet looked away, slightly embarrassed by her impulsive public display of affection. A warm glow spread across her face as her stomach twitched. The guilty pleasure of J.T.'s kisses were getting to be a habit. "I'm gonna go and see if I can help in the kitchen," she said as she backed away from J.T. He pointed her in the direction of the living room and dining room, then toward the rear of the house. She nodded and followed his directions.

As she headed through the house, she stopped at a large oil painting that hung above a white baby-grand piano against the opposite wall. She read the signature, *Taylor Evans*, and nodded appreciatively at the vibrant colors, balance, and texture of the brush stroke. She could see why her paintings usually sold for so much.

Continuing in the direction J.T. had pointed her, she passed six columns at the entrance of the dining room. Noting the subdued and muted light from the sparkling chandelier above the dining table, she glanced up as she passed. The ceiling was a vaulted dome of blue frosted stained glass, giving the room a blissful glow.

She continued on, now following the laughter that radiated from the kitchen. She peeked inside as Taylor and Louise prepared the meals. "Hi, can I help?" Two heads guiltily popped up.

"Of course, join us," Taylor said.

Juliet happily walked into the kitchen and stood by Taylor, who tried not to burst with delight as she opened several of the containers that the caterers left in the refrigerator. "Looks like you had a feast this evening."

"Yes, we did. It's a shame you two came so late," Taylor said as she opened the chilled meat container. She slid the container to Juliet, who peeked inside and, following Taylor's lead, took a peeled, seasoned shrimp, dipped it in a horseradish cocktail sauce, then popped it into her mouth.

"Umm, this is delicious," Juliet said as she grabbed another, suddenly starving, "I love the sauce."

Taylor pulled out several more containers. She placed half on the counter with serving spoons, then put several more in the microwave and pushed the low heat button. She grabbed two china plates, silverware, glasses, and napkins setting a place at the counter.

"Everything was wonderful, Taylor. Thank you again for such a wonderful evening filled with delightful surprise," Louise said. "Lately I've been getting so lonely at the manor now that Tony and Raymond are married and away so much."

"Oh," Juliet said nodding and munching on a medallion of chilled lobster dipped in warm butter that Taylor had just removed from the microwave. "Are they your sons, Mrs. Gates?"

"Oh, heavens no, and call me Mamma Lou, everyone else does," she said leaning over to Juliet and patting her hand. "Tony and Raymond are my grandsons."

"Tony is married to my daughter Madison. They live in Philadelphia and are expecting their first child."

Juliet smiled brightly. "Congratulations, you both must be extremely happy."

"We are," both Taylor and Louise said in unison, beaming like true grandparents.

"Raymond, my other grandson, is a doctor in New York. He just married a wonderful young lady, also a doctor. They've just returned from their honeymoon."

"Ooh, a honeymoon, how romantic. Where did they go?" Juliet asked, accepting a plate of pasta and salad from Taylor.

"Switzerland," Louise answered.

"Switzerland, that's an odd location for a honeymoon." Juliet said, filling her fork with pasta curls.

"I hear it was a great place to stay warm." They laughed at the implication just as Colonel Wheeler, Jace, and J.T. arrived.

"Hey, I'm starved, where's the food?" J.T. asked as he entered the kitchen first.

"Looks like the ladies are in here having their own little party," Colonel Wheeler said, following J.T.

"No wonder the food's not ready yet," Jace said coming in right behind Colonel Wheeler.

J.T. leaned over Juliet's shoulder and grabbed a shrimp from the container. She motioned for him to dip it into the spicy sauce. He did, then popped it in his mouth.

"Umm, that's good."

"Have a seat, everything's ready," Taylor grabbed a bottle of wine from the refrigerator and placed it on the counter. "Anyone else hungry?" she asked.

Colonel Wheeler patted his stomach and said no thanks. Jace walked over to Taylor and hugged her warmly.

Taylor looked back to the empty doorway. "Where's Trey?"

"He said his good-byes. He has an early flight and a week-long business trip."

"Actually, that sounds like a great idea," Louise said. "I'm getting a little tired myself. It's been a long and exciting day filled with wonderful surprises." She looked to J.T. and Juliet, who were nearly connected at the hip. "I'm going to call it a night," Louise said as Colonel Wheeler helped her down from the counter chair.

"Sounds like a great idea," Colonel Wheeler said. "Jace and I have an early flight in the morning. I'm right behind you, Louise."

"Count us in, too," Jace said, as Taylor grasped his hand and they followed the older couple. "You're right, we have a long day tomorrow."

Jace and Taylor said their good nights as they followed Louise and Colonel Wheeler upstairs. "I won't be in the office tomorrow, but don't forget about tomorrow evening," Taylor said to J.T. as she followed Jace upstairs.

"I won't, good night," J.T. said as he poured wine into their glasses.

As soon as everyone had left Juliet turned to J.T., "They're nice people."

"Yeah, they are," he said proudly.

"Your father mentioned that he and Colonel Wheeler were going fishing. Where?"

"Up in Canada. They both love fishing and try to go as often as possible. This is the first time that they are going together."

"Just the two of them?"

"No, Mamma Lou's two sons, Matthew and Ray, are also going along with a few of Colonel Wheeler's retired military buddies."

"Military, I wondered why he goes by colonel."

"Colonel Wheeler is an ex-Marine Special Forces. But fair warning—don't get him started on telling his old war stories. They're almost as shocking as the stories he tells about the restaurant he owns on Crescent Island."

"Mamma Lou mentioned Crescent Island. Where is that?"

"Just off the coast of Virginia, about twenty miles in the middle of the Chesapeake Bay. It's got a wonderful history and is the most beautiful place in the world. As a matter of fact, the brochures refer to it as *God's Garden of Eden*."

"It sounds beautiful."

"It is, maybe we'll get there one day."

Juliet bit her lower lip and smiled as she quickly changed the subject. "Yeah, maybe. So, do you fish?"

"No, I don't have the patience."

Juliet nodded her head, understanding. "What's tomorrow night?"

"My mother's gallery is opening a new exhibit. I'd like you to attend with me if you're free. Mamma Lou will be there."

Juliet smiled. "Sure, back to work, right? Sounds like fun."

Chapter 16

Laughter filled the car as they drove down interstate 95 back to Taylor's home.

Juliet sat in the darkness and listened as J.T. and Taylor joked about computer programs and their family computer contests. Taylor explained that J.T. had developed a series of games as a way for each family member to keep in touch. She also said that even though it was J.T.'s program and he designed the systems, he had never actually won a single game in six years.

That evening, Taylor was the guest speaker, and since Jace and Colonel Wheeler were out of town, she had asked J.T. to escort her and Louise to the affair. The event, a fundraiser at Union Station to raise scholarship money for area children majoring in fine arts, was a great success.

Juliet sat in the front of the car next to J.T. and listened to Taylor and Louise talk. Their conversation shifted from their gardens, to new plantings, to Crescent Island history, to family, then to art and galleries and back to dance and the theatre. Then, as usual, the conversation shifted to her relationship with J.T.

Keeping their answers short and to the point, J.T. and Juliet had so far, after four evenings together, managed to avoid the major relationship questions until now.

"J.T. you never told us how you and Juliet first met," Taylor said.

J.T. looked over at Juliet in the darkness and smiled. "We met about ten months ago in New York," he answered.

"So you had seen her dance before."

"No. We met during the blackout," J.T. began deciding to finally get this conversation over with.

"We had dinner together out on the sidewalk," Juliet continued. J.T. reached over and took her hand and brought it to his lips. The smile on their profiled faces caused Louise to reach over and pat Taylor's hand knowingly.

"How romantic," Louise said.

"It was romantic, very romantic," Juliet added.

"And you two have been together ever since?" Taylor asked.

"No, not quite," J.T. injected. "Actually our schedules didn't allow us to get together much until recently, when I moved back to the area."

"Well you two look happy together," Louise added. "I couldn't have put together a more perfect couple."

"Really," Juliet said. "How so?"

"Mamma Lou is a matchmaker," J.T. said to Juliet needlessly.

Juliet pivoted in her seat to look at Louise, "He's joking, right, Mamma Lou?" Juliet said, keeping up the pretense of not knowing about Louise's matchmaking. "Are you really a matchmaker?"

"I've been know to introduce more than a few couples in my time."

Juliet turned back to J.T., seeing his unease with the conversation. "Really, how does that work?" She delighted in the conversation since it had shifted from additional relationship and personal questions.

"It's not rocket science, like some seem to think. It's more biology than anything else."

"Really?" Juliet queried.

"Oh yes, it's a matter of finding two people with just

enough differing and opposing qualities to make the positive ones come together. Matchmaking is all about balance."

"Have you ever tried to match J.T. up before?" Juliet asked as J.T. grimaced and turned to her in the darkness.

"No," Louise answered truthfully.

J.T. looked up in the rearview mirror. Questions washed over his face. He'd been certain that Mamma Lou had him next in her target. But knowing her as he did, she'd never lie about matchmaking. So what was all the mystery with her sudden visit, and why all the added interest in his return to the area?

Quietly Taylor beamed with pride. Even though she hadn't been the one to initiate their first meeting ten months ago, she was obviously responsible for them coming together since it was her idea for Jace to name J.T. CEO sooner than expected. She had known from the start that Juliet was the perfect one for her son. Her conversation with Lena as she discussed Juliet gave her the sense that Juliet belonged in the Evans family.

"Juliet, Lena mentioned that you two were related."

"We are. Lena is one of my stepmothers."

"One of your stepmothers," Taylor repeated. "How many do you have?" The new information surprised her. She knew that Juliet's father had been remarried after his divorce from her mother, she just didn't realize that he'd made a career out of it.

Juliet smiled in the darkness, having always received that question when she mentioned her extended family. "Seven and counting. My father's been married seven times. As a matter of fact, he's getting married again next weekend in Florida."

"Good Lord," Louise said, surprised by the sheer volume. "Mother's Day must be hectic."

Juliet smiled and laughed. she'd never though of it that way. "You're right."

"He sounds like a very interesting man," Taylor said.

"He is."

"And what about your mother?"

"She passed away last year after a lengthy illness."

"I'm sorry," both Taylor and Louise said. J.T., being unusually quiet as he inadvertently learned more about Juliet, reached over and grasped her hand to his. A gently comforting squeeze opened her heart to him even more.

Taylor nodded then continued, "Lena speaks very highly of you."

"Lena is more like a second mother to me. I often spent weekends with her in New York watching her dance from the wings at the American Ballet Theatre and teach at the Dance Theatre of Harlem. As a matter of fact, Lena was the one who started me in dance when I was a child. She and my mother were more like sisters than ex-wives to the same man. I don't know what I would have done without her. She's a wonderful woman."

"Yes, she is."

"How old were you when you began dancing?"

"I was about five years old. I started right after my parents divorced. Lena was my father's third wife. She was a ballerina. My father took me to one of her performances and I fell in love instantly."

"Lena is a magnificent dancer," Louise began. "I remember her stage performance. I saw her dance *Giselle* just before she retired. I'd never seen anything as graceful and lovely."

"She is exceptional," Taylor agreed. "But now as a choreographer, she has truly found her calling. She has rejuvenated the old classics, giving them a more modern translation and bringing in the audiences in droves."

J.T. turned into the circular drive in front of the Evans family home. "Here we are, ladies, home at last."

"Oh my, are we here already?" Louise asked as she looked up at the well-lit house.

Everyone said their good-byes as J.T. got out and opened

the car door for Louise. He took her arm and they walked to
the front door.

"Juliet," Taylor said as she watched J.T. help Louise down
the brick path to the door. He opened it and stepped inside,
turned the alarm off, then helped Louise over the threshold.
Taylor reached over and gripped Juliet's hand. "Thank you."

Juliet looked puzzled as she turned and tilted her head to
the side. "What do you mean? Thank you for what?"

"For making J.T. so happy," she smiled lovingly as only a
mother could. "For caring and loving him. I can see in his
eyes that he feels the same way. Louise was right, you two are
perfect together."

Juliet swallowed hard. This part-time job was definitely
getting too complicated. "Mrs. Evans, Taylor," she began, but
couldn't continue. There was no way that she could tell Taylor that she and J.T. were nothing more than a couple of con
artists out to fool a sweet old woman into leaving him alone.
But the truth was she did have feelings for J.T. And that troubled her even more than lying. She squeezed Taylor's hand
gently. "You're welcome."

"Good night dear," Taylor said as she slipped out of the car
and walked down the path to the front door.

Juliet watched as Taylor whispered something to J.T. He
smiled then glanced back to her in the car. He nodded his
agreement, then hugged her close. After closing the door he
waited to hear the alarm click, then turned and walked back
to the car.

Emotion welled up inside of her. She hadn't realized until
that moment how much she really missed her mother. They
had always been close, but after her diagnosis they were
nearly inseparable. Juliet had sold her condo, moved back
into the family home in Old Town, and stayed until her
mother's death.

After his mother and Mamma Lou were inside the house,
J.T. got in the car. They sat in the darkness for a few minutes before he started the engine. Silence drifted between

them as he pulled around the drive and drove back toward the main highway.

He reached up, plucked a CD from the sun visor, and eased it into the player on the dash. The smooth, swaying rhythms of soul and spirit filled the car. J.T. sang the words as he drove.

Juliet nodded her head to the slow, rhythmic beat. "This is nice, Earth Wind and Fire, right?"

"Yes, they're one of my favorite groups. They're timeless. This is called 'Love's Holiday.' "

She nodded and smiled, "I remember." Juliet closed her eyes, sat back, and listened to J.T.'s voice blend melodiously with the lead singer. It was as if they were singing to her. She felt his hand grasp and hold hers. The gentle softness of his touch and the rich tenor of his voice opened her heart more than ever.

She drifted on the emotions of the words, feeling them touch her like never before. She turned to J.T. as he glanced over to her. Suddenly she felt shaky and her stomach quivered as a flush of warmth sank into her body. She breathed heavily.

Thankful for the muted glow of the dashboard lights, she turned and looked away at the blur of traffic around them. There was no way she wanted J.T. to see her at that moment. Love had indeed found its way into her heart. Ten months ago, three days ago, when, she wasn't exactly sure, but she did know that she loved him, and it was the best and worst feeling in the world.

"You have a nice voice," she said, changing the subject away from her heart.

He nodded his response and continued singing until the song drifted off. A slow, soothing instrumental was next. "Why dance?" he asked.

"Why not?" she answered.

"You're obviously an intelligent woman, you could be and do anything. Why did you choose dance?"

She smiled in the darkness. "Actually, dance chose me. At first it was my way of escaping the pain of my parents' divorce. Then it became a kind of an addiction, with its flawless technique and exacting positions. There's nothing more beautifully erotic and powerfully thrilling than dance."

"So, why are you leaving ballet?"

Juliet opened her eyes, surprised by the new topic of conversation. "What do you mean?"

"I've heard it mentioned that you'll be leaving ballet at the end of the season. I want to know why."

"I'm not leaving ballet. I'm just retiring from the stage."

"What's the difference?"

"Ballet will always be a part of me. I'll never give that up. But I am giving up my position as principal ballerina."

"Why?"

"Age," she simply stated.

"What about it?"

"Ballerinas, particularly principal dancers, have a relatively short stage life. Ten to fifteen years is about it. After that, your body begins to slow down."

He chuckled. "That's ridiculous. You're beautiful on stage. I've never seen anything as graceful and exciting. How can you be too old just because the clock says so?"

"I am slowing down, I can feel it," she whispered timidly, half afraid to even speak the words aloud. "The intense training and the nomadic lifestyle have taken their toll. The limelight isn't as bright as it used to be. My body can't do the things it once could."

"Your body is perfect," J.T. assured her, "It's more than perfect, it's what keeps me awake at night."

Juliet smiled at the compliment. "I have a question for you."

"Okay."

"How can you be your mother's son and still not love the arts?"

"Because I'm also my father's son."

"But she's an artist, didn't you grow up with it?"

"At times, but you'd be surprised what you can avoid when you're extremely good with computers."

She smiled, off guard. "When am I going to get tired of you?"

"Is that what you're waiting for, the other shoe to drop?"

"Yeah, something like that."

"Why?"

"It always does."

"Maybe not this time." He drove around to the front of the building, pulled into a parking space, and turned off the ignition.

Juliet hadn't been paying attention to his driving. She became aware when he pulled up to a gated complex. He lowered the window and waved at the guard's booth. The uniformed man acknowledged him and allowed him to pass immediately.

"Where are we?" she asked.

"E-Corp, Evans Corporation, the family business."

He got out and opened the door for her. He escorted her through the main lobby to the executive elevators and then to the top floor. They walked down the hall with J.T. explaining the basics of his position and E-Corp's place in the computer industry.

"Sounds nice. Where did all this come from initially?"

"What do you mean?"

"Old money, new money, trust funds, great investments?"

J.T. nodded his understanding. "New money. My father was in the computer industry long before there was one. When it broke wide open with the dot-com's he was there, and we've been on the cutting edge ever since."

"What about you?" she asked as they continued walking.

"I've always been into computers. I was actually a pseudo-hacker as a teen. I back-doored into some pretty interesting places. But ultimately, you could say that I got in and out of the dot-com's in plenty of time to make a nice chunk of change."

At the end of the hall, J.T. stopped. He opened the door with a plaque on the side wall that read, *J.T. Evans, Chief Executive Officer*. As soon as the door opened, a soft glow surrounded them. Juliet stepped inside and looked around at the cool, sterile environment. She walked further into the office, then over to the desk. She sat down and spun the chair around once, then stopped with her palms on the desk. She looked around again, then focused her attention on the panel of buttons on his desk. "What do these do?"

J.T. leaned across his desk and pushed a button. Instantly four computer monitors appeared from inside his desktop and a rectangular cover slid back, revealing the most extensive keyboard she'd ever seen. Juliet ran her finger across the tops of the screens. "Impressive, what are they exactly?"

"It's a multiscreen system."

"A computer?"

"Yes, basically it's a computer system with four interconnected monitors."

"That sounds simple, what does it do exactly?"

"It allows me to access a number of programs and networks simultaneously, giving me greater access to information."

"Cool."

"They're prototypes called thinking systems or basically a modified artificial intelligence."

"Artificial intelligence, as in robots?"

"Yes, in its simplest form."

"You have robots on your desk?"

"Something like that."

She nodded, not sure she actually believed what he had told her. She leaned in and looked over the keys on the keyboard. "How do you turn it on, or should I refer to it by name?"

"No name, there are several security checks before the operating system accepts a command." She looked at him, questioning, as he continued. "Voice print, access codes, and a retinal scan."

"All that?"

"All that," he confirmed.

"What happens if someone else tries to turn on the system without having all that?"

"There's an intrusion system that automatically engages when there is unauthorized access. For instantance, the system will completely lockdown and go into search-and-retrieve mode."

Juliet smiled. This was sounding more and more like a sci-fi thriller. "Okay." She decided to leave that line of questioning alone. "What about hackers?"

"This is a stand-alone system with limited cyber-modem access to the mainframe. It can gain information via the net without exposing itself to hackers."

"And that's good why?"

"The more information, the faster I do my job."

"What exactly is it you do?"

"I run the company."

"You're the CEO and you run the company, that's it? No job description?"

He smiled, remembering his mother's threat of writing his job description for him. "As a matter of fact, I understand that there's one in the works. But officially, no, according to my schedule, I basically create program codes and make sure that everything runs smoothly."

"Really?"

"Lately I've been working on a new program code that would allow an encrypted cipher to denote a predetermined digitized code. The code would then develop into an A-linear cryptographic system to arbitrarily transpose units according to a predetermined binary code."

"Sounds like fun, but I thought E-Corp made computer games."

J.T. smiled at the usual question. "We do that, too, at least one division does. They're located on the West Coast."

"How many offices do you have?"

"There are three satellite offices—in California, Seattle and New York. This is the main facility."

"And who runs them?"

"I do, but up until about a month ago I ran the satellite offices directly. I worked out of three different offices and lived out of different hotels in three different cities. The demands of the position required me to travel constantly. But now we've consolidated and brought more work in-house at this location."

"Are you here at this site permanently?"

"Yes."

"Good."

"So, do you approve?"

She looked around the office again. "It's not what I expected."

"Really, what did you expect?" He asked as he walked around to the front of the desk and sat down in one of the two seats. She didn't answer, but instead bit her lower lip causing a ripple through his stomach. It was a habit of hers that he was beginning to recognize well. He first noticed it in New York, then later when she walked into her dressing room and found him standing there. She was intrigued.

"Something softer, warmer, less harsh."

"Ouch," he feigned hurt over her insulting his decorative taste.

She shrugged and twitched her nose, another habit he knew well and found captivating. "You put on the straight-laced, corporate-man-of-business armor. I guess I expected to see the real you someplace in your life."

"What if this is the real me?" he asked.

"It's not."

"How can you be so sure?"

"If it were, I never would have talked you into sharing a hotel room with me."

He chuckled softly. "You're that sure?"

"I'm positive." She nodded and casually glanced down at the folder and papers on his desk. The yellow and black *Carmen* playbill instantly caught her eye. She picked it up and looked it over. "Not exactly Fortune 500 reading, is it, or does it have the Dow Jones and NASDAQ listed on the back cover?"

"My mom gave that to me when she gave me the invitation that first night."

Juliet nodded finally understanding. "Your mother, Taylor, the woman you said was at home that first night at the Ritz-Carlton." He nodded. She nodded. "Funny."

"I thought so."

And it's been on your desk since then?" She stood and slowly walked around to his side of the desk.

He leaned back, watching her approach. "Housekeeping has been slack lately."

"Liar," she said standing in front of him. Then impulsively she rose up on her toes and spun around several times, her arms gracefully rounded in front of her in *port de bras*. When her final rotation was complete, she ended facing him with her arms open. "Dance with me."

J.T. smiled, still admiring her perfect movements even in street clothes and heels. "I have a better idea, you dance for me." His thoughts instantly went to the first night when he watched her private dance in the dark studio.

"Like the night in the studio," she said, sliding onto his lap. He nodded slowly, not at all surprised that she was able to read his thoughts. She kissed him softly.

"You were very good that night."

"Yes, I was."

"It was amazing to see you holding some of those positions for so long. Your balance was remarkable."

"It's all in the mind."

"Funny, I though it was in the body."

"Line, clarity, elevation, dynamics, and balance."

"What are those?"

"They're all aspects of dance. And in the ultimate sense, they're aspects of the universe."

"You want to try that again?"

"Everything has balance. For every yin, there is yang. Positive and negative. Male and Female. Up and down. Right side of the brain, left side of the brain. One side is lost without the other side."

"I see."

"Knowing that every action has an equal and opposite reaction keeps all life in balance."

"Fascinating, one of Isaac Newton's theories used in dance. That's an interesting concept."

"The idea of balance is all around, even in the no-name robot computer sitting on your desk. Each time you open a program, you must close it, thus a universal balance."

"Since when are dancers so analytical?"

"Balance. The body and brain live as one."

He wrapped his arms around her, pulling her closer to his body. He kissed her as the passion he felt deepened. Tasting and teasing, they relished each other as the building desire burned. His hands touched her body as his heart had touched her soul.

"I love your body," she said.

"I love your brain," he said.

"Balance," they said in unison as their lips came together again. When the kiss ended, she tucked into his embrace. "This is getting complicated, isn't it?" she said breathlessly.

"No, this is getting interesting."

"I grew up alone. I have one best friend. I know how to be one. I don't know how to be two."

"I'll teach you." He kissed her again.

"Tell me something, why does Mamma Lou want to match you up with someone so badly?"

"That's what she does." He nibbled her neck through the silky softness of her dress.

"So she has played matchmaker with other people?"

"Yes," he continued with his pursuit of pleasure.

"Who?" She tensed, her body pulled back slightly.

"She's matched my sister, and two of my friends, and apparently about a dozen others."

"So she's good."

"She'd say she is."

"So her saying earlier that you and I looked perfect together, and that she couldn't have chosen any better, was a confirmation that she was satisfied."

J.T. leaned back to see Juliet's face. "What do you mean?"

"I mean, was that the end? Is this over?"

"Not yet. Are you trying to get rid of me already?"

"I'll let you know when I'm ready to get rid of you." He smiled, sending an anxious tremor through her. This pretend thing was beginning to get too close to the truth. "What's my next assignment?"

"There's another cocktail party tomorrow night at my mom's gallery. I'd like you to attend with me."

"Okay," she stood and stepped away.

"I'll pick you up at seven-thirty."

"No," she objected too quickly. "I'm not sure what time I'll be leaving the studio. It's better if I meet you there."

Puzzled, J.T. grimaced at her sudden change. "Okay. If you like, I'll get you the directions."

She nodded. "We'd better go. It's getting late, and I have an early rehearsal." He stood and followed her to the door. Moments later she stared in the passenger side rearview mirror and watched E-Corp vanish into the darkness. She breathed a heavy sigh. *This is getting way to complicated.*

Chapter 17

J.T. sat at his desk piled high with proposals, marketing strategies, and schematics for the latest computer programs and peripherals. But instead of focusing on the material at hand, he sat flipping through the *Carmen* playbill once more.

He studied and examined the cover art thoroughly, and then turned to read and reread the biography on Juliet. Afterward he took a few seconds to focus on her photo and flip back to the cover art. The act had quickly turned into an obsession for him each time he paused to think.

Suddenly he tossed the playbill into his top drawer. Now, determined to refocus, he opened the marketing proposal and scanned the points he wanted to consider. Detailed and defined by his standards, the program suggested an intense focus on nationwide advertising while initiating marketing programs specifically focused on colleges and universities.

He looked up at the computer screen he'd been working on to check the schematics. His focus slowly drifted. A contented smile spread wide across his face as he sat at his desk and handled his tie purposefully. He loosened it and wrapped it around his hand as Juliet had done a few nights before, and then he released it, smoothing the tie's edge flat against his chest. He smiled and chuckled, thinking that he would never casually think of his ties again as just accessories to his business suits.

He closed his eyes and leaned his head back against the high leather chair. It felt good to be back with Juliet, even if it was just for a short time. She was an enigma wrapped in a seductive temptress. Talented and smart, she was an exhilarating and vivacious woman with an arousing spirit that had him awake all night with images of their love-making.

The passion that he felt for her had gone way beyond a passing attraction. There was something more, something more intense, something that he couldn't shake. The seed of his yearning grew the moment that he'd laid eyes on her. And each moment after that, it kept growing and building, until finally it was beyond anything he could have imagined. He knew what it was. He just didn't want to admit it.

He'd called her earlier, as soon as he got into the office, but she was already in rehearsals. Impatiently he called twice more. He looked at his watch. It was late afternoon and she hadn't called, but he knew she would. He picked up the next page of the proposal and scanned its contents. He needed to get his mind off of Juliet and back on work.

Hours later his private cell phone rang, interrupting his flow of concentration. Usually he'd just let it ring, particularly if he was in the middle of something. But this time he looked at the number. Recognizing it instantly, he answered. "Lo," his deep, rich voice answered.

"So, what should I call you: dear, darling, honey, sweetheart, or maybe lambchop?"

"Whatever you'd like," he said as the sound of her voice caused him to smile. He relaxed back in his chair and pulled the playbill from the top drawer. He flipped to Juliet's photo. "You decide."

"Actually, you don't look like the pet name type."

He chuckled. "What type do I look like?"

She took a deep breath and paused a second. "Honestly, I'm still trying to figure you out."

"I'm not that difficult to figure out, am I?"

Juliet glanced over at Roger standing in the opposite wing. He motioned for the chorus to line up for the last act, last scene. "How do you think we did last night?" she asked, changing the subject while still anxious to get his feelings.

"You were phenomenal, as usual."

She bit at her lip and hesitated. "Are you talking about the fundraiser at Union Station or the conversation in the car on the way to your parent's house?"

"Both." His smiled widened.

Juliet blushed like a schoolgirl, then frowned, surprised by her reaction. "I have to go, I'm on stage in a few minutes."

"Juliet, we need to talk." He sensed the apprehension in the silence from the other end of the phone. "About our arrangement," he added. "How about a quick dinner before going to the gallery tonight?"

"I never eat after a performance," she stalled, avoiding the moment she knew would come.

"Not even dessert?" he asked, noticing the sudden chill in her voice.

"No, not even desert."

"What do you do after a performance?" he asked.

"I walk. It helps with the adrenaline rush after a performance."

"Sounds good, we'll go for a walk together."

"I usually walk alone."

"A ritual?"

"Yes."

"I did, too, but things change."

"Seasons change, J.T., people don't."

"You'd be surprised how quickly people can change when they want to, when they need to."

The conversation was beginning to go in an uncomfortable direction. Juliet opened her mouth to respond but nothing came out. He was right, things do change. People change. She had changed. The woman she was ten months ago wasn't the woman she was now. She looked over toward the stage. The music began and the curtain rose slowly.

"I have a curtain, I have to go now. I got the directions you sent. I'll meet you at the art gallery." She hung up quickly without giving him the opportunity to respond. This was getting too complicated. Maybe Patricia was right. She'd never had a serious relationship and let it actually run its course. She was too much like her father for that.

He'd been married and divorced seven times. Each time, the marriage lasted less and less time. He was married to his seventh wife only three months. His charisma and charm had always found him the perfect mate, but when it came time to making a lasting commitment, he'd find some excuse to end the relationship just as she herself had done time and time again.

She looked over to Roger. He nodded as the music began to play. *Focus,* she admonished herself, trying desperately to shake J.T. from her thoughts. But she couldn't. Ultimately she took him out on stage with her and danced like she had never danced before. The passion in her movements gave her dance an exhilarated fervor.

She danced for him even though he wasn't there. And each step sent a wave of joy through her soul. Her heart leapt. There was no other place she ever wanted to be than right here on the dance floor, feeling the music and letting her body move to its melodious form. Juliet closed her eyes and sank into the dream. Her body soared, filled with a never-ending emotion that flowed in every step she took.

It was the perfect feeling she got when she danced. It was the ultimate high, beyond pills and powders. Empowered by the movements, the more she thought about J.T., the more exacting her dancing became, until she imagined that he was the only person in the audience, just as he had watched her that first night. The intensity of emotion she felt as she danced raised her performance to near perfection.

Like liquid silk, she moved across the stage, graceful and elegant; she was pure magic. The audience couldn't take their eyes from her. She was brazen and bold as the character and soft and subtle as the dancer.

When the performance ended, she realized that she could have danced another two hours. Three ovations later, she watched the curtain fall for the evening.

Richard turned and engulfed her in his arms. "I don't know what got into you tonight, love, but you were brilliant this evening. I've never seen you so dynamic."

"Thanks," she said, still breathing hard from the performance.

"It's gonna be hard giving this up," he said, air-pecking her forehead and walking away.

Juliet looked around the backstage area and nodded, emotionally. He was wrong. It wasn't going to be hard giving this up. It was going to be damn near impossible to give this up.

"Somebody's positively glowing," Nadine said as Juliet took the towel she offered and draped it over she shoulders. "You were brilliant. I don't know what got into you, but I've never seen you dance so perfectly. Every step, every turn was perfectly pitched."

Juliet stood and waited for the inevitable. It came. Nadine turned and smiled coyly. "Whatever you're doing," she winked, "keep doing it."

"That's it? No smart remark, no hidden lesson?" Juliet asked.

Nadine nodded, "That's it."

"Thanks," she smiled happily as she watched Nadine walk over to Vanya. The grimace on Vanya's face told her exactly what Nadine had said to her.

Juliet walked over to Vanya, "Nadine doesn't mean any harm. She has an eye for perfection, and it's her way of helping you. Believe it or not, she's usually right."

"I don't need her help or yours," Vanya insisted.

"Actually you do. You just don't know it yet, but you will."

"You're old, Juliet. Retire now and save yourself and the

company the embarrassment." She rolled her eyes and stomped off in the opposite direction.

Juliet stood looking after Vanya, shaking her head. She definitely had a thing or two to learn.

Chapter 18

That night, as on stage earlier, Juliet played her part to perfection. To the world, and in particular to Louise Gates, she and J.T. were a loving, devoted, couple with eyes only for each other. They played their romantic roles until pretending and reality blurred into one. That night, they more than proved to Louise that they were a couple. They showed her that they were in love.

By that following afternoon, Jace and Colonel Wheeler had returned from their fishing trip. A welcome-home fish fry and cookout celebration was planned. Taylor, Louise, and Juliet cooked a feast while Jace, Colonel Wheeler, and J.T. prepared an elaborate meal on the outside grill. That evening, the three couples laughed and joked as Colonel Wheeler and Jace concocted outrageous tales about their weeklong Canadian fishing trip.

The following morning, after long hugs and fond farewells, Colonel Wheeler and Louise left to return to Crescent Island. Louise embraced both Juliet and J.T., giving them special hugs and telling each to always cherish and nurture their love. She was obviously beyond elated.

It was finished. The plan had worked, and J.T. patted himself on the back the remainder of the next day. He called Juliet at the theatre and asked her to join him in celebrating their success. She accepted. He gave her the directions.

* * *

Patricia looked at her watch, then picked up the phone on the second ring. "Hello?"

"Why am I not surprised you're still in the office?" Juliet said.

Patricia smiled, removed her glasses, and tossed her pen down. It had been a long, exhausting day and she deserved a break. Talking to her best friend was the perfect remedy. "Hey, girl, how are you?"

"Fine. What are you still doing there?"

"I had some paperwork to catch up on. Pierce is working late tonight, and Kimberly's visiting Jasmine. The last thing I wanted was to go home to that big, empty house."

"Are you kidding? That place is a palace."

"It's an empty palace sometimes. So what's going on with you?"

"Same old, same old. Richard and I are doing *Don Quixote*. Vanya still wants to break my legs. In a few days I'll have no idea what I'm going to be doing with the rest of my life. I fell in love with J.T. Evans and I think he loves me, too, and finally, I've decided to attend my father's wedding in Florida with Randolph." Juliet exhaled quickly, feeling like a burden had been lifted from her chest.

Patricia went completely silent. "What did you just say?"

"Richard and I are doing *Don Quixote*. Vanya still wants to break my legs—"

"No," Patricia interrupted. "The last part."

Juliet smiled. "I've decided to attend my father's wedding in Florida with Randolph."

"Don't be a smart-ass, you know what part I'm talking about."

"Don't make me say it again."

"Have you told him yet?"

"No."

"Are you going to?" Juliet remained silent. "Don't you think you should? You owe it to yourself and to him."

"Exactly how am I supposed to do that?"

"Simple. Just tell him."

"You don't understand. Telling a man that I'm in love with him isn't exactly me. You know that."

"Yes, and I also know that you've been in love with J.T. since New York ten months ago. And chances are he fell in love with you at the same time. Tell him," Patricia insisted.

"I'm still debating that issue."

"And what conclusions have you come to, if any?"

"That's why I called you. I need your help."

"You don't need my help, Juliet. Do what's in your heart," Patricia said.

"You don't understand, this wasn't how it was supposed to be. We made a deal. We were only supposed to pretend. What am I supposed to do now?"

"How about talking to him, telling him how you feel?"

"Is that the only idea you can come up with?"

"Juliet, call him, talk to him."

"He wants to meet with me tonight, to talk."

"Perfect. Tell him that you love him tonight."

"This wasn't part of the deal," Juliet lamented.

"It never is." Patricia smiled, looking up and seeing her husband open her office door and walk inside. He crossed the room and gently pulled her up from her chair.

"What do I say?" Juliet asked.

"That's the easiest part," she smiled and paused, looking into her husband's eyes. "I love you," Patricia said to her husband. Pierce kissed her hands and mouthed the words back to her. Patricia blushed. She would never get tired of hearing those words from him.

Juliet sighed heavily. "I'll call you later."

Juliet hung up and stood at the barre. She looked at herself in the mirror. It was getting late. The decision to go to the celebration party J.T. planned weighed heavily on her mind. She needed to end this now, before it was too late. Who was she kidding, it was already too late. The moment they met, it was too late for her. She looked up at her soft brown eyes. Love at first sight, thanks a lot.

She picked up her purse and grabbed the address J.T. had e-mailed over. She was supposed to meet him at the party; she was fine with that. The last thing she needed was to have J.T. drive her home again. She was barely able to resist him last night.

This whole thing had gotten out of hand. She knew from the start in New York that she had gotten too emotionally involved. There was no way she could continue to play this part. Love had trapped her, and there was no way out.

She grabbed her keys and walked out the door.

Following the detailed directions, she drove just a mile or so from her own house. Checking the address she pulled into the driveway and parked as instructed. Admiral's Way. She got out of the car and glanced around the quiet neighborhood.

The three-story riverfront town house was beautiful, stately, and majestic. Built directly across the street from the Potomac River, it had an ideal view of the waterway as it overlooked the harborside.

Juliet paused for a moment to look across the street. A small cruise ship was passing by and several people waved at her from the top deck. She waved back, then waited as it silently drifted away. She turned and walked back across the street to the house. She rang the bell.

"J.T.?"

"Welcome." He stepped back, took her hand, and guided her into the house.

"This is home now?"

"Yes, for the time being at least. It actually belongs to my brother-in-law. He recently moved to Philadelphia. I'm just staying here until I find something in the area. Although," he looked around casually, "this place is pretty phenomenal. I just might consider making him an offer now that he and my sister have permanently moved to Philadelphia."

Juliet looked around nodding. "Not bad, what's he do?"

"He owns a few antique shops."

"This is gorgeous," she picked up a beautiful gold inlay vase. "Business must be good."

"It's very good."

"So, you don't live in New York. You don't live here. Where do you live?"

"Actually I did live in New York for about six years. I had an apartment on the Upper West Side. I just sublet it."

"If you had an apartment, why'd you go to the hotel that night?"

"I got stuck in traffic. There was an accident and traffic wasn't moving, and I wasn't walking fifty blocks to my apartment, so a hotel room seemed like a good idea at the time."

She nodded. "So where exactly is home for you?"

"I have a place in Virginia Beach."

"On the beach?" she asked, he nodded yes. "You're a beach bum, I love it." She laughed. "I knew it. I knew there had to be someplace in your life where you were totally free to be yourself."

"Is that Old Town for you?"

"Yeah, that's home for me, it's where I grew up."

"Come on, I'll give you an abbreviated tour." The first stop was the lower level. A two-car garage, mini gym, laundry, and game room loaded with every imaginable activity.

The next level up was the main entrance with a large foyer, glamorously adorned living room, and eat-in kitchen. Rich dark mahogany and deep green and blue hues extended from the vestibule through to the formal dining room and full kitchen, which were professionally decorated and accented with the finest antiques.

Above that floor were two spacious bedrooms, complete with Jacuzzi bathrooms attached to each, and a small library and home office. And the top floor was an elegant master bedroom with an attached balcony, and an alcove seating area.

The home was beautiful. They went back to the second

floor. J.T. checked dinner in the kitchen and Juliet stood and marveled at the scenic view from the living room balcony. To the left was King Street and its festive atmosphere, to the right was the majestic Woodrow Wilson Bridge, and straight ahead, the Potomac River lay before her. She could have stood at the spot the rest of her life. It was perfect. Here with J.T., she was in her own personal heaven, she was in love.

Her heart slammed against her chest as the realization continued to dawn on her. She was in love. For the first time in her life, this was the real thing and there wasn't a thing she could do about it. *So what, I'm in love, I'll get over it eventually.*

J.T. came out and stood behind her, slowly running his hands up and down her arms. Then he encircled her nuzzling her neck. They stood in silence looking out at the dark star-studded sky. "Did you ever wonder how we ended up like we did?" he asked.

"In a hotel room together?"

"No."

"A dancer?" she asked.

"No," J.T. paused. "Alone, looking for someone special to share our life with, someone to love." He looked down at her tenderly.

She turned to him. "What makes you think that's what I'm looking for?"

"Aren't you? Aren't we all?"

"My mother was in love until the day she died, still heartbroken over my father."

"But you see yourself differently, don't you?"

"Yes. I'm nothing like my mother—I don't mind being alone. It's what I'm good at."

"How can you not mind being alone, not having someone to wake up to every morning, someone to share your joys and troubles with, someone to have children with and grow old with?"

Juliet looked away. "You mean someone to cook and clean

and take care of the babies while he's out in the world on the career track. If that's what you're looking for, why didn't you just let Mamma Lou do her matchmaking thing?"

"I don't need Mamma Lou to match me up with someone."

"Why not, you seem to want all that domestic tranquility stuff. I'm sure she can find you someone suitable if you ask her."

J.T. smirked at her insinuation. "First of all, I'm a very good cook, I have a cleaning service, raising my children is a *we* thing, done together, and as for being out in the world on the career track, the world of computers is a remarkable one. You can be in the Orient, in London, in San Francisco, or at home in bed with your wife, and still be completely connected to the office."

"You make it sound so simple."

"It is if you want it to be, do you?" A sudden chill shot through Juliet. She shivered. "Are you chilly?" J.T. asked.

"No," she choked out, then cleared her throat. "I'm fine," she looked away quickly. "It's so beautiful here."

They stood in silence and looked out into the blackness of the night sky, each pondering their conversation. "Come on, let's eat, dinner's ready," J.T. said as he took her hand.

He led her to the formal dining room where the table was set for a romantic dinner for two. Scented candles, soft music, and fresh flowers added to the romantic ambiance.

"It's lovely," she said as she casually fingered one of the two gold-rimmed plates. "I presume that by the two place settings, I'm the only guest for this evening's celebratory festivities?"

"I assumed you figured that one out."

"It wasn't exactly a no-brainer. So, what is all this?"

"It's my way of saying thank you for your help, and also I wanted to talk to you about our arrangement."

"An amendment to the deal?"

"Yeah, something like that." He poured champagne into

her crystal flute, then into his own. He sat down at the head of the table and looked across to her.

Backlit by the glow of candles, she was an angel. He reached over and stroked the side of her face. "You are so beautiful." His voice was tender, loving, and filled with raw emotion.

Juliet looked away. The intensity of his gaze caused a chill to flutter through her again. Her heart opened up completely, and for the first time in her life, she realized that there was no escaping it, and no doubt about it, she had fallen in love.

Juliet purposely swayed their dinner conversation to center on him: his youth, his career, and his dreams. When it shifted to her, she evaded all of his questions and directed them back at him. She didn't want tonight to be about her. She wanted to know everything there was to know about him: his likes, his dislikes, his desires, and his fantasies.

She decided that if tonight would be their last night together then she was going to make it one for the memory books. "Tell me about your fantasies."

He nearly choked on his drink. "What?"

"Your fantasies, you must have them."

"You never cease to amaze me," he said as he placed his drink down. He tossed his napkin on the table and stood up.

"You're stalling."

"I have a better idea," he pulled her close to face him, flush with his body. "Tell me about yours."

He dipped his mouth into hers but the emotions welled deep inside of him gave him pause. He pulled back, reached up, and stroked her face gently. "I need to kiss you."

"Need, or want?" she asked flippantly.

"Need, as in have no choice, need as in the air I breathe. I need to breathe, I need to kiss you."

Juliet opened her mouth to speak but the kiss came. Long and soft, sweet and moving, with all the tenderness he felt, he kissed her. With gentle strokes and tiny loving caresses he held her close. In still repose they melted into each other's arms. In sweet submission, she gave what he beseeched, and he surrendered what she implored. In a perfect union of one, they stood swimming in the sensation of each other.

"Are you trying to seduce me?" she asked as his lips traced tender kisses on her neck and shoulders.

"Um-hum," he hummed as he closed his eyes, feeling the pleasures of her body.

"Then I need to warn you, this might be dangerous."

"Um-hum," he hummed.

"Once we go down this road there may not be any turning back."

"Um-hum," he hummed.

"Are you getting serious?"

"Um-hum," he hummed as he opened his eyes and looked up to see her reaction. In truth, he was well past serious.

Juliet backed up, seeing the emotion in his eyes reflecting what she felt inside. She stepped away from his embrace. "Maybe this wasn't such a good idea. I'd better go."

"Don't go, stay with me. I told you that I wanted to talk about our deal. You did your part," he reached into his pocket and pulled out a check and handed it to her. "Here, our deal is complete."

She took the check, looked at it, and placed it on the table. "You broke the deal, all bets are off."

"Yes, I did," he said, knowing exactly what she meant, "but so did you."

"I told you I don't do the love thing," she told him.

"Love wasn't supposed to be part of the deal, it just happened."

She shook her head no. "I gotta get out of here."

"Juliet." She stopped. "I don't know what love is. I've never felt it for anyone other than my family. But if what I feel for you is love, and what I see reflected in your eyes is love, then we owe it to ourselves to see this through."

"Regardless of how I feel about you, J.T., this has to be

over. I'm not the 'til death-do-us-part kind. You'll only wind up hurt."

"Let me worry about that."

"No, not this time," she reached up and stroked his face tenderly. "I love you too much to hurt you." *There, I said it.*

"Juliet."

"No, J.T.," she said. "Not even if you offered me the world. Good-bye."

Chapter 19

It wasn't like he didn't know it or see it coming. Eventually it would end. That was how he'd always set it up. That was the deal. Unfortunately, for the first time he'd gotten emotional. J.T. tossed his pen on the desk and walked away. Who was he kidding? He'd been emotional about Juliet since the first moment her saw her enter the lobby of the hotel months ago.

It was pure luck that they were all out of rooms and that they shared the last one. He remembered how they had walked into the hotel. They reached for the door at the same time. He held it for her. She nodded politely, walked in, and went straight to the line at the front desk.

He waited in line behind her, on the phone, yet watching every move she made. The curve of her suit and the sway of her hips held his attention longer than he expected. He definitely liked what he saw.

J.T. reached over and pressed a button on the keyboard. If she wanted the world, he'd give it to her. A few keystrokes later he looked at the Tiffany screen and chose the perfect gift. Several keystrokes after that, he cleared the screen, then sat back in his chair, satisfied with his accomplishment as he picked up the phone on the second ring.

"I think it worked," Trey began, finally back from his business trip. "I think your preemptive strike did it. Mamma Lou was so stunned when she saw Juliet the other night I thought she was going to pass out. You, my man, are my hero. And that stunt you pulled by not arriving to the house until late was a stroke of pure brilliance." J.T. nodded mutely as his cousin continued. "How on earth did you come up with that? You strung them along waiting for you and your guest all night. It was absolutely brilliant."

"Thanks," J.T. said as he repeatedly clicked his pen on the desk. The success of his plan was inevitable. Juliet was going to be out of his life again, this time by his insistence.

"You are genuinely diabolical, a true Machiavellian. You actually stopped the famous Mamma Lou before she even got started. That has to be some kind of record."

"You're giving me too much credit, Trey," J.T. noted.

"Now you're being modest." A stilled silence drifted in through the connection. "Are you okay, man? You sound hesitant?"

J.T. took a deep breath. "No, yeah, I'm fine, just distracted by a program code," he lied while looking at four blank screens on his desk that had gone into sleep mode. "I've been so busy with Juliet that I've let a few things slip."

"So is it over?"

"Not quite. To tell you the truth, I'm not completely convinced that Mamma Lou's matchmaking plans are officially and completely closed down. But it seems that for the time being she's turned her attention in another direction."

"Speaking of which, have you given her the line yet?"

J.T., still absently focused on Juliet, resigned himself that what he was about to do was for the best. "Who, what line?"

"Juliet, the *my work comes first* line."

"No, not yet, I'm stopping by her place later. I'll tell her then."

"Well, my brother, welcome back to the bachelor life."

"I'm back, count on it," he said, trying to reassure himself of his resolve. But his assertion that it would pass left an empty feeling nonetheless.

"Great, let's celebrate. I just got an invitation to a fundraiser on Capitol Hill tomorrow night. I understand that there'll be dozens of single women in attendance."

J.T. moaned inwardly. The last thing he wanted right now was to be in a room filled with marriage-minded women. Not when all he could think about was Juliet.

"Sounds great," he finally committed.

Juliet put on her dark sunglasses, slung her bag over her shoulder, and walked to the front entrance. She was exhausted, but a strenuous rehearsal was exactly what she needed to get back on course. Thankfully she didn't have another performance for a few days.

Just as she waved good-bye to the receptionist, she was called back to the desk. She walked over questioning. "You have a package," the receptionist said, as she handed the clipboard to her. "Perfect timing. It needs your signature."

Juliet took the clipboard and signed her name. As she handed it to the express delivery man he handed her a small, taped box, Looking at it oddly, Juliet took the box and read the return name on the top. She hadn't ordered anything in months.

"Aren't you gonna open it?" the receptionist asked.

"Later," she dropped the small box in her bag, placed it back on her shoulder, and continued on her way.

Her first stop was at the children's dance workshop she sponsored and taught at the local recreation center. It had been awhile since she was there, and as soon as she stepped through the doors, she felt the warmth and comfort of home surrounding her. She climbed the steps to the main level as a buzz of excitement grew.

"Juliet is here. Juliet's back. Juliet's here," the young girls excitedly whispered, then called out louder as the wave of enthusiasm grew. Juliet smiled and joked fondly with them. Like a celebrity coming home, she was welcomed with open arms.

Some of the younger girls ran up to her and grabbed her around the waist, hugging tenderly. They excitedly all talked at the same time, telling her of their latest success on point or at the barre. Soon the mob of excited little faces energized her. It felt good to be back.

"Ladies, ladies," Juliet began, "you're going to be late for your classes, and remember, a ballerina is never late."

As the young ones obediently hurried off, the older girls, most of whom had been in the program for years and were like little sisters to her, hurried over. They'd been to her house and watched her perform on stage, as well as toured the backstage areas of the Cultural Center.

With collective awe, the girls hurried off to their classes as Juliet changed into her workout gear in preparation to teach her next class.

Afterwards, she picked up her dry cleaning, stopped at the grocery store, then went to the post office to get her mail. It wasn't until she was at home and tossed her bag on the bed and the package tumbled out that she even remembered she had it.

She plopped across the bed, grabbed the box and began peeling the mailing tape away. She opened the box, removed the packing tissue and reached inside and pulled out a ball.

Her mouth dropped open. It was stunning. She held it in her hand and slowly turned the heavy sphere over and around. It was a jeweled encrusted lapis replica of the world—every country, every ocean, perfectly represented in mother of pearl, ruby, sapphire, and emerald shavings. Juliet smiled, then laughed aloud at the odd gift. She literally held the world in her hand.

She rolled it around, seeing a small golden clasp in the center just above the equator. She unfastened the lock and opened the sphere. Resting on a soft satiny cushion was a note. *I give you the world, J.T.* She had no idea what to make of it until she remembered her last words to him.

Juliet dialed his number. It rang once. *No.* She disconnected before he could answer. She was losing control. She quickly placed the note back in the orb, placed the orb in the box, then put the box in the nightstand drawer beside her bed. She needed air. The suffocating feeling of love surrounded her. She needed to walk.

A rush of warm air hit her as soon as she opened the front door. She inhaled deeply, letting the fresh air fill her lungs. She walked to the end of her brick path. The streets were empty. She looked up at the threatening sky. A light drizzle of rain. Perfect, she needed the rain to wash away the feelings she had. She headed toward the waterfront.

This was getting too personal, and she was losing herself to an emotion she couldn't afford and couldn't control. J.T. had stirred something inside of her that was taking over and weakening her concentration.

Her last performance, she had danced the best she had danced in months. The freedom she felt on stage was like nothing she'd ever experienced. After hearing his voice, she stepped out on stage and became one with the music. Her body flowed and moved in fluid perfection. She was flawless, energized, composed, and in complete control of the audience. She had rarely felt anything as perfect.

Juliet stood at the dock and watched the night sky. Gray clouds thickened, and the rumble of thunder hummed in the distance. It was late, too late to be out. But she needed to walk. The crowds were gone, and a heavy drizzle began to fall. Leaning over the wooden rail, she looked into the blackness of the Potomac River as raindrops caused tiny drops to grow into giant ripples.

It was exactly how J.T. had grown and affected her life. One moment in time, months ago, had forever changed something inside of her. She knew it even then. The moment she touched him she felt the change. The firm strength of his body had left an unyielding ache inside of her, a hunger forever wanting.

She closed her eyes and raised her jacket hood as the rain began to pour. Needing the control, she focused on the end.

They always ended, but then none of her relationships had ever been like this one. J.T. was different.

Lost in her dreams she barely heard the phone in her pocket ringing. She answered on the third ring. "Hello."

"You called."

She knew his voice instantly, and she paused to think. "Yes." They sank into silence. "I don't know why."

"Don't you?"

"Yeah," she whispered. She knew exactly why she'd called. It was a moment of weakness; she wanted to see him.

"Where are you?"

"Out, walking," she said.

"This time of night? Where are you exactly? I'll come get you."

"No," she paused, still fighting the war inside. "I'll come to you." Moments later, she looked up at the familiar three-story building. She rang the doorbell. He answered immediately. "Make love to me," she said as she stood on his stoop in the rain.

J.T. brought her into the living room by the warmth of the gas fireplace and went upstairs to get towels. When he returned, Juliet had taken her wet jacket off and was sitting on the floor staring into the fire. He sat down by her side and draped a big, fluffy towel around her shoulders. She sat mute as he unclipped her barrette and rested her wet hair on her shoulders.

"What were you doing out walking this time of night?"

She turned to him. "Make love to me."

J.T. saw for the first time the desperate pain in her eyes. "Juliet, what's wrong? What's going on? Tell me, I can help."

She shook her head. She was confused and angry and frustrated and in love. She was trapped. How could this happen to her? She had always stayed her heart from this. No man had ever gotten to her. She never allowed it, until now.

Her heart had been in jeopardy since the moment she laid eyes on him. She knew the instant it happened, when she woke up in New York alone in the bed they'd shared. The familiar feelings of being left and discarded scared her so much that she needed to get out. She needed to purge the feelings before it was too late.

Now those same feelings had entrapped and confused her again. It was already too late. She was losing the battle for her independence, for her freedom, and for her heart. Love had won, but tonight she didn't care.

"Make love to me," she repeated again.

"No, not like this," he tipped her chin and kissed her forehead.

Humiliated, she stood and grabbed her jacket to leave. "Not exactly the response I was looking for."

"Where are you going?" He stood and blocked her path.

"Home," she said as she continued around him to the front door.

J.T. reached out to her and took her in his arms, holding her securely. "I don't know what you're going through, but I know it has something to do with me, with us. Talk to me Juliet. Tell me."

The love she felt grew stronger as he encircled her in his arms. "Thank you for the world, it's beautiful," she said weakly.

He rocked her slowly. "You're welcome."

Juliet relaxed into his arms, feeling safe and warm and comforted. The loving power of his embrace collapsed a shadow of doubt in her heart. She knew that she had opened her heart to him, and he had accepted it willingly. Inwardly she pleaded for the strength to go all the way.

The invisible space between their bodies forged a gentle reminder of the setting around them. The soft music playing in the background, the crackling fire ablaze in the fireplace, and the dimmed lighting all added to the simmering burn inside of her. "Make love to me," she muttered into his chest.

She could feel his muscles tighten and retract with restraint but this wasn't the night for his puritanical gentility. She needed him, and she knew that he wanted her. She offered her body to his stoic armor. His noble willpower would have to take the night off. She'd come there tonight for one purpose, and one purpose only. She wanted him inside of her, and to feel the closeness of their bodies as he connected with her one last time.

She began to move her body enticingly against him, arousing the repressed desire she knew he felt. Slow and steady, in determined action, she tempted and teased him, drawing his passion to the surface. She nuzzled her face against his chest, while her hands stroked the strong length of his firm arms and back. A low, guttural moan rumbled through his chest. She was getting to him like a lit match tossed on gasoline. She intended to ignite his passion.

He dropped his hands to his side and leaned away, but she was there to hold him to her. The war of wills had begun, and Juliet had no intention of losing this battle. She would have him tonight, all night, their last night.

She pulled the knit shirt from the band of his pants and dragged her nails beneath, against his bare back and chest. He moaned again as his eyes closed, and, as the last of his willpower crumbled, a satisfied smile increased her assault. She lifted the shirt up over his head and pulled it from his body, tossing it on the floor by the sofa.

His chest was bare and beautiful. She reveled in the treasure she had uncovered. She touched his body, kneading the firmness and feeling the tremble of strength seething below the surface. His perfectly formed pectorals eased flawlessly into his hard, impeccably packed abdomen. The excitement of victory urged her to dare further.

She grabbed the hem of her sport top and pulled the tight elastic band over her head, freeing her breasts to him. His chest heaved in full expanse, sending a rush of air through his lungs, prompting his pounding heart to beat faster. He exhaled slowly. He was teetering by the thinnest thread.

"Make love to me, J.T.," she whispered near his ear again.

"Juliet."

"You want me, don't you?" she asked, reaching up to drape her hands around his neck. "Don't you?"

His chest expanded again and a shattered ragged breath sputtered out. Juliet placed her hands on his shoulders and began pulling him down. He resisted at first, but the force of her determination overtook his willpower. He came to his knees before her.

She gathered his face to her stomach then tipped his head upward to rest between her breasts. The silence of the moment was interrupted by lyrics of "Reasons." There were no more love games, no more illusions, only love remained for just one night. Juliet stood still, watching, waiting for him to yield. Then she felt it. Slowly his arms encircled her as his eyes opened. She smiled down at him, accepting his surrender to their love. She kissed him and the creation of passion began.

J.T. had fought hard against the inevitable. He focused his mind on everything from mathematical equations to computer-generated formats. Nothing worked. Juliet's pull was too strong. She was too irresistible. Through a labyrinth of determined logic, she had reached in and captured his heart. His mind faltered, for the first time losing the control he had spent a lifetime developing.

Like lava flowing down a molten peak, a flood of passion burned through him in uncontrollable desire. The blinding acceptance of her body was all he felt. He reached for her, holding onto the only person able to satisfy his burning need.

Still kneeling, he pulled her into his cupped arms and gently laid her on the cushioned carpet warmed by the heat of the fire. He ran his hand down her body, causing a gasp to escape her open mouth. Juliet arched her back as his hand neared the band of her sweatpants. He dipped his finger inside the rim and pulled the elastic, gently tugging the pants down her long legs.

She sat up and unfastened the button of his jeans and pulled the zipper down. He lay back as she helped him remove his jeans. As if for the first time, they looked at each other as the glow of the fireplace reflected the golden red and brown tones of their bodies. The crackling sound of the fire, the hushed drizzle of the rain outside, and the sweet soft sounds of Phillip Bailey and Maurice White gave them to pause.

He looked up at her as she sat there looking down on him. Her hand absently stroked the length of his chest and stomach. He reached up and stroked the smooth underside of one breast, feeling the weight cupped in his hand. She was small compared to other women he'd been with, but he'd decided earlier on that she was just the right size for him. To prove the fact he reached behind her and pulled her body toward him, bringing her cupful into his waiting mouth.

He suckled the sweetness of her body, filling his need with the honeysweet orbs of desire. Tasting one drove his desire for more. He lifted her further across his body and sandwiched both orbs between his hands, licking and teasing the sweet brown taut nipples to pointed fullness.

The ache of his torturous tongue caused her to gasp aloud. This was exactly what she wanted, and this was exactly what he was going to give her. In exotic splendor, his actions proved that this would be a night she would never forget.

He angled her body as he sat up, bringing her with him. She reached out to her purse and pulled it down from the sofa. She dug through, finding a disc-shaped packet. She pulled it out and tore it open.

Then she grabbed a sofa pillow and dropped it on the floor behind him. She placed her hand flat on his chest and slowly pushed him back onto the pillow. He yielded, and in what was more like an erotic striptease than a safety act, Juliet pulled the contents out of the packet and extended it through her fingers.

She dangled it over her body, then his body, traced the covering over his pecs, then down his chest to the firmness of his stomach. She drifted lower and circled the latex around the small hairs below. A sizzling sound hissed from J.T. as his body instantly twitched with anticipation as she slowly sheathed his hardness.

She was tucked nicely across him until he rolled over, positioning her beneath him. Juliet reached up to touch J.T.'s face. It was hot to the touch. She softly scratched her nails down the sides of his neck, shoulder, and finally, over his chest. She watched as the dull tingle caused J.T.'s jaw muscle to tighten. She reached up again and caressed his neck as he leaned down to kiss her.

Kneeling, he pulled her legs up to straddle his thighs. She wrapped them around his waist, feeling the firmness of his need beckoning. Eye to eye, he nibbled her lips with caressing kisses, leaving a trail of burning passion.

J.T. circled his palms against her nipples. She moaned in ecstasy as the heat of his mouth found the tiny, pebbled nipples and devoured each.

Juliet reached between their bodies and found him hard and throbbing. She guided him closer to her core, feeling him tense. Then in one powerful thrust, he entered. She gasped in delight. The exquisite pain of pleasure filled her completely.

Together they danced the ancient rhythm of lovers as gentle kisses rained down on her face, neck, and shoulders. She held firm, feeling the strength of his muscles as they stretched and tightened across his back.

He looked down into her eyes. They burned with seething passion as they rocked their hips in unison, slowly at first, then picking up the pace to a fevered frenzy. Their bodies thrust together in a frantic fury. Deeper and deeper he plunged into her as her inner muscles tightened around him, adding more to his already soaring pleasure. Closer and closer they came, perched just to the edge of the crescendo.

Then in unison they exploded as the sweet, savored climax they sought brought them to the brink of pleasure and sent them reeling over the edge into absolute ecstasy. Breathless and winded, he collapsed onto her. Weak with sated bliss, he gathered her into his arms and rolled to the side, bringing her on top of him, reversing their position.

She lay there in perfect contentment, never wanting the world to return. J.T. wrapped his arms tighter as he brushed her wayward hair aside with his lips. He realized that he would never have enough of this woman in his arms. The thought of not having her by his side sent a tremble through him. Juliet closed her eyes and drifted to the peaceful place she always found when she was with him.

Sometime later J.T. had picked her up, turned off the lights, and climbed the stairs. He laid her on his bed after coaxing her to put on one of his company T-shirts to prevent a chill in the night. Reluctantly she accepted it, then drifted right back to a deep sleep.

J.T. sat awake for hours, sitting out on the balcony staring out at the night sky. The rain had passed, and a sweet, clean scent filled the air. The dawning of a new day came too quickly. He watched it break against the sky's horizon.

Hearing Juliet stir, he stood and returned to her side in the bed. She instantly curled her body to fit him. He accepted her intimate closeness willingly. Moments later, he drifted to a light sleep with dreams of the woman beside him in his bed.

Juliet woke up the next morning tucked comfortably in J.T.'s bed. She looked around, remembering the masculine décor of his bedroom. She tossed the sheets back and smiled. She was dressed in an oversized E-Corp T-shirt. She got out of bed and walked to the balcony doors. The bright, sunny day promised a new beginning. The rain had gone and the sweet, fresh smell of peace filled her.

"Good morning," J.T. said as he stood in the doorway behind her.

Juliet turned. He was the ideal *GQ* man, wearing an open white French cuff dress shirt and denim jeans, with bare feet and a broad, winning smile. "Good morning," she replied. She'd never get enough of seeing this man's chest.

He walked to her and handed her a cup of hot coffee. She took it, sipping tentatively, then sighed. It was exactly as she liked it. "Thank you, it's perfect."

"Good, breakfast will be ready in about fifteen minutes. Are Spanish omelets okay?"

"Perfect. I'm gonna grab a shower first," she said. He nodded and turned to go. "J.T., about last night—" she began.

"We'll talk about that later. What do you have planned the rest of the day?" he asked curiously.

"I'm teaching a class this morning at the dance workshop in town, then meeting some friends. Then we'll probably do some shopping."

J.T. nodded and smiled. "Your clothes are clean and are hanging up in the closet or," he smiled, "since that shirt looks so good on you, there're more in the armoire."

"Thanks." She watched him leave, then turned back to the balcony. *How perfect is this?* After a few moments to reflect on her day, she went inside and grabbed a quick shower. The hot water and steam on her body felt wonderful. Refreshed and rejuvenated, she walked into the closet and easily found her sweatpants and jacket in with his suits.

She ran her finger along the perfectly hung line of suits, jackets, and pants. He had dozens of them, all lined up at attention. She sat down on the cushioned bench in his dressing room and slipped into her sweatpants. As she prepared to put on her shirt, she remembered J.T. mentioned the company T-shirts. She grabbed one from the armoire and wrapped her jacket around her hips.

She smelled the food before she hit the stairs. Her stomach grumbled and her mouth watered. If this is what J.T. meant by being domestically self-sufficient, then he was one exceptional man. The men she knew—her father, her half brother and others—couldn't boil water if their lives depended on it.

But truthfully, neither could she. She chuckled to herself at the reality of her totally un-domesticated state. As a cook, she'd be terrible. As a housewife she'd be horrendous. And as a mother, she thought happily, she'd be wonderful. The last step brought her to the open kitchen area where a breakfast table placesetting had already been laid out.

"I hope you're hungry," J.T. said as he saw her enter the kitchen area.

"Starved." She walked over to the stove and grabbed a piece of bacon. Munching, she looked around at the ordered disarray. He was mixing eggs while twisting orange halves on a grinder and flipping hash browns. He reached over, picked up a knife, and began chopping onions and red and green peppers to mix into the egg mixture.

Juliet was completely lost. The whole idea of having more then one pan on the stove at a time was mind-boggling.

"You look lost," he said noticing the bewilderment on her face.

"I am. I'm not exactly B. Smith in the kitchen, or any other part of the house, for that matter."

"No problem, as long as one of us knows what he's doing."

She looked at him oddly. *What was that supposed to mean?* She opened her mouth to ask, but thought better of it. She wasn't sure she wanted to know at this point.

"I see you're talented in the kitchen."

"I'm talented in several other rooms."

"So I've noticed," she said, playing along.

"Want to help?"

"Dangerous question. How close is the nearest stomach pump?"

He chuckled. "Take this," he handed her the small cutting board, "and drop these into the bowl. Mix it all up with the fork and pour it into the pan once you see the butter beginning to bubble."

"Are you kidding? How am I supposed to do all that?"

"Brilliantly, like you do everything else."

She began her chore slowly, inching the cut vegetables into the egg mixture. "You have way too much faith in me."

"On the contrary." He wanted to say more but paused. She

was skittish, and the last thing he wanted to do again was scare her away.

When she had poured all the batter into the pan, J.T. stepped up to the stove as she took the bowl and cutting board to the sink. She let the water run in the bowl, washing out the last remnants.

"About last night—" she began.

"I think we need more thyme," J.T. interrupted, as he sprinkled parsley and other herbs into the pan.

Her heart jumped instantly at his suggestion. "Time?" she asked nervously.

"Yeah," he said absently distracted by the skillet.

"Fine, time apart is probably best."

J.T. turned to her. "I meant thyme, as in the herb. It's over there on the far counter." He pointed at a small bunch of fresh thyme bundled together. She walked over, grabbed the bunch, and handed it to him. He pulled a few leaves, chopped them, and then tossed them in the pan. An awkward silence filled the room. As the pan began to sizzle, he turned to her and took her hands. "Juliet if you need time, I understand, take all the time you need."

"Thank you." She placed her hand on his and squeezed gently. "And thank you for the world, it's beautiful."

She picked up the herb bunch, looked at it, then tossed it back down on the counter. "They really should change the name of this stuff." J.T. smiled and shook his head, chuckling inwardly. He loved the woman, every quirky, smart mouth, and temperamental part of her.

"Let's eat."

Chapter 20

A long, white, oblong box with a bright red ribbon lay on the side of steps. Although it would be unseen from the street or sidewalk, Kimberly Franklin noticed it a soon as she opened the wrought-iron gate and walked up the brick path.

"Juliet, you got a delivery," Kimberly said as she hurried to the front steps, carrying a shopping bag in each hand and her dance bag over her shoulder. Jasmine Penbrook, her best friend since third grade, followed closely.

"Ooh, let me see," Jasmine, said as she hurried to Kimberly's side. "Who's it from?"

Kimberly leaned over to whisper in Jasmine's ear. "I bet it's the same guy from last night." At fifteen years old, Kimberly and Jasmine were as close as two friends could be. Just like Patricia and Juliet at their age, they were always in and out of each other's homes and lives. What one knew, they both knew.

"Ohh yeah, that's right, I forgot about him," Jasmine agreed.

Juliet, overhearing, looked at Patricia, then at Jasmine and Kimberly. "What same guy from last night? What do you know about last night?"

"Well, since Uncle Pierce is out of town this week, and Jasmine was spending the night at our house last night—" Kimberly began.

Jasmine immediately chimed in, ending Kimberly's sentence, "We all decided to go to the movies, so we picked a movie and then we decided that we should ask you since we figured since you were off today, we could grab a bite to eat then hang out—"

"So Aunt Patricia called you a couple of times—" Kimberly continued.

"Even on your cell phone—" Jasmine added.

Kimberly nodded. "But we didn't get an answer, so we drove over here last night, and your car was still here, so we rang the bell, but there was no answer so—"

"Aunt Patricia opened the door with her key—" Kimberly said.

"'Cause we were really worried—" Jasmine interrupted again.

"And we looked around, but you weren't here, so we figured that you had a date and we went to eat, then saw the movie, and it was really good."

Having looked at each girl as they spoke, Juliet and Patricia turned their heads nearly a half dozen times. It was more like a tennis match volley than a conversation.

"That was exhausting," Patricia said, chuckling.

"I'm sorry I asked," Juliet said, opening the door.

"So what's in the box?" the girls said in unison.

"Can we at least get in the house first?" Patricia said.

Sullenly, Kimberly and Jasmine walked inside. They dropped the shopping bags at the base of the steps and hurried back to Juliet with the coveted white box.

Juliet took the lid off, plucked the card for the box, and gave the box to the girls. They immediately tore at the green and white tissue paper. Juliet opened the envelope and chuckled as she read the card aloud: "All the thyme in the world."

"Yuck." Kimberly turned her nose up.

"Oow, that's disgusting," Jasmine added. "Who would send you weeds?"

"Someone who doesn't like rivals, obviously."

"Ya think?"

"Maybe?"

"Like a lovesick fan?" Jasmine asked beginning to look around the empty living and dining room.

"No, no," Kimberly corrected, "like a serious secret admirer who's broken-hearted now that Juliet has a new man in her life."

"Ohh yeah," Jasmine added, "so he pines away for her unrequited love."

"He probably still lives with his mother."

"With two dozen cats."

"And Juliet's new man will have to rescue her after the nutcase goes to the center and professes his love for her."

"But then Juliet chooses true love."

"Would you please do something about them?" Juliet said, turning to Patricia. Patricia started laughing. "Thanks," she said to Patricia, who was laughing too hard to speak. "Alright, alright ladies," Juliet finally said. "I don't know how much more of this I can take." Patricia continued laughing. "This is all your fault."

"Me?" Patricia said astonished.

"Yes, you."

"How is this my fault? What did I do?"

"It's all those happily-ever-after novels and movies you keep giving them."

"Don't blame me, you dance the stuff."

Moments later they began a playful argument, challenging each other, back and forth, just as they had done all their lives.

"Hello, adults," Kimberly said, getting Juliet's and Patricia's attention. "Who sent the thyme?"

"My date from last night."

Patricia peeked over the girl's shoulders and pulled a stem of thyme from the box. "That must have been some kind of interesting date."

"Don't you start again!" Juliet said, lifting the box to her nose and inhaling the woodsy, aromatic scent. She shook her head in disbelief as she reached into the box and pulled out a sprig of thyme. Apparently J.T.'s gift giving continued to evolve into more than the usual flowers and candy.

Patricia noted Juliet's odd expression. She pointed to the bags at the base of the stairs. "Okay, girls, why don't you go try some of those outfits on?"

Instantly dismissing the box and choosing clothes over weeds, Kimberly and Jasmine grabbed their bags and ran up the stairs to try on their new clothes.

While the girls tried on their new outfits and listened to music in the spare bedroom, Juliet hung up the clothes she purchased in her bedroom and told Patricia about her evening and morning at J.T.'s house. Patricia remained uncharacteristically quiet the whole time.

"I'm waiting," Juliet finally said, prompting her friend.

"This is absolutely beautiful. It must have cost a small fortune, look at all the jewel inlay," Patricia said as she examined the first gift closer, running her fingers over Africa and North America. She looked past the small globe to Juliet. "I promised I wouldn't say it."

"Then I'll say it: you warned me, you told me so."

"So how did you end it with him this morning?" Patricia asked as she placed the orb back into the box.

Juliet smiled and gave Patricia the card from the bouquet box. "I told him that we both need time." Patricia smiled and nodded her head, understanding the inside joke. "So naturally J.T. sent me a box of thyme, the herb."

"He's got your warped sense of humor, you gotta give him that."

"What am I supposed to do?"

"Do you love him?" Patricia asked.

"I don't know, maybe, I guess," Juliet fudged.

"Do you love him?" Patricia asked again.

Juliet frowned. Admitting that she was in love with J.T. to someone else was a lot easier then admitting it to herself. She wrapped her arms around her body for comfort and sat down on the bed beside her friend. The answer was so simple, but it was the hardest thing to say. "Yes, I do."

"Does he love you?"

She shrugged. "Yes."

"Then what's the problem?"

"I don't want to get swallowed up in his world and lose myself like my mom did. Cancer or no cancer, she still died of a twenty-year-old broken heart when Wyatt left."

"What makes you think that's gonna happen?"

"It happened to Mom. She stopped her career when she and Wyatt married. When they divorced she had nothing. She never really recovered. She lost everything, herself included."

"I'm married. I still have a career and my job, and it's even better with the *Dr. Patricia Franklin, Child Psychologist* shingle hanging out front."

"That's different. Pierce is one in a million. There aren't many men out there like him."

"You'd be surprised, Juliet. There are a lot of good men out there. You just have to look. But in your case you already found one, and he cooks."

"Can you believe it?"

"At least you won't starve."

"Hey, I beg your pardon," she said with added indignation. "I'm not that bad in the kitchen."

"You're talking to your best friend here. You need a recipe to boil water, and then you burn it. You don't even know where the kitchen is."

Juliet opened her mouth in shock. "I do so. It's where the coffee machine is." They burst into laughter as each began recalling the times that Juliet had tried her hand at cooking. The laughter continued, eventually drawing a curious Kimberly to the bedroom doorway. She looked at them, rolling on the bed, laughing, and tossing pillows at each other, as if they'd lost there minds.

"Hello, adults," she interrupted sarcastically. "Impressionable teenager in the room, proper decorum please." Still giggling like teenagers, Juliet and Patricia stopped tossing the pillows long enough to at least give the appearance of maturity.

"Jasmine's sister is here to pick us up."

Still chuckling, Patricia and Juliet followed Kimberly downstairs to the front door. Jasmine was already showing her sister the box of herbs and telling her the story of last night's movie adventure. Her sister peeked into the box and had the same reaction as Kimberly and Jasmine. Kimberly and Jasmine grabbed their shopping bags, hugged Patricia and Juliet, said good-bye, and then hurried out of the door and down the path to the car.

Juliet stood in the door waving as Jasmine's sister drove by, with the girls in the backseat already talking a mile a minute. She turned back to Patricia, who was busy smelling the aromatic thyme. "Were we ever that young?" Juliet asked wistfully.

"Younger."

"Do they ever actually separate and sleep at their own house?"

"Hardly ever. It's just like when we were their age, I was either at your house or you were in D.C. at mine."

Juliet looked at Patricia oddly as she bent over and smelled the herb again. "Why do you keep smelling those herbs?" she asked, her nose crinkling at the strong, woodsy scent.

"I don't know," Patricia said. "Believe it or not, so far, it's the only thing that's settled my stomach. Lately I've been so queasy. I think I must have a mild case of food poisoning or something. But I don't know how, I haven't eaten your cooking in years."

"I can so cook," Juliet insisted.

"You can burn," Patricia topped her, "water."

"Very funny," Juliet said as she headed to the kitchen. "I need a cup of coffee if I'm gonna be awake all night. Do you want a cup?"

"No thanks," Patricia said as she picked up the white box

of thyme and followed Juliet to the kitchen. She propped up on the stool at the counter and began pulling the thyme branches out of the box as Juliet poured water into a crystal vase.

Juliet placed the vase in front of her and Patricia began inserting the thyme branches one by one. Juliet leaned her nose near the closest branch. "Umm, they do smell pretty good, kind of woodsy with a hint of mint." Patricia watched Juliet pour cold water in the dispenser, then add coffee to the filter.

"How about a cup of tea?" Juliet asked when she finished.

"That sounds good," Patricia said as she hopped down from the stool and grabbed a cup from the cabinet, added water, then put it in the microwave. She grabbed the tea canister on the counter and opened it. She found coffee beans. She opened the flour and sugar ones, also finding coffee beans. "Where do you keep the tea bags this week?"

"There might be some tea bags in the refrigerator."

Patricia opened the refrigerator door and scanned its contents. She found three square Styrofoam takeout containers: a plastic-covered tin and two Chinese cartons. She opened one of the take-out containers and looked inside. "Yuck, what was this?"

Juliet peeked over the refrigerator door and into the container. "I have no idea. Trash it."

Patricia pulled the trash can over to the open refrigerator and began opening and disposing of the contents of the refrigerator. "Found them," Juliet said, holding a box of decaffeinated tea bags she purchased the last time she and Patricia went shopping together. She pulled one out and dipped it into the steaming hot water.

When Patricia finished dumping the contents of the refrigerator, Juliet moved the trash can back, then filled a cup of brewed coffee.

Patricia took a sip of her tea, "How's your protégée?"

"Who, Vanya?" Patricia nodded while blowing on her hot tea. "Vanya is hardly what I'd consider a protégée."

"She's a pretty good dancer."

"She's an excellent dancer, and given time, she will rock the ballet world. But she's too impatient. She wants everything right now. She doesn't realize that it takes years to get to the top and hard work to stay there."

"So tell her."

"Not the easiest thing in the world to do. She's out of control, stubborn, arrogant, and paranoid. She actually thinks that everyone's out to get her. It probably has something to do with her Russian father."

"Isn't she supposed to take over as principal when you leave?"

"Maybe, they haven't decided yet. Truthfully, I don't think she's ready."

"Will she ever be ready?"

"I hope so; she's very talented. With a little coaching, she could be awesome. The funny thing is, she reminds me of myself when I was that age."

"I remember. Couldn't tell you anything. Still can't."

They each chuckled, then Juliet stared pensively into her black coffee. "Mom's illness helped me to stop focusing so much on myself."

Patricia reached over and grasped her friend's hand. Juliet looked up, smiled, and nodded that she was okay. "I miss her," Patricia said.

"I do too."

"Have you decided if you're going to go to your father's wedding?"

"Yes, if Randolph can still get away, I'm going down to Florida with him."

"It was good to see him today. He looks tired."

"He's been working hard. I was surprised that he even had time to stop by the workshop this morning."

"It was so sweet of him to invite me to tag along with you

two tonight. With Pierce away and Kimberly over at Jasmine's, I was just going to eat popcorn and watch a DVD."

"I'm glad you'll be there. These political parties are as dull as watching paint dry."

"What time's your brother picking us up tonight?"

"Stepbrother," Juliet stated, then looked at her watch. "He said around eight o'clock."

"Half brother," Patricia purposely corrected as she glanced at her watch to confirm the time. "Three hours, good, that gives me just enough time to grab a quick nap. I'm beat; all that dancing and shopping really wore me out."

"The girls looked really good out there. Kimberly's turning into a genuine ballerina, isn't she?"

"She loves it."

Patricia nodded in agreement. "How did it feel to be back at the workshop teaching again?"

"Wonderful, I missed it. I get such an energy boost just being there with the girls and seeing their joy when they're dancing. It was really exciting."

"And exhausting. I forgot how strenuous dancing could be."

"Correction, Kimberly danced. Jasmine danced. I danced. You, however, sat on your bottom in the corner and typed on your laptop all morning."

"I danced, you just didn't see me. Anyway, I'm beat." She yawned for emphasis. "Wake me up when you get out of the shower," she said as she grabbed her tea and the vase of thyme and headed through the empty dining room through the empty living room then upstairs to her favorite guest bedroom.

Unlike her friend, Juliet was too wound up to sleep. Instead she changed into her leotard and decided to dance off the excess energy. But an hour into her routine, the chime of the doorbell drew her attention. She grabbed a towel and went to the door.

"J.T., hi," she said surprised to see him. She tipped up on toes to kiss him but noted his noncommittal response.

"May I come in?" he asked, seeing her dressed in leotards, a tight fitted tank top, and ballet slippers. His mouth dried with the impulse to pick her up and take her upstairs to the bedroom and make love to her for the rest of his life, but he firmly resisted.

He'd gone to the children's dance workshop that she'd mentioned earlier to surprise her. Yet when he arrived, she'd surprised him. He'd walked through the main entrance and spotted her instantly with her arms lovingly wrapped around Senator Kingsley and bestowing on him an overzealous greeting.

He'd immediately turned and left. Seeing Juliet embrace another man had stunned him. "I just need to speak with you, it won't take long."

"Sure, come on in," she said, sensing his distance.

"Am I interrupting?"

"No, not at all." She closed the door behind them and followed him into the living room. "Thanks for the thyme, it was a cute idea."

J.T. half smiled. He'd forgotten all about the florist he'd called earlier. "You're welcome."

"So, what's up?" she asked. "Another invitation?"

"No," he said and turned. "Not this time. I came to thank you."

"For what?" she asked as she tucked herself close to his body.

"It's over, we did it."

"What do you mean?"

"Mamma Lou was more than convinced. We're done."

"But I thought," she swallowed hard then paused, "or was it just me?" Suddenly the dream she had had for months had vanished right before her eyes as the finality in his voice shocked her into reality.

He shrugged. "All good things must come to an end."

"That's lame even for you."

"I have something for you."

"A parting gift, how sweet," she said dryly as she stepped away.

J.T. reached into his pocket and pulled out the check from last night. He offered it to her. "It's the check from last night."

"I don't want it. Give it to your next decoy."

He offered it to her again. "You need it for the school or studio or whatever you're going to do next. Take it."

"No, you keep it, donate it, give it away, whatever, I don't care."

"Take it, you earned it."

The seriousness of his tone gave her pause. A quick intake of breath sent Juliet's head spinning. How could she have been so blind? Of course, this was the big breakup. She glared at him as a heavy feeling sank to the pit of her stomach. "You're right. I did earn it." She reached out and snatched the envelope. "Anything else?"

"Just to say thanks for your assistance." He began walking toward the door.

"*My assistance*," she repeated, "Was that all it was?"

"That was the deal."

"And I suppose everything else that happened between us was also part of the deal."

Here it comes, the big, emotional scene. "No strings, no attachments, no expectations, no exceptions, remember that. I told you, my work is my sole commitment. I was never looking for a relationship."

"Yeah, I remember that, cash for services rendered."

"It wasn't like that," he began.

"Really, then how was it?"

"You make it sound—"

"Exactly like what it was, a business proposition," she replied and fingered the envelope in her hand. "Thanks for the payment in full. I don't suppose I got a tip for service beyond the call of duty," she added sarcastically.

"You're being irrational."

"On the contrary, I think I'm handling this quite well." She began tapping the envelope against her hand. "You know, I've been considering what I would do after I leave ballet in a few weeks. Thanks to you I've opened myself up to a whole new career opportunity."

"This is exactly my point. You're not being logical about this."

"Oh, please, your magnanimous compensation and donation to my new career option is more then enough."

"Juliet, this relationship has never been about guilt. We both went in with our eyes wide open."

"Relationship?" she stammered. "The word implies that emotions were involved, and we know that wasn't in the deal. So saying "relationship" is a bit presumptuous, don't you think?"

"Juliet," he began.

She held her hand up to silence him. "I think you've said everything that needed to be said." She smiled painfully and chuckled. "Funny, the last time we made a deal you walked out, and now here you are again at the same place. I guess I was right, after all some things never change."

"There are extenuating circumstances."

"There always are, I'd bet. Now if you'll excuse me, I have another engagement this evening."

"There's no performance tonight."

"I never said there was."

"Juliet."

"Good-bye, J.T." She walked over and held the door for him to leave. He did. She refused to cry.

Chapter 21

If you've been to one political function, you've been to them all. Dry food and plastic people, or plastic food and dry people. Either way, Juliet was bored stiff. She looked over to Patricia who was having a lively and animated conversation with a senator about of school vouchers and privatizing public schools.

She looked across the room to see Randolph speaking pointedly to one of his constituents about his opinion on something. She was sure they had no idea what he was talking about. She shook her head. He was definitely a charmer. Politics was truly his calling. In a lot of ways he was so much like her father.

Maybe that's why she always came when he called and needed a date for a particular function. She was his safe date, and he was hers. At first the papers made a thing about it, but now it was readily accepted that she would be on his arm whenever he needed her.

The stiffening air inside was beginning to make her dizzy. Juliet walked over to the patio doors and stepped outside into the night air.

J.T. felt more than a little possessive. As soon as he walked into the room he noticed her standing by his side. Tall and stately, Senator Randolph Kingsley was obviously several years older than Juliet. With temples brushed with gray, he had a youthful smile that seemed to belie his distinguished position.

In contrast, Juliet, not smiling, not entertained, was just there, exactly where she stayed for most of the evening. Time, she needed time. And like a fool, that's what he was giving her.

J.T. finally tore his eyes away when he felt a hand on his sleeve. He looked down to see a familiar face smiling up at him. "Nice to see you again, J.T."

"Vanya, how are you?"

"Good." She paused, seeing his eyes drift across the room. "So, J.T. are you into politics?"

"No, not much."

"I just wondered, since you're here."

"I came with my cousin," he said, nodding to Trey, who was casually leaning on the bar talking to two pretty women.

Vanya's interest elevated. "He looks familiar. Would I know him from politics?"

"No, Trey's an investment banker."

"Oh, I see. He does the money."

"Yes."

"He must be very smart."

"He is."

J.T. found his interest in the monotonous conversation waning quickly. Vanya said something, some small talk about being at a political function, then asked if he enjoyed politics. He said no, then excused himself, seeing Juliet go out on the patio alone. He followed.

She stood by the edge of the garden path alone.

"Too crowded inside," he said as he stood a few feet behind her.

She knew the voice. She turned. "J.T." Her heart pounded wildly; he was the last person she expected to see tonight. "What are you doing here?"

"I could ask you the same," he said keeping his eyes firmly

on hers. "I noticed that you're here with your senator friend."
He knew she'd know to whom he was referring.

"I see you're here with your dancer friend." Juliet watched
as Vanya stepped outside, looked J.T. up and down, planted
her fists on her thin hips, then returned to the party.

J.T. turned around in time to see Vanya glare at him angrily,
then huff inside. "It's not what you think," he responded, turning back to face her.

"Ditto," she said pointedly.

"I came with my cousin," he said quickly.

"I came with my brother," she tossed back just as quickly.

Hearing her lame excuse and lie, he shook his head.
Everyone knew that she was seeing Senator Kingsley. "I just
wanted to tell you that New York wasn't just another night for
me. Our time together was special. I felt something, you got
to me, and it scared the hell out of me." He took a step back
to walk away, then paused. "Our deal is done, but I thought, I
hoped, we could remain friends."

Seeing the hurt on his face broke her heart. "J.T.," she
called out, then walked to him as he turned. "I felt it too. You
have a restless spirit. You're always searching for something,
in your computers, in your life, and in your heart."

"Does he make you happy?"

"I hope someday you find what you're searching for," she
said instead of answering his question.

"I have." He took a step toward her, then stopped cold.

"Good evening." Both Juliet and J.T. looked. Senator Randolph Kingsley walked up beside Juliet and placed his arm
around her waist protectively. He reached out with his free
hand to shake, "How do you do, Senator Randolph Kingsley."

J.T. obliged: "J.T. Evans."

"Yes, of course, it's good to meet you. E-Corp has very
generously contributed to my campaign and been a welcome
partner in a few of my public school computer-related programs. Thank you for all your support, it's greatly
appreciated."

"Don't mention it." J.T. nodded but kept his eyes on Juliet.

"Juliet, are you ready to leave?"

"Yes," she looked at J.T. She could explain right now and end this misunderstanding, but having J.T. believe that she was involved with Randolph was better. That way he'd let go easier and she could get back to her life. "Good-bye, J.T. All good things must come to an end. An old friend told me that."

A muscle visibly tightened in his jaw. He nodded curtly while accepting Randolph's hand again.

"A pleasure meeting you," Randolph said and guided Juliet back into the main hall. They met Patricia waiting in the doorway. She'd caught the last part of the conversation. She leaned toward Juliet as they prepared to leave. "What was all that about?"

Juliet sighed with frustration. "That was the aftermath of J.T. dumping me earlier this evening."

"Are you okay?"

"Apparently not."

J.T. turned his back and stared out at the darkness. *Women.* He was beginning to think that Trey and his numerous theories on women and love were beginning to make sense. How desperate was that?

Chapter 22

"Five card stud, play 'em like you see 'em, nothing wild," Trey said as he tossed cards around the circular table and four red chips piled into the center.

"J.T.?"

"J.T., yo man, you all right?" Dennis Hayes asked. J.T. finally looked up. All eyes around the table were staring at him as Trey continued dealing the cards. He looked at Dennis, questioning.

Trey looked up. His eyes connected with Raymond Gates, sitting right next to him. Raymond nodded, questioningly. Trey smiled and shook his head sadly. He knew exactly what was up.

"The pot's light," Dennis said as he pointed to J.T.'s stack of chips.

J.T. nodded and tossed a red chip into the center of the table. It rolled several times, then stopped and fell alongside the others already there. He picked up his cards and absently glanced at them.

The conversation quickly turned back to Raymond, the recently returned newlywed. Tony had led the pack in teasing him mercilessly all evening. "Black men do not go to Switzerland on a honeymoon," Trey said as he dealt out the last five cards to each man sitting around the table. He placed the remaining cards in a neat pile near him, "It's just not natural. Tahiti, Brazil, Hawaii, even Paris as a last resort, but not Switzerland."

"Why not Switzerland?" Raymond countered.

"Simple, Switzerland is cold, with a lot of chocolate and a lot of watches. A honeymoon, my friend," Trey said notably, "means having your new bride in as many skimpy outfits as possible one hundred and fifty percent of the time."

"Another theory?" J.T. asked, plucking two cards from his hand and tossing them in the center of the table. Trey replaced his two cards with those from the pile.

"Precisely," Trey confirmed and pointed to Tony.

A collective moan sent the room into a boisterous debate on the perfect honeymoon location, led by Tony and Raymond, the only two married men in the room.

"I hear Buenos Aires is perfect for a honeymoon," Trey said, pointing across the table to Dennis.

"St. Thomas." Dennis followed suit, tossing three cards in. Trey replaced them from the pile.

Tony tossed two cards down. "A honeymoon can technically be on the moon as long as you're with the woman you love," he said as Trey gave him two in return.

"Switzerland was perfect," Raymond smiled knowingly. He tossed two cards and accepted two in return. "Snow-capped mountains, beautiful scenery, chilly crisp fresh air, skiing in the morning, shopping in the afternoon, and sitting close by the fire, drinking champagne and eating chocolate while coming up with interesting ways to warm each other. Cold nights, hot love, sexy, and sensuous, believe me, Switzerland was the perfect honeymoon spot."

Trey pulled three cards from his hand, tossed them, then replaced them with cards from the pile. He collected all the tossed cards and set them aside. The room hushed as each man looked at the cards in his hand, studying and calculating the possibilities, as they nodded, accepting that Switzerland might not be a bad location after all.

"I'm in," J.T. said and tossed two chips into the pile.

"I'll see you," Dennis said, following suit with two chips, then adding another two. "And I'll raise you ten more."

Tony eyed the men at the table and glanced at each one's face card. He shook his head, conceding, "Too rich for my blood. I fold." He tossed his hand into the pile. "Egypt," he continued to the silent room, citing his own honeymoon location. "The Pyramids, the Sphinx, Cairo museums, golden treasures from ancient times, traversing the Nile by moonlight, and following in the same footsteps as our ancestors. Egypt was perfect."

"No way, who wants to honeymoon in a thousand degrees? You and Madison got that roaming-the-desert-on-a-camel stuff. Give me a cool breeze, but not Switzerland's twenty below," Trey said, pointing to Raymond. Raymond tossed four chips into the pile as Trey continued. "And give me warm temperatures, not Egypt's hundred and ten degrees. I'll take something nicely tucked in the middle, maybe with a little gambling just in case I get adventurous, maybe something like Aruba or Rio," Trey said as he tossed his chips into the pile and pointed to J.T.

"We've decided to go to St. Thomas," Dennis added.

Heads nodded. St. Thomas was an excellent location for a honeymoon, they all agreed, although Trey added that to party, a short ferry ride to St. John would definitely be in order.

After the discussion finally slowed, Tony looked at Trey, questioning. The poker game had noticeably come to a complete halt.

"J.T.," Trey said, getting no response. He shrugged and nodded his head toward his distracted cousin.

"J.T.?" Tony said.

"J.T., yo man, you all right man?" Dennis asked. J.T. finally looked up. All eyes around the table were staring at him again.

"J.T., man, what's up? You feeling okay? You've been distracted and moping around here all night." Raymond said.

"I know that look," Tony said.

"Don't mind him," Trey answered. "He's got a virus."

"Why didn't you tell me?" Raymond said as he laid his cards on the table face down. "What kind of virus?" The doctor in him immediately took over.

"Call," J.T. said as he added two chips and turned his hand over. Each man followed suit, revealing their cards. After sizing up the hands, Dennis chuckled and pulled the colored chips in front of him. "I knew you were bluffing," he said as Trey gathered the cards, shuffled, and prepared to deal again.

J.T. glared at his cousin sitting beside him. Trey instantly began laughing as Raymond cut the cards. "Doctor, gentlemen," Trey began, "my dear cousin here has contracted the worst of all viruses, no cure, no medicine, no treatments, no known antidotes, and always completely fatal." He began dealing the cards out. "It leaves you mindless and whipped for the next seventy-plus years. Two words my friends, *lovicuois jonesious*."

"What?" Dennis asked, looking at J.T., concerned.

"Love Jones," Raymond said, deciphering Trey's meaning.

"Exactly, and he caught it from Ms. Juliet Bridges."

"Who's Juliet Bridges?" Raymond and Dennis asked.

"You two have to get out more," Tony said jokingly. "She's a dancer."

"Ooh, a dancer," Dennis said tossing three cards to Raymond. "Nice."

"Not bad," Raymond said as his fist tapped lightly with Dennis's.

"Actually she's a ballerina, and she's infected our comrade here," Trey said.

J.T. glared at Trey. "Can we please just play the game?" he said, suddenly interested in playing their monthly game of poker. His tone only aggravated the situation as the four men sitting at the table burst into laughter.

"J.T., we're not laughing at you, man. We've all been there. We're laughing with you," Raymond said picking up his three cards and shuffling them into his hand.

"Speak for yourself. I'm laughing at him," Trey said as he tossed two cards toward Tony.

"Okay, wait. Guys, let him talk," Tony said. "How'd you meet her?"

"Mamma Lou, how else?" Trey said.

Laughter erupted instantly as finger-pointing and howls of amusement surrounded J.T. Dennis pulled out his Blackberry and started scanning to see who'd won their wager. "I knew you were next. I knew it," he repeated several times.

"Now it makes sense. My grandmother strikes again," Tony said, well aware of his grandmother's expertise in match-making, having experienced her skill with his wife Madison. "She's got a better record then Walter Payton, Kareem Abdul-Jabbar, and Hank Aaron put together.

"Take my advice," Raymond began. "Mamma Lou's matchmaking is like going down in quicksand. The harder you struggle, the quicker you fall in love. You wind up fighting a losing battle, just relax and let it happen."

Laughter continued as each man fondly remembered Louise's efforts, and, in the end found their soul mates.

"Well, sorry to disappoint you all, but not this time," J.T. called out above the laughter. "Mamma Lou had nothing to do with me meeting Juliet, so all the bets are off."

"As far as you know," Raymond said, remembering well how Louise got him and Hope together by purposely eating almonds and winding up in the emergency room under Hope's care. "My grandmother can be very deceptive."

"True, that," Tony began as he reached for his beer bottle across the table to tap Dennis and Raymond's bottle lightly. "Remember, Madison came to Crescent Island and stayed at the cottage for rest and relaxation. Even she was in the dark when it came to Mamma Lou's plans for the two of us."

"Well, unless she can black out an entire city and a good part of the East Coast and Canada, she had nothing to do with this."

"Okay, okay, wait," Dennis said, waving his hands to calm

the loud, rowdy bunch. "If it wasn't Mamma Lou who set you up, then who was it?"

"Nobody set us up," J.T. confirmed.

"So, how'd you meet her? Let's face it, you're not exactly the kind of guy who hangs out at the opera and the ballet," Dennis questioned.

"There was a blackout about ten months ago in Manhattan when I was there to speak at a conference. Everything was eventually cancelled. I couldn't get back to the apartment, so I checked into a small hotel. Juliet was in line at the desk in front of me. Because of the blackout, the hotel only accepted cash. She didn't have enough. I didn't have enough, so we pooled our resources and got the last available room."

Trey, Raymond, Tony and Dennis all looked at each other. "Mamma Lou," Tony said. The room erupted with laughter again.

"There's no way," J.T. assured them, finding it difficult to be heard over the howls, hoots, and whoops of joy.

"Better you than me," Trey said, bragging.

Raymond, Tony, and Dennis all looked at him, nodded, and chuckled. "I wouldn't be too sure, Trey, your time is coming."

"No way, not in a million years, I have my bachelor-for-life certificate laminated and framed over my bed. I can't deal with the whole monogamy thing."

"I said the same thing," Dennis confirmed.

"We all did," Raymond said looking around the table at the nodding heads. "Don't get me wrong, I had fun when I was single and out there. But being married has, like, somehow completed me." He and Tony bumped fists as Dennis raised his bottle and they all clinked.

"It's just not for me," Trey said firmly. "My theory is simple—"

"Ohh, no." A collective moan rose again from the table.

"Not another theory," Raymond interrupted.

"This ought to be good," Dennis added.

"I've heard it before. I'll pass," J.T. added.

"No, no listen, give the man a chance, this just might be profound," Tony said.

"They're all profound. Trey's got about two dozen theories, he collects them like he collects gold coins," J.T. said.

"Bring it on."

"Gentlemen, my brothers, may I continue with my theory," Trey said.

"By all means, continue."

Trey stood and cleared his throat. "I'm sure we can all agree that without a doubt, these women nowadays are slammin' with serious soft bodies, sweet smelling, gorgeous eyes, luscious legs and, well you get the picture." The men all nodded in unison. "They look good, they smell good, they feel good, and they know exactly what they're doing. They're dangerous, they have all the power, and they can seriously screw a brother up if you let them. Now I'm not saying all women are like that. But, bottom line, a brother's got to be careful."

"In other words, love 'em, then leave 'em?"

"No, not at all. Here it is in a nutshell, my brothers, women are like an investment, you put the time, the energy, and the emotions into a money market relationship—"

"Don't forget your heart," J.T. spoke up.

"Yeah, and your heart, you put all that in a relationship money market. And over time it pays off, sometimes. Other times it doesn't and you have to divest, regroup, and then eventually, if you've lost everything, get back into the market. That's why as an investment banker I suggest that my clients invest in several markets at a time. Blue chip, certificates, bonds, S&P, stocks."

"What was that?" Raymond asked as he chuckled.

"Sounded like an E.F. Hutton television commercial to me," Dennis added with laughter.

"A trash-talking E.F. Hutton." Laughter continued.

"So you think that monogamy is here to stay?" Trey asked.

"There's nothing like being with just one woman, a strong, independent black woman," Tony stated proudly.

"Definitely," Raymond seconded.

"Hear, hear," Dennis agreed.

Trey shook his head sadly at his lost comrades. "Better you than me. One woman, one man is played. you can count me out, and trust that it'll never, I repeat, never happen to me."

Tony shook his head. "You can't fight destiny."

"So what you're saying is that a billion or so years ago, J.T. was destined to fall in love with Juliet and never look at another woman?" Trey said.

"God knew exactly what he was doing when he took man's rib and created woman," Raymond interjected. "We've been searching ever since for our soul mate."

"No," Dennis spoke up. "It's a cosmic thing. You put the energy out there and your perfect partner responds. It's all chemistry and energy."

"So you and Faith are energized?" Trey asked. Everyone chuckled.

"What about Mamma Lou and her matchmaking?" J.T. asked.

A silent reverence fell around the room.

"She's old," Tony began as grimaces etched into the foreheads around him. "No, not in a bad way. Listen. She's been around a long time. She knows how love works. And she's a master at this. I've found a new respect for her matchmaking, or cosmic connections, or her God-given talent. Whatever it is, she knows what she's doing, and I respect that."

"Hear, hear," the men said, uniting on one point.

Tony stood and picked up his bottle. "To Mamma Lou."

Everyone else at the table stood and joined in the toast. "To Mamma Lou," they said in unison.

As they sat, Trey began another one of his theories on love. Tony and J.T. got up, shaking their heads, and went into the kitchen to get another round of drinks and more food.

"I never thought I'd say this but, your cousin is actually worse than mine," Tony began.

J.T. looked back at the dining room table seeing Trey standing up, loudly professing yet another theory, as Raymond and Dennis laughed hysterically. "I'm inclined to agree. Although sometimes I find it hard to believe that we're actually related. Then, as soon as he steps into his office he becomes this brilliant machine that literally cranks out money for his investors." He went into the refrigerator and grabbed several bottles of beer.

"You've got a point there," Tony agreed, "He's like Dr. Jeckyl and Mr. Hyde, only he's more like Mr. Stock-Broker and Dr. I'm-a-Player."

J.T. chuckled. "Tell me something, Tony, when did you know that my sister was the one woman for you?"

"From the first moment I laid eyes on her at the ferry platform." He smiled, remembering exactly what she looked like as she walked toward him while she took the time to fully scan his body behind her dark sunglasses.

"If you knew she was the one, what stopped you the whole summer?"

"Pride, arrogance, stupidity. There was no way I was gonna admit what I was feeling to myself. She had me running scared from that first moment I saw her."

"But you knew?"

"Without a doubt."

J.T. shook his head, remembering the first time he laid eyes on Juliet. "But still you procrastinated."

"Until I finally stopped and realized that love and death weren't the same word. Madison is my destiny. She's the mother of my soon-to-be-born child and the only woman who could capture my heart." He paused. "Juliet might well be yours."

"If she doesn't kill me first. I can't sleep, can't eat, and I haven't touched a keyboard in twenty-four hours."

"Whoa, wait, you not in front of a computer keyboard," J.T. nodded. "Damn, she is good."

"Have you seen her perform?"

"Oh yeah, she's talented, beautiful, sexy." J.T. looked at

Tony and grimaced. "Hey I'm married, I'm not dead. Yes, she's hot. The question is, is she the one for you?"

"Truthfully, I don't know. Sometimes when I'm with her, I feel like we're the only two people in the whole world. When we were in New York during the blackout she was," he paused and shook his head, "irresistible. But now it's over. She's with Senator Kingsley."

"A little romance goes a long way. You'd be surprised how far it'll get you."

"No, not this time, I blew it. I walked out on her in New York and then yesterday I gave her the line about work being my number-one priority and told her that the deal was over."

"Not very smart."

"I panicked. Then last night, Trey and I went to a fund-raiser and she was there with her senator friend." J.T. rubbed his temples roughly.

"Presumably the new man in her life?" Tony questioned. J.T. nodded. "Are you sure? Because of all people, believe me, I know that appearances have been known to be deceiving. I actually thought that your sister Kennedy was a man that Madison was talking to on the phone. When she shortened her name to Keni, I panicked."

"I'm positive. I saw them together all night and then they left together."

"Which means absolutely nothing. If you really want to get her back."

"How?"

"You know better than anyone."

"What was the turning point with you and Madi?"

"Simple, happiness was on one side, and commitment was on the other. Love is where the two become one."

"That doesn't answer the question."

"You can't rationalize love logically, J.T. It just is."

"The thing is what we had, had grown into something special. But I let it get away twice. After last night, she'll never trust me again."

"She's scared."

"Undoubtedly. So what am I doing wrong?"

"Show her that there's nothing to be afraid of. Be patient, give her time."

J.T. chuckled thinking of the herb bouquet. "I felt it. I know she felt it, if she wasn't so damn stubborn."

"That's what makes her perfect for you."

"You sound like your grandmother."

"Are you sure she didn't set this up?"

"Hardly, we met during a blackout."

"Mamma Lou can be very determined when she wants to be."

"That's not funny," J.T. warned.

"Who's joking?" Tony said as J.T. grabbed five beer bottles and followed him with another round of snacks back to the dining room. The game had completely broken up and Trey was still standing, giving more of his theories on love.

"My brothers," Trey began again, "May I continue—"

"Check please," someone called out, filling the room with laughter again.

Chapter 23

The hotel's ballroom was lavishly decorated with ice sculptures, white roses, and yards of ribbon. The seats, numbering over one hundred and fifty, were neatly in place, with a rolled carpet center aisle. The minister stood beneath a makeshift floral arbor with his Bible open to the appropriate verse.

The familiar scene brought a chuckle to Juliet as she looked around at the deliriously happy faces. If they only knew. Another chuckle threatened to escape, but she held it back. Sitting on the groom's side afforded her the perfect view of the elaborate waste of time. The bubble was released she chuckled again, louder this time.

Two women in front of her turned and smiled pleasantly, presuming that she was just giddy with joy. They were so wrong. It seemed like she'd been standing on the groom's side of the chapel, church, and judge's chamber all her life. She chuckled again. "What are you doing?"

"Nothing," Juliet whispered.

"What's so funny?" Randolph asked quietly.

"Just like old times."

"Number eight and counting."

"Do you ever wonder why he keeps doing this?" she asked in a hushed voice.

"He's in love—"

"Yet again," she added dryly.

Randolph looked over to Juliet, sensing her disposition. Her mood had grown from bad to worse then to downright miserable ever since they'd arrived in Florida earlier that morning. "You've been in a lousy mood ever since we got here. Look at this place, it's gorgeous. Palm trees, sandy beaches, serenity. Why don't you just relax and enjoy it?" She looked at him, sneered, then looked away. "What is wrong with you lately?" he asked.

She looked across the room, seeing her father arrive and take his place beside the minister. "Love is impossible."

Randolph followed her line of vision to their father. "Not for Wyatt. It's always been simple for him."

"But that's just it. He doesn't have a clue what love really is. Love is the hope of spending forever with someone, the dream of waking up in that special someone's arms every morning, and thanking God for bringing them into your life. Love is twenty-four, seven, 'til death do you part. Love is," she paused, gathering her thoughts.

"Never having to say you're sorry," Randolph said with a chuckle as Juliet jokingly slapped at his arm. "I couldn't resist." She slapped at him again. "Okay, okay, I know what you mean, and you're right. Love is all those things."

"It seems that for Wyatt falling in love is a lot easier than being in love," Juliet said.

"Of course it is, falling is the easy part, staying in love gets a bit trickier. That's where the reality of love begins to blur."

"And that's when he bales out," she added.

"We all do."

Juliet looked at Randolph. "You're right, we do. I guess it's the Bridges gene. When's the last time you fell in love and actually worked to make it last?"

Realizing that she wasn't going to let the issue drop, he sighed heavily and shook his head. "Fine, I'll bite." He glanced across the room to the happy groom. "I'm not the falling-in-love type. It's just a fact, and I accept it."

"Don't you think that's because of Wyatt and our ever-endless parade of stepmothers over the years?"

"Wyatt has always been emotionally distracted. He's got a

short attention span when it comes to commitment," Randolph began in all seriousness. "My mother to yours, your mother to Lena, her to number four, four to five, and so on. And now he's at number eight."

"He's like a *Sesame Street* dropout."

"I don't even remember their names anymore."

"Rachel was four, Dolly was five, Brenda was number six, and Wanda was seven."

Randolph smiled. "You always took the stepdaughter thing seriously. I could never figure out why, they come and go so quickly."

"Because I knew our dear father would eventually dump them like he always has, and I guess I wanted them to have some good memories of the Bridges family."

"And they all still adore him," Randolph said in complete wonder.

"Yes, they do. Maybe it's a good thing that he ends the relationship before the yelling and screaming starts. Come to think of it, I'm still friends with most of my old boyfriends."

"And the majority of my exes still keep in touch."

"So why even bother? We are our father's children. Falling in love and making a commitment to someone isn't in our genes. We're just like him."

"You are kidding, right? Juliet, we're nothing like Wyatt. Just because he doesn't stay around long enough doesn't mean we won't."

"We never have."

"Maybe the right person hasn't come into our lives yet."

"It's a moot point."

"There are marriages that last a lifetime. As a matter of fact, Wyatt and your mom lasted longer then most."

"Until he needed his freedom," she sighed heavily. "Let's face it, love doesn't last for us. It's not the Bridges' destiny."

"How can you say that?"

"You and I do the same thing he does. We break off the relationship before the other person gets hurt. I guess it's kinder that way. We save them the pain of being hurt twice."

"You make it sound so noble when actually it's being cowardly."

Juliet shook her head in desperation. "Freedom and independence are not cowardly."

"Where is all this coming from?" Randolph asked.

"I've just been thinking lately," Juliet said.

"Just because you've never truly been in love doesn't mean it won't happen."

"Oh, it'll happen," she nodded assuredly, remembering J.T.'s hurt face at the party. "I just refuse to do anything about it, and I even knowingly discouraged it. That makes me just like him." She nodded toward the altar as the bride's music began to play. The assembled guests all stood. "So why even bother falling in love in the first place and condemn someone else's life to hurt and pain?"

"So after all this, your answer is to simply what, fall in love but get out early?"

The wedding march continued to play, and all heads turned to the back of the hall. The bride started walking down the aisle. Juliet looked back at her dress, a lovely white suit with lace trim. She looked beautiful, she looked so happy. It was a shame it wouldn't last.

The ceremony was thankfully brief. The vows were exchanged and the key question was asked. *Does anyone here see fit why this man and this woman should not be joined together in holy matrimony, speak now or forever hold your peace.* Randolph looked at Juliet, she looked at him. The hopeful expressions of *maybe this time* covered their faces as they smiled, knowing better, and the minister continued.

The pronouncement of man and wife only added more confusion to Juliet's already annoyed state. She watched as her father stood at the hotel's makeshift altar beaming happily, just as he always did. After eight weddings, he was an expert at saying I do. Randolph was right, the wedding was apparently the easy part. It was the actual commitment to being married that he seemed to have problems with.

An hour later, Juliet and Randolph sat at the main reception table eating chilled salmon and caviar and drinking champagne. *What exactly do men want*? Having just met her latest stepmother half an hour ago in the receiving line, Juliet sat at the reception table and pondered her brief relationship with J.T.

It had started easily enough, but even then she felt that there was going to be trouble. That's why she left when she woke up and he was already gone.

"If I live to be a hundred, I will never understand men," Juliet ranted absently as she sat watching her father smile liberally, then kiss and hug his new bride.

Randolph rolled his eyes to the ballroom's ceiling. "Are we back to that again?" Randolph whispered after hearing more of Juliet's half rages, cryptic outbursts, and obscure rants. She'd been going on and on since the two of them had flown down for the wedding. "If you didn't want to come to the wedding you should have said so."

"He wanted a simple favor, I did a simple favor. No attachments. That's what he said. That was the deal." She sipped from her champagne flute.

"And?" Randolph prompted.

"And what?"

"And who was the he, and what was the favor?"

"Never mind," Juliet said.

"No way," Randolph said as he poured more champagne into her glass. "You're not gonna begin a statement like that and just say never mind."

"J.T. Evans."

"Of course," Randolph said nodding and remembering their meeting on the patio the night before. "I should have guessed. He looked like he was going to knock me down when I escorted you out last night. So what happened between you two?"

Juliet told Randolph the whole story, beginning with their first meeting in New York and ending with the afternoon that J.T. came by to drop off the check, including J.T.'s misconception of their relationship. "Don't give me that overly protective big-brother stuff. It was your idea not let people know that we're related."

"What were you thinking?"

"Don't you start. Patricia has already blasted my ears about New York and this whole thing."

"Good, you deserved it. You realize, of course, that I have to get involved at this point."

"Don't you dare. This has nothing to do with you. You getting involved will only make things worse."

"How much worse can they possibly be? What exactly were you thinking when you agreed to this?"

"It was a simple deal."

"Obviously, it didn't work out like you planned."

"Obviously," she said miserably.

"So what are you going to do now that you're in love with him?"

"Is it that obvious?"

"Only to the trained eye," he paused and smiled widely, "and of course everyone else on the planet," he added. "Is he in love with you?"

"Yes."

"I don't get it, go live happily ever after."

"It's not that simple, and you know it. I told him that I needed time. Then he saw you and me together last night. He doesn't know that we're related."

"And you didn't clear up the misconception."

"No."

"Why not?"

"You of all people should know the answer to that." Juliet looked over to their father as he proudly danced with his new bride on the dance floor. "It would never last."

"You don't know that."

"I have a pretty good idea."

"Juliet, you're not meant to be alone. You can't live your life hiding under a rock because of your mother and Wyatt's marriage. Falling in love is rare. When it happens, treasure it for as long as you can. Don't be afraid that the other shoe is going to drop. Not every man is like Wyatt. Do you want him back?"

"It's too late for that. Even if I told him the truth, he'd know that I let him believe the worst."

Randolph thought for a moment. "What about that matchmaker you were trying to fool?"

"Mamma Lou?"

"Yes, why don't you talk to her, maybe she can help."

"I have no idea how to contact her. All I know is that she lives someplace off the coast of Virginia called Crescent Island."

Randolph reached into his suit pocket and pulled out his phone. "Let me make a few calls." Ten minutes later, he had the exact address for Louise Gates on Crescent Island.

Chapter 24

The planning of the Arts Community Center start-up process took all afternoon, leaving Lena and Taylor to continue late into the evening. By six o'clock they had discussed the strategy of location, and construction and had narrowed down a workable timeline with a feasible target date. The conception of the new programs took more detailed scheduling.

With the major decisions taken care of, the two women relaxed and enjoyed the early-evening dinner that Taylor ordered and had delivered to the office. They sat at the small, comfortable conference table in Taylor's office and continued their discussion over salads, chilled pasta with steamed vegetables, and iced tea.

After refilling hers and Lena's tea glasses, Taylor sat the carafe down and opened the last container of food, two slices of cheesecake. Full from the meal, both women decided to pass on the dessert.

Their discussion went on to focus on Taylor's art gallery and works in progress, Lena's ballet school's mid-summer recital in New York, and then, finally, the Arts Council, the Washington, D.C. Cultural Center, and the Capitol Ballet Company. After the conversation, Taylor confessed to the real reason she needed to speak to Lena.

"Lena, there's actually another reason I asked you to stop by this evening," Taylor said as she gathered the empty plates. Lena helped. They each grabbed empty containers and walked them over to the trash can.

"Really," Lena said as she sat back down and picked up her iced tea. "What is it?"

Taylor walked over to her desk, shuffled through a pile, then pulled a folded newspaper from a folder and handed it over to Lena. Lena took the paper, grabbed her reading glasses from the table next to her, then glanced at the grainy black-and-white photo and caption at the top of the page. It was a picture of Juliet and Randolph standing smiling side by side at a political benefit.

"I was more than a little surprised to see Juliet and Senator Kingsley pictured together again. I presumed that their relationship had ended a while ago."

"Why were you surprised? They're just as close as they've ever been."

Taylor's concern about Juliet's and Randolph's renewed relationship weighed heavily. "That's unfortunate."

"Why do you say that?"

"I was under that impression that Juliet was seeing someone else."

"Really, and who might that be?"

Taylor smiled half-heartedly. "It doesn't matter now, not since she and the Senator are back together."

"Taylor, Juliet and Randolph are very close, they practically grew up together."

"I understand. She's a wonderful person. I hope the two of them will be very happy together." Taylor said, but her troubled expression showed the pain she felt inside for her son. She knew that J.T. had seen the photo, and she knew that he must be hurting. It was the only explanation for his stolid mood all day. She saw him around noon and he barely said a word, just briefly waved and kept going. When she saw him later and asked to speak with him, he brushed her off, citing an important conference call. He hadn't moved from his office all day.

Apparently there had been a spark, at least on his part. Now he looked like a man who had just been sucker punched.

Lena, seeing her friend's needless distress, sighed heavily, then decided to enlighten her. "Taylor, may I tell you something in the strictest of confidence?"

"Yes, of course."

"They're related."

"Excuse me?"

"They're brother and sister."

"Juliet and Senator Kingsley are brother and sister?" Taylor repeated.

"Yes, to be more specific, they're half brother and sister. Wyatt, my ex-husband, is their father. As a matter of fact, the two of them are in Florida attending Wyatt's eighth wedding as we speak."

"I had no idea."

"Oh, very few people know. Both Wyatt and Randolph wanted it kept quiet in order to protect the family. And, well, you know politics can be extremely ugly at times."

"Why doesn't the Senator have the last name Bridges? Isn't it the family name?"

"Yes, but Rita Kingsley, Randolph's mother and Wyatt's first wife, took her maiden name back after their divorce. Neither actually knew that Rita was pregnant until well after the papers were signed and filed."

"Oh my goodness," Taylor said stunned by the extensive and tangled Bridges family tree.

"Wyatt didn't actually meet his son until Randolph was nearly five years old. By then Wyatt was married to Juliet's mother and she was expecting."

"Are they the only two siblings?"

"Yes."

"I can't tell you how delighted I am to hear this. When I first saw the photo of the two of them, I didn't know what to think." Lena looked at her, questioning. "I have to tell you I was more than a bit concerned when I saw it since I was under the impression that Juliet and my son were seeing each other."

"Your son?"

"Yes, J.T.," Taylor said.

"That explains it."

"Explains what?"

"I just recently met J.T. at a closed rehearsal at the Cultural Center."

"I'm not surprised. The two of them have been practically inseparable the last week."

Taylor went on to relay the meeting at her house when J.T. and Juliet arrived late. She added other occasions when they were together and that she had personally witnessed the apparent intimacy and closeness of their relationship.

Lena smiled but kept silent. So that's what Juliet had been hiding when they spoke earlier in her dressing room. She was having an affair with J.T. Evans, a company patron, one of the worst possible things she could do, particularly at this point in her career.

The company considered fraternization with patrons questionable ethics and split loyalties. It was one of their staunchest rules. Written in each dancer's contract, they restricted and frowned upon the interaction because ideally the relationship could take funds from the company if ever a dancer wanted to start his or her own company.

"How long have J.T. and Juliet been together?"

"As I understand it, only a few months. Apparently they met during that East Coast blackout last year. Whatever happened apparently left a lasting impression, because as soon as he came back into town they started the relationship up again."

"Although I only just recently became aware that they knew each other, I can't say that I'm completely surprised."

"Actually, I had every intention of introducing the two of them myself. I always thought they'd be the perfect couple, but I guess destiny beat me to it."

"You mean matchmaking." Taylor nodded. "Taylor, you've been around Louise too long."

"Guilty."

"And you're positive that they're together?"

"Yes, why?"

"Is it serious?"

"I don't know. I'd hoped so."

"It's just that Juliet never mentioned anything to me when I spoke to her earlier. As a matter of fact, she completely avoided talking about him. And when I met J.T. earlier, he was just as evasive."

"Really, that's odd," Taylor said, knowing how close and genuine Lena and Juliet appeared to be. "I would have thought you would be the first to know. But initially, I didn't find out myself until last week, when Juliet and J.T. came to the house for dinner."

Lena paused for a moment to consider her options. Talking to Juliet was mandatory. She just hoped that it wasn't too late and that Juliet had some idea of what she was doing.

"Well, I'd better go. I have an early flight in the morning." Lena stood to leave. She gathered her folders into her briefcase, but her mind stayed on Juliet. She needed to speak with her as soon as possible. What could she be thinking? Her entire career could be ended by a brief, meaningless fling, if indeed that was all it was.

Taylor and Lena said their good-byes and Lena left.

Taylor packed her briefcase and gathered the papers Trey needed for their proposals. She placed them on her assistant's desk so that they could be faxed out in the morning. She grabbed the dessert container to take home to Jace, then took one last look back as she turned off the office lights and closed the door.

Taylor walked past the elevators and headed to Jace's office in the executive suite. As she headed down the hall she noticed that J.T.'s lights were still on in his office. Not at all unusual, he was a night owl when it came to dedication to his job. But she also knew that tonight, in particular, he might need to talk.

She knocked softly. Then, receiving no answer, she turned the knob and entered. She looked around the lit office, finally finding J.T. standing at the window looking out.

"J.T." she called out.

He stood with his back to her, still staring out into the evening sky. She walked up behind him. "J.T." He didn't move and didn't respond. "J.T.," she called out again and tapped his arm. He turned, surprised to see her standing just a few inches away.

"Sorry," he leaned over and kissed her forehead, "I didn't hear you come in." He looked troubled.

"Looks like you were deep in thought."

"I guess I was. Did you need something?"

"No, you've been overly quiet all day. Is there anything wrong?" Taylor asked as she followed him back to his desk. He sat down heavily as she remained standing.

J.T. frowned. He hadn't realized that he was that obvious. "No, just business concerns," he said.

"Anything I or your father can help with?"

"No, not this time," he said.

"I just had a meeting with Lena." Taylor said and placed the container of cheesecake and a fork on the desk in front of him.

"Oh," he said as he peeked into the food container. Cheesecake was his favorite. He picked up the fork, stuck it in the creamy dessert, and scooped up a mouthful. But instead of eating it, he lowered the fork, rested it on the side of the container, and pushed it away.

Taylor watched her son carefully. He'd been pensive and brooding all afternoon and she knew the reason why—the photo in the paper. Apparently Juliet never told him that Randolph was her half brother. "How's Juliet?" she asked.

"Fine, I guess," he replied too quickly. He was supposed to be doing damage control. He knew that his mother and father had seen the newspaper photo of Juliet and Randolph. He was just thankful that Mamma Lou was already back on Crescent

Island or he'd have to explain it to her as well. And the last thing he needed was to have her back on the matchmaking trail. Not now, not after Juliet. Not ever.

What was she thinking, having her photo taken with Randolph so soon after their deal had been complete? She must have known that his parents might see it. And now here he was, trying to salvage what was left of a very good plan gone wrong.

"I suppose you saw the photo of Juliet with Senator Kingsley in the paper this morning," he began, deciding to just jump right in and get the conversation over with.

"Yes, I saw it."

"And you're wondering why she's with him?"

"As a matter of fact Lena and I were just talking about that—"

"Actually there's an excellent explanation for it," he said, having no idea what he was going to say.

Taylor exhaled a huge sigh of relief. She didn't want to break Lena's confidence, but she had no intention of seeing her son distraught over a simple mistaken-identity issue. But now, since he apparently already knew, she was thrilled. "Yes, I know, Lena already told me." She walked over to the orchid on his desk and felt for any dryness. Satisfied, she continued to the windowsill and checked the jade, bonsai, and rubber plants. All were well-watered and doing fine. Apparently that little talk she had with housekeeping had worked wonders.

"Really," J.T. said absently, only half listening.

"Oh, yes, Lena told me everything, including that fact that the two of them left for Florida together late last night. Can you imagine? Not even members of his staff know."

J.T. sat staring at his mother as the words "Florida" and "together" continued to ring in his ears. *They went to Florida together late last night.*

J.T. watched absently as Taylor continued to admire the little touches she'd recently added to his office. She rearranged the silk angora throw she tossed over the back of his new sofa, adjusted the three paintings she had hung, and turned on the two lamps she had delivered and placed on his new end tables in his new corner seating area.

"J.T., I have never told you how to run you life," she began.

"I know."

"And I'm not gonna start now."

"But," he prompted and waited for her to continue.

"But, Juliet is a wonderful woman and I know you."

"Meaning?" he asked, already knowing the answer.

"Your father has always enjoyed a loving family and a very successful and rewarding career. There's no reason in the world that you can't also."

"You're referring to my relationship with Juliet, I assume."

"Yes."

"And where exactly do you see this relationship going?"

"Give it a chance J.T., hold on to her."

"Mom, I'm not the one who let go." She looked at him, questioning. "There's something I need to tell you about my relationship with Juliet."

"No, not again, please don't tell me you've dumped her because you don't have the time and work is more important to you. Honestly J.T., look at you. How long do you intend to be alone? This happens every time. At this rate you'll never get married." She crossed her arms over she chest and huffed.

"Are you done?"

"Yes," she said disgustedly.

"First of all, I have every intention of getting married someday, just not right now. I know you want the best for me, and I love you for that. But some things are just out of my control."

Taylor sighed heavily, "I realize that, just be patient. Now it's time for me to make a confession."

"What kind of confession?" he asked, curious as to what she might say.

"I have never meddled in your romantic life." He nodded at the truth in her words. She paused. "Until now."

"What do you mean?"

"Remember when I suggested that you take me to lunch last week?" He nodded. "And the playbill and invitation to the ballet," he nodded again, "that was my very subtle way of getting you and Juliet to meet. But it was apparently unnecessary since the two of you had already met months ago."

"You were matchmaking?"

"Yes."

J.T. chuckled. "So all this time I was focused on Mamma Lou, and it was you I should have been looking out for."

"Louise helped me plan a few things, but as I said, it seemed fate had already done the job. I guess you and Juliet were just destined."

"At this point it doesn't matter. She's no longer interested. And you know that I never pursue something or someone that's not already accessible and obtainable. She doesn't want me."

"Do you want her?"

"Yes."

"Then it's not over, encourage her."

He began laughing. "And how do you suppose I do that?"

"Simple. I went to Crescent Island and Louise helped me. She can help you, too."

"Mamma Lou?" he groaned inwardly, bemoaning the fact that he was actually considering asking Louise Gates for help with his love life. "She's the last person I'd talk to about this."

"Who better to match you up with Juliet again than the matchmaking queen herself? Avail yourself of her vast knowledge. Listen to her. She knows what she's talking about."

"I'll think about it."

Taylor kissed J.T.'s forehead, picked up her briefcase, and said goodnight. Alone again, J.T.'s mind whirled. He was in love with a woman he'd just dumped. She was away in Florida with another man, his only recourse was to go to Crescent Island and talk to Mamma Lou. How did his life get so complicated?

"Oh boy," J.T. said, knowing he was never going to live this down at the next poker game with the guys.

Chapter 25

Juliet and Richard had been dancing in the studio for nearly five hours. Sweat dotted her brow, and her knitted leg warmers were soaked. She'd changed clothes during the last break, but now even that outfit was drenched. The intense rehearsal was one of the last few they expected to have before her final performance and Richard's eventual return to London. She changed clothes again during their last their break while Richard met with Phillip and Peter.

Juliet's retirement and her final performance date had officially been announced at the beginning of the season. What management hadn't expected was to lose Richard at the same time. His contract was up, and he had decided to accept a limited engagement with the London Ballet Company to be a guest performer there next season. There were a number of companies vying for the honor of sponsoring his last performance with the CBC, but he had requested that his last performance coincide with Juliet's and keep her same sponsor, E-Corp.

Phillip, Roger, and Peter were all stunned when Richard told them of his decision earlier in the day. They had met with him and his agent, anticipating that he would continue on with the company long after Juliet had left. Much to their regret, he had rejected their offer. His name in the ballet world was a strong pull at the box office. His name linked with Juliet's guaranteed a full house at every performance.

After changing, Juliet walked down to the main stage just

as a chorus rehearsal had ended. Since the full cast and crew had been assembled, the stage was essentially packed. Juliet found an open space and sat down in the rear of the stage just as the mandatory daily cast meeting commenced. Scheduled during the last rehearsal break, announcements and notices were usually ignored as most of the cast used the thirty-minute downtime to rest, keep warm, and stay limber. A quiet chatter among the cast continued as Roger read his usual notes.

"How did they take it?" Juliet asked as Richard came in and sat down beside her.

"Disappointed, but they'll live."

"You're gonna be a hard act to follow."

"You're absolutely right, love," Richard said in complete agreement. "Ditto."

From the wings Peter and Phillip walked on stage and stood next to Roger. He looked at the two men and nodded. A hushed silence hung over the crowded stage. The sight of Phillip at a daily meeting caused attentive interest.

Juliet, having already known about the upcoming announcement, waited patiently as Phillip began his with a typical speech congratulating the cast and crew on another superb performance series. Ten minutes later, he asked Richard to come up front. Once Richard had arrived, Phillip grasped his hand and thanked him personally for dedication and excellence, basically the same thing he had done when Juliet told him she had decided to retire. He finished by announcing Richard's decision to return to London at the end of the season. A collective shock swept through the cast and crew.

Afterward, the stage was sectioned off in two areas, one for the two principal dancers and one for the rest of the cast. The principals took center stage and began the rehearsed routine as members of the cast stood around discussing the choreographer's latest ideas.

Juliet crossed the stage in a flurry of pirouettes, jumping

higher and higher each time. She soared into the last jump and came down hard. Her weight pulled to the side and a popping sound echoed. She crumbled to the hardwood floor in pain. Richard rushed to her side along with Roger, Peter, and Phillip.

"Get an ambulance." Roger called out to the backstage crew.

Nadine immediately picked up the phone and dialed for emergency services. After the call was made she hurried to the now-crowded floor. "Everybody stand back, please," she ordered, then told her assistant to bring her a pillow and several ice packs. "Give her some air." She knelt down to assess the injury. "Where exactly does it hurt?"

Juliet took a deep breath and exhaled raggedly. "My ankle, I think I twisted it when I came down."

Nadine nodded. Having had the same career-ending injury, she gently grasped Juliet's leg and felt around for any broken bones. Satisfied that there were no broken bones she took the pillow and placed it under Juliet's leg to elevate the foot, then placed the ice packs on Juliet's quickly swelling ankle.

She leaned down to Juliet. "It looks like a slight sprain. I didn't feel any broken bones. Hopefully you'll just have to stay off of it for a few days."

Juliet, having never been seriously injured, nodded then bit her lower lip in pain.

Peter immediately canceled rehearsals and dismissed the cast. Only he, Richard, Nadine, and Juliet remained on the stage for fifteen minutes more.

"Right this way," Juliet heard Roger say as he directed the emergency technicians to the stage. "She fell," he said stating the obvious since she was still sitting on the stage floor.

The medical team instantly took over as soon as they arrived. They commended Nadine on her quick thinking with the pillow and ice pack. Then they rolled a stretcher next to Juliet. They gently placed her on it, then rolled her out. Nadine followed.

Ten minutes later, wasting little time, Vanya marched into Peter's office and stated that she was prepared to replace Juliet in the evening's performance. Before he could open his mouth, she continued with her list of qualifications. "I am the only one here capable of replacing her. I'm as good as she is, even better, some say. I'm a soloist, second lead, and I know the routine. I can even dance with Richard."

The heartless way she presented her case gave Peter pause. "Vanya, I know you're looking at this as your big break, but we haven't even heard from the hospital yet."

"Why?" she asked in all seriousness. "What can they possibly say that you don't already know? Juliet will not be dancing tonight, that much is obvious."

Peter winced. Vanya's vulture-like demeanor was cold and calculatingly cruel, even for her. "As soon as Nadine calls with a report, we'll know what our options are. Believe me, we realize that as soloist and Juliet's primary understudy, you are the likely choice to replace her in tonight's performance. But before we make that call, we need more information."

Vanya, not nearly as satisfied as she expected to be and on the verge of a full tantrum, looked at Peter strangely. "What exactly are you waiting for? Juliet left here on a stretcher. There's no way she'll be dancing tonight. It's simple, she's out, and I'm in."

Peter stood and came around to Vanya. "As soon as we know for sure, we'll call you."

"This is absurd," she complained. "I'm the only likely dancer you have."

"I'm not saying you're not. Vanya, please, we'll let you know one way or another."

A quick knock on the door turned both of their heads as it opened and Phillip came in. Looking from Vanya to Peter, Phillip asked Vanya to excuse them a moment. She huffed, sucked her teeth childishly, and marched out.

When the door slammed soundly Phillip turned to Peter. "I presume Vanya wants tonight's performance."

"You presume correctly. She was just about to have another one of her full-blown operatic fits before you can in."

"Is she capable of the performance? Can she do it?"

"She knows the moves, and technically she extremely proficient. She just needs more seasoning and confidence. Kitri is a demanding role."

"Maybe this opportunity will give it to her."

"Maybe, hopefully," Peter said looking more concerned than assured. "Has Nadine called yet?"

"Yes," Phillip said. "Juliet will be out for the next week and a half, looks like she'll be back on stage just in time for her final performance."

Peter walked back around his desk to sit. His brow furrowed. He had one last performance in the spring series, and Juliet was his lead dancer. Vanya was the obvious choice, but he wasn't particularly confident in her ability to carry the entire performance. "I'll talk to Vanya."

"Good," Phillip nodded in agreement as he turned and walked to the door. "Don't forget to send flowers to Juliet."

Juliet stood in the wings with a soft cast on her foot and crutches under both arms. She had insisted on returning to the theater amidst staunch objections from her emergency room doctor and Nadine.

She watched with angst as Vanya danced. Her performance was nothing less than a struggle. She glanced across into the opposite wing and caught a glimpse of Nadine shaking her head miserably. She knew that look all too well. Vanya, with all her self-proclaimed brilliance, was a nervous wreck.

Juliet sympathized; holding a performance together was difficult. She had learned that years ago. It took patience, understanding of the character, and an icy calm to go out on stage and dance. Knowing the technical movements was one thing, feeling the dance in your heart and soul was another.

In the quintessential role of Kitri in *Don Quixote,* Vanya's performance was detached and emotionless and lacked the needed energy to make the character truly memorable. The character, sexy and flirtatious, was instead cool and distant. For such an extremely difficult and complicated role, the principal dancer must be on cue with allegro agility each and every second.

Danced to exacting steps, choreographed to fast-paced music, the dancer was expected to perform beyond ordinary standards. The dance demanded soaring leaps, split-second turns, and animated vivacity. Each movement required extreme quickness and follow-through. Paired with Richard in the pivotal scene, the fanciful *Pas de Duex Mauesque*, she should have been brilliant. But instead she was robotic and stiff.

Vanya's showing was technically good but lacked the sparkle and energy usually seen in the character, Kitri. She focused her attention on the choreography and lost the feeling of playful romance in her movements. Filled with spirited frolicking, *Don Quixote* the ballet required more of the dancer's personality than most.

When Juliet danced Kitri, she incorporated the entire repertoire of movements in her characterization of the role. Her maturity gave Juliet the experience and knowledge needed to grasp the subtle line between sexy vamp and brilliant dancer, while giving her partner an opportunity to shine.

As Vanya's solo sequence began, Richard exited the stage. Juliet handed him a few tissues to wipe his face. He looked at Juliet and shook his head. "I've never seen her dance so poorly. She's like a zombie on a Thorazine drip."

Juliet nodded. There was nothing she could say. Vanya had begged for this opportunity and she failed had miserably. When the performance was over, the audience applauded as usual, delighted at seeing the ballet, but the joy and exuberance was missing, and Vanya knew it.

She had tried too hard and had failed. When she left the stage, Nadine walked over to her and handed her a towel. She didn't say a word, she just walked away. Vanya turned in the other direction and headed for her dressing room.

Juliet congratulated the cast and stopped a few minutes to speak with Peter and Richard before leaving. She walked to the back stage door, then paused, remembering this same performance nearly fifteen years ago. She turned and headed back to the dressing rooms.

Juliet knocked on the dressing room door and waiting until she heard the door knob jiggle. Vanya stuck her head around the door and peeked out. Her eyes were red and bloodshot. She had been crying. "What do you want?"

"To talk." Vanya began closing the door. "Vanya," Juliet called out, holding the door at bay. The door stopped and Vanya walked away, leaving the door half ajar.

"If you've come to gloat, make it fast."

Juliet walked into her small dressing room and stood just beyond the mirror, watching Vanya's reflection as she removed her makeup.

"I didn't come to gloat. I came to offer my assistance."

"I don't need your help," she snapped.

"I think you do."

Vanya looked at Juliet for the first time. "Why are you here?"

"I'm here because I was exactly where you are about fifteen years ago. I got my big break when the lead principal broke her foot. The break never healed properly, and she never returned to the stage. I went out on stage in her place and I stunk, just like you did tonight. But, I was lucky; she came to my dressing room and told me something I've never forgotten."

Vanya turned around and looked up at Juliet. "What?"

"She told me that I had forgotten something."

"What, some kind of good-luck charm?"

Juliet bit her lip but decided to be patient with Vanya. "No, she reminded me of why I was out there on stage in the first place. I'd forgotten that I loved to dance more than anything else in the world. And that the next time I went out on stage I needed to remember why I was there. I needed to feel the dance in here, in my heart, in my soul."

"I was horrible," Vanya said as a slow tear crept down her thin face.

"Yeah, you were. But you forgot why you were out there. Try remembering that next time. It's not the dance that makes the dancer, it's the heart." Juliet turned to leave. Just as she opened the door and passed through, Vanya called out her name. She stopped and turned.

"Who was the dancer, Lena Palmer?"

Juliet smiled. "No, it was Nadine."

Chapter 26

The doorbell's chime sent her heart racing. She already knew who was standing on the other side, J.T. She'd been avoiding him for days with one excuse after another, knowing of course that one day she'd have to face him. Apparently today was the day. He'd called earlier and said to expect him later that day, and he refused to accept any more excuses.

She hobbled to the foyer door, placed her crutches behind it, and cautiously limped to the front door. The doctor in the ER told her to stay off her foot for the next week or so and she should not have problem.

Juliet opened the door. Her mouth suddenly went dry as they each stood staring. "Vanya?"

"Hi, Juliet, I hope you don't mind. Richard told me where you lived a long time ago when he and I were," she flushed red, looked away and shrugged, "together."

"Come in," Juliet said, finally getting over the shock of seeing Vanya standing in her doorway. Vanya took a few steps and waited for Juliet at the entrance of the foyer. "And for the record, there's no need to be embarrassed about your relationship with Richard. I think it was pretty much obvious at the time. The two of you seemed suited."

"I know," she stuttered quietly. "It's just that you and Richard are . . . were . . ."

"Are the best of friends and that's all we ever were and ever will be."

"But, I just assumed that . . . Well, you know . . . I mean,

Richard never actually said anything . . . I mean, I thought that since you two were so close . . . Doesn't everybody think that you and he . . ." she said in broken half sentences that never actually completed a single thought.

"Vanya, you haven't been with this company for very long. There's a lot you have to learn, and not all of it takes place on stage. You've been a dancer for a long time, I'm sure, but being a dancer and knowing the business of life are two different things."

She nodded in understanding. "I know I should have called first, but I wasn't sure that you'd talk to me."

"Why wouldn't I?" Juliet motioned for her to continue walking through the foyer and into the living room.

Vanya slung her dance bag over her shoulder, turned, and walked into Juliet's house. She stopped short in the living room admiring the wall of mirrors and the dance barres on both sides of the room. "This is magnificent," she remarked with enthusiasm. She grasped the barre, looked at her reflection in the one mirror, then turned slightly and looked at herself across the room. "I love this idea. How did you do this?"

Juliet watched as she continued to observe her body in the mirrors. She was like a kid in a candy store. "Simple, I hung mirrors. Seemed like a good idea at the time."

"Aren't you gonna miss this?"

"Yes, terribly, but lately I've realized that life goes on, yes, even off stage," she paused for a second, then shook her head slightly and smiled. For the first time in a long time, she actually believed it. She knew that she'd survive her last performance on stage just as she had survived her first. The new life awaiting her afterward, whatever she chose to do, would be just as exciting and stimulating as nightly ovations.

"Is there something I can help you with?"

"Yes," Vanya said. "I just wanted to thank you for the other night. I guess I was pretty bad out there. It was just so hard. I thought that—"

"It would be easier?" Vanya nodded. "It depends."

"On what?"

"On how prepared you are."

Vanya nodded. "Anyway, thanks for afterwards. It really got me thinking. When I was growing up, my mother and father were very strict. I had to practice for hours and hours every day. I never had any friends. I was always too busy and," she paused a moment and shrugged, "scared. Ballet is all I know. It's all I ever wanted to do. But then I realized that I couldn't do it."

"Who said you couldn't do it? You just need a little trust."

"In what?"

"In yourself."

"But I am confident."

"No, Vanya, I didn't say being confident, I said having the kind of trust inside that takes your heart to another level. Once you're there, there'll be nothing you can't do."

"I don't think I understand."

"You were nervous when you were on stage last night. It's understandable. Being the center of attention and carrying the entire performance is a massive responsibility."

"You did it at my age."

"I had help."

"Nadine and Lena."

"Yes, among others. They gave me a sense of trust in my ability. I filled my heart with dance, and the emotion flowed outward from there."

"I still don't think I get it."

"I'll tell you what, if you like I could show you a few things to help."

"Would you really?"

"Of course, any time."

"How about now? I have my tights and shoes in my bag, and since you have this room," she said, motioning around the emptiness of the living room and dining room areas, "maybe you could show me now?"

"Great idea, why don't you go upstairs and change and warm up, and I'll put some coffee on."

"Are you sure you don't mind?"

"Of course not. The guest bedrooms are upstairs rear. It doesn't matter which one you use."

"Thank you, Juliet," Vanya said happily and hurried upstairs.

Vanya danced for the next three hours, listening to Juliet's input and altering her actions accordingly. Two pots of coffee later, they were sitting on the floor as Vanya stretched to relax her tightened muscles. She'd gone upstairs and changed back into her street clothes and returned to Juliet's side. "I have to dance Kitri again tonight."

"You'll be wonderful."

"Not as good as you," she offered.

"I've been doing this a long time. Believe me, you'll do just fine. Just trust in the love of the dance. The performance will come naturally. Did you get a chance to speak with Nadine?"

"Yes, this morning. She gave me a list of things to work on for tonight's performance." Vanya smiled the smile of a young girl with optimistic assurance. She pulled out a piece of paper and began listing the points that Nadine suggested she work on. "Line, elevation, and purity."

"Sounds like my first list." They both smiled. "Listen to her, she knows. She's been where I am and where you will be in time."

"Thank you. No one's ever helped me like this before. It's like you know exactly what I'm going through." Vanya looked down at Juliet's Ace-bandage-wrapped foot. "I'm sorry about your ankle. Is it very bad?"

"I'll be back just in time for my finale."

"I can't wait to see it. Everybody's talking about it. I just know it's going to be incredible."

"I hope so."

Just as they stood to leave the doorbell rang. Juliet's heart jumped—J.T. She and Vanya walked to the door. A delivery man stood with a clipboard. "I have a delivery for Juliet Bridges. Sign here, please."

J.T. stood and paced in his office like a caged lion. He walked over to the window, stood a moment, then walked back to his desk and sat down. He punched a few keys on the keyboard and rebooted a program he was currently developing. The four monitors that made up the multiscreen system on his desk simultaneously came to life. He typed in his digital access code and began.

Five hours later, he glanced at his watch. It was six o'clock, and although he'd been highly productive, the day had crawled by. He looked at the four monitors in front of him. They were filled with crypto codes, display files, and verification ciphers.

Then, surrendering to the inevitable, he began initiating the sequence of shutting down his system. His original intrusion, lockout system was designed to crash and trash any hacker's system by synchronizing a trapdoor outlet and reversing the damage by way of following and entering their system through digital footsteps, allowing him to enter their system exactly the same way they had tried to enter his.

Half an hour later he decided that it was time to see Juliet. He drove to her house, parked, and then rang the doorbell. She answered the second time he rang.

"Hello, J.T."

"Juliet," he said, then paused and glanced behind her through the foyer, "may I come in?"

"Now really isn't a good time."

"We need to talk," he said, stepping closer.

"About what, there's really nothing left to say."

"Our deal isn't over yet."

"It is for me, you made your point very clear, and I agree. I think it's best if we just go our separate ways."

"You can't do that any more than I can."

"Watch me."

"Ten minutes," he requested.

She inhaled deeply. This was getting her nowhere. She needed to purge him from her system once and for all. "Fine, ten minutes." She stepped aside, let him pass, and closed the door behind him.

J.T. walked into the bare living room and noticed that an extra-wide lounge chair sat in the middle of the living room floor. He turned to her, seeing her leaning against the barre on the opposite wall. She decided to ignore his questioning expression. He opened his mouth to speak but the doorbell took both their attention.

Juliet turned, startled by the sudden distraction. She gingerly walked over to open the door, then heard keys in the lock. Although she was expecting to see her friend Patricia, Randolph walked in. "Hey, are you okay?" He hugged her while looking down the length of her body. "Sorry I didn't get here sooner, I was in California in meetings all day and just heard. Why are you standing?"

"I'm fine, really," she said, then turned to J.T. who stood staring. "You remember J.T. Evans."

"Yes, of course." Randolph walked to J.T. and they shook hands. They both turned to Juliet, who had resumed her previous position of leaning back against the barre again.

"Thanks for the chair, it just arrived."

"Good, don't you need to get off your feet?"

"No, I'm fine," she said, brushing his suggestion aside.

J.T. noted Randolph's concern. "Why does Juliet need to get off her feet?" he asked Randolph, knowing Juliet wouldn't tell him.

Confused, Randolph turned to Juliet, then back to J.T. "Juliet fell in rehearsal yesterday and was taken to the ER."

J.T.'s eyes widened, half in concern and half in anger at not being told.

"It was minor," she assured them.

"How minor?" J.T. asked.

"The doctor said it was just a sprain with partially torn ligaments. It's not a debilitating injury. It happens all the time to dancers."

"But not to you," J.T. offered.

"No, not to me."

"What exactly did the doctor suggest?" Randolph asked.

"Restrict my movements for a bit, and I should be good as new."

"What else?" J.T. asked.

"That's it. It's just a simple sprain."

"You're a dancer, I'm sure that there's more to it than just a simple sprain," J.T. said.

"What do you mean?" Randolph asked.

"Bone is connected to bone by ligaments. When an injury occurs to the ligament, either a pull or tear, then you have a sprain. A sprain, according to its severity, can be as damaging and as painful as a broken bone."

"It's a second-degree sprain, it's not that bad."

"What does she need to do?" Randolph turned to ask J.T.

"Nothing," Juliet insisted.

"How about complete immobilization, elevating the injured foot, ice-cold compresses, and keeping the injured area wrapped tightly to reduce additional swelling?"

Both Juliet and Randolph looked at J.T. after he finished. "Dabbling in the medical profession, are we?" She asked sarcastically.

"My sister fell into an open tomb in South American once. I remember what she went through with the bruising and swelling, it was extremely painful."

"Do you have pain medication?" Randolph asked.

"I had a prescription."

"Where is it?"

"I don't need it, and I'm not taking some Vicodin smoothie. I'm fine."

"Juliet," Randolph warned as only a big brother could.

"I'm getting tired. If you two will excuse me, I'm sure you can see your way out." She grabbed her crutches from behind the door and walked to the stairs.

The two men watched as she easily maneuvered herself up the staircase. When they heard the bedroom door close, they eyed each other suspiciously.

"You want to tell me what that was all about?" Randolph asked.

"Not really."

"Oh, but I insist."

J.T. chuckled. "Somehow discussing our relationship with her new boyfriend is a bit more progressive than I care to be at the moment." He walked to the front door and opened it to leave.

"You and I need to talk, J.T." Randolph followed, closing and locking the front door behind himself.

"I have to get back to the office," J.T. said.

"Now," Randoloh reiterated more firmly.

"Some other time," J.T. said as he continued to walk down the street to his car. Randolph watched and shook his head. His sister and J.T. were making a huge mistake, and apparently it was up to him to rectify the matter.

Chapter 27

The following morning, after a sleepless night, J.T. entered his office and went directly to his desk. He sat down and turned on the computer. The screens came to life. Just as he was about to begin entering data, his secretary interrupted. She peeked her head into his office.

"Excuse me, there's a Senator Randolph Kingsley in the outer office asking to speak with you."

J.T. went still, stunned by the absurdity. Apparently the good senator didn't understand the subtle hint of mind-your-own-business. "Send him in."

Randolph marched in seconds later. "I'm not a man who's used to being dismissed. I didn't get where I am today by taking no for an answer."

"Obviously. But I think you should be speaking with Juliet."

"I will, in time. But it's you I'd like to speak with first."

J.T. motioned for Randolph to take a seat as he returned to his chair behind the desk. He pushed a button on the keyboard and the screens went black. He keyed in a few more buttons and the four screens lowered into his desk.

"Impressive," Randolph remarked at the innovation.

"Saves time in the long run, and my time is valuable," J.T. prompted Randolph to get to the point.

"My sentiments exactly, so I'll get right to the point. Juliet is a grown woman, and I seldom find myself intruding in her affairs, so to speak, but it seems I have no choice in the matter. She told me about your little arrangement, or deal, or whatever."

"Really," he said surprised that she'd reveal that to her current lover. "Did she also inform you that our arrangement was complete?"

"No, although I presume that that's a more recent occurrence." J.T. nodded. "In that case, since you obviously intend on spending more time with her, I'd like to know what your current intentions toward Juliet are."

"There are none."

"I find that hard to believe, particularly since you were just at her home last night."

"I needed to speak with her."

"About what, may I ask?"

"It doesn't concern you."

"I beg to differ. What concerns Juliet concerns me."

"Enough."

"Excuse me?" Randolph questioned.

"I said, enough. This little senate interrogation is over. You need to go run the country, and I need to run this business. As far as I'm concerned you and Juliet are perfect together. You're both—"

"Careful," Randolph warned.

"Impossible," he continued. "With that said, if you'll excuse me, I have work to do."

Randolph stood, accepting his dismissal, knowing that J.T. would eventually listen. "I have a feeling that this isn't over J.T. Juliet's happiness is my concern and she's obviously not happy about something. And I think that that something concerns you. In a career of fifteen years, she's never been distracted or injured on stage. And now you enter the picture three weeks from her finale and she's injured. I find that very curious."

"Not at all, I'm sure Juliet's injury had nothing to do with me. You, on the other hand—"

"Am not as impossible as you seem to think."

"As I said earlier, you need to speak with Juliet."

"I intend to," he walked to the office door, "but for the time being I suggest you stay away from my sister." He closed the door soundly behind him.

It took all of a fraction of a second for J.T. to process what he had just heard, and another fraction to reach the office door. He bolted outside, surprising both his secretary, who was speaking on the phone, and his father, who was about to knock on his door. Randolph continued walking toward the bank of elevators.

"Senator," J.T. called out. Randolph paused and turned, smiling inwardly. Then J.T. looked to his father. "Dad, can I get back to you in about half an hour?" Jace nodded agreeably, noting the senator's smug expression, then walked back toward his office. "Senator," J.T. called out again. "If I may speak with you again," he offered, motioning to his office and the open door.

Randolph glanced around, seeing that all eyes were on him. He nodded graciously. "Of course."

Both men walked back into the office. As soon as J.T. closed the door behind him, he began: "Your sister?"

Randolph smiled smugly, "I thought that might get your attention."

"Fine, you've got it. Now explain it," J.T. said as he walked to his desk.

Randolph remained at the door. "Actually your assessment of my time was quite accurate. I do have a country to run. I suggest you discuss whatever you need to discuss with Juliet. But make no mistake, if you hurt her again, I will personally see to it that you, this company, your entire family, and your pet bird are audited for the rest of your natural lives. And then I'll get angry." Making his point extremely clear, he opened the door and left. J.T. stood and watched Randolph leave a second time. He felt as if he'd just been sucker punched. "Sister."

A million and one thoughts raced through his mind in an

instant. Juliet knew exactly what he thought when he witnessed them together at the political fundraiser, and she never said a word to correct the misunderstanding. She just let him believe that she and Randolph were together as he stood there looking and spouting off like a jealous teenager.

Of course, now it all made sense. Juliet was Kingsley's date just like he had sometimes used either Madison or Kennedy as his last-minute fill-in. Sisters were the perfect bailouts.

J.T. smiled knowingly. She did love him. Why else would she go through so much trouble to make sure he had the wrong impression and to get rid of him? But why? She knew that the feeling of love was mutual. Why purposely run away from love?

Speculation was one thing, he needed answers now.

Interstate 95 was a blur and the speed limit meant nothing to him and he arrived in Old Town Alexandria in record time. He parked right in front of her house, slammed open her iron gate, and stomped up to her front door.

The loud and determined knocking startled Juliet at first. She hopped to the foyer and there, seeing J.T., stopped to consider her mood. Was she in the mood for more of this? *Why not?* She opened the door. "Welcome back." She turned and left him to close the door behind himself.

"What happened, Juliet?"

"What do you mean?" she asked.

"We were supposed to follow the plan."

"I did follow your plan."

He nodded slowly. "Who's Randolph?"

"He's not part of this."

"Who is he?"

She remained silent then answered, "A friend."

He smiled, humored that she still refused to divulge that Randolph was her brother. "Why didn't you tell me that Randolph was your brother?"

She smiled and shrugged. "He's my half brother," she said matter-of-factly.

"Why didn't you tell me?"

"What difference does it make? You and I wanted the same thing, and we got it. The problem is, J.T., you've changed your mind, I haven't."

"Oh, I know what I want. It's the same thing I've wanted for ten months." His jaw tightened again.

"And I need my freedom, so everything worked out for the best."

"The best for whom?" he questioned.

"Wait a minute, your deal was very specific."

"Enough! I can't take this any more." He grabbed her by her arms, pulled her to his chest, and kissed her soundly. "I love you, Juliet, and you love me, and you and I are going to finish what we started," he promised her breathlessly.

She shook her head no. "Not now, not ever."

J.T. remained silent and just looked at her in shock.

"Don't look at me like that."

"Like what?"

"Like that."

"Why not?"

"Because it makes me feel—"

"Wanted, needed, desired, loved—"

"Uneasy." He reached out and gently stroked her face.

"What do you want now, J.T.?"

"To end this."

"I believe you already did." She stepped back.

"No, that was only the beginning. I love you, Juliet, and whatever happened before doesn't matter. No more deals, no more arrangements, and no more agreements. I suggest a simple beginning, you and me in front of a minister and hundreds of invited guests. Will you marry me, Juliet?"

Juliet shook her head slowly, seriously. The memory of her father's wedding was clear. J.T. had just proposed, but she had no choice but to turn him down. "No, I'm sorry, J.T. But I realize that you were right. I think it's best that we go our separate ways. And since our circles have never crossed in the past, I don't suppose we'll have a problem in the future." She walked over to the front door.

"No."

"Yes, plus I've decided to either go to New York with Lena or to London. Either way, it's for the best."

"No."

"Yes. Good-bye J.T." She opened and held the door for him.

He passed without a word. Then when he got to the gate's entrance he turned. "To be continued," he promised. She closed the door softly.

Juliet leaned against the door frame and watched J.T. get into his car and drive away. Wyatt Bridges may have perfected the walk-away, but today she was truly her father's daughter.

"Senator, there's a gentlemen by the name of J.T. Evans here to see you. He said that you were expecting him, but I don't have him in your appointment book or on your calendar. And you have a committee meeting in half an hour."

Randolph chuckled and shook his head. "Send him in."

J.T. marched in angrily, slammed down in the nearest chair, stood and walked across the room, turned to Randolph, then got right to the point. "She's killing me."

Randolph laughed joyfully, "Welcome to my world."

J.T. looked at Randolph murderously. He had no idea why he had even come to the Senate building. But he had to do something.

When he left Juliet, he drove back to the office. But instead of going inside, he sat out in the parking lot. Then he drove to the town house, to McLean, and finally he found himself driving in D.C. traffic on his way to Capitol Hill.

"I presume you've spoken to Juliet."

"I have."

"By that remark, I presume you two are *not* back together then."

"You presume correctly."

"Pity, if you ask me you deserve each other."

"Thanks," he said sarcastically. "Your concern is heart-warming."

Randolph laughed openly.

"She's killing me. I proposed, she turned me down. Did you know that she intends to go to New York with Lena, or possibly to London?"

Randolph continued laughing. "Yes, she told me."

"And you're just going to allow her to leave?"

"I understand your concerns, but I assure you Juliet is a grown woman and capable of making up her own mind. She'll be fine whatever she chooses."

"But she loves me."

"Yes, I believe she does, but again, it's her choice."

J.T. looked at Randolph as if he'd gone mad. "What about money? In a few days she'll be without an income. What is she going to do?"

"I'm sure she won't suffer job offers. In case you haven't noticed, Juliet is very good at what she does. Besides, she has money," Randolph assured him. He noticed J.T.'s confused frown. "Apparently she didn't tell you everything." Randolph chuckled to himself. "Juliet has a trust fund from our grandfather worth, conservatively, one and a half million dollars. I assure you, she'll be fine."

J.T. shook his head. This day just kept getting better and better. "I don't get it. What did I do wrong?"

"Do you want the list alphabetically or chronologically?"

"Alright, so my grand scheme, even though it worked and got Mamma Lou and her matchmaking off of my back, wasn't exactly the best idea. And in the process, I lost the only woman in the world for me."

"You do learn quickly," Randolph said, applauding and impressed. "I give you that."

"Apparently it's too late. I told her that I wanted to start over. I asked her to marry me. She shot me down cold."

"One thing about love," Randolph noted. "It's never too late. Be patient, give her time, she'll come around."

"She doesn't want to see me. Why?"

"Our father, Wyatt Bridges, got married last weekend, it was his eighth marriage. He's the only man I know who falls in love, marries, and divorces in the span of twelve months. Not much of a role model, granted, but that's how he's chosen to lead his life. The reason I'm telling you this is because Wyatt is Juliet's only real model for relationships.

"She knows what it feels like to be hurt by love. Her mother never really got over Wyatt, and I guess that transferred to Juliet. She doesn't want to wind up like that, bitter and heartbroken for twenty years."

"So Juliet sees that as typifying relationships and marriage?" J.T. asked.

"Correct. Also she's been on stage dancing as a principal ballerina all of her adult life. Dance is her passion, her love, and her escape. In two days all of that's going to come to an end. She'll have to walk off into the sunset . . ." He didn't finish.

"What?"

"Her future, change isn't easy for any of us."

"And she's anxious about it."

"An understatement, but accurate. Then you show up, and apparently complicate matters. I think time and patience are in order."

J.T. shook his head and stood to leave. "She's killing me, " he said as he opened the door to leave.

J.T. returned to his office and worked the remainder of the evening. He'd taken too much time away from his job already. But he was sure that nothing was over.

Later that evening, J.T. sat at his desk in quiet darkness listening to the hushed tones of his computer program filtering through his latest development. He felt nothing. The utter elation and joy he should have felt at the successful implementation of his latest design was dampened by the chilling of his heart.

In a state of emotional disarray, he stood and walked away from his desk. The program he'd been struggling with for the last two years was brilliant and had come to life over the past two days.

He looked back at his desk, then turned his head away from the screens. Saying it out loud was futile. But there was no other rational explanation for it. She was right, he needed balance.

Since he and Juliet had begun their little charade, he had seen the program from a completely different vantage point. Then something she had said that night here in his office had completely altered his perception. He'd been going about the design from the opposite direction. Then he reasoned that searching for purely analytical solutions had only compounded the process. His usual problem-solving strategies had gotten him nowhere. It wasn't until the idea of tying the creative side to the analytical side came that the project seemed to work. The program was flawless in its performance, at the cost of his heart.

He looked down on the coffee table and picked up the familiar playbill. Juliet had been his inspiration without even knowing it. The clear and exacting way she saw the solution had eluded him. For two years the obvious had been hidden by the stubborn, unyielding idea that logic didn't need anything else to perform efficiently.

He had kept his distance for the last two days as all rational thought slipped through his fingers like sand. He'd done his job, he went to meetings, he organized, he recommended, and basically ran the company, but emotionally he was a disaster.

His thoughts were suddenly interrupted by a knocking on the door. He looked at his watch. It was late, too late for anyone else to be working. Then it occurred to him that it had to be the cleaning crew. "The office is fine, come back later," he called out as he plopped down on the new upholstered sofa his mother had purchased. The door opened anyway. "I said come back later," he insisted.

Trey stuck his head in the office, then came all the way inside. "I tried calling you last night, then again this afternoon," he said as he walked into the darkened office and looked around.

The room was completely different from what he had expected. It was comfortable and plush and warm. Trey, expected to see J.T. sitting at his desk with his terminals blaring their eerie blue light. Instead he found him sitting on the cushioned sofa with the playbill in his hands. He walked over and sat down in the chair across from him.

"Nice job," he began as he continued to look around the comfortable room. "Warm, cozy, very nice. I'm surprised. I expected something a bit more," he thought it over, searching for the right word, "sterile."

J.T. absently looked around the room. Trey was right. The room was nice and cozy and a far cry from where it had begun just a few weeks earlier. He smiled and shook his head as he thought about where his life was a few weeks earlier. Then he had been happily on his way to corporate bliss.

Now look at him. He was frustrated, disheartened, and miserable. He had proposed to a woman who was as different from himself as possible, and finally he was so in love he couldn't see straight.

"As I said, I called earlier, but your very efficient secretary told me that you were unavailable until further notice."

"I am."

"You don't look unavailable to me."

"Look closer," J.T. grumbled. "Better yet, I have work to do, I'll talk to you later."

"Not so fast, rumor has it that you could use a little cheering up."

"I have no idea what you're talking about."

"A friend of mine suggested that I stop by and check on you."

"What friend?"

"Doesn't matter. The point is, it looks like he was right, you could use a little cheering up. Why don't we go out tonight and see what kind of trouble we can get into?"

"I'll pass."

"My friend told me that there's a very interesting party on Embassy Row this evening."

"Maybe next time."

"Okay, how about a little gala at the Treasury Department?" J.T. shook his head as Trey continued with his suggestions. "Let's see, there's a party at the main post office, a soirée at the Department of the Interior, and a fundraiser at the Department of Justice?"

"I'm really not in a partying mood."

"There are a lot of lovely ladies just waiting to meet the CEO of E-Corp."

"No thanks."

"So, do I have to see you moping around the rest of your life feeling sorry for yourself, or are you going to get up and do something about this mess you've created?"

J.T. looked at Trey with annoyance as he tossed the playbill on the glass coffee table. The answer to his question was obvious, J.T. intended to mope. "You could just go and leave me alone," he said.

Trey casually picked up the playbill and scanned it. "Nah, not exactly the answer I was looking for, so let's try again." He opened his mouth to continue.

"You have no idea what you're talking about."

"Which part, the senator who's really Juliet's half brother, the marriage proposal, or the definitive turndown?"

"You knew about Randolph and Juliet?"

"I just found out. Kind of puts a different slant on things, don't you think?"

"Don't you have stock options to buy, or an investor to annoy, or something else constructive to do?"

Trey looked at his watch, confirming the time. "Actually

no, at least, not at the moment. However, now that you mention it, I do have a theory about all of this."

"No," J.T. said, warning him.

"But it's a good one," Trey assured him.

"No. I'm not in the mood to listen to any of your page-from-a-player-handbook theories."

"You're gonna kick yourself for not listening to me."

"In what world does the word 'no' disappear from your vocabulary?"

"Good, I'd be delighted to share." J.T. looked at him with murderous intent. The last thing he was in the mood for was Trey's ridiculous pearls of wisdom. "In a nutshell, old habits die hard, so it's time for some new ones." The look from J.T. continued as the sincerity of Trey's expression revealed that he was completely serious.

"Like what, she doesn't want to see or hear from me."

"Well then," Trey added, "as far as I can see there's only one way out of this."

J.T. looked to him with interest. He had racked his brains for the past two days searching for an answer to his problem. How was he going to get Juliet back in his life permanently?

"You know what you have to do," Trey said.

J.T. looked at him lazily. "What?"

"Go to her, she's the only one who can help you now."

"Juliet won't see me, I've tried. Besides, she's been in some kind of intense rehearsal for the performance tomorrow night."

"That's not the who to which I'm referring."

J.T. looked at him in wonder, having absolutely no idea who Trey was talking about.

"Sorry it took so long to get here," Patricia said as Juliet opened the door and greeted her warmly. "I've sort of been under the weather lately."

"How do you forget a man who was never yours in the first place?"

"Awe, sweetie," Patricia consoled Juliet as she opened her arms to take her in. They hugged for a long time until Juliet slowly backed away and they walked into the living room.

Patricia immediately stopped short. "Nice chair."

"Thanks, don't ask," Juliet said seeing her questioning expression.

Juliet took a deep breath and sighed as she walked over to the oversized lounge chair. "It's the old feelings all over again. I thought that I'd finally gotten through it. But here it is again, with happiness comes pain."

"No, Juliet. It doesn't have to be like that."

"Who was I kidding?" she plopped down heavily on the seat. "What was I thinking? Dad left me. Mom left me, and the first time that I stand up and refuse to walk away, I got left anyway. The Bridges' curse once again has reared its ugly head."

"That's it," Patricia began as she stamped her foot on the wooden floor, getting Juliet's attention. "There is no such thing as the Bridges' curse. There's only you, scared to death of leaving your cozy little world. You have gone way beyond the passive-aggressive tendencies and abandonment issues, and you're seriously heading for clinically nutzo, young lady. You finally get over leaving the stage and changing careers, and now this." Patricia shook her head, crossed her arms, and tapped her toe parentally. "Psychologically speaking, you have just invented your own Juliet-phobia, fear of finding love, falling in love, being in love, and lovingly living happily ever after," she breathed finally.

Juliet opened her mouth in shock. She looked at her friend with a mixture of surprise and annoyance. Then a smile began to crack her expression as they both instantly broke into laughter. Patricia collapsed on the roomy chair beside Juliet and they hugged again.

"Clinically nutzo? Juliet-phobia? I can't believe that the medical board actually gave you a license to practice psychiatry with that line." They laughed again. "So what medication are you taking for your recent mood swings?"

"Is it that obvious?"

"Only to all life on earth and the known universe."

"But you said that he proposed, Juliet," Patricia said.

"Yes, he did," Juliet smiled slightly with lost hope.

"So what are you going to do about it now?" Patricia asked.

"Sit," Juliet said.

"And?"

"Stare."

"And?" Patricia prompted again.

"Bask in my glorious triumph."

"Juliet, I still can't believe you turned him down. He asked to marry you, for goodness' sakes, and you said no."

"Seemed like a good idea at the time."

"He loves you, you love him. Get over the 'Bridges curse' and marry the man. Please, for me. I'm getting emotional-roller-coaster burnout."

"Another medical term, I presume?" Juliet teased, jokingly then turned serious. "I couldn't even if I wanted to. I was a fool. I can't go back and change my mind now."

"Go get your man."

"He's not my man, he never was. Don't you get it? It was all a sham, a scheme to fool a nice old lady, and it worked. Unfortunately too well, 'cause I got scammed too."

"I have hope."

"You always do." They smiled in a brief moment of tranquility. "Okay," Juliet took a deep breath. "Enough of this pity party, I don't have time for this. I have a performance in two days, my last stage performance as a principal ballerina for CBC."

"Are you ready?"

Juliet thought a moment, then nodded her head assuredly. "Yes, I'm ready. So, what did you want to talk to me about? Your call sounded important."

Patricia smiled and instinctively held her stomach. "I'm pregnant."

The idea was pure insanity, and even though his mother suggested it first, only Trey could have actually talked him into going. On an impulsive whim, he decided to go to her, the only woman in the world who could help him. He got in the car and headed south to his destination, Crescent Island.

When he took the ferry over, he had no idea what he was going to say. All he knew was that he needed Mamma Lou's help to win Juliet's heart again.

J.T. stood at the rail and watched as the Virginia shoreline slowly came in to view as Mamma Lou's words played in his heart.

He had confessed that his relationship with Juliet had been a sham and his only intention was to prevent her from matching him up with someone.

"It doesn't matter how it started," her voice gently urged with wisdom. "What matters is how it ends. Follow your heart, it will always lead you to love."

She fed him lunch, gave him a tour of her prized begonia garden, then sent him on his way. J.T. smiled and shook his head. His respect and love for Mamma Lou had grown, but now he realized that, just as Tony, Raymond, and Dennis had said, she had a wisdom for love beyond most.

Chapter 28

Juliet sat at her dressing table, the lights dimmed and candles lit. She looked up at her reflection in the mirror. Her hair was down, with a large red silk flower pinning it back on the side. She reached over and dropped a CD into the player. A slow, smooth, tranquil song played sending a relaxing rhythm through the room.

She closed her eyes, going through her usual ritual. This was her time for meditation. She used the few moments before a performance to get into character and let the ballet flow through her. She closed her eyes to let go of her anxiety, find peace, and let the music wash over her.

Unfortunately, the only thing she saw when she closed her eyes was J.T. She cupped her face in her hands and focused until the sound of light knocking on her door caught her attention. "Come," she called out to the umpteenth interruption as she turned in her seat.

Dressed in her costume, Vanya peeked around the open door. She smiled genuinely. "Hi, I just wanted to stop by before stage to say good luck and break a leg."

"Thanks," Juliet said, "I'll see you on stage."

Vanya nodded and closed the door behind her.

Juliet turned and picked up a make-up brush and dusted it across her cheeks. She dabbed the bristles into the powder and prepared to brush her face again when another knock on the door got her attention. The constant parade of cast, crew, and well-wishers had made her more nervous. "Come."

"You look wonderful," Lena said as soon as she closed the door behind her.

"Thanks," Juliet said. "This is it, the final stage."

"Don't be ridiculous, you'll be on stage again."

"As a guest dancer maybe, possibly, probably, but never again as a principal for a company."

"Regrets?"

Juliet smiled brightly and answered from the heart, "No, not a one. I had a fantastic career."

"Yes you did, and the best is yet to come."

Juliet nodded, too emotional to speak. She picked up a tissue and dotted the corner of her eyes. This was the fifth time she had to refresh her makeup.

"Juliet, I wanted to talk to you about J.T. Evans."

"What about him?" She looked up, tossing the smudged tissues in the trash can.

"Juliet, I know all about your relationship with him. Having a private liaison with a patron is one thing, but your public displays are quite another. The cocktail parties, the dinners, and the gallery openings, I know it all."

"Apparently," Juliet said, realizing of course that in the larger scheme of things that had happened in the past few weeks, Lena knew absolutely nothing.

"What happened to discretion?" Juliet remained quiet. "You are literally moments away from a graceful retirement, and you initiate a relationship with one of the company's biggest patrons. What exactly were you thinking?"

"I don't know, why don't you tell me?"

"This is serious, Juliet. Something like this could ruin your reputation in the dance world. This could be a major scandal, and for what, an infatuation, a few laughs and a good time? Is it worth it? Honestly, if you were at least serious about this relationship, then maybe it would spin differently. But you've always played this dangerous kind of game when it comes to relationships."

"Lena," she turned around, her makeup beginning to

smudge again. "There's really nothing to be concerned about."

Lena looked into her eyes and realized that there was much more to the situation than a minor fling. "Oh, Juliet," she hurried over to her and took her in her arms, "you fell in love with him."

"Lena, the relationship with J.T. is very much over."

"But—"

Juliet shook her head, "It's over between us."

Lena nodded her understanding, "I'm so sorry."

"Me too," she took a deep breath and exhaled slowly. "I have to finish getting ready. There's a curtain call with my name on it in about twenty minutes."

Lena gave her a hug and smiled, gently fluffing her hair back. "I'll see you out there, enjoy."

"I will." Just as the door closed Juliet turned, grabbed another tissue, and began retouching her makeup again. As she expected, someone else knocked. "Come."

Juliet watched as he walked in and stood in silence.

"Jace Taylor Evans."

She looked at him oddly, expecting him to say more about his parents. But he didn't."

"What about them?"

"My name, J.T., stands for Jace Taylor."

Juliet's despondent expression softened. The obvious answer had eluded her. She nodded, "Thanks."

He nodded, "I'll see you out there. Good luck."

Fifteen minutes later, Juliet peeked out from the wings. The house lights were uncharacteristically bright for the occasion. She squinted in the orchestra seats and boxes. No J.T. The hesitancy she felt had turned into anxiety. Her entire career had come down to this moment, and she had no one to share it with except in her heart.

The orchestra started, Roger cued her, and her final professional stage performance began. She danced to perfection.

Every step, every movement, every gesture was sharp, clear, and precise. The finale of her stage career was flawless.

When the final curtain dropped, the audience stood to their feet and thanked her for over a half an hour. Flower petals floated down from the rafters and were brought onto stage by luminaries in the ballet world.

Phillip came onstage and began an uncharacteristically short tribute to Juliet's career with the company. He was followed by Peter, Richard, and finally, Lena. Their tributes were spoken with such heartfelt sincerity that she broke down and cried. She looked out into the well-lit seats. J.T. was nowhere to be seen.

As the applause finally died down, all eyes turned to the wings for the next orator. J.T. walked out on stage as the spotlight followed his every step. Juliet turned to him, stunned to see him standing by her side. He took her hand and pressed it to his lips as he slowly dropped to one knee. The audience gasped in surprise, excitement, and eagerness. The anticipated act infused the room with a feel of romantic intimacy as the onlookers became witnesses to their pledge of love.

He reached into his pocket, pulled out a small box, and opened it to her. "Juliet, will you please do me the honor of becoming my wife?"

"Yes."

J.T. stood and wrapped his arms around her. The euphoric feeling of joy was eclipsed only by their love.

Epilogue

The receiving line had finally dwindled down to the last few well-wishers. After they congratulated J.T., they moved on to Juliet. J.T. reached up, loosened his tie, and relaxed for the first time in a long time. He had done it, and it felt good. He took Juliet's hand and brought it to his lips. She turned to him and smiled. "I love you, Mrs. Evans."

"I love you, Mr. Evans."

They held the moment as their eyes sparkled in wonder. No one could possibly be as happy as they were. "Did I tell you how beautiful you are?"

"You might have mentioned it once or twice."

"You are so beautiful." He curled a loose ringlet around his finger, then let it go. It immediately bounced back into position as he laid his hands on her bare shoulders, reached down, and kissed her lips gently.

"You're not so bad yourself," Juliet said pulling at his perfectly knotted bow tie. One end came loose, and she smiled seductively as they both remembered their playful adventure with another one of his ties.

"We throw a nice party," J.T. said, his eyes still on his new bride's face.

"Yes, we do." Juliet looked around at their family and friends. A gathering of two worlds were united as one to witness the blessed occasion of their union. This was the day of her dreams, the day all of her fantasies came true, and the day she became Mrs. Jace Taylor Evans.

"So, you just had to do it," Trey said as he walked up to J.T. and reached out his hand. "You just had to go and get yourself married."

"Yep," J.T. said, nodding happily as he took Trey's hand in congratulations.

"You know what this means, don't you?"

"Another theory, I'd say," Tony said as he, Raymond, and Dennis walked up and stood beside Trey.

"Sorry, gents, no theories, just heartfelt congratulations."

"Looks like we have to chalk another one up to Mamma Lou, she does have her ways."

"How could you do this to me?" The woman's voice was stern and demanding. "How could you leave me like this?"

J.T. turned to around see his sister Kennedy standing behind him. He immediately grabbed her up in his arms. "When did you get in? Did you miss the ceremony?"

She hugged him, holding on as he literally picked her up off of her feet. "Of course I didn't miss it. I came in and sat by Madison just before you entered with your best man. You know I'd never miss your wedding, even if I did have to come from halfway around the world to get here. Well?"

"Well, what?" he asked.

"Aren't you going to introduce me to my new sister?"

Laughter surrounded them as J.T. finally remembered that Juliet and Kennedy had never actually met. He made the introductions, and Kennedy welcomed Juliet with a big hug. Afterward she leaned over and kissed Tony, Raymond, and Dennis. Then she turned to Trey. "I believe you have something for me?" She held her hand out.

Trey reached into his jacket pocket, pulled out an envelope, and handed it to her. Madison, Hope, and Faith walked up just as Kennedy opened it up and pulled out several hundred-dollar bills. Juliet looked at J.T. as Kennedy dropped the envelope in her purse.

"It's the payoff. We all made a bet after Raymond and Hope

got married and when Dennis and Faith got engaged, who Mamma Lou would match up next."

"And you lost," Juliet said to J.T.

"No, actually I won," his meaning clear as he leaned down and kissed her. The assembled family and friends all sighed.

Patricia, the matron of honor, her husband, Pierce, and Randolph walked up just as Tony began explaining their wager in more detail. Juliet made introductions as Raymond continued the story with his initiation into the world of matchmaking and Dennis ended with his tale of Mamma Lou's matchmaking.

"So did Mamma Lou match all of you up?" Patricia asked. She looked around the gathering as heads nodded all around her until she got to Trey.

"Never," he said emphatically. "It will never happen to me. I'm not the marring kind. There's not a woman out there who can catch and hold me," Trey said, proudly.

"I have to agree with Trey," Randolph said. "I can't see it happening for me, either. I just don't have the time. Politics barely gives me enough time as it is. I can't see having a wife and family to also contend with."

J.T., Tony, Raymond, Dennis and Pierce all laughed, knowing better. They had each proclaimed the same thing just before their lives turned upside down when love took over.

"Well, Kennedy?" Trey said, hoping for another ally. She shook her head.

"I'm not even going to start that again. From all of this I've learned that love and Mamma Lou work in mysterious ways. So leave me out of it this time."

"Too late, you're the only one left," Trey said. "Looks like the only betting will have to be on the time frame. I'll take four months."

Before anyone else said a word or upped Trey's wager, Kennedy interrupted, "No way. I'm on my way back to Africa in a few days. Mamma Lou is good, but even she can't play matchmaker if I'm not even in the country."

"She's good, very good," Tony warned. "If I remember correctly, I was also out of the country when she started working on hooking me up with Madison." He reached over and pulled his wife into his arms, embracing both her and her large, round belly.

"A few days, that ought to be just enough time for Mamma Lou to have you well on your way to walking down the aisle," Madison said as those around the small group began chuckling and nodding their heads in agreement.

"Less sometimes," J.T. said, and Juliet agreed.

"Mamma Lou's matchmaking can be a bit complicated, look at everything she went through just to get Hope and me together," said Raymond.

"I don't know about that. Randolph and I did a bit of matchmaking toward the end to get J.T. and Juliet together. It's not that difficult," said Trey.

"True, as a matter of fact, it was our final push that turned the whole relationship around," Randolph added.

"So technically, if it weren't for us, you two might still be off in your separate corners pouting and moping."

"Exactly," Randolph concurred as they congratulated themselves by shaking hands.

"Excuse me, mind if I borrow these two?" A stunned gasp traveled from Trey to Randolph as all eyes turned to the petite older woman now standing between the two men. She entwined her arms with each man's and smiled happily. "So Trey, Randolph, tell me a little about yourselves." Because they were so completely stunned by her sudden appearance, they stood with their mouths wide open.

Mamma Lou backed up and began walking away, taking Trey and Randolph with her, one on each arm. Everyone else standing in the group burst into laughter as both Trey and Randolph turned around with worried, frightened expressions on their faces.

"Looks like another doubleheader," Raymond said.

"I give them six months," said Dennis.

"Two," Tony contradicted. "I think another wedding would be a nice birthday gift for the baby." He reached down and rubbed Madison's seven-months-pregnant stomach.

"Here we go again." Kennedy said and she pulled out her envelope and began taking bets.

Dear Reader,

I've always thought that there was something innately sexy about a blackout. So when the unimaginable happened on a warm Friday afternoon in August in New York City, it got me thinking, what would happen if an anonymous rendezvous with no rules and no names suddenly became love at first sight? From there, the possibilities were endless and the idea of *Irresistible You* was born.

J.T. Evans and Juliet Bridges, given their respective careers, were perfect for the situation. And, of course Mamma Lou was right there in the center of it all. I hope you enjoyed reading *Irresistible You*. As always, it was a pure pleasure to write. The new characters I added in this book, stockbroker Trey Evans and U.S. Senator Randolph Kinglesy, add a new dimension to the usual suspects.

So it seems that Kennedy Evans has dodged the matchmaking target once again. But she can't hide out in Africa forever. How long before her luck runs out and love comes knocking at her door? The Mamma Lou series continues.

In the meantime, watch for *Only You* in March, 2005.

As always, I thank you for your continued support. Please feel free to contact me at conorfleet@aol.com or Celeste O. Norfleet, P.O. Box 7346, Woodbridge, VA 22195-7346. Watch my Web site (www.celesteonorfleet.com) for contests and special surprises.

Best wishes,
Celeste O. Norfleet

ABOUT THE AUTHOR

Born and raised in Philadelphia, Pennsylvania, critically acclaimed author Celeste O. Norfleet currently has over six novels to her credit. An avid reader and writer, she lives in Northern Virginia with her husband and two children.

BOOK YOUR PLACE ON OUR WEBSITE AND MAKE THE ARABESQUE ROMANCE CONNECTION!

We've created a customized website just for our very special Arabesque readers, where you can get the inside scoop on everything that's going on with Arabesque romance novels.

When you come online, you'll have the exciting opportunity to:

- View covers of upcoming books

- Learn about our future publishing schedule (listed by publication month and author)

- Find out when your favorite authors will be visiting a city near you

- Search for and order backlist books

- Check out author bios and background information

- Send e-mail to your favorite authors

- Join us in weekly chats with authors, readers and other guests

- Get writing guidelines

- AND MUCH MORE!

Visit our website at
http://www.arabesquebooks.com